Praise for Lynn Mar……

'A fabulous read…just magical'
Becca's Books

'A lovely, funny and sexy modern "upstairs, downstairs"
story. Prepare yourself for a Christmas like you've never seen
before'
M's Bookshelf

'A classy, witty story with lots of laughs, a few tears and most
importantly heartfelt romance'
Jane Hunt Writer Book Reviews

'One of my favourite romantic comedies'
Reviewed the Book

'Christmas at Thornton Hall easily makes it onto my list of
my most favourite reads of 2013'
Cosmochicklitan

'A good debut novel that I really enjoyed'
Chick Lit Chloe

LYNN MARIE HULSMAN

Author Lynn Marie Hulsman's varied employment background includes stints writing at a direct marketing agency specializing in casino advertising (Loosest slots in town!), ushering at Manhattan Theatre Club, where she saw John Slattery naked (onstage) over 50 times, editing for big pharma companies (Ask her anything about the prostate: she knows), creatively ideating for major global brands (I'm in it for the catered lunches) and passing out cheese cube samples (a decided low point). As a performer she's done comedy at places like Caroline's, Stand Up New York, The Big Stinkin' Comedy Festival in Austin, TX, and Boom Chicago in Amsterdam. She can't tell you what she's ghost written (obv!) but she's co-written two books on cookery, and authored The Bourbon Dessert Cookbook. She does not believe in white chocolate.

Lynn Marie lives and writes twenty-six floors above 42nd Street in New York City with her husband, children, and two elderly terriers.

www.lynnmariehulsman.com

@LynnMarieSays

A Miracle at Macy's

LYNN MARIE HULSMAN

Harper*Impulse* an imprint of
HarperCollins*Publishers* Ltd
1 London Bridge Street
London SE1 9GF

www.harpercollins.co.uk

A Paperback Original 2015

First published in Great Britain in ebook format by Harper*Impulse* 2015

A catalogue record for this book is
available from the British Library

ISBN: 9780008164348

This novel is entirely a work of fiction.
The names, characters and incidents portrayed in it are
the work of the author's imagination. Any resemblance to
actual persons, living or dead, events or localities is
entirely coincidental.

Automatically produced by Atomik ePublisher from Easypress

Printed and bound in Great Britain

For Rosie and Wolfie, the best presents I ever got.

Chapter 1

They say dogs are man's best friend and that a woman's not a woman until she's a wife. *Wrong!* I'm here to tell you that the most natural match in the world is a girl and her dog...end of.

Take me and Hudson, for example. We couldn't be happier. Ever since the magical day I found him wet and skinny, huddled in the back of a Macy's shopping bag. You know the one. With the big red star on it? Since the day I saved him, we've been each other's family. Well, that's not the whole story. I mean, the family part is. But if I were to be honest, I'd have to admit that he saved me as much as I saved him. Maybe more.

"Harf! Harf, harf!"

"Quiet, Huddie," I scold, as he comes tearing into the kitchen, claws skittering over the polished wood floor, launched from his cozy nest on the sofa. "It's early. You'll wake the whole building."

"Worf!" Not only does my little mutt keep barking, he also has the nerve to start jumping against the kitchen island where I'm up to my elbows grating frozen beef fat (suet, to those in the know) so I can test a recipe for traditional English mincemeat Christmas pies.

"It's a marshmallow world in the winter...when the snow comes to cover the grouuuund..."

"Oh, the phone! Of course. You are a wonder dog, aren't you?"

1

My December ringtone is the jaunty Dean Martin rendition of one of my favorite retro holiday songs. I should have guessed. Hudson has a knack for barking right before my phone rings. I chalk it up to being a version of that thing animals do when they sense earthquakes and tsunamis.

"Rowf!"

"Yes, the phone. I hear it, Huddie. I'm getting it. It's not life and death," I say, wiping my hand on a freshly bleached, extra-large Williams-Sonoma kitchen towel. "I do have voicemail, you know."

"Hello darling, I scarcely have a minute to breathe, never mind visiting the loo, but I promised I'd ring you this week. I'm told you're in my diary, so here I am."

It's Aunt Miranda. If she were Native American, her name would be more "Bursts in Frantic," than one of the more traditional, serene names like, "Walks with Nature" or "Drifts on Clouds."

"Good morning, Aunt Miranda," I say, slipping Hudson a pinch of the suet. He's considerate enough to nibble it gently out from between my fingers. I know that took disciplined restraint on his part. "I've missed you too." Hudson finishes his morsel, and rubs against my leg to give me a hug.

"Now Charlotte, don't be like that! You know I always miss you, it's only my hair's on fire with the Rockefeller Tree Lighting tonight. As you know, those early December blizzards really threw a spanner in the works. We had this planned for the week after Thanksgiving, the way it has been for years and years. But they've only just managed to resurface the skating rink after the weight of the snow caused that massive crack. The commissioner only just declared it safe to the public. Pulling off this huge event this close to Christmas Day will be the triumph of my career. Between you, me, and the lamppost, it's going to be spectacular."

It amazes me how Aunt Miranda can talk a mile a minute when she's downloading information to me, but the second she's in the presence of a client or celebrity, she's as measured and gracious as the Queen. Her chameleon-like ability to adapt has catapulted her the top of her field. My Aunt Miranda is a party planner on steroids. She produces major events all over the globe, ranging from celebrity weddings, to movie openings, to charity marathons, to high-profile ribbon cuttings. Her company, Nichols Bespoke Events, is, as they say, a major player.

"Sounds awesome."

"Awesome? Honestly Charlotte, one would imagine you were born in the States and educated on a Disney cruise ship, rather than born in England and educated in the finest public schools."

"You mean the finest boarding schools where you could chuck me on the Northeastern coast. I've lived in America longer than in England. I moved here when I was twelve."

"I know very well when you moved here. I raised you, if you'll remember."

"Sort of," I mumbled.

"What's that?" Miranda shouts, not bothering to muffle the phone with her hand. *"NO! Shandelle, the horse blankets belong in wardrobe! And tell craft services to track down those cases of NutriWater. If we don't have Pomegranate-Acai, then we don't have Miss Miranda Lambert in a fringed jacket and cowboy boots handing over a billboard-sized check to Toys for Tots in front of millions of television viewers! No. I said pomegranate! It's the pink one. Do you enjoy being employed?!!"*

I pick up a microplane grater and calmly begin shaving nutmeg seeds into a bowl. It's been my experience that Aunt Miranda's tirades can go on so long that she forgets about me and walks away from her phone. I shouldn't have picked up. This call is throwing me off my schedule. I have a plan for the day, as usual. There is very little that makes me happier than a solid plan.

Today's agenda:
1. Test the recipe for mince pies
2. Update *The Cozy Brownstone Kitchen*, (maybe a blog post on potted meat?) and respond to questions from my followers

3. Go to the butcher to pick up the crown roast I ordered for my next recipe test
4. Make lunch for myself and Huddie and eat it together while watching the end of *You've Got Mail*
5. Research the origins of the preservation of potted prawns in the days before refrigeration
6. Prepare said crown roast, with an array of winter vegetables
7. Test a recipe for a Bakewell tart,
8. Watch some *Animal Planet* with Hudson, and maybe the first part of *Love, Actually*
9. Early bedtime with my fat new Harlequin Superromance novel and Hudson (he never judges what I read)

Perfection!

"*...and the baby for the crèche scene needs a laminate,*" Aunt Miranda is still shouting. "*Strangling hazard? So remove the cord and pin it onto his pyjamas, do I have to solve every problem? What? Then Velcro it! It's not rocket science. Of COURSE the mother needs an all-access pass as well. Do you think the baby is going to climb up into the manger and swaddle himself? Why are you still standing here? GO!*"

"Right then, sorry about the interruption," she says smoothly transitioning back to me. "Charlotte, dear, I'm ringing to respond to your invitations to Christmas Eve brunch and Christmas dinner. I have some very big deals in the works, and I'm not at liberty to discuss them at this point, confidentiality agreements, meow meow, etcetera. At this point I'm afraid I still can't commit."

None of this comes a surprise, of course. Aunt Miranda may be my only family, apart from a few very distant cousins numerous-times removed who live in far-flung tiny villages dotting England and Wales, but she is first and foremost a businesswoman.

"Oh," I respond, trying not to sound disappointed, "it's just that I've already blogged that I might have a crowd here in the brownstone so I can serve the traditional English feasts I've been working on recently. I mean, this is a really good way to test the recipes for the cookbook I'm researching. I'm told by my agent, Beverly, it's expected to sell big." This latest cookbook, *The English Manor Cookbook: Traditional Meals for Holidays, Shoot Lunches, and More*, is due out next year.

Hudson takes advantage of my being distracted by climbing onto a kitchen chair and straining his pointy little muzzle toward the bowl of beef fat. I swat him away. "Hey you, you had your share."

Sometimes I forget he's a dog and treat him like a person, but his animal instincts come roaring to the forefront when there's raw meat within smelling distance. "Huddie, shoo!" Disappointed, he hops down, and slinks to his basket in the corner of the kitchen.

Aunt Miranda sighs down the phone line. "Why can't you just fly off to Saint Thomas like other sane, single young women and forget Christmas is even happening?"

I hear the subtext: *Because that would be so much more convenient for me.*

"That's what I'd do…" she continues. "A few frozen cocktails, a chaise lounge, a bottle of tanning oil, a personal butler. Before you know it, Christmas will be done and dusted, and you'll come home bronzed and more relaxed than you've been in years, if you catch my meaning."

"Subtle, Aunt Miranda. Is that how you speak to the Dalai Lama when you're overseeing his blessing ceremonies? Anyway, I don't want to leave New York at Christmas time. I'm planning to put up my tree tomorrow." I feel a frisson of pleasure buzz up the back of my neck. I love everything about having a real, living Christmas tree. I love choosing it, I love springing the branches free from the bundling, I love the herbal floral fragrance, and I just adore draping it in lights. "You should try it some year."

"What's the point? I'm never at home. Besides, if I wanted a sticky pine tree swathed in handmade ornaments and drugstore tinsel, I have people for that. You know, Charlotte, you could have people, too."

"I don't need people." I lean over and give Hudson a little

scratch on the belly. He twitches, and bicycles his stubby legs. He smiles a blissed-out smile.

"I'm saying that I have connections. I could give you a leg up to a real career."

"I have a real career." I pick up my nutmeg and begin grating with renewed determination.

"Pfft! When are you going to stop testing recipes for cookbook authors, and write a cookbook of your own? For heaven's sake, how many awards did you walk away with when you graduated from the Culinary Institute of America? I'd never have sanctioned your turning your back on university in favor of the CIA had I known you'd toss out any chance of success and waste your time with that little blog."

"This recipe testing and my 'little blog,' happen to pay my bills, thank you very much. I'm getting more and more paying sponsors every day. Since last month, thirty-seven more members have signed up."

"Ah, yes, your 'Charlotte's Chefs.' Has it ever occurred to you, young lady, that you spend more time with the followers on your blog than you do with live humans?"

"'Charlotte's Chefs' are live humans."

"Technically, yes, but you must see my point. A twenty-six-year-old girl shouldn't rely on online friendships and a stray dog as her entire social sphere. She should be out in the city, getting dirty and making mistakes. Speaking of dirty, have you heard from James?"

My back stiffens as I accidentally hack a large chunk of skin off of my knuckle. "Ouch," I cry, chucking the microplane and the nutmeg into the sink. "No, I have *not* heard from James, and I've asked you repeatedly not to bring him up." I crouch down on the floor, gather Hudson into a hug, and suck on my wounded finger.

"With your talent and his star-power, you could be someone by now. I know you blew your chance by turning James down way back when, but I've an idea he'd welcome you back with open arms. Team up with a real player like that firecracker, and you'd be a New York

Times columnist and a leading restaurateur in short order. Your literary agent, the one who gets you all those testing jobs… what's his name? Beverly Chestnut! That's it. He's said as much a number of times. What a character that man is! Ha! The bolo tie he wore to the World Literacy Fund Charity Ball slayed me. *Genius!* All I'm saying, darling, is that you could be someplace in this world."

"I am someplace in this world." I look around my cozy kitchen, decorated just the way I like it with a combination of French country touches, and mid-century appliances. "I'm where I want to be." Hudson turns in a circle, and snuggles into my lap, burrowing with his little, pear-shaped head. I give him a scratch behind the ears. He fusses a little, then settles in the crook of my knee.

Aunt Miranda sighs. "I care about you, Charlotte, I truly do, but I'll never understand you."

I notice the clock, and see that the day is getting away from me. "So, is there a chance you'll come to Christmas brunch or dinner, or is it an absolute 'no?'"

"One moment Charlotte… *I beg your pardon! Of course we cannot supply cocaine to the on-air talent. Who do you think I am? The concierge of the Chateau Marmont.*"

I put the phone down on the counter. Maybe I can make some apple butter, I think to myself while Miranda rants on, with lots of clove. That'll be so warm and yummy for the winter. Hmm… when will I be able to hit Fairway to see what they have in the way of decent New York State apples…?

"Charlotte, are you there, darling?"

"I'm here," I say firing up my Nespresso machine to make a nice, steaming double-shot cappuccino.

"As I was saying Charlotte… Actually, hold the phone. *You'd better tell that talent wrangler that if any pop star, politician, or for that matter, Muppet, is too high to sing in the final number, he'll be looking for a job come New Year's!* Sorry darling, it's a madhouse here. Tell you what, come down to the tree lighting tonight and we'll discuss. I really can't stay on the line."

"No thanks," I say, pulling my antique, hand-cranked food mill from under the sink. "I'm going to watch it on TV."

"Darling, you must come. It's the pinnacle of my event-planning career to date, and I'm not going to be very English about it and pretend it's really nothing. Taking a leaf from the Americans' book, I'll simply say it. If I pull this off, I'll frankly be one of the top global Production Directors, period. Hello Cannes! Hello coronation of Prince William! Say you'll pop round."

I glance over at Hudson snoring lightly in his warm bed. I don't want to go out for walkies today, much less eject myself into one of the single-most crowded events on the island of Manhattan.

"I don't know…"

"Super. The broadcast starts at 7, and the lights go on at 9. I'll phone or text you later. I won't take no for an answer."

Before I can argue, she's put down the phone. I'm on a schedule, too, you know. Maybe I'm not organizing the lighting of the tallest tree in the Northeastern US, but I have responsibilities. I stomp my foot and let out a scream of exasperation, waking Hudson.

He leaps out of his bed and runs from the kitchen to the hallway. I hear a *ching ching* and I don't even have to turn my back to know that my determined little roommate is rattling his tags, leaping up against the wall under the little blue plastic IKEA hook shaped like a dog's rear end. He's trying to grab his leash.

"Seriously? I have a countertop covered in mincemeat and dough waiting to be made into tiny pies. You'd love a mincemeat pie, wouldn't you, boy?"

He doesn't rise to the bait.

"Besides, I haven't had enough coffee yet. Do you really need to change the game plan?"

With one concerted leap, he snatches the loop of the leash in his muzzle. He stands there, staring.

"No, I won't do it." I cross my arms in defiance.

"Both you and Aunt Miranda need to learn to respect my boundaries."

No response.

"I know you don't need to do business. You always hold it until 11:30."

More staring.

"The answer is no." I turn my back on him. "Schedules are healthy. I read that all the best parents keep their children on schedules. I had no parameters when I was little, no rules. I read in *Psychology Today* that can make you feel unsafe." I peek over my shoulder.

Hudson hasn't moved a muscle. I wonder if he's breathing. He doesn't even blink.

"Hudson…"

Still as a statue.

"Oh, *OK!*" I heave myself out of my desk chair and pull my coat from the rack.

Hudson breaks his freeze, and begins a frenzy of circling, first one way, and then the other. I crack up. "Do you love me?" I ask him. He runs at me, and banks off my calf. He's scratching frantically at my leg, as if to climb me. I know he wants to give me a kiss, so I bend down so we're nose to nose. He gives me a bounty of face-licks, then stretches his neck out so it fits in the crook of my own. He rubs his cheek against mine, with a few upward jerks. "Aw … huggies!" I say. It's a thing we do. "You do love me! Sweet boy. OK, we're going out," I explain, pulling on my knit hat, "but we're not going to the dog park. This is just a quick relief break, then I'm coming back to make coffee, and get back to work. Got it?"

I click the ring of his leash onto his harness, and hold open the door.

"Did you hear me? Five minutes. That's final."

For a quick second, his eyes twinkle before he bounds onto the landing, and skitters down the stairs.

*****

9

Scratching to get in the park gate, Hudson pulls hard on his leash as I juggle my Starbucks flat white. It spills all over my mittens.

"Huddie, there's a reason we make coffee at home. You talked me into leaving the house against my will, can you at least be patient?" I fumble with first one gate, then another. There are always two gates at dog runs: Opening them one at a time contains the "flight risks." Once we're inside, I squat down try to unfasten the ring on Hudson's leash, while maintaining my balance. A man with sunny reddish-blonde, curly hair and warm, brown eyes smiles at me. "Looks like you've got your hands full."

"He's a handful, all right," I mumble. Hudson whines impatiently.

"Doesn't the run look fantastic? The community board pitched in funds for all these twinkle lights and the decorations. I hardly recognize the place with all the Christmas trimmings."

I take a minute to glance around. It's breathtaking. The chain-link fence is festooned with glowing shapes made from strings of lights: A dog bone, the outline of a dog, a dog's face, a dog dish that says "Spot" on it. And there are various sizes of Christmas tree in every corner, decorated with strings of popcorn.

"Oh, wow," I whisper involuntarily.

"I know, right? I heard they chose popcorn for the trees since it's biodegradable. Peeing on them is encouraged. By the dogs, of course. Merry Christmas to them."

Now I'm on my knees in the dirt and gravel, still struggling to free Hudson. I perch my coffee carefully on a large rock.

"Listen, Puppy Dog," I say, "you have to stop pulling if you want me to undo this." He's spied some of his neighborhood dog friends and he's eager to get into the mix.

"Hold still," I tell him. "And before you run off, remember this: We're only staying five minutes. Don't look at me like that. I know I said that before, but I really do mean it. Pay attention to the time. I don't want to have to embarrass you in front of your friends."

He's panting with expectation, and his curled tongue and open mouth form a goofy grin. I finally manage to free him from his restraint, and he races toward the clump of canines like a shot. He jumps up to nip the nape of a young Great Dane's neck, and the oversized pup swings around playfully, nearly taking out a couple of Chihuahuas with his huge feet. The look of sheer joy on Hudson's face as he throws himself into the throng of dogs makes me smile. The blonde guy catches my eye and raises an eyebrow. *He thinks I was smiling at him!*

"Oh, no," I mumble, waving my hand as if to erase the moment. "I was… well, my dog…" I say pointing.

Embarrassed, I take a seat on one of the benches along the edge of the fence. The air is cold, but it's warm in the midmorning winter sun. I loosen my scarf and take in the twinkly scene, trying to relax. I can't help looking at my watch. I really wanted to start baking by now. I eat lunch at 1 and this unplanned trip is throwing off my schedule. There is no way I'm going to the tree lighting. Relax, I tell myself. Five minutes, I promise myself. Five minutes.

Not far away, groups of school children are filing off of yellow buses and up the path to the Natural History Museum. They're nearly as frisky as the puppies in the park. I don't imagine much schoolwork gets done in the run-up to Christmas.

On the corner of 81st, a group of musicians circle up and take out instruments, setting their cases in a bunch near a handler. A mom sits on the bench opposite me, and lifts her toddler out of a stroller. He's wearing a knitted hat with reindeer antlers attached. The baby babbles and points at me. I can feel my cheeks start to turn pink.

"Yes, that's a pretty lady," the mom says. The baby squeals, delighted, and points again. I wish the baby would focus on someone else. I pretend to be concentrating on picking Hudson out of the pack. Four more minutes, I tell myself, picking at a thread on my sweater sleeve.

Hudson comes tearing toward me, running so fast that he's scooping up gravel and flinging it behind himself with every bound. He comes to a stop and bangs into my knees. He shakes

11

all over, and looks up at me, tongue still curled, goofy smile still in place.

"Hello, my baby," I say, scratching his ears. "Are you having fun?" My shoulders drop. Maybe we can stay for ten minutes. It makes him so happy.

"Who's a good boy?" I bend down to let him lick my cheek and I nuzzle his whiskery snout. "You're a good boy, right Hudson?"

"His name is Hudson? That's my son's name!" The guy with the curly blonde hair comes walking up to the bench. I straighten up, and look at his face. He's handsome, and I cannot pull my eyes away. Seconds pass as I try to think of something to say that won't sound weird.

C'mon Charlotte, I coach myself, he's waiting. It's been awhile since I've made conversation with a guy. Or anyone, really. I try to think of the last time I talked to someone face-to-face. Was it yesterday? The day before? I'm still staring. He's still waiting. Just say something, I tell myself. Anything.

"I named him after the deli where I found him," I finally blurt. "He'd been living in the trash."

"Hey, that's what happened with my son!"

I stiffen, and suck in some air. "Really? I'm so sorry...or I guess, I mean, that's great...?"

He bursts out with a deep belly laugh. "I'm *joking!*" He sits down on the bench beside me. "Hudson is my ex-wife's surname, so we thought, you know, since he'd have my last name, that it was nice that he'd have something of hers. Do you have kids?"

"No," I say simply. I don't elaborate, but I feel like he's waiting for more of an explanation. He probably thinks something's wrong with me. I want to tell him that I'm not even married, but saying that might sound like I'm coming on to him. I try to think of something else to talk about. "No," I say again. Good one, Charlotte! I notice that Hudson has jumped up onto the bench beside the man, and is nuzzling his snout into his armpit. "Just... no."

"Well," he says "this little Westie must keep you busy." I don't bother to mention that Hudson is a mutt. Everyone who meets him assigns him a breed. It's like they see what's familiar, and decide that's what he is. The man leans back against the fence and stretches out his long legs. "Does your mommy spoil you, Hudson?" The way Hudson is pushing his head under the man's arm makes it look like he's nodding in agreement. "Yeah, thought so."

My heart is beating fast. Aunt Miranda might be right. I think I've lost the art of having to hold up my end on of the conversation with a live human. When my agent Beverly or book editors take me out to lunch, they're always happy enough to do the talking, filling the space with business details. And when I make an appearance at Aunt Miranda's parties or opening-night events, I stick to the background. Anyone who's had a drink or two generally relishes the chance to monologue, I've found. My strategy is to stand next to the champagne guzzlers. No need to say a word.

Hudson is now fully seated in the guy's lap. Should I scold him playfully? Is that the way dog people banter? I pull off my knit hat. My scalp is starting to sweat.

"That's my girl over there," he says, pointing.

He has a girlfriend and he's flirting with me? It's James all over again.

"The spotted one."

I look at a klatch of dogs engaged in a ball game, and spy a Dalmatian.

"Oh, your dog," I try. "She's lovely."

"Yeah, she's a good girl," he says. I exhale. I'm making this harder than it needs to be. Deep breath, Charlotte. OK, this isn't bad. This is what I should want, right? To sit and chat with what anyone might call a good-looking man. He's friendly. He's not creepy. Look at me! I'm being normal.

"Your dog is gorgeous," I tell him, stretching myself. She really is. She's all legs and flapping ears, filled with energy. One thing I never mind talking about is dogs. Hudson jumps off of the guy's lap, and heads off to the waste bin, sniffing around.

13

"Hudson," I call, "leave that alone. Here, Hudson. Come!"

The brass band at the west side of the museum strikes up, and we're treated to a loud, merry rendition of *Let it Snow*.

I check my watch again. It's been over twenty minutes. I'm itchy to get home.

"Huddie! C'mon boy. We should get moving," I call.

"Oh, are you leaving?" He looks disappointed. "I was hoping you'd stay for a while."

"We should go soon," I tell him and I risk stealing a glance. He smiles. Breathe, Charlotte. This is how people meet people. I don't feel a particular spark with this guy, even though he's nice, but maybe this is how it's supposed to be. Maybe slow and steady wins the race. "Soon-ish, anyway." I lean my back against the fence. 'Ten minutes won't throw me off my schedule too badly."

"People say Dalmatians aren't the brightest bulbs on the tree, but that's not true about Daphne." There's no rush in the man's voice, no tension. It's like he has no other plans for the day. He beams out at his dog. "She's an angel, smart as a whip," he says, his voice filled with affection.

He's so relaxed, I think. Are other people born like that? I wonder. I sip my now-cold coffee, just to have something to do with my hands. Am I missing a gene?

"What do you do for a living?" he asks, scanning the playing field.

"I'm a food writer, and I test recipes on the side. I have a blog."

"Do you have a card? With your website on it?"

"I do," I say fumbling in my bag. I'm down to my last one, it's a bit damp, and crumbs from the bottom of my purse are clinging to it. I brush it off, and wonder if he'll think it's too gross if I hand it to him.

"Cool. I'm an art director," he says, taking the card and pocketing it. "My name is Ken by the way. My friends all call me a foodie. I hate that word, but it's kind of true. I like cooking, and I really love eating out."

14

"Food is… really great," I say awkwardly. He smiles encouragingly. "Really. I eat it all the time." I'm starting to sweat. Not pretty. I try to scratch surreptitiously under my arms. Beneath my coat, perspiration is making me feel all prickly.

"Glad to hear that. I was just thinking that I'd love to take you out to dinner some night. Do you like Ethiopian?"

Oh my God. He's asking me on a date.

I see Hudson bounding up, holding something in his mouth.

"Hudson! Put that down. We don't pick up trash in our mouths," I say. I hear my rigid, school-marmish tone. Does this guy think I'm a stick-in-the-mud? "Hudson," I try again, "bring that to me. That's right. Come here. *Good boy*. I'll take that." I hope I sound less uptight. My peppy little angel is headed right toward me, so I bend over and hold out my hand.

At the last minute, Hudson veers and lasers in on the guy. He drops the magazine from his mouth, onto the guy's feet, and sits down, looking very pleased with himself.

"I'll get that," I say quickly. I don't want him to think my dog and I are litterbugs.

"Don't worry." He's already reaching for it.

"No, really, I've got it." I bend over to grab it and smack my skull into his.

"Ow!" I say, rubbing my head. "I'm so sorry!"

He's got the magazine in his hand. "Don't worry." He points to his head. "Hard as a rock," he says with a laugh. "Hey, you didn't answer. Would you go out to dinner with me?"

I reach for the magazine, but the guy is examining it. He turns it over, and to my horror, it's *American Bride.*

Hudson's on his feet, with his expressive tail high in the air, wagging like metronome on the verge of exploding, looking from one to the other of us.

The guy laughs out loud, and points to the magazine's cover. "You have to go out with me now. Your dog obviously has big plans for us."

I can feel my whole face go red. Could I go out with this guy? I wonder to myself. It's been a long time. Why not? It's crazy that I'm a food blogger and I haven't eaten out at a nice place in... how long?

"I guess dinner would be OK," I say, doubting that's the truth, even as I say it. I'm talking slowly, turning the possibility over in my head, thinking through any potential pitfalls. What would we talk about for two hours?

"Great! Have you heard of that new place in Chelsea? *The Fork?*"

"No, I haven't." I'm embarrassed. The truth is, I don't know what's hot or new on the city restaurant scene. "Is it new?"

"Really new. It's James Keyes' latest. American comfort food. He's the chef behind *Four Chairs* and *East 4th.* Do you know of him?"

I feel like someone just dumped a bucket of ice water down my back. "Oh, I definitely know of him. In fact, I *know* him."

"Cool! How did you get to know someone so famous?"

"We went to culinary school together. You know what?" I say, scrambling to pull on my gloves and gather my belongings. "Thanks anyway, but I'm super busy. I really don't think I can work in going out to dinner any time soon. I'm sorry, we have to go now," I say, lunging toward Hudson, and snapping the leash onto the ring of his harness in one swift motion. I snatch the magazine from the guy's hand, and zoom for the gate, dragging my unwilling canine behind me.

"Wait!" the man calls. "Your coffee!"

By the time he says it, I'm locking the second gate behind me. I chuck the copy of *American Bride* into a trashcan, and cut around the museum instead of taking the shortest route home. Hudson won't stop tugging in the opposite direction.

"Huddie, no," I pant. "We're not going back."

He sits down on his rump and gazes at me. It looks like he's raising his one black eyebrow.

"It's just a bad idea. I just want to keep things simple right now.

Let's go boy," I say, gently tugging on his leash. When I hit the avenue, I'm just starting to slow from a jog to a normal gait. My phone buzzes on my coat pocket, and I pull over in front of the German bakery in the middle of the block. I can smell the butter and raspberry from the Linzer tarts and my stomach starts to rumble. I've missed breakfast, now I just want to get home, make myself lunch, and maybe, just maybe, slip into my PJs.

Pulling out my mobile I see a string of text messages waiting for me.

Can't phone, so texting. Utterly mad on Rock Plaza. Our life-sized Elf On A Shelf developed sudden-onset agoraphobia and won't leave her trailer + pranking flash mob dumped buckets of marbles onto skating rink

This just in: Xmas Eve at yours is no-go. *Big* celeb getting engaged onstage with the Rockettes. Say you'll come to Radio City that night, and we'll order in from Mangia. Still hoping to make it for Xmas dinner at yours. I don't want you to be alone. x

OH, and don't think you're skiving off on me tonight. You can be my date. I expect to see you here by 7 sharp. If you behave, I'll bow out and fix you up with Kermit the Frog. xo

I guess I've finally hit bottom. It's come to my aunt accepting the fact that the only dates anyone can see me having are with a spinster or a puppet. Of course, I just threw away a chance with someone who seemed like a nice guy. Maybe I have become a crazy dog lady. But isn't that OK? Is there a law that says I have to put on a coconut bra and dance on barroom tables every weekend? Why can't I just be me, by myself, the way I want to be?

"Excuse me," a man barks, pushing past me to get in the door to the bakery. "Nut job," he mutters under his breath before pushing into the shop. I look at the phone in my hand, and realizing I've been staring at it for quite awhile now. I glance down to see Hudson doing a little dance, hopping from one foot to another to another.

"Sorry boy, are you getting cold? Let's go."

I turn downtown, the shortest route to my apartment, but Hudson won't stop tugging in the opposite direction.

"Huddie, no," I tell him. "We're not going back."

He sits down on his rump and gazes at me. Raising his eyebrow at me again.

"You'll freeze your tail off."

He jumps up and down, smiling, as if to say he's fine.

"It's just a bad idea, OK. I just want to keep things simple. Now come on," I say, gently tugging on his leash. "Sorry, boy, I really want to be home right now. I'll make it up to you, I promise. How does a snuggle in your blankies and a nice, big bone sound? I'll even turn on the TV for you. *Animal Planet.*"

He doesn't look back at me. He seems resigned. He just pulls me to the crosswalk that he knows takes us home. I swear he sighs, before he steps off the curb. We walk home together in silence.

*****

My arm is going numb from being held high in the air, trying to beckon a cab on Central Park West at shift-change time.

Three yellow taxis have already slowed down, clocked that I have a smiling, be-sweatered little dog on the end of my leash, before speeding off. My high-heeled wedge boots are pinching my feet, and I feel constricted in my good wool dress coat. I had to haul myself into the shower, blow my hair dry, and put makeup on my face to leave my apartment. I wouldn't dare show up to one of Aunt Miranda's events without making an effort. It won't be to her standards, but at least she can't say I didn't try.

Believe me when I tell you, I decided that I wasn't going tonight no fewer than 50 times but I always circled back to the hard truth: Aunt Miranda's haranguing would be harder to endure than an hour at Rockefeller Center. Like I told Hudson, we're going late, showing our faces, staying for half an hour… an hour max… and then home to my jammies and Netflix. With any luck, we'd be burrowed into the couch with the TV on by the time they actually flicked the switch to light the 100-foot Norway Spruce.

Just as I can no longer feel my fingers, a taxi swoops up to the curb, and shouts out the window, "Where you going?"

"Rockefeller Center, 50th Street between 5th and 6th."

"I know where the Rockefeller Center is. I'm a New Yorker. I've lived here for twenty years since I moved from Delhi as a kid."

"Sorry."

"Your dog, is he a good dog?"

Hudson lets out a little whine, culminating in an affirmative yelp.

"Yes, very good."

"I like good dogs. I do not like bad dogs."

"Fair enough," I say. "Yes or no?" I can no longer feel my left foot.

"OK, get in. I take you."

"Oh, thank you!" Hudson and I pile into the cab. I spy myself in the rearview mirror. My nose is pink with cold.

"They make the tree lights tonight. Very big crowds, very crowded."

"I know," I say, voice filled with dread. "I have to go. My aunt is producing it."

"She's a movie producer? Like Steven Spielberg? I look very handsome on camera. Very handsome indeed."

"No, she's in charge of the tree lighting. Production Manager, that's the title. She's in charge of the guests, everything that happens onsite, coordinating with the television crew, just… everything."

He whistles a low whistle. "Your dog is VIP. Or shall I say VID? Understand? Very Important Dog? That's funny, I think! Very funny!"

I laugh. "Yes, it is."

"I do stand-up comedy. Here," he turns around, and shoves a

card through the little tray that tunnels through the plastic between the front and back seats. "Vijay Singh, this Monday night, Broadway Comedy Club. Next week, Caroline's Comedy Club."

Impressed, I tuck the card in my handbag. "From what I hear, getting into Caroline's is a big deal."

It just goes to show if you take the time to speak to your taxi driver, you never know who you're going to meet. Once I even met an opera singer though this guy was my first comedian.

"It is a very big deal! I'm hilarious. Very funny. Trust me when I say this to you."

"I believe you."

The sparkle of multiple flashbulbs going off catches my eye from the little TV screen affixed to the back of the seat in front of me. It's a *New York One* live report from the tree lighting. Hudson tries to stand and sniff the screen, but Vijay is driving like a maniac, so my little dog looks like he's surfing. "Sit, Hudson." I scooch over and put my arm around him. "Look, here's Aunt Miranda's event. See the tree?"

A tiny country singer with long blonde hair and a powerful voice begins belting out *O Holy Night*.

Suddenly, the cab slams to a stop and Hudson goes careening into the footwell.

I fish him out from the floorboards, and kiss his little head. As the singer is reaching the crescendo of the song, the camera cuts to a woman holding a sleeping baby, and singing along, sincere and misty-eyed. My heart does a little jig. The impact of the soulful song, and the beauty of the swaying crowd among all of the festive decorations, send a frisson of holiday excitement through my body. Now I'm glad I made the effort to get out of the house.

A Christmas feeling from when I was a little girl washes over me. I feel the safety and joy of when our cook, Bridget, baked up a storm, and my parents stayed around the house instead of going out all the time. That was before the car accident. Before I moved to the states to live with Aunt Miranda. Hudson stands up, putting all the weight of his pointy little feet onto my thigh.

On the television, other musicians, sports stars, and the mayor of New York join the singer on the stage in front of the soon-to-be brilliantly illuminated tree. The camera pans the audience. People are holding up their phones and tablets to snap photos. Suddenly, I'm glad I'm en route. I can't believe I almost passed up this opportunity.

When the camera pans to the very edge of the stage, I see Aunt Miranda.

"Look, Hudson, there she is!" I wave frantically, as if I'll really get her attention. "Hiya, Aunt Miranda! Hi!" Hudson barks.

"No barking in the taxi," Vijay says. "Look, there is your Radio City Music Hall."

"I'm a New Yorker, I know where Radio City Music Hall is."

"Touché," he says.

Hudson pants and smiles, eyes on the TV. Can he see Aunt Miranda, I wonder? She looks impeccable in a classic winter white wool coat with a large golden brooch, reminiscent of the bronze *Titan Prometheus* statue that graces the lower plaza of Rockefeller Center. I'm sure it was no accident. Aunt Miranda is the very essence of style. Standing next to her, typing into an iPad is a young man I've never seen before, with wavy light-brown hair falling over the edge of his roundish tortoise-shell, horn-rimmed glasses. He has a neat, close-trimmed beard. He's smiling, I think. Is he? I can't be sure, since the shot isn't a close-up. Maybe it's just the way his heavy eyebrow arches. He looks like he's thinking of an amusing story or a joke.

It's usually Cerie who assists Aunt Miranda, but I recall that she's on maternity leave. If her right-hand assistant is gone, no wonder my aunt is more tightly wound than usual.

"Look Hudson, look at that man with Aunt Miranda. Who do you think he is?"

The guy is wearing a deep oxblood-colored leather pea coat with a chunky forest-green scarf twined around his neck. It looks hand-made. I wonder if he chose his clothes, or if Miranda "styled" him. He looks up at the scene onstage and smiles a satisfied smile, unmistakable this time. It's so unrestrained, it makes me smile too.

For half a second, I wish I were there, smelling the pine scent of the enormous tree, and enjoying the rumbling of the bass singers in my chest during the carols. I feel wide-awake, even though usually it would just about my bedtime.

The guy's eyes twinkle behind his glasses for a moment before Miranda points to something up in the tree, and his eyebrows knit together. I can't see his face anymore, because he's furiously scrolling through his tablet. I wonder what's wrong. All of the sudden, the man disappears and the screen is blue, demanding that I touch a button declaring whether I'd like to pay with cash, credit, or debit. I have the sensation of the film breaking in an old-time reel projector. I feel a bit robbed. I wanted to watch him longer; to know what changed his mood.

"Here we are, as close as I can drive," says Vijay. "There are police barricades, so I'm very sorry, but you must walk the rest of the way." Hudson stands up on his back legs, front paws against the window, eyes bright and expectant.

"That's fine," I say, tapping the touch screen and sliding my card into the machine. "We expected that." I tip him 25%. He did, after all, rescue both me and my little dog from frost bite.

"Thank you, miss," he says, pushing the receipt through the slot.

"Merry Christmas!" I tell him, opening the door to a crisp blast of wintry New York air.

"I don't celebrate Christmas." He waves a hand indicating his turban and dark skin. "The nativity story isn't sweeping Punjab, if you hear what I'm saying."

"Oh, I'm sorry, that was rude…"

He cuts me off, smiling. "No need to apologize. Many, many people confuse me with Brad Pitt!"

I open my mouth to respond, but my brain is working hard to catch up. He really doesn't look anything like the Hollywood actor.

"Joking! Of course I don't look like Brad Pitt."

I laugh uncertainly. He should probably work on his routine. Hudson leaps onto the sidewalk and is straining on his leash.

"Well, happy winter and good luck with the stand up," I say, just before slamming the door hard to make sure he's not heating the whole of the outdoors. I hear, "Don't forget! Vijay Singh at Caroline's. Very funny!"

I feel a smile spreading across my face as I walk across the sidewalk on 50th street toward the huge crowd. "This is fun, isn't it Huddie?" I call above the din of the throngs and the amplified Muppet version of *All I Want for Christmas is My Two Front Teeth* that's coming from the ceremony site. There are tourists everywhere, and to a person, they are all wide-eyed and beaming. As we approach, I spy the hundreds of flags surrounding the ice rink. Normally, the flagpoles fly the colors of every country in the United Nations, but this... I have to catch my breath. To herald Christmas, all of the flags have been replaced by red, green, and gold banners. Against the majestic gold flagpoles, and the myriad lights draped in the potted trees, shrubbery, and along the walls and fences, it makes my heart soar with the promise of what Christmas will bring. And that's to say nothing of the lush, towering evergreen, standing at the ready to be set aglow. There's no other word for it, I feel uplifted. Hudson scrapes ahead of me as if he's trying to dig up the concrete; he's clearly eager to get into the mix.

As we get closer to the tents from which stars, PAs, and Teamsters emerge, the crowds become thicker. I bend down to scoop Hudson up, and clutch him to my chest. "Ready boy?" His skinny tail thumps against the front of my coat, and I give him a big smooch on the muzzle.

People are clearly here to celebrate. The attendees range from bare-legged young women in filmy coats and cocktail dresses, who are so fashion-forward they wouldn't dare don tights with their stilettos, even in this cold weather, to families wearing matching parkas and knit caps declaring, "Wheeler Family Reunion—Xmas

NYC," to young couples who have such eyes for one another it's a wonder they can even see the skyscraper of an evergreen.

A door to what looks like the holding area catches my eye, and I set my sights on beelining through all the bodies to get there. The surprise at my enjoyment of being here is pumping adrenaline through my body, and making me feel like I've had a split of champagne, though I'm stone-cold sober. I have to admit, I'm kind of loving it. Maybe I'll become the kind of girl who goes to the Macy's fireworks along the river, or dresses up and boards a Halloween float in the West Village.

One thing's for sure: Hudson is in his element. Chest-to-chest, I can feel his little heart drumming rapidly, and his curled tongue is out and bobbing up and down with each step I take. I call that expression his "perma-smile." I love that he's happy, but I could do without the wet dog saliva on my already freezing ear. Note to self: Next year, wear earmuffs to tree lighting.

We shoulder our way through the revelers, and finally make it to the door of a white tent. I hear general buzzing inside, with the occasional shout. I've been on enough "sets" of Aunt Miranda's events to know that tension will be high as the stage managers inside are ruled by the stopwatch, and the talent is marking time, waiting to be led to the stage. I approach a refrigerator of a man, wearing a black suede overcoat, dark glasses, and a formidable headset.

"Hello, sir," I begin.

"You can't be here, move to the right, miss," he cuts me off.

"I'm supposed to be here, you see..."

"No entry without a laminate."

I saw that I was going to have to pull the Aunt Miranda card. I hated myself for what I was about to say. "I'm on the list."

"Name?" he barks.

"Charlotte Bell."

He picks up a clipboard from the director's chair beside him, and traces down the column of names with the wrong end of his pen.

"Nope. Move it to the right."

The buoyant holiday bliss I'd recently experienced was fading rapidly. Without warning, the throbbing in my feet resumes.

"Can you check again, please," I said, full of sweetness and light. Aunt Miranda wasn't much in the way of motherly, but she had taught me a few essential life skills. Her top tip is never to piss off the gatekeeper, i.e., the receptionist, the secretary, the personal assistant, or the hotel clerk. That was a pure guarantee, she said, of being separated from what you hoped to gain or achieve. "My aunt works here. Maybe you know her?"

He gives me a hard once-over. At least I think he does. It's hard to tell behind his menacing shades. At any rate, he's standing still and facing me.

Hudson lets out a little whine, and bicycles his front legs. I give him a squeeze to warn him not to blow it. To my surprise and relief, a slow smile spreads over the Refrigerator's face. "That's a good-lookin' Jack Russell," he says. "Real cute dog."

He presses a button near his chest, and says, "We need an escort at A4. Send a PA right away."

He reaches out, and says, "May I?"

Bemused, I hand over Hudson, and the big teddy bear of a bouncer snuggles my dog, cooing, "Who's a handsome dog? You are! That's right. You're a handsome dog!" Hudson wriggles gleefully, twitching and contorting his body into a near backbend, burrowing into the multiple chins of the big softie. I look on, smiling. I smell coffee coming from inside. My stomach rumbles. I can't wait for Aunt Miranda to walk me in, show me where the craft services table is, and sit me down someplace with a view of the tree. I have to confess, I do love a craft services table. I hope they have pastry. Something sweet and fruity would hit the spot about now.

"Who did you say your aunt was?" the bouncer asks, setting Hudson down on the floor.

"Miranda Nichols," I tell him.

25

We both squat down to play with Hudson.

"Aw, hell no. For real? You're not messin' around." He presses the button near his chest a second time. "Escort to A4, pronto." Hudson nuzzles the man's huge, ham of a hand. "Heh, heh. Real cute dog."

Huddie's extra-frisky tonight. Maybe it's the cold weather or the snow on the ground, but I suspect it's from being out in the melee. Guilt nudges at the corners of my heart. I really should bring him out more often. I mean, I make sure he gets exercise, and he has plenty of opportunities to relieve himself and all, but he's such a social butterfly. I wonder if he ever regrets being saddled with a homebody like me.

Even though he's a dog, Hudson is a "people person." He rolls over on his back, writhing like an alligator, flapping his paws above him. This elicits a big belly laugh from our formerly foreboding friend. We take turns pretending to nip at Hudson's hindquarters with our forefingers and thumbs, and each time, he whips around pretending to snap at the offender. He couldn't look happier if he tried.

Without preamble, two impeccable men's Italian leather boots appear in my field of vision. Hudson romps over, and moves in to give them a sniff.

"Can I help?" demands a stern, disembodied English voice from above.

I struggle to rise from my position on all fours, but find that now, not only are my feet numb, my knees are stiff from the cold. My new friend, the bodyguard, has nimbly risen and is back at his post, stiff as a statue, staring straight ahead. Hudson thinks I'm still playing a game. He keeps leaping up, punching me in the legs with his two front paws. I teeter, trying to stand, but there's nothing solid to grab onto. "I need to see Miranda Nichols," I say, trying to push up with my hands from the ground. Hudson licks my face with glee.

"Miranda Nichols?" He barks out a short laugh before

recovering. "She's a bit busy at the moment." There's no sarcasm colder than an Englishman's sarcasm.

"I'm sure, but could you, just, uh," I stammer. "Could you please go and get her for me?" I'm hoping by the time she gets here to meet me, I won't still be scrabbling around on the floor.

"That won't be possible. She's unreachable at the moment."

I see his feet shifting impatiently. I'd better get up quickly. He's grouchy, and obviously has better things to do. Like Aunt Miranda says, you don't annoy the gatekeepers. The harder I try to get up, the more the pins and needles prick my feet, and the more Hudson bounces off of my hip like a circus poodle.

"Huddie, no! Down!"

If I could only push off from something... I grab at the man's knee, but the physics of lifting are all wrong. I strain to re-position my arms. Maybe if I can just crab walk to the director's chair, I think. Hudson notices my struggle and begins springing up and nipping at my ear.

"Huddie, cut it out," I say, breathless from trying to maintain my yoga-like position. He barks playfully in response. I try to gain equilibrium, woefully aware that my backside is pointing skyward.

My dress coat, cut quite close through the shoulders, is effectively functioning as a strait jacket. Miranda convinced me that sleek was in last winter. I think I hear fabric ripping. I'm dizzy from hanging my head downward, and Hudson's sharp barks so close to my ears are making them ring. In a valiant leap, he winds up on the flat of my back, and teeters there for a proud moment before we both tumble over in the snow. I land hard on my bum. It smarts a bit, but I can't help laughing as Hudson flails like a bug on his back.

"For heaven's sake," the man says impatiently. He hooks his hands under my arms and, with seemingly little effort, pulls me up to standing. I'm face-to-chest with an oxblood leather coat, and green knit scarf.

"Oh! It's you." Behind his glasses, his eyes are a startling clear blue. I've never seen eyes that blue before. I look closer, trying to see if there's a corona of gold, green, or even turquoise around his pupils. Nope, just bright Grecian blue.

"Have we met?" he asks, holding my gaze.

Oh God, I've been staring. "I know you. I mean, no. You're one of the production assistants I saw on TV."

I hear a high-pitched little gasp. I whip around to look at the Refrigerator, but he's cool as a cucumber, arms crossed, eyes straight ahead. If the gasp came from him, he's not letting on.

"I most certainly am not a production assistant," he assures me in a Little Lord Fauntleroy voice. He stands up taller, which is a feat. I mean, he's pretty tall in the first place. "I'm the Assistant Production Manager." He looks at his watch. "And right about now, I'm responsible for seeing that the mayor of your fine city is briefed before she goes on live television. So, if you'll excuse me," he says, turning crisply to walk away.

"Wait!"

"I'm sorry, there's no access through this door. You'll have to queue by the barriers for autographs." He turns again, and Olympic race-walks in the other direction, deftly dodging crates, printers, and myriad interns as he goes.

Hudson lets out a low, slow whine, ending in a bark. He wants the man to play! He's bowing down with his rump in the air, shimmying. Clearly, he isn't as offended by the man's rudeness as I am.

"I'm not here for autographs, I'm going backstage."

"No dogs allowed. Please exit through the front with your animal. This is a restricted area," he says, still walking.

No dogs allowed? I just saw the outlines of a camel and what appeared to be two fully grown sheep through the far tent wall. As if Hudson's going to infect the place!

"Not for us!"

"Goodbye," he calls not bothering to turn around. "Marlon, please escort the lady *and her dog* out to the public plaza." His snootiness ignites a fire in me. Is that the way he talks to the minions in his fleet of servants back home on the manor in Jolly Olde England, I wonder. I think it's time he was taught a little respect.

I hate to do it but he's left me no choice.

"Miranda Nichols is my aunt," I fire, just as he's exiting through a flap door on the other side of the tent. All of the fresh-faced young people hunched over their laptops around a table littered with coffee cups, stacks of papers, and wires for days look up with interest.

The Assistant Production Manager freezes. Slowly, he turns back around, one eyebrow raised.

I scoop Hudson up in one arm, plant my other fist on my hip, and raise my eyebrow right back.

"I see. Very good, would you follow me, please?" he asks, in a clipped, efficient voice. Butter wouldn't melt in his mouth.

I don't make a move. Tilting my head toward Hudson, I dare Mr. Blue Eyes to say he's not welcome.

He walks back to meet me, and gently takes my elbow with an elegant protocol that would rival a Buckingham Palace butler's. "I beg your pardon, Ms. Nichols. Would you *both* follow me, please?" Before I know it, all of the PAs have their eyes back on their computers, and I'm gliding through the tent with him like we're Fred Astaire and Ginger Rogers.

I have to give it to him. He's good. But I'm not soon going to forget the spurn. Sure, he's nice to me now he knows I'm connected. But where was his common decency before? It's James's world all over again — only the rich, titled, or famous count. And it goes without saying that any enemy of dogs is an enemy of mine.

"My name isn't Nichols," I declare crossly, and set Hudson down on the floor as if throwing down a gauntlet. I itch for this pompous ass to complain about Hudson's muddy paws. He doesn't say a word, but instead leans down to scratch Hudson's ear, which infuriates me.

Ms. Nichols! How lazy of him. Didn't his fancy boarding school or wherever he crawled out from teach him better than that? I'm just about to lecture him about the folly of making assumptions when we pass through a tent flap serving as a door. It's like day and night. One moment we were in a grubby production office, and now suddenly we're standing on a richly patterned, claret-colored Persian rug, adorned with a full tapestry-covered living room suite dotted around with hundreds of votive candles. There's nothing above our heads but the New York City skyline and a pinkish smear of stars gilding the remnants of the day's clouds. From the bustling streets of Manhattan to this... It was like a genie had transported me to another land. I can't help myself. "What is this place?" I breathe.

"VIP holding. It's where we seat the talent right before they go on stage." A warm smile spreads across his face. He looks at me for a long time, seeming to take me in for the first time.

"It's beautiful, isn't it?" he asks, eyes sparkling.

His gaze makes me feel shy. "It is," I agree, turning away and running my hand along the wood of one of the bookshelves along the wall.

"Welcome to the wonders of high-budget, network television," he says. "May I offer you a glass of wine?" He gestures to a carafe surrounded by crystal glasses on a substantial mahogany sideboard. The magic of the scene is throwing me off-kilter. I surprise myself and nod.

"By the way," he asks, the shadow of a smile turning up one corner of his mouth, "what is it?" He hands me a ruby-hued drink, which I accept. I don't make a habit of drinking alone, so it's been awhile since I've had wine. I take a tentative sip. His eyes are on my lips as I drink. The wine is very, very good, as I suspected it would be.

"What is what?"

"Your name." He takes a step closer to me. He doesn't seem as harried as before. "If your name isn't Nichols, what is it?"

"It's Bell. Charlotte Bell."

He tilts his head, considering me. "It suits you." He pauses, and looks straight into my eyes. "Charlotte Bell."

Ding-dong, ding -dong! Ding, ding, ding, ding-ding ding-a dong ding-ding ding-a-dong diiiiiiing...

Hudson freezes and cocks his head at a high-pitched chiming noise. "What's that?" I ask.

The man's eyes widen. He looks down at his tablet and scrolls to wake it up. The harsh artificial light of the screen cuts through the glow of the candles. "That, Ms. Bell, is the Sonos Handbell Ensemble playing *Sleigh Bells.* Right on cue. And my signal to be on the alert."

He's halfway across the carpet, and nearing the door of the adjacent tent. "The mayor is due on set in four minutes." He stops to pull his phone from the pocket of his leather coat. "Send a PA to VIP holding to escort a young woman and an animal to Area J. It's a canine. No, she's ordinary. Thank you."

Ordinary?

"My apologies," he says curtly, "but I'll have to ask you and your dog to clear the area." His eyes keep flicking to an actual wooden door leading from a diaphanous tunnel coming from yet another tent. "Strictly for security reasons, you understand."

He now has the palm of his hand on the small of my back, and he's pushing me to a flap in a tent opposite the wooden door. I barely have time to set my half-full wineglass on a Chinese cabinet as we hurry past it. What does he think I'm going to do? Lunge at the mayor, and threaten to take her hostage? Sic my dog on her? Burn out her retinas with my *ordinary*-ness?

Within 5 seconds, a thickly bundled young woman with a knit toboggan emblazoned with the network's logo under her headset slips through the flap door and grabs me by the arm. "You'll need to come with me."

I short-leash Huddie to make sure he doesn't get stepped on. Talk about having a bucket of cold water thrown on you.

I look behind me, and catch a glimpse of the man's broad back, and call out, "Thanks a *lot!*"

"It was my pleasure," he says, looking over his shoulder. Apparently he gives better than he gets in the old sarcasm department; he didn't seem to clock my annoyance at all. I'm quivering with irritation. His face is all business but I detect a twinkle in his eyes, and the slightest bit of mischief around the eyebrow. Or do I? I can't read him.

Four men in long, black coats stream through the door, and line up to form a tunnel. I didn't know the mayor traveled with that kind of entourage, but to be honest, it had been years since I rubbed shoulders with anyone with more status than the check-out clerks at Whole Foods or the Nook support crew at Barnes & Noble.

"Connie, see that Ms. Bell gets my card," he says just before turning around and stepping forward to receive not the mayor, but – oh my God – the president!

Connie pulls me through the flap, hard, and I tug Hudson behind me. In a shocking change of circumstances, we're now standing in what appears to be a men's dressing room for the lowest rung of extras. A couple of guys dressed as reindeer are playing poker on a milk crate. A skinny man wearing nothing but a snowman's head and a pair of tighty-whiteys hollers, "Hey! You can't be in here. I'll call the union."

"Don't get your panties in a bunch, Frosty," Connie says. "We're just passing through." She pulls me through another flap, and my nostrils are assaulted by the fertile smell of dung. All around me are stalls reminiscent of a fair, in which sheep, goats, a cow, and a small elephant loll and recline.

"There's a bench. Have a seat. Someone will be with you in a minute. Oh right," she says. She rifles through her breast pocket and fishes something out. "Here." It's an off-white card, engraved in black letters. There are only two words on it.

HENRY WENTWORTH

Underneath his name should also be written, Pretentious Jerk. I fling the card as hard as I can, and it lands in a puddle next to the hoof of a donkey. I watch as it soaks through and sinks.

Chapter 2

By the time we're up and out the door bright and early the next morning, Henry Wentworth and his pompous insults are a distant memory. Hudson woke me up bright-eyed and bushy-tailed, so I promised him a real walk this morning. He's been extra restless, and the tree lighting didn't seem to quell his appetite for adventure.

I'm just glad to be in my deliciously comfortable, if not exactly trendy, Uggs this morning. Last night, after half an hour of enduring a freezing cold tushy on a hard plank bench, I decided I couldn't spend one more moment inhaling *Eau de Farm*, so I stumbled off to try to find Aunt Miranda on my own. Here's an insider tip: when the president of the United States is on the premises, one is not at liberty to wander around a venue. I was denied at every exit.

In the end, I gave up and managed to make it to the edge of the Plaza just as the ceremony peaked. Hudson and I may not have been up close and personal as originally promised, as we finally waded through the throngs to reach 51st Street and find a cab, the sky caught fire. Not only did great bursts of fireworks tear through the blackness of the night sky, we were bathed in blanket of "oohs" and "ahhs" as everyone within sight of the spectacle joined in a shared moment of awe. We could smell the gunpowder's tang as it cut through the scent of evergreen and hot chocolate.

Huddie and I stopped in our tracks and looked upward, mouths hanging open when the statuesque spruce was set ablaze, lighting up the New York City skyline, and everyone joined in to sing *Joy to the World*. Honestly, it stole my breath.

As much as I appreciate having experienced it, I am nothing if not a creature of habit. I won't lie to you. Once I was home in my cozy apartment, swathed in flannel and curled up on the sofa, I was a very, very happy girl. Hudson was my star, as usual. He crawled up into my arms, burrowing into my bathrobe, and lay on my chest. His heart beat fast against mine, as it beat slowly. Still, except for the comforting in-out of his breathing, Hudson lay on me without falling asleep. It's like he knew I needed the soothing after being so exposed out in the chaos of the city.

I thought it was odd that Aunt Miranda hadn't gotten in touch, but I'd chalked it up to her perpetual business duties and frankly, her self-centeredness. Well, maybe that's not entirely fair. She did want me there. It's just that she's always on the job.

AT&T doesn't do well in that part of Midtown, and when I checked my phone, ten texts that never reached me last night flooded in from Aunt Miranda all at once. They ran the gamut from **Beavering away, can't catch my breath**, to **R U here yet?** to **Don't miss the mini marble cheesecakes in craft services. They're a triumph.** And lastly, **About to hit "go" on the tree! Find me! In a cherry picker 20 floors up on the west side of the plaza!**

In a flash of anger born of wounded pride, I dashed back a quick text selling Henry Wentworth up the river and ratted to Aunt Miranda about how abysmally he'd treated me.

Didn't bail on you last night! Was there, but held hostage in a pig pen by security, no thanks to that plummy ASS of an assistant of yours. But glad I saw lighting. Congrats. You nailed it, naturally! Will call later today x C

I hit send, but immediately regret being so hotheaded. I know

35

Aunt Miranda all too well, unfortunately. On a good day she fires three people before her first cup of tea. I don't want that kind of blood on my hands. Left alone, I'm sure in short order that pompous poser would have dug his own grave. I push it out of my mind, and take a deep breath of the frosted air, laced with the promise of snow to come. The less I think about him, the happier I am.

This morning I decide to detour to Broadway to my favorite coffee place, Zabar's, to pick up a latte and a bagel before we hit the park. The sky is a clear, bright blue, and the air is crisp and cold. Walking briskly feels good; my muscles warm as my blood pumps. Hudson's short legs are moving a mile a minute. The chill seems to make him even friskier than usual.

Several passers-by call out "Cute dog!" and "What a sweetie!" I beam with pride. I have to admit he looks extra-dapper today in his quilted red tartan coat.

I tie Hudson's leash to a bike rack outside the big front windows of the cafe so I can keep a careful eye on him. Pushing open the door, I am enveloped in the smell of warm, yeasty bagels, and strong, black coffee. My mouth literally starts to water. When it's my turn to order, I get an oversized everything bagel with lox so I can give Hudson a few treats. He goes wild for salmon.

We stand on the corner, basking in the warm sunlight, and taking bites of the fresh-from-the-oven bagel and creamy Nova lox while I drink my coffee. The breakfast gives me a pep, or maybe it's the sun, so I feel like stretching my legs and start walking south, toward 57th Street, where we'll enter Central Park. Work can wait just a little while longer today.

"It's still early, Huddie. Let's take a long walk down to Columbus Circle, and we can cut into the park and walk home on the paths." He's not even listening to me. He's too busy greeting every dog that passes, and trying to hoover up food scraps from the sidewalk. He looks so happy; it melts my heart. Just then, a burly man, staring at his cell phone, smashes into my shoulder.

36

"Watch where you're going!" he growls, and keeps on walking.

Spun around in the opposite direction, I wind up jerking Hudson's leash, and halting from the shock of it. Hudson lunges out after the guy to protect me.

I open my mouth to yell after him, willing the people around me to brace themselves for hair-curling profanity, but what's the point, really? I breathe in a cleansing breath, scratch my dog's head, and plod on. People are going to act how they act. Nothing I do or say can change that, and trying is a fool's errand. Better to keep to myself. I learned that a long time ago.

I look at Hudson's little half tail, spiked up in the air on high-alert, as he trots ahead and I feel a smile rise from my heart to my lips. I love him so much. So what if people can be jerks? Dogs never are.

All along Broadway, the shops are displaying the holiday spirit. Wreaths and garlands adorn the windows, and snippets of festive holiday music push out onto the street with every determined customer. Even New York City itself has started to deck the halls, so to speak. Arches of lights in snowflake patterns cross the wide avenue, and greenery flows down the polls of the gas lamps and the signs declaring the names of streets and avenues.

We pass Fairway Market, with its outdoor stalls featuring brightly colored cranberries, pumpkins, cabbages, red potatoes, and myriad other fruits and vegetables shining like jewels on the sidewalk. Live trees of all heights and shapes are being unloaded from a huge double-parked truck and piled into a much-coveted parking spot. The balsam scent gives me itchy fingers. I can't wait to get home to dig into a mixing bowl full of pie-crust dough. Some make their crusts with a stand mixer or a food processor. Not me. I like to feel the texture of the pastry between my fingers. It's how I know it'll turn out perfect from the oven.

The smell of Christmas trees makes me think of spiced apple tart with plenty of clove. I'll make one of those when I get home, I think to myself, shivering with excitement, and since I have apples, I'll do a platter of apple-stuffed pork chops with rosemary too. The thought of spending the afternoon in my oven-warmed kitchen with my Pandora radio to the Vintage Christmas Carols station gives me a lift till I'm practically skipping.

The blocks melt away as I enjoy the feeling of sunlight on my chilled cheeks, and watch Hudson delight in the sounds and aromas of a New York pre-holiday morning. As we near Columbus Circle, we veer toward the park. The crowds thicken as we approach the Trump International Tower Hotel, and holiday tourists are gathered around the impressive Globe sculpture snapping shots. There's the entrance to one of Manhattan's most famous upscale restaurants, the sublime Jean-Georges, and I remember ducking in there out of the rain one summer afternoon. James and I had planned to rent bikes and ride around the park, maybe grab a hot dog from a cart. The shower hit fast and hard, and we ran for the awning. Before I could protest about the state of my elderly sundress and wet hair, we were standing at a desk with two models in white blouses and black suits in front of very discreet three-inch letters lit by a subtle golden spotlight, spelling out *Jean-Georges*. Every seat in the place was reserved, but we didn't mind eating at the bar. We shared charred corn ravioli, and line-caught hake in lemongrass consommé. It was early on, and I felt flirty with James. I remember telling him I could cook better, and he threatened to call for the chef. The bartender comped us several rounds of cucumber-mint martinis, and when we emerged sated and buzzy into the sunshine, I had felt loose-limbed and hopeful. It's funny how things don't always turn out how you expect them to at first. James, summer, and living spontaneously feel like long-ago daydreams as the chilly air tickles my nose and freezes the tips of my earlobes.

Across the way, I see The Shops at Columbus Circle. It's hard not to lose track of time when shopping in the uber-luxurious glass-fronted building with panoramic views of Central Park. If heaven had a trademark scent, it would be the comingled aromas of the merchants there. Shampoos from Aveda, bath salts from Crabtree & Evelyn, the rich leather smells from Coach and Etienne Aigner, the rich cocoa notes floating out from Godiva and La Maison du Chocolat, the tangy fresh fruit smell from Jamba Juice, the wonderful cooking smells like curry and sautéed onion rising from Whole Foods Market in the basement… even the sweat and freshly showered man-smell from Equinox intrigues.

Visually pleasing at any time of the year, the shops have been amped up to the Nth degree, decorated with fourteen-foot three-dimensional hanging stars that hang from the 150-foot Great Room. Lit during the day with blue and purple lights, they're easy to see from the park. Like an ice palace, the whole Time Warner Center, with its Shops on Columbus Circle, acts as an ornament to Central Park's festive greenness.

"Look, Hudson," I say, pointing. "See the stars? I heard that they do the world's biggest projected light show there, from the time the sun goes down to midnight, and that they play Christmas music and everything." He cocks his head, body poised to pounce. He's on high alert. "Oh, not now, Huddie. In the evening. Probably not tonight," I tell him, "but maybe sometime. We'll see."

And there's *Per Se*… How long has it been since I've eaten at Thomas Keller's sublime restaurant, I wonder. A long time, I think, as my mouth waters. I sigh, remembering passing through the simple, classic, blue painted doors and entering the serene, intimate restaurant. On paper, it would seem to be everything I hate, with its artfully arranged dishes, infusions, foams, and sugar cages over exquisitely shaped meringues. But the food won me over. In spite of the upscale presentation and cheffy techniques, the emphasis was on the simplicity and goodness of the food. The butter-poached nova lobster, humbly prepared with leeks, carrots, watercress and the most eye-wateringly brilliant sauce — a sauce bordelaise — remains to this day one of the top dishes I've ever tasted in my life.

My shoulders stiffen as I recall, Oh, right. That was with James,

39

too. I walk on, doing my best to concentrate on cut-diamond brilliance of the meal and tease it away from the memory of James scheming and plotting, and eventually wangling his way back into the kitchen to shake hands with Keller himself. Even though James had been with me, I'd dined alone that night.

At the light, Hudson and I turn and drift with the herd across the street to Merchant's Gate, the entrance to the park at 59th and Central Park South. As we wade into the crowd, I notice the array of food trucks selling delicacies ranging from warm roasted chestnuts, to sugared Dutch *stroopwafels*, to fragrant Indian samosas, to your basic New York hot dog with that world-famous onion sauce. Even though it's freezing, there's still a Mr. Softee truck out, and there's even a line for the creamy cones.

"C'mon Hudson, let's go into the park and start home," I say, tugging his leash toward the path. "Time to head back." He sits down, panting and taking in the crowd. "You are a stubborn thing, aren't you? You're going to freeze your little tail off sitting on the concrete in this weather. I have work to do. Recipes to test. You can have a quick sip of water, and then it's go-time."

I pull a collapsible water bowl and small metal bottle out of my coat pocket, and pour him a drink. He perks up, and helps himself with gusto.

"That salmon was salty, huh boy?" While he drinks, I people-watch. Sitting in a chair by the base of the fountain, an elderly man with a wispy gray beard plays a warbling, Asian-inspired *Rudolph the Red-Nosed Reindeer* on an *erhu*, pulling the bow back and forth with the grace of a ballet dancer. He's competing with a group of Madrigal singers in full Renaissance garb, standing behind a sign proudly declaring *Skidmore College Glee Club*.

Further out, I hear hip-hop strains coming from an oversized boom-box. Glancing over, I see that five fit youths in futuristic tracksuits and Kabuki masks are breakdancing. People dressed as cows are handing out individual Greek yogurts from refrigerators attached to oversized tricycles.

"Elfies! Come take a free holiday Elfie, compliments of Takasaki Worldwide. Takasaki: On the cutting edge of global technology! Free Elfies! No money to pay!"

Hudson, chin dripping from his drink of water, lasers in on the high-pitched voice piercing through the din from a crowd of Japanese youngsters, dressed as Manga-style elves. They're so hip it hurts, with the red and green streaks in their hair, black-and-white striped tights, off-kilter ponytails, and pointed high-heeled elf boots. That's girls *and* boys, mind you. I feel tragically frumpy in my brown puffer coat.

Hudson strains toward the Elfie tent, standing on his back legs, paws bicycling in the air, chest supported by his harness.

"Wait, Hudson! Stop." I shake out his dish, fold it up, and pocket it. Once I'm upright, he's scraping his claws on the pavement, pulling me toward the tent.

"Huddie, I'm not getting my picture taken," I explain as I walk him over to the teeming gaggle of elves. One by one, revelers and tourists sit on the brightly colored sleigh situated in the center of the staging area, allowing Santa's Helpers to drape them in festive scarves and to plop pointy hats with jingle bells atop their heads. There's a mirror, so all newly ordained Christmas Troopers are able to see themselves. To a person, they all laugh when they catch sight of themselves transformed into elves. Upon exiting, they're given a lapel button declaring, "I can't ELF myself — I jingle for Takasaki!"

"You want photo?" one of the elves demands, pointing straight at me. "Step up here. Take a seat on the sleigh! Sit now! Free, from Takasaki."

Hudson climbs the first step to the dais where the sleigh sits empty.

"No thanks," I call. "We were just looking."

"Come on! You take photo now. No one else waiting. Your turn. Come!" He picks up a scarf and a hat, and gestures toward the sleigh.

41

"Not today. Thanks anyway. Come on, Hudson, time to go home."

"Oh, hello, little dog! Oh, cuuuuuuuute." The elf comes toward me, arms outstretched, and Hudson starts dancing like a loon. "Mai, Sparkles, come! Come and see this little dog." Before I know it, we're surrounded by elves. "Let's take an Elfie of this doggie!"

Another elf picks Hudson up, and holds him high in the air à la Simba in the Lion King, and there's a cacophony of Japanese phrases spoken in excited, high-pitched baby voices surrounding us.

Like a flock of birds, the elves drift toward the sleigh, and I'm swept along, still holding the end of the leash. I can't even see Hudson above all of the pointed hats, and I trip on the step leading up to the sleigh. I couldn't fall down if I wanted to, though, because I'm shoulder-to-shoulder in a herd of Santa's Finest.

"Hudson!" I call, as I find my footing. The leash goes slack in my hand. I can't see my dog anywhere. As if on cue, the crowd parts like the red sea to reveal my dog up on the sleigh being fussed over like Dorothy just before she meets the Wizard. They've stripped him of his harness and collar, and two elfin stylists are brushing back the wispy hair around his face. Is that hairspray? From the look on his face, he's enjoying the fuss. An elf takes out a baby-sized green-and-red scarf and winds it around his neck, and another sets about fitting his little head with a tiny elf hat with jingle bells on top. A girl pulls an elastic headband from her own hairdo, and from what I can see, fashions a chinstrap out of it and… what is that? Maybe safety pins?

A crowd of impossibly tall and impossibly blonde tourists presses in front of me.

"Look Astrid! Gus! See the elf dog?" They're all wearing huge, thick sweatshirts that say, "Lincoln Nebraska Future Business Leaders of America."

"Excuse me," I say to a tree of a farm boy, "I just need to get to the front to pick up my dog." I can see the elves, phones out, taking turns leaning in to get in shots with Hudson. He has a smear of lipstick on the white part of his muzzle from all the elf kisses.

"That's your dog?" The towering teen asks me. "He's hilarious. He oughta be on TV or something."

"Thanks," I say, trying to muscle past. The crowd is closing in, and I just get a glimpse of the chair Hudson was sitting on. It's empty.

"Excuse me," I holler. I'm eye level with the shoulders of all the Midwestern giants. I stand on my tippy-toes to see if I can spot Hudson. I can't. "Move!" I yell, garnering lots of affronted looks.

"You don't have to scream, ma'am," one of the boys admonishes. "It takes more energy to be rude than to be nice. Here, I'll help you through." He uses his body like a barge in an icy river in order to part the crowd, and I walk in his wake until I hit the step up to the dais.

"Hudson!" I call. I don't see him. My chest starts to feel tight. "Hey, where's my dog? Where's Hudson?"

The elves all begin to look around their feet. Smiles melt from their faces as it's clear he's not there.

"Where is my dog?" I demand, starting to feel dizzy.

Their voices rise in a cacophony of panicked Japanese sentences, and a tall boy-elf holding Hudson's collar and harness points. "There! There is the dog!"

I swing around only to glimpse Hudson's tail disappear between the tall Uggs of a teenaged girl and out toward 57th Street.

"Hudson!" I scream. "Someone, grab my dog! Help!" I start to push my way into the crowd, but I'm like a salmon swimming upstream. "He doesn't know what to do in traffic!"

"Wait lady," the boy-elf shrieks. "You forgot your selfie!" I don't stop, but he manages to catch up with me. He lurches into my back, propelled by the sea of bodies, and says, panting, "All this yours! Take!" and shoves Hudson's leash and harness, along with a piece of cardboard, into my hand. I think I spy some fur, down by a man's expensive leather brogues, but I can't be sure.

43

I see a hole in the crowd, and take off into a run, but I lose sight of him. I keep calling, and launch my body like a bottle-rocket in the direction I last saw him. He must have crossed the street. My lungs constrict. What if he gets hit by a car? Out of nowhere, a horse and buggy speeds into my path, and almost runs me over. By the time it's gone, I can't see Hudson anywhere.

"Hudson, here Huddie!" I cry over and over again. "Someone help me!" My blood is icy. I'm running in wide circles, paying no attention to cars and bumping into bodies everywhere. I'm too terrified to cry. I hear myself screaming Hudson's name, and feel rawness in my throat. I stumble at the entrance to the subway, and almost go headfirst down the stairs. Shaking, I lower myself to the top step and sit down, even though there is a sea of humanity ascending from underground. If he went down these stairs, anyone could have snatched him and hopped the A, C, B, D, or 1 train in the blink of an eye. He could already be in another borough. It hits me. It's possible I could never see him again.

I hang my head between my legs and sob.

*****

"Miss?"

Through a fog I hear a husky, male voice. It sounds impatient.

"Hey, miss. Are you listening to me? You can't sit on the stairs. You need to move, now, or I'm gonna have to move you."

I take my face out of my hands, and look up to see a muscular, dark-skinned New York City cop, clad in traditional deep blue. The gun on his hip is inches from my face. Scrambling to me feet, I wipe my running nose. "Sorry, Officer. I'm moving. There. I'm up."

Hands in his belt loops, he gives me a stern once-over.

I try to tell him I've just lost my dog, but my face crumples, and I know that if I talk, nothing will come out but a wail. I clamp my lips shut.

His stern demeanor turns to concern. He leans in. "Did someone hurt you?"

"No, it's just..." I swallow the lump in my throat, and manage to say, "My dog was stolen."

He pulls a pad from his utility belt. "What did the perpetrator look like?"

"OK, I don't know if he was *stolen* stolen, but he wouldn't run away. I know that." A shiver skates through my body. He wouldn't, would he?

"Miss, in New York City, there are leash laws. Your pet should have been properly restrained." He slides the pad back into his belt, and stands in front of me with his hands on his hips. He's solid. His silver badge reads simply "Curtis." I can only assume no one messes with this guy. Still, he does sport a tiny candy cane pin on the collar of his turtleneck sweater. Maybe he has a soft side.

"Yes, I know." Weakly, I hold up the leash in my hand. "I live here. It's just that he was taking a selfie…"

"Your dog was taking a selfie?"

"They dressed him in a hat and scarf… I need to get his collar from the elves… the giants kept me away from him…"

"Miss, are you on drugs?" Officer Curtis whips out his flashlight, shines it in my face, and peers deep in to my eyes.

"Of course not! Wait, you're a police officer, right? Can you help me find my dog?"

"Miss, this is New York City," he barks. "I'm not exactly Fireman Joe from Podunk, Nowhere who spends all day getting cats down from trees. We have serious crimes to deal with."

Another cop, this one skinny as a whip, with an angular face and pink cheeks, sidles up to us. "Everything alright here, Curtis?" he asks, checking me out sideways.

"I lost my dog. I need help," I interrupt.

"That's right up your alley, Curtis," the other cop says. "What kind of dogs do you and your mother have up there in the Bronx? Sporks? Porkies?"

"Morkies," Curtis mumbles.

"That's it! What are those little fellas a mix of?"

45

"Maltese and Yorkshire Terriers."

"Yeah, that's right, Curtis and his mom rescue little mixed-breed dogs. Tiny things. Pretty cute. Curtis loves dogs, don't cha' Curtis?"

"Well, yes. I do. But we are on duty, Scrivello." He pulls his partner to the side. I hear him whisper-hissing, "How's it gonna look if at the end of the day all we have to show for ourselves is a citation for public urination and a found puppy?"

"It's gonna look like we made people keep it in their pants, and like we helped the distraught citizens of our fair city. You worry too much, Curtis. Probably why you don't have a girlfriend. Help the young lady! We'll crack the Columbian drug ring after Christmas. Come on, show the girl a picture of your dogs. You know you want to."

Without having to be asked twice, Officer Curtis pulls out his wallet, and flips it open. "The big bruiser there is Apollo. Don't let his size fool you, though. He's a teddy bear."

From what I could tell, Apollo could fit in a loaf pan and probably didn't weigh ten pounds soaking wet.

"And here's a picture of the girls, Aretha and Tina, from last Christmas."

"Lemme see," Scrivello said, craning his neck. "Ah yeah, that's when we took 'em to see Santa Claus and hang out at the senior center."

I feel a surge of adrenaline. These men love dogs. Maybe there's hope I could find Huddie today. "Please, Officer Curtis? Help me find Hudson."

"Oh, all right. You're in this, too, Scrivello." He puts his phone away, and takes his pad out again, letting out a big sigh.

"Name and description of the missing person?" he asks me, pen poised.

"Atta boy, Curtis," Scrivello says. "Never fear, lady. You have the finest of New York's finest on the job."

My heart lifts, and I begin to tell the story. "Hudson Bell. He weighs about twenty-two pounds, his hair is smooth and wiry…"

"What color?"

"Pretty much every color a dog can be… he has a pointy face, and bright eyes…"

"Do you have a photograph?"

"I do on my phone… wait!" I root in my backpack where I'd shoved the leash and cardboard the elf had given me. It was a picture frame, and inside was a fabulous photo of Hudson all decked out in his elfwear. "Here he is. That's my Hudson," I say, with a little crack in my voice.

"Aww…" Scrivello says. "He's a cutie. Looks like he's smiling for the camera."

Curtis takes a long hard look at the photo, as if he's memorizing every detail. Meeting my eyes, he says, sincerely, "I'm going to do everything in my power to find your dog, Miss."

In no time, we are combing the south side of the park, the way the police officers had been trained to do for a missing person. I look at my watch. It's still morning. The sun is shining. I feel a smile spread across my face. Hudson and I would be safe and warm at home by lunchtime. Dinnertime at the latest.

*****

"Sit down there," Officer Curtis, or Craig as I now knew him, said to me, motioning to a park bench around Central Park West. "You need some water. You're going to make yourself sick if you don't slow down. That won't do you or Hudson any good at all."

New York starts getting dark in the winter at about four thirty in the afternoon. We're sitting in the ever-increasing blackness, and I have no clue what time it was. The only real light is coming from the twinkling snowflake decorations on the west side of the Natural History Museum. My feet are throbbing, and I am so frozen through I can't feel my limbs anymore. Still, Hudson's out there alone somewhere in the city. I can't just give up. He needs me.

"You want a hot dog?" Craig calls from the steaming cart half

47

a block from where I sat. I shake my head "no." We'd been all over the south side of the park, east and west. The officers had radioed all their friends on beats on the north side with Hudson's description, and they sent a report in to the station. There's was nothing left to do.

"Drink this," Craig said, handing me a bottle of water. He munches hungrily into his hot dog. "Listen, Charlotte, you need to go home and get some rest. Hudson has an identity chip. Someone will probably find him and bring him into a vet, or he could wind up at the pound. The first thing they do is scan. Plus, we have all kinds of people out there looking for him now. I'd keep on going, but my mom has bingo night at her church, and I promised I'd go home and take care of our dogs. There's a houseful. We have three fosters right now, on top of our own three." He chuckled. "This one, I call her Fang, is a puppy and she can't stop gnawing on me with those little needly teeth."

I think about how little and frail Hudson was when I brought him home, and tears pool in my eyes. I will myself not to cry.

"No, of course you need to go. You aren't even on the clock." I turn my back and wipe my eyes with the back of my hand. "I'm fine. Thank you for everything. You've been amazing."

He stands up. "Well, I'm not done. I'll make some calls, and tomorrow Scrivello and I will keep looking and asking around. Plus, we scanned that photo of yours, and my crew at the station's been passing it around to the other precincts. I have your card, and you have mine." He wads up the paper from his hot dog, and takes a step toward the 86th Street subway station. "Don't worry. As a cop, I see things like this work out lots of times."

And the other times? I think to myself. I need to be alone. I can't feel all of this in front of someone I'd just met. To be honest, I can't feel this much in front of anyone. I'm more comfortable being alone when things are going badly. It's what I'm used to. "Go!" I tell him, forcing a smile. "It's all going to work out."

"Sure it is," he said, smiling back. "You go home, now, and call

all your friends and family. The more people you got working, the sooner you'll find that dog of yours."

"Right!" I said brightly. My gut feels hollow as I take mental inventory of my friends and family. Apart from my online friends, Charlotte's Chefs, there was... Aunt Miranda. And, of course, Hudson.

"Will do. I'm fine. Go home and take care of your pups." I make myself start crossing the street toward the west side, so he could feel free to go.

"Alright then. You have a good night, Charlotte, and keep the faith."

"I will!"

I watch him disappear up the block before I let my body sag. I know I have to get home and take some kind of action, but every step feels like dragging a bag of lead weights without my furry little friend by my side. I plod on. There's a little dog out there who needs help, and I'm the one to help him. Just like before, just like when he came to me. He's mine and I'm his.

When I finally reach my building and start up the stairs of my brownstone, I feel the loneliness right down to my bones. It's like climbing Everest. I know why. When I open my apartment door, I know there will be nothing there to greet me but darkness and silence.

Chapter 3

I wake up with a start in the half-light of the early Manhattan morning, facedown on my sofa in a puddle of drool. Panic electrifies my body as I re-remember Hudson is gone. My eyes feel like they've been doused in a combination of lemon juice and glue. They sting, but I can't quite pull them open. I'd spent the early part of the night alternately laying down, feeling like a freight train was racing through my brain, then leaping up and pacing the apartment. I wonder how many hours of sleep I'd I've had. Two or three? I had been sure the police would call, or that someone at the shelter would get in touch to say that Hudson had shown up. My cell phone never left my hand.

As I moved from room to room, filled with an energy to act, but having nothing to do, I'd stop and pick up a squeaky toy here, or a morsel of kibble there, each time calling, "Huddie!" before realizing again and again, like Groundhog Day, that he wasn't there. Everywhere I looked was another reminder of our life together. The framed photo of us at the Chelsea Piers Mixed-Breed Dog Show, the prescription bottle of antiseptic the vet had given us when he stepped on that nail on Amsterdam Avenue, the fluffy donut bed I'd splurged on from Orvis with his name embroidered on the front.

Awake now, and at the end of my tether I punch Aunt Miranda's number in via "Favorites." Actually, it should be "favorite," since she's the only one. Despite the pre-dawn hour, she picks up before the second ring.

"Oh hello, darling," she launches in immediately. "I only have a split second, but I've rung to say I'm mortified I haven't gotten in touch since the fiasco at the tree lighting."

"You didn't call me, I called you."

"Be that as it may, I'm standing in the Russian Tea Room overseeing the set-up for an informal meeting of the G8 leaders, but you didn't hear that from me. Would you believe the Prime Minister of Canada flat out *refuses* to sit at a table where smoked sable is being eaten? Claims it makes him gag. Usually Canadians are the least of my worries, always so polite."

"I don't care about the tree lighting," I interrupt her, stripping off my sweaty clothes from the night before, and pulling on sweat pants and a sweatshirt.

"That's the attitude!" she bursts in. "Shake it off and move forward. Let it go, or get revenge. No point dwelling. By the by, I'm still not up to speed with what happened, but rest assured when I find out, heads will roll. Say you aren't cross with me."

"I'm not, but…"

"Well, I should think not," she cuts me off. "Doubtless you got some underling's back up, and in the short term that can only lead to a dead end. Until you're prepared to shoot through the heart, never show your gun. Have you still not read that copy of *The Art of War* that I had Cerie ship to you?"

"You are not listening to me. I'm trying to tell you that Huddie is missing."

"He's quite small…have you checked under the bed? You know, at one time Cerie was a warrior. I once watched her bring Joan Rivers to tears! I loved Joanie, God rest her soul, but Cerie was right. The Gucci bootlets were too youthful."

I sense that she's in the middle of a monologue, and not about to come up for air any time soon. I take the time to run into the kitchen and pop a capsule into my Nespresso machine. I'm going to need coffee today, and lots of it if I'm going to find my little needle in the haystack that is New York City.

"Aunt Miranda, do you even care that my dog is missing? Do you?"

"Of course, darling, but I'm in the middle of a story. Just let me finish my thought. Losing Cerie was like losing my right arm, let me tell you. I will never, as long as I live, understand how she could have chosen to take leave just as I was on the brink of locking down the curation of Caitlyn Jenner's world debut."

"Didn't you say she was in labor?" I demand in exasperation. "For God's sake, Aunt Miranda." I slam down my coffee cup.

"We all make our choices, don't we? Any old hoo, I'm calling to break the news that Christmas Day lunch at yours is defo a no-go. I'm sorry, darling, it's just the event planner for the Vatican Christmas Dinner quit in a huff. It seems the new pontiff is a good deal more humble than previous ones, and he's insisting on keeping it simple."

"Aunt Miranda! I called to talk about Hudson. I don't have time to talk about Christmas."

"Several cardinals are in an uproar, and Jacques Desmaisson refuses to work with such a low budget, 'low' being in heavy inverted quotes, you understand." While she rattles on, I pour milk in the frother, and watch it swirl and foam.

"Aunt Miranda," I say, cutting in where there's a breath, "I need you to focus. On me, for a change."

"Oh, but don't you want to hear my genius plan to make this disaster an opportunity by introducing a shabby-chic element? Picture it: The Vatican meets Pottery Barn meets Summer in Provence! It goes without saying that all of the gold staffs and mitres could distract from the theme, but my new assistant has some ideas that could tie it all together."

"You are seriously not going to listen to me, are you?"

"Hold the phone, darling. *You cannot put silver spoons in the*

52

Beluga caviar, you nitwit! That's why we special-ordered an entire crate of mother of pearl ones! Sorry about that, as I was saying, Henry did a short stint in Connecticut last summer for Martha Stewart, you know. During the Post-Prison Renaissance. I stole him from under her nose. She's furious. Suffice it to say, I won't be shucking clams at her beach house any time soon. Still, it was worth it. Henry is a hungry young thing who works like a machine. I have him here through to New Year's when he's promised himself to Nigella Lawson for some launch or another. I'll be sorry to see him go, even though he's in the doghouse with me at the moment for the way he treated you at the tree lighting."

I feel a stab of guilt. "Don't punish him on my account. Even if he is a puffed-up jerk."

"Don't try and defend him! I'll think of a little lesson to teach him. If you give the brilliant ones too much rope early on, they don't learn discipline. If I check his ego, he'll respect me for it and take it like a man. He's the closest thing to a mini-me I have. No offense, darling."

"None taken. Believe me."

I slurp down my second coffee in one hot gulp, the bitter burn no match for the hole in my heart left by the fact that Aunt Miranda is continuing to ignore me. It's no secret she has always been disappointed that I don't click around behind her in high heels and a form-fitting pencil skirt barking orders at catering staffs around the globe. But you'd think she'd be on deck for me in a time of crisis. As if I'd want to be a robot like that stick-up-his ass Englishman she had toadying for her. I wish I didn't need her. It would feel so good to just hang up on her. But today I do.

I can hear crystal tinging, and people shouting in Russian.

"Aunt Miranda! Hello? Are you even listening to me?" Why won't she just pay attention to me and let her little shadow handle whatever is going on at the Russian Tea Room. He's probably lording his power above PAs and waiters as we speak.

I'm not sure if my heart is pounding from the two shots of

espresso I just chugged, or from abject fear of never seeing my dog again.

I check my circa 1955 red Bakelite kitchen clock, and see that morning is now fully upon us. "All right. No more monkeying around. It's go time. You have to listen to me, now. Hudson is *gone*, Aunt Miranda. As in not here. As in lost!"

There's a beat of silence on her end of the phone. "Well, surely if he were dead you'd have heard by now, wouldn't you?"

I burst into tears with the force of someone turning on a jet-powered spa shower. Grabbing a kitchen towel to contain what has unexpectedly come forth from my nostrils, I consider what I hadn't even allowed myself to think last night. That Hudson might be dead.

"There, there, darling, I'm just trying to be practical. I didn't mean to be insensitive, but it seems to me that this is an awful lot of fuss to make over a dog."

"He's *not* just a dog," I cough out, still sobbing. "I know you don't like him, Aunt Miranda, but I can't believe you'd say that. He's my *family.*"

"Oh, there, there Charlotte," she says awkwardly. Aunt Miranda doesn't do tears. "It's not that I don't like him, exactly. I'm just not a dog person, as they say. Cheer up. If you don't find him, I'll order you another."

The heaving sobs threaten to squeeze my heart till it stops. I'm gasping for a full breath. In the background, I hear someone calling, "*Ms. Nichols, you're needed in the staging area. The vendor sent 30 pounds of cheesecake instead of cream cheese.*"

"I hear that you're upset, Charlotte. And truly, I am sorry, it's just… hang on, I'm so sorry, one more mo… *Then get your arse down to Food Emporium and buy every block of Philadelphia's finest in the dairy case! In 20 minutes, we'll have the heads of the most powerful countries on the planet sitting on those rococo chairs to inhale their breakfasts while they solve world war! Are you going to be the one to tell them they're going to have to eat naked bagels???*

I thought not!"

I put the phone on speaker, set it on the counter, and splash cold water on my face. A glimpse of my kitchen calendar tells me I'm falling behind on the recipes for *The English Manor Cookbook* and I haven't responded to Charlotte's Chefs on the blog in two days. My regular fans, like Martha26 and GrillDadNJ will be worried. I'm meticulous about responding to my blog followers. I consider them friends. But I can't think about that right now. It'll keep till Hudson is back safe and sound. I dry my face on my dishtowel and steel myself to move forward. All by myself.

"Hello? Hello, darling? Are you there?"

I consider just hanging up, and pretending the connection was lost but I take a breath, and answer. "Yes, I'm here."

"As you can tell, sweetheart, I'm swamped, but I've put you on my list. I'll see what I can do. I'll check in after the last chancellors and presidents are out the door and on their way to see *The Book of Mormon.* You cannot imagine how I had to move heaven and earth to get them orchestra seats for the matinee. Hottest ticket in town!"

"You know, Aunt Miranda, I've learned not to expect much from you but this time I'm truly disappointed."

"Charlotte, please don't say that. Really, I am trying to think of a way to solve your little problem."

"I thought talking to you might help. I feel worse than I did before I called."

"Darling!"

"Maybe if I were a country star or the prime minister or something, you'd give me the time of day."

"Not another word, Charlotte. I promise you, the minute I've put the butts of the most powerful leaders in the world in their seats, I will solve your little dog problem. You have my word." There's a little pause. "Please. I want to help."

"Fine." I doubt she'll remember to call back, but it doesn't matter. A lightbulb has gone off in my head, and I don't want to

55

waste another minute. "I have to go now."

"That's better, then. Keep your pecker up. As I said, I will find a solution… *Not Clamato! Are you out of your gourd? Two words. Shellfish allergies. Do you want to kill off a leader of the free world…*" Aunt Miranda trails off and I hang up the phone.

I pad in to the bathroom to quickly brush my teeth and twist my dirty-blonde hair up into a clip. I don't dwell for a minute on my blotchy skin and swollen eyes. In my heather gray sweat suit, I'll be nothing but invisible today. That's just how I want it. Then I won't have to slow down and explain myself to anyone. After the car accident, people always wanted me to talk. I hated that. I like being a grown-up. No one can make me share how I'm feeling if I don't want to. "If you want help, look to the end of your own arm," isn't that what they say?

"Everything will be fine," I tell myself in the mirror, just as I have nearly every day since I was twelve, "Believe." It's been my mantra ever since Bridget, our cook and my nanny, packed me up from the old house in England, and waved goodbye. I look myself straight in the eye.

"You will find Hudson." I get ready to go.

*****

"Geek Squad!" answered the cheerful tech support girl on the other end of the phone line. "What's your problem?"

What's my problem? My problem is that my tiny dog is lost out in the freezing cold in one of the world's biggest cities.

"I can't make my computer talk to my printer. I need to be able to scan and print. It's urgent," I reply. For over an hour I'd been trying to make flyers from the cardboard-framed Elfie that the young man from Takasaki had pressed into my hand. Time was ticking. I can just about manage my blog, and Microsoft Word, but no one could accuse me of being tech-savvy.

"We can help you with that. Can you explain exactly what's

going on? Let's, uh, start with the computer part."

Sighing with relief, I recount the frustrations of trying to make my "Lost Dog" flyer with the planet Mercury taunting me from its position in retrograde, making all of my electronics and technology go pear-shaped.

"Please hold." She clicks off, leaving me to listen to the Geek Squad's hold music. It's a syrupy Muzak version of the Carpenters' *Close to You*. I would have expected someone cooler from the Geek Squad. I sit at my writing desk, in the little maid's room off the kitchen, and drum my nails on the desk. For something to occupy my mind, I click on to my blog while I wait. Yes, I said maid's room. Yes, my brownstone is Pre-War. Yes, I know how lucky I am. I managed to buy it with what was left of Mum's money after all the debts were paid. I needed a place with a big kitchen, and this one came kitted out with a Chambers stove and an industrial, French-doored refrigerator. It was a match made in heaven, so I splurged. I haven't regretted it for one single day.

I can't stop looking at the photo of Hudson in his holiday garb. It's clear that he had liked the elf who was snapping the photo. The goofy smile on his scruffy little face is evidence of that. His one black eyebrow is sky high, and he appears about as happy as he's ever been. He looks so vital, like he's just about to burst out of the picture and land in my lap.

Tears prick at the backs of my eyelids. My arms ache from the emptiness of not having him to squeeze. Wow, I have been on hold a long time.

My phone beeps and I grab it quickly, in turn putting the Geek Squad on hold. If I can wait, they can wait. Maybe it's Officer Curtis with some news from the police department?

"Hello?" I say breathlessly. "This is Charlotte."

"Ms. Bell. This is Henry Wentworth ringing from Nichols Bespoke Events, on behalf of Miranda Nichols."

I feel my shoulders rise to ear level. "Did she make you call to apologize? Because I don't have time for this. My dog is missing." I stab at various keys on my computer, hoping that a technological miracle occurs so I can skip the whole Geek Squad appointment, and take action.

"Erm, no. The nature of my phone call is to offer my services, not to apologize." Then, with a slightly prickly tone, he says, "I wasn't aware that I had anything to apologize for."

"You wouldn't, would you?" My patience is wire-thin. "Listen, I have another call on hold, so goodbye..."

"Wait! Ms. Bell, please," he says.

"It's MISS Bell." I'm aware that my mouth is a tight line. If I didn't like this man before, I really didn't like him now. "I have a call on the other line."

"Your aunt, that is, Miranda asked me to ring you to see how I might help you find your dog. To start, I think we should report the animal missing."

"We? Since when are we 'we?' I've already reported him missing. Thanks for the inventive suggestion." Great, this was her "machine"? Her right arm? Her mini-me? I'd do better hiring a tween with a smartphone and a bookshelf full of Nancy Drew Mysteries. "I've even filed police reports, if you can imagine. Now, if you'll excuse me, I'm in the middle of an important phone call!"

I click over to the Geek Squad.

The girl is gone, and they're playing a wordless jazz version of *Close to You*. I didn't think it was possible for that song to get any sappier or more maudlin, but they made it happen. I drum my fingers on the desk. Geez, how long are they going to leave me hanging? I try to hang up so I can call back, but the other line is still engaged. I wind up clicking back to Henry, and he's in midsentence. He is just like Miranda! She never listens when I speak on the phone either.

"...given your fragility due to your parents early deaths, may I express my condolences, she felt that you might be a danger to yourself if your dog were to be found, pardon me, deceased and you were left alone."

Oh, no. No, no, no. I'd had enough pity back when I was twelve years old. Nonstop pity from everyone, starting with the police lady who gave me the news, to the social worker who was assigned to get me through the school term, to the air hostesses who watched me on the flight to America, to the headmistress of the boarding school where Aunt Miranda dropped me off that fall. It's exhausting to be pitied. People want you to make it OK so they don't have to feel worried for you, so they don't have to consider that life is fragile and that terrible things could happen to them, too. It's hard work being the object of pity. I had to nip this right in the bud.

"Don't worry about me," I told him breezily. "I'm fine. Tell Aunt Miranda that she's absolved. I am noting that she did something to help. She sent an assistant. Box checked. I'm officially releasing you from duty. She's off the hook, and so are you. Have a nice day!" I hang up the phone, for real this time. If I didn't need Aunt Miranda, I certainly didn't need some random lackey who was being paid to be my fake friend.

I switch back over to the hold music. They're now playing a peppy Latin-inspired version of Toni Braxton's *Unbreak My Heart*.

"Geek Squad. Thank you for holding," a voice says, breaking through the knock-off pop song. "We've considered your case, and we think the best course of action is to deploy remote crisis intervention."

"Wow." I realize I'm no Steve Jobs, but that sounds intense. "Yes! I want that. Does that mean you're coming here?"

"Yes ma'am. We can launch a vehicle within the hour."

Launch? That's taking their branding a bit too seriously, if you ask me. Unless they really are going to launch something.

"Fine!" I concede. "Launch away." I don't even ask what this personalized service is going to cost me. It simply doesn't matter. All that matters is getting Hudson back. I give the Geek Squad rep all my details, and hang up.

I can't shake the itching feeling of needing to do something other than wait. I consider calling Craig to check on the police department's progress, but I don't want to slow him and Scrivello down. I know they'll get in touch if they have news. Calling the shelters this early in the morning could backfire. If I interrupt while they're getting to their desks and setting up for the day, they're more likely to blow me off. I'll call after the lunch hour, when people are in a good mood and more willing to go the extra mile. I can't make flyers until my printer is fixed. I can't go search on foot since I have to wait for tech support. There's nothing to do but distract myself.

I head to the kitchen and pull out the homemade pie-crust dough that's been chilling since my Christmas Mince Pie operation got thwarted.

Out of habit, I turn my vintage chrome-and-lacquered radio's dial to "on" to listen to WNYC on National Public Radio. Maybe it'll take my mind off things.

"…And if you're just joining us today here on 'Last Chance Foods,' we're talking with frequent guest food writer, blogger, and chef Melissa Clark. Today on the show, we're discussing one-dish meals and holiday tables. Welcome, Melissa."

"Glad to be here, Amy."

Even though she's decades her junior, Melissa Clark reminds me of Bridget, my parents' cook. They both delight in all aspects of food: The sensual feel of it in the hands during preparation, the libertine delight of allowing something delicious to melt in the mouth, and the warmth and pride of sharing good food made well with delighted guests. When I was in cooking school, my favorite teacher said that I must have cooking in my blood. I remember nodding, unable to answer because of the knot in my throat. Bridget may not have been blood, but she was more family than my own kin in many ways.

For a while, I'm able to push away the fear of never seeing Hudson again, and get lost in the rolling and pinching of my pie dough. Melissa Clark shares her secrets for simple, crowd-pleasing holiday hors d'oeuvres while I scoop spoonsful of the now-integrated mincemeat mixture into tiny, prepared tins.

"Don't be afraid to offer simple crudité," Melissa encourages. "During the holidays, people are overwhelmed with rich, complicated meals. Don't get me wrong, I enjoy them, too. I'm just advising you to let yourself off the hook so you'll have time and energy to enjoy your guests."

"So not every dish has to come from the Cordon Bleu cookbook, am I right, Melissa?"

"Absolutely."

While I listen, I'm soothed by the familiar actions of baking. A kind of Zen rolls over me. When thoughts of Hudson push their way into my brain, I feel positive. I'll have him back soon, I'm sure of it. This Christmas, I'll make him a special savory pie made with chopped steak. He goes nuts for steak.

I check the clock; there's half an hour left until the Geek Squad is due.

Since I have pie crust at the ready (insider tip: I make and freeze enormous batches, storing the dough in patties suitable for single-crust and double-crust pies. When it comes to pie crust, very cold butter is the secret to flakiness.), and leftover roasted vegetables from testing a Sunday Lunch recipe from the cookbook, I roll out what I need to make a deep dish winter veggie-and-egg pie. My stomach is starting to growl, and this delicious recipe is the closest thing to "slow" fast food that I can think of, apart from an omelet.

I spend a chunk of time listening to Melissa Clark's take on canapés and skewered meats while I assemble the pie and pop it into the oven along with the tartlets.

The voice of the radio presenter interrupts my Zen.

"Cuisine innovator and owner of highly rated restaurants such as Four Chairs and East 4th, James Keyes, is here today to share his recipe for sweet green pea guacamole. Welcome, James."

"Thank you, Amy. Happy to be here."

I dive to turn off the damned radio. And just as I was starting to feel calmer.

I'd managed not to hear his voice for nearly four years now, the last time being when he left that voicemail before I'd gotten my number changed. Now, the last thing on earth I needed today of all days was to be transported back to James Land. No thank you. Feel free to live your celebrity life, but do it far from me. Besides, putting peas in guacamole is just stupid. It's just like James to do something over-the-top just to get attention. Sure, it's nutritious, but they're *peas!* In *guacamole!* It's the most unholy union I can think aside from James and me. I wipe my hands, and set a timer. No time like the present to move on.

I check the clock again. Where was the Geek Squad, anyway? What did they launch? A skateboard?

I survey my mutinous computer and realize I never actually looked in on my blog. According to my schedule, I always post and reply to comments three times daily, and often once more before bed. Firing up the site, I can see that my negligence has caused a backlog. Charlotte's Chefs are in a tizzy wondering where I've been. Martha26 writes, *Dear Charlotte. I'm still waiting for your answer about substituting mint for rosemary in my Christmas Compote. It's a bit worrying that you've disappeared. I hope you're off on a grand adventure, or better yet, a romantic weekend ;)*

There must be twenty or more inquiries about where I've been and whether I'm all right. I debate telling my online friends how horrible the situation is, but they all know Hudson. There will be an outpouring of concern and pity. While I ponder my next move, blog-wise, I check the mince pies to see if they're done. As I open the oven door, I'm wrapped in a blanket of steaming, fragrant winter spices. The tops of the tartlets are a perfect golden brown, so I hustle to de-pan them to cooling racks.

No, I think, heading back to my desk. I'm going to keep the whole Hudson situation to myself for the time being. I can't handle reassuring everyone when I'm on shaky ground myself. I'll just act as though everything is hunky-dory. Where on *Earth* was the Geek Squad?

Dear Martha,' I answer. Either seasoning will do! Fruit loves herbs, and doesn't differentiate. Keep on baking, and please post a photo when you've made the recipe. Cheers! Charlotte.

I'm just about to dig into GrillDadNJ's question about marinades, when the buzzer goes. Oh, thank God! I run to press the button by the door. "Who is it?"

"It's BrrRR-UUUUumph." I hear nothing but the Doppler effect of a motorcycle speeding across what is supposed to be my quiet Upper West Side street. I push the button, and it emits the sizzling-sounding electric noise that opens the outer safety door down at the top of the stoop. I rush over to tidy up my desk in preparation. First, I want to get my printer rolling so I can make flyers. Then, I'll ask them to help me hook up the scanner I bought last month, and promptly chucked back in the box. Sure, the Geek Squad guy might think I'm an idiot, but I deal with food, not electronics.

Ding dong.

I race across the room, my chunky knitted socks skidding on the bare parts of the floor as I go, and fling open the door.

"Oh! It's you." Standing in front of me is not a uniformed Geek Squad representative, as I'd expected. It's Henry Wentworth, all six-foot-three of him, dressed casually in jeans and a Sherpa-lined suede peacoat. His face is like thunder.

"You say that a lot. Now, please step aside so I can come in and help you find your dog."

*****

I'll be honest with you. I'm a peaceful person, but I can get ugly when I'm backed into a corner. Ask Penelope Granger. If Lulu Wong hadn't stepped in when she did, not only would Penelope's art final have been ripped to shreds, she'd have had a fat lip as well. I'll bet it's the last time she ever tried to extort money from an underclassman at boarding school.

It's only by the grace of God, and Henry Wentworth's lucky stars, that the sweet-faced, mild-mannered Geek Squad guy arrives at precisely that moment. He looks nervously from Henry to me. I bite my tongue. Unleashed, the string of expletives backed up behind my teeth would have made Amy Schumer blush. I can feel that Henry is as near to bursting with rage as I, but we both swallow it out of common courtesy to the socially awkward young man who is clearly just trying to do his job. Still, he's like a little kid when mom and dad are arguing. He can sense the tension.

"Smells great in here," the young guy tries, shuffling from one foot to another. "Like my granny's at Christmas." I offer him a wan smile, and he smiles back and breathes out with huge relief. "Good! Great! Let's fix that machine."

Henry steps aside while I lead Blake (as his nametag proclaims) to the computer, and explain my issues. Out of the corner of my eye, I see Henry surveying my abode. He peeks around the corner to the kitchen. I watch him eyeball the cooling tartlets with interest.

"Do not touch those!" I hiss quietly, irritated to have been interrupted during my computer consultation. Who does he think he is, pawing through my house?

Like the commander of a starship, Blake has lowered himself into my chair and has taken charge of his domain. He finally looks comfortable in his own skin as he flicks switches, and plugs machinery into sockets.

Henry ignores me, pushing aside one of the curtains and looking at the windowsill. He's pretending to be all CSI about it, picking up a framed photo of Hudson and nodding his head, but I think he's just nosey. "Psst! Why are you even here?" I whisper, trying not to distract Blake. The faster the Geek Squad expert gets my computer up and running, the better off I'll be.

"Go!" I whisper-hiss, making huge motions with my arms indicating shoving Henry out the door. "Just go."

He mouths "No!" then picks up notebook I left lying on the arm of the couch. It has thoughts on favorite recipes and lists of dishes that I want to cook next, along with perfect menus for different occasions. "Put that down," I mouth, pointing to the couch. "Down!" I feel like I'm talking to Hudson.

"Lamb chops for Valentine's Day," he mumbles, tilting his head in consideration. "Maybe," he says, bobbing his head up and down, reading the pages. I tear across the room, snatching my notebook from his hands. "Give me that!" He holds up his hands in surrender, and is off to the next corner, poking and prodding.

Comfortable in his wheelhouse, Blake continues typing in long strings of characters. From time to time, he roots in his messenger bag for items to plug into ports in my computer that I wasn't aware existed. I leave him to it, and turn my attention to His Snobby Highness.

"Now, if you'd go and get yourself dressed, I can supervise your computer technician." He makes a big show of averting his eyes from my worn tracksuit.

"I *am* dressed," I huff. "I'm in my own home looking for my lost dog, not gearing up to walk the red carpet at the Oscars."

He looks me up and down. "Very well." He looks unsatisfied, but shakes it off. "Let's get down to business, then, shall we?" He's halfway through slipping off his coat, when I pull him aside.

"Don't get comfortable. You aren't staying." I whisper so as not to make it even more awkward for the boy.

"To the contrary, *Miss* Bell, I will indeed be staying as your aunt has given me explicit instructions that I'm not to report back to the Russian Tea Room, or for that matter, any of our soundstages, party venues, or offices, until I locate your pet. It is now my *job*." Underneath his closely trimmed beard, I see a muscle twitch in his jaw. His blue eyes are blazing, but other than that, his face is placid. "So calm down."

There is nothing, and I mean nothing, I hate more than being told to calm down when I'm already calm. Or even if I'm not calm. Jot this down, it's a sure way to make me punch you in the nose. I ball up my fists. "Get out," I say. "Leave."

"You need help, and I've been dispatched to offer it. Relax, and put yourself in my capable hands."

Relax! That's even worse than calm down. "I have hands of my own, as you can see." I show him my quivering fists. "I've been on my own since I was twelve. I'm good. I've got this. You can go now."

I pull out my phone and stab in a text to Aunt Miranda.

Dear Aunt M, I appreciate the offer of help, but am fine on my own.
You can tell HW to come back to the office.
If I need to talk to you, I can contact you directly. I really hope to find H today. x C

"Listen to me, Charlotte," he says in a soft voice full of urgency, "you haven't 'got this.'" I don't even raise my eyes from my phone. I just keep on texting. "Look at me," he says. Begrudgingly, I do. He nods in Blake's direction. "Case in point: Your big plan of the day is to run off some scrapbook-level flyers and…and what? Attach them to telephone poles with pushpins? Slide them under the doors of the people in your neighborhood? Maybe wear a sandwich board declaring 'I've lost my dog'?"

I'm starting to sweat around my hairline. Maybe I haven't fully thought this through.

"What do you know?" I fire off, knowing I sound like a testy adolescent. I need to get Hudson back and I've been doing everything I know how. "How dare you…you snobby *asshat,* come into *my* home and tell me I don't know how to find *my* dog? I'm figuring it out."

Henry Wentworth puts both hands on my shoulders, and fixes my eyes with those Aegean blue lasers of his.

"You'll burn hours and hours of precious time, and to no avail in the end. Meanwhile, your dog is God-knows-where, far from home and hearth. Now, allow Bill Gates, Jr. to finish up, and I'll come up with a real plan of action." I hear the buzz of a phone.

Henry sighs loudly. "Hang on, I have to check this."

He pulls out his phone and listens to the message. From my vantage point, all I hear is a high-pitched yelling. Is it Aunt Miranda? I strain to hear, but he sees me listening and turns his body away from me. His face closes off, then blooms into an expression of irritation. I scrutinize him, thinking about my next move.

On the one hand, I don't trust this pontifical, self-important *Englishman,* emphasis on 'man'. Being treated like the proverbial fragile little lady has always chapped my ass. Add to that his ulterior motive: He'll say or do anything to get back under Aunt Miranda's wing, where the action is. Come to think of it, Aunt Miranda shouldn't trust him either. I'm getting a real *All About Eve* vibe from this one.

On the other hand, if I need to swallow my ego to get Huddie back, so be it. I owe it to him to take advantage of every opportunity, no matter how distasteful.

"Charlotte, please," Henry says in a low voice. His posture has softened. "Your dog could be shivering on the street somewhere, cold and scared. And I hardly want to hint at it, but people have been known to steal animals." A tiny cry escapes my throat.

"Shh." He squeezes my shoulders. "Stay with me. The faster we find him, the better. Wouldn't you rather he were here, being fed home-cooked morsels off your plate, and shoving you over in the bed till you're teetering on the edge while he snores peacefully?"

Oh, Huddie. I let my eyes drift to the floor. I don't want Henry to see my fear.

"All right, ma'am," Blake breaks in, standing up and gathering his equipment. "You're all set to print and scan, and I ran some diagnostics and cleaned off some malware. Today's visit is $349.99. You should bring her into the shop soon if you want us to run updates."

"Never mind, that won't be necessary" Henry says, brandishing a credit card. Before I can intervene, the card is run through a swiper. "I can do the updates myself."

"Wait a minute," I begin.

"That will be all for today, thank you," Henry breaks in.

"Well, great then!" says the boy, moving toward the door. "If there's anything your husband can't handle, just stop in or give us a call."

"He's not my..."

"I can handle quite a bit, can't I, my dear?" Henry cuts me off, giving the young man just the lightest shove out the door, and closing it. "And at 350 dollars a visit, I'd certainly offer you more than fifteen minutes of fiddling around!"

I feel my eyebrows hurtle skyward, and my mouth drops open.

"That is to say... Miss Bell, what I mean to say, is..."

"*Bing!*" Saved by the oven timer. I hurry to the kitchen to take out the egg-and-vegetable pie.

Heading into the kitchen, I grab my heavy-duty silicone oven gloves. As I'm bending over to heave the substantial pie from the oven, I'm aware that Henry is behind me. Why won't he stop following me around? I need a minute to think. Whether it's from panic or lack of sleep or the distraction of having a person in my apartment, I cannot cut through the fog. I'm edgy, and I know it. I have to keep my cool. I want my dog back, and as Henry has pointed out, two heads are better than one. Especially when one of the heads isn't firing on all cylinders. I slide the pie onto a cooling rack, and turn around.

Henry is leaning, arms crossed, against the door jamb. "Did you make that?"

"Of course I made it. Do you see anyone else around here?" Easy, Charlotte, my inner voice tells me. Keep your eye on the prize.

"I mean, did you bake that? From scratch? And those little, what are they, mince pies, as well?" He sidles up to the counter, inspecting my wares.

"Yes, I did. Why?"

"It's just I don't know any women, apart from my mum, who do that." He looks at me with that maddening eyebrow lift. "All the women I've dated have only ever known how to pick up the phone to order food."

"Well I made them. Any other questions before you help me find my dog. I mean, that is why you're here, isn't it? I mean," I suck in my breath and let out a long sigh, "I'm sorry I snapped at you. It wasn't fair. Please, help me find my dog."

"Apology accepted. I do have one question…any chance of a cup of tea? I was ejected from the offices first thing in order to come to your rescue."

I stare at him. I can feel my breath rising and falling at a rapid rate, and I remind myself not to make an angry face. "One quick cup, then we get to work. OK?"

"Perfect."

"Sit down at the table," I bark. "I mean, please. Have a seat." I flick on the electric kettle and in short order, I'm setting a cup of strong, milky tea and a plate of mince pies in front of him.

"Thank you," he says. He bites into one of the pies, and moans. "God, this is unbelievable. What are you, a witch?" He takes a drink of tea, and greedily pops the rest of the pie into his mouth. "Heaven!"

I can't help feeling proud. Half the time when I bake, I just do a ring-and-run, leaving the leftovers at the door of the elderly couple in apartment 1F. They always leave an index card under my door thanking me, but it's not the same as watching someone appreciate my food.

"Well done, really. This is absolutely superb. You've got quite a talent."

"Thank you." I'm starting to warm to him a little. "Hudson loves my cooking. I like to think I'm pretty handy around the kitchen."

"The kitchen, yes, but you were taken to the cleaners with that house call."

I feel steam rising. "It was an emergency."

"I could have fixed your computer problems easily." He bites into a second pie. "Oh, mmm. These may be better than my mother's," he marvels. "And I meant to mention earlier, a single woman like yourself shouldn't open the door to complete strangers. This is, after all, New York City."

"I didn't open the door to a stranger. I opened it to the Geek Squad."

"Perhaps, but who was standing there? I could have been a common psychopath."

"Could have been…" I mumble under my breath.

"At any rate, I'm here to help. You've made the right choice. Now, we can finally do something that will work." He mutters something that sounds like, "…pleased you've come to your senses." I grit my teeth and smile. "Thank you for helping," I manage to cough out.

Ooh, it would feel so good to smack him across his smug, beardy face right now, but I can't afford to be emotional.

"We have an understanding. I'll use you to get what I want. Just as you're doing with me. I need my dog; you need Aunt Miranda's approval. One hand can wash the other. It's a win-win, right?"

"Sounds perfect," he replies.

I push away the little voice in my head that reminded me that, in a nutshell, this was James's *modus operandi* and the reason I wasn't standing next to him at the openings of his top-shelf restaurants. But today was a new day. As they say, "All's fair in love and war." At least I think that's what *The Art of War* said. I don't know, I really only skimmed the first few pages. Or maybe that's from a Humphrey Bogart film. It doesn't matter.

Henry Wentworth has something I need and I'm not going to give up until I get it.

Chapter 4

"Slow down there," Henry calls. I'm already halfway up the block. Once my feet have hit the sidewalk, my body kicked into high gear. I couldn't slow down if I wanted to. Henry does a little jog, and catches up with me, panting slightly. "It's a good thing I wore trainers today. Now, tell me again, where exactly was Hudson when he slipped away? We're going to retrace your steps."

It didn't matter to me that I'd been all over the park with Officers Curtis and Scrivello. Today was a new day, and Henry Wentworth had a new perspective. If I had to pretend to trust him to find my dog, then that's what I'd do.

"Hello there, what's that?" he said, gesturing to Paws & Claws, a mom-and-pop pet supply store on the avenue. "Have you ever been there?"

"Yes," I tell him, "that's where I get Huddie's food. I know the lady who owns the place."

"Let's make a detour, then. Follow me." I swallow the urge to tell him not to boss me around, and I do as I'm told. After all, it's not the worst idea.

He surveys the complimentary water bowl that Mrs. Rabinowitz leaves out for passing dogs. This time of year, it's deep blue with a yellow Star of David painted on the bottom. I see Henry take in the kitty-cat menorah sitting in the window, waiting for sundown when she'll turn on the right number of bulbs for this night of Chanukah. She spies me through the window, and waves enthusiastically, gesturing for me to come in.

Once Henry pushes open the door, tinkling the shop bell, Mrs. Rabinowitz races over, pumping her elbows and leading with her ample, pigeon-shaped bosom.

"Come in! What, you never visit anymore? Don't tell me you've been getting Hudson's food from the internet, God forbid, puh puh puh," she spits. "We haven't seen you in weeks!"

I open my mouth to ask if she's seen Huddie, but before I can form the words, she holds up her hands in surrender.

"I get it," she says before I can speak, "you're a young girl, you're busy with the young men, and the social life, and the this and the that." She gives a not-subtle-at-all nod to Henry. "Where's my little bubbeleh?" she asks.

"That's the thing, Mrs....?" Henry replies.

"Rabinowitz," she offers, scowling. "Everyone knows that. But what? What's the thing? Is something the matter? Talk to me."

Henry pulls a card from his pocket, and gestures toward a cup of pens on the counter. "May I?" She nods her head, and he chooses one, and scribbles on the back of the card.

In the name of all that is holy, why doesn't he just print his phone number, email, and Twitter handle on his cards like everyone else in the 21st century? From the way she's eyeballing him, I get the sense that Mrs. Rabinowitz is as suspicious of Henry as I am.

She loses her patience and quickly blurts out, "Forgive me for being a buttinsky, but there's something you're not telling me. Out with it, already."

"Hudson has gone missing," I whisper.

She looks horrified and then Henry informs her briskly. "Here's my card. If you hear anything from pet owners in the neighborhood, I'd appreciate it if you'd give me a call."

She takes the card without looking at Henry. "What happened, my Shayna Maidel?" she asks me. I feel a lump rise in my throat.

"Was he stolen? You poor dear."

I shake my head no, pinching my lips together so I don't cry. I don't like to cry in front of people under the best of circumstances. I sure as hell wasn't going to cry in front of Henry Wentworth of the Heavy Cardstock Wentworths. But Mrs. Rabinowitz's eyes are wells of pure concern. I look away. There's nothing worse when you're trying not to cry than having someone be nice to you. "Talk to me. What happened?"

"We're not sure. He was last seen around Columbus Circle. He slipped away without his collar and tags," Henry says.

"Tsk, tsk, tsk. How long has he been gone?"

"Not quite twenty-four hours," Henry supplies. Mrs. Rabinowitz shakes her head and says a quiet string of what I think are Hebrew words, ending in A-meyn. She sighs a ragged sigh. "May God help the poor little thing. Lost in a big city such as this one."

Bustling over to the bulletin board on the wall with photographs of her furry customers, she zeroes in on one and pulls out the staple. Some of the pictures were brought in by the pets' families; others were taken with the old Polaroid camera she keeps behind the desk.

"Here, take this, and use it in health. She shoves a photo of herself clutching Huddie to her ample chest. Eyes at half-mast, he's resting his head amongst her multiple chins and his face reflects pure bliss.

"You could show this to the police, maybe?" Henry accepts the photo, and studies it. "We have a flyer to hand out. If you wouldn't mind, Mrs. Rabinowitz, would you keep this here? To show your customers, and inquire about whether they've seen Hudson?"

"Mind? Why should I mind? I love that scraggly little treasure like he's my own!"

I'm afraid an ugly sob might escape if I open my mouth, so I simply hand over one of the fliers made from the Elfie photo.

"Look at the little boychik! Give me a stack of those. I'll have my delivery boy, Sheldon, leave one behind with every order. Oy, my heart is going to break and fall out onto the floor," she wails. "My dear," she says to me, "tell me your name."

I take a deep breath. "It's Charlotte," I manage. There. No sob. Back on solid ground.

"Listen to me, and listen to me good, Charlotte." She cups my jaw with her hand and tilts my head, and looks me in the eye. "I'm saying this as a mother." Her faded brown eyes start to blur as the tears pool. "There are people out there, not nice people, if you understand me. I hear all sorts from this one who rescues, and that one who works at a shelter. Enough said, am I right?"

I nod.

"We're not going to let that happen to Hudson, *kayn ayin hara*," she turns her head and spits through her fingers, "puh puh puh."

I shake my head no.

"We have to find our boy, and find him fast. I'm going to get on the horn and phone every pet shop owner in the book and tell them to keep their ears to the ground. It's good to have friends." She pulls me into a squishy hug, and I stiffen in surprise. She's having none of it. She squeezes tighter until I relax, then rubs my back. "Have faith, my Charlotte. Hope is needed most when times are the darkest. I know you're not Jewish, and neither is Hudson, but *Hashem* watches over all of us."

My heart lifts in my chest. I almost believe that it's all going to work out.

"Now, what is the plan?" she asks Henry.

Henry tacks the photo back up in its place on the board. "We're headed back to where the dog escaped to retrace Charlotte's steps."

She narrows her eyes. "Not *the dog*. His name is Hudson. And believe you me, he didn't escape. Why would he? Look at her! Would you escape from a gorgeous girl like that?" She waits for an answer. "Would you?"

Henry takes a long look at me. "No. I certainly wouldn't."

"That's right you wouldn't! And neither did Hudson. Charlotte, my dear, didn't you tell me Hudson loves the fountain at Lincoln

Center?" Her eyes light up. "That he likes to jump and bite at the fronds of water?"

I feel myself smiling when I picture Hudson with his front paws in the water. Technically, dogs aren't allowed up on the rim of the fountain, but I always let him sneak on. "Yes, he can't get enough of it."

"So, boom. You'll have a little look around Lincoln Center. You," she says accusingly, poking her finger into Henry's chest. "You take care of this one. Make sure she eats. Make sure she rests." She takes a card from the display tray and thrusts it at him. "You call me twice a day until you find Hudson, no excuses."

He pockets the card, and assures her he will.

"Go on, dear," she says to me. "See that bin of bones by the door? Walk up there and choose a nice one for when you find Hudson. Go."

She watches me walk away before addressing Henry.

"Remember," she says, pulling him to the side, and whispering. "The sooner the better," she says. I strain to hear. "There are sick people out there," she says even more softly. "I hear they take them to Canada. If you can, find him today."

*****

I'm practically hyperventilating as we hop in a cab to head downtown. "Lincoln Center, please, driver," Henry says crisply. "We'll start there and if we come up short, we'll head back to where you last saw Hudson."

I can hardly hear what he's saying. My blood roars in my ears. Against my will, images of animals in danger play like film clips across my brain. I wish I'd waited outside the pet store for Henry. Now I can't unthink about creepy animal-nappers. I lean back against the seat, and try to close my eyes, but that just makes it worse.

"Listen Henry, we've got to do something! We've got to do

something now!"

"We are doing something. We're going to check out spots that Hudson knows. Animals have an excellent ability to return to places familiar to them. First, we're going to the Lincoln Center."

"But what if he's not there? I mean, I know this is crazy, but what if some scientists found him, and they want to take him to a lab, for you know, experiments?"

"Yes, that is crazy. Calm down, no mad scientists are roaming New York City's streets searching for lab animals."

"Lab animals! A-ha. You said it yourself," I say, sitting up on my tailbone. "What if, you know, cosmetics companies are sending out interns to find strays? It's illegal to test on animals, right?"

"Not exactly…"

"So they'd have to do it undercover, like, by dark of night."

He squints his eyes and tilts his head. "Didn't you say Hudson was lost late yesterday morning?"

"That's not my point." I could feel my blood start to race. He wasn't listening to me *at all*. "What I'm saying is, they'd have to steal animals because they couldn't buy them at a pet store or online because they'd get arrested." The cab takes a sharp right, and I'm flung across Henry's lap. He sets me upright and untangles his arms from mine. We're hip to hip.

"Again, I don't think you understand the regulations for cosmetics companies." He looks down at our touching thighs. "I'd feel much more comfortable if you were to fasten your safety belt."

I shift over. I can't keep my hands still. I'm bubbling over with nerves. Now my brain is functioning on high speed. Suddenly, I feel like I see the big picture.

"I know what we have to do," I say, buckling my belt. A strange calm settles over me. "We have to contact the FBI." I pull out my phone and punch in the number for information.

Henry snatches my phone from my hand, and hangs up.

"Charlotte," he says with exaggerated patience, "the Federal Bureau of Investigation is not going to get involved with finding a lost dog."

"They might if we tell them he's being experimented on."

"Charlotte, please," he says. "Driver, could you let us off on the right-hand side, please? In front of the steps. Thank you." He takes some bills out of his wallet, and pushes them through the slot. "May I have a receipt, please?"

"What if they do take animals to other countries? Probably the laws are more lenient in places like South America or the Ukraine."

"Shh. Just a minute." He takes the receipt. "Thanks, keep the change."

He climbs out of the cab, and extends his hand to help me. It's larger than I expected, and warm. I pull hard on it, and scramble out of the back seat. I demand my phone back, but he pockets it. "If Hudson's in international waters, it may already be too late."

"We're going to look around here, then we're going to spread out in concentric circles. We are not calling the FBI."

"I'm going to call my cop friend and ask him which department handles open water crimes. I've read about Scientologists taking people eight miles off shore...You know, they could have just sailed him right up the Hudson River."

"Charlotte," he says, warily. "Please look at me."

"I heard what Mrs. Rabinowitz said. It's just that if Hudson is already across the border, we have to act now."

He's holding me firmly by the shoulders. I reach in his coat pocket to try to fish out my phone, but he holds my wrist in his big hand.

"Shh, shh, shh. Take a deep breath."

"I have to find Hudson," I break his grip, and burst into a jog, taking the famous Lincoln Center steps two at a time. Lit internally by LED lights, they welcome me in dozens of languages.

"Charlotte, please wait," Henry calls, chasing me.

I have to get this energy out of me. I just keep thinking of Hudson being blindfolded, and tied up by James Bond villains. I run into the horseshoe-shaped space of the center among glass buildings advertising *The Nutcracker* ballet, and the opera *Aida*. I'm passing the fountain, when Henry overtakes me, wrapping both his arms around mine. "Stop. Just stop."

"I can't stop, don't you see?" I search his eyes, looking for confirmation that he understands me. "He's my baby. If he's gone for good, or hurt, or worse, then I don't know what I'll do. Do you get it? Do you?"

"Listen to me," he says softly, and loosens his grip. "I understand." He leads me over the edge of the iconic water feature. "I know what it's like to lose something you care about." His eyes cloud over, and he goes very quiet. I listen harder.

"You feel off balance right?" Gently, he pushes my shoulders till I'm sitting. "You feel like someone's pulled the rug out from under you, don't you?"

I nod.

"Right." He sits down opposite me. "Have you ever heard the term 'mania'?"

"Yes, of course."

"That describes the state you're in at the moment."

Of all the condescending things to say! I can't help but bite back. "Because I suppose you're England's answer to Sigmund Freud? I don't need to sit here and be criticized. I need to find my dog." I hop down, but he catches me by the arm.

"Hear me out."

Reluctantly, I take a seat.

"It's not a criticism. Not at all. It's an acknowledgement that what you're feeling is perfectly natural. The highs, the lows. The wild rollercoaster feeling. You're in a crisis. I know what that feels like."

I collapse a little. That's a good word for it. Crisis.

"And people in a crisis need others to take over." I huff out a little noise of protest. "Temporarily," he says in a soothing voice, as if he's trying to hypnotize me. "Give me a chance. Allow me to think logically for you while you can't do it for yourself."

"I seriously cannot believe you just said that. Do you know women at all?"

I cross my arms. I'm aware I'm making a nasty face, but he's doing a poor job of convincing me to go along for his ride.

"How many people have you known who are truly bad?"

"Lots!" I cross my arms.

"No really. I mean truly bad people."

I think. Mum was flighty and negligent, but she loved me. I know that. She just never learned to be a grown-up, and she died before she had the chance to redeem herself. There's the freak that tried to send me porn through my blog, but it was garden-variety topless lady stuff. It was creepy, but not truly, truly evil. I think harder. Penelope Granger? Now I was scraping the bottom of the barrel. James maybe.

"See? You know people who are annoying, nasty, maybe even manipulative or unethical, but no one truly sinister. And the ones you hear about on the news are the exception to the rule. It's like sharks. Everyone goes around thinking that the minute someone dips their toe in the sea, they'll be eaten alive by Jaws. It's sensationalism. Do you know how many people actually die each year at the hands, or rather, mouths, of sharks? Eight. Only eight people. But the Discovery Channel people and the news media would have you believe differently."

"Go on. I'm listening."

"Now," he says, gesturing around to the flush-cheeked people around me, dressed in bright winter coats, fluffy scarves, and quirky wool hats. "How many people do you know who are good?"

Most of them.

I look up, blinking my eyes. I hadn't even noticed the giant, glimmering ice sculpture of The Nutcracker rising from the center of the fountain. A second ago, it was like I was seeing New York through reverse binoculars. I breathe in. Everything felt so much more spacious all of the sudden.

"See? Think about all of the people you know who would

79

help Hudson, and never dream of harming a hair on his head." I conjure up a parade of smiling faces. All of the people at the dog park, Mrs. Rabinowitz, the Refrigerator, taxi driver Vijay Singh, my agent Beverly, Aunt Miranda. I even think of people I don't know well, like the checkout girl with the orange extensions from Zabar's, and my super, and all of Charlotte's Chefs. They'd all do the right thing if they found a dog like Huddie.

"OK. You win," I tell him. "I'm calm. In my own way."

He breaks into a wide, crooked grin. I haven't seen him smile yet. He looks so different. Suddenly, he looks familiar, like I should know him from somewhere. I can't help smiling myself.

"Do you trust me?"

I think about it. "No," I answer honestly. "I don't know you."

"Do you believe I'm on your side?" he asks.

"Yes. I can believe." For now.

*****

Henry takes the lead, and I follow, as he approaches tourists and city dwellers bustling across Lincoln Center's plaza on their way to do last-minute holiday shopping. If you haven't spent much time in New York City, I'll fill you in on a fact. Most of the time, when a stranger approaches, New Yorkers keep on walking. It's not that New Yorkers aren't good people, it's just that we generally have someplace to be.

That said, if a New Yorker susses out that you need help, and aren't going to A) weave a story about how you were robbed on the way to Penn Station and need $40 for the train, B) distract them while you ever-so-gently lift their wallet, or C) commandeer their much-needed public privacy by glomming on and following them wherever they're going, they are largely very generous.

Henry does a masterful job of coaxing people in while being brisk enough not to waste their time. I'm heartened by the number of men and women who stop to answer his questions about having seen a lost dog. The majority take a flyer and promise to get in touch if they see anything. His harshness has fallen away. In stark contrast to how he was the night we met, he's inviting. It's probably all an act. You don't get to be Aunt Miranda's partner in crime without a certain amount of salesmanship.

"Excuse me, ladies?" he asks. Four very young women eye him, then stop and turn around. They're all wearing thick puffer coats over what seems to be nothing. On closer inspection, I see that they all have on double-thick tights that match their respective skin tones. To a girl, they all have tight buns perched atop their heads, interlaced with sparkling red and green ribbon. As a group, they look surprised. I realize that's less a function of their emotional states, than the ostrich-like false eyelashes they all sport. Not one of them is as tall as my shoulder.

"Yes?" The leader of the bird-like pack answers. "Are you lost?"

"No, nothing like that." Henry beams a charming smile at them, and they all answer simultaneously with wide smiles and batting eyelashes like a flock of flamingoes. I examine Henry. It goes without saying that he's handsome. I mean, he's tall, and he has that broad shoulder/slim waist thing going on. And there's his beard, and the glasses. I know certain girls like that type. But really! These girls can't be more than nineteen or twenty, and Henry is, what? Thirty? Thirty-three? I watch with interest. "I was wondering if perhaps you've seen this little lost dog?"

They all huddle over the flyer with a chorus of "Aww!"

He has them in the palm of his hand.

From a cacophonous burst of high-pitched baby voices, I can pick out the phrases, "He's so cute," "I had a dog like that when I was little," "Poor baby!" and "When did you lose him?" When the din dies down, the ringleader tells Henry, "We're ballerinas, so we're here every day. We can keep an eye out for him." She looks up from beneath the canopy of lashes and says, "Have you ever seen *The Nutcracker*?" She gestures toward the five-story high banner, which features a delicate ballerina dancing among life-sized toys and giant wrapped presents, hung in front of the architectural wonder of Lincoln Center's crystal palace windows.

"Almost, but not quite." His cheeriness fades, and is replaced by what appears to be deep thought. "Never mind, though," he brightens again. "I'm sure the performance I missed would have paled in comparison to the current run with you ladies dancing."

"You were in New York years ago?" I ask.

"Yes, but that's a story for another time," he tells me.

"Here's my number," the smallest of the girls bursts forth from the sidelines, literally pushing me aside to get to Henry. The ringleader shoots daggers at her. "If you want house seats, I mean," she continues, duly cowed.

"We'll ask around about your dog," the ringleader tells Henry. Not one of them has cast so much as a glance in my direction. The whole invisibility thing I had working for me this morning is obviously doing its job. "And I'll call you if we hear anything. Is that your number on the flyer?" she simpers.

"That," Henry says, "is the number of Nichols Bespoke Events. I work for the firm."

"I've heard of them," she says. "They did Fashion Week here last year, didn't they?"

"Very good." He bestows his grace on the girl, and she receives it with beaming pride. "We'll do it again next year. Contact me ladies, if you'd like passes."

His offer is rewarded with a bouquet of high-pitched shrieks that I suspect might call to every lost dog in the city. "And remember, if you hear anything, please do get in touch."

"Did you look back there?" the smallest one asks, bravely asserting herself. She points in the direction of a tent at the back of the sprawling plaza. "I heard some barking earlier."

"I was going to say that!" the ringleader chastises. "Anyway, we have to go now. We only have half an hour for lunch and it takes ten minutes to walk to Jamba Juice. Wardrobe will be furious if we're late. We still haven't been fitted for the candy cane costumes."

"Thank you for your time, ladies. And thank you for being my eyes and ears on the ground." He bestows one last smile, as they glide off in a graceful swoop.

"Right then, that's a few more soldiers in our army."

I'm not sure if I'm impressed or disgusted.

He gestures toward a tent city, not unlike the staging area at Rockefeller Center, situated to the left of the sumptuously bedecked rooftop Christmas tree. In my daze, I hadn't noticed it before.

"Shall we?"

I nod, and follow him.

*****

Henry pushes back a flap at the back of the cavernous, multi-roomed tent and peeks in.

"We should go in the front," I tell him.

"We'll just be told they're not open for business." He motions for me to follow him. My nerves are already pulled tight without having to worry about being arrested for breaking and entering. I peek over his shoulder at what appears to be a locker room. He's inside and crossing to the next door before I can stop him. A low, thunderous rumble stops me dead in my tracks. I'm sure my eyes must be as big as saucers when I look to Henry for direction. Another basso eruption, this time culminating in a neck-prickling roar sends me running toward Henry. I press myself against him, clutching his arm.

"What was that?" I whisper.

"Lions," he says matter-of-factly.

"*Lions?*"

"Could be tigers."

"What the hell?"

"It's a circus," he says, shrugging me off, and peeking through the next door.

"In Midtown?"

He turns around and stares at me hard. "Yes, in Midtown. It's the

83

Big Apple Circus. Didn't your aunt ever bring you here as a child?"

"She did not."

"Well, surely you've walked past? It says it on the tent, larger than life. Big Apple Circus." I shrug. "Do you or do you not live here?"

"I don't go out much at night," I mumble.

He assesses me, cocking his head. "I know more about Manhattan than you do, it seems."

"Fine. You win. But now that I am at a circus, I'd really rather see any large African cats from the safety of a theater seat." I pull him backwards. "Let's go."

"Shh!" he tells me, freezing in place. "Did you hear that?"

There's a growl, but this one sounds much less threatening than the previous noise.

"Listen!"

A high, loud bark cuts through the silence.

"Come on," he says, taking my hand and pulling me through to the next makeshift room. Seated at a makeup table is a man in a clown suit, but no makeup, reading a newspaper. Off to the side, there's a stylist curling the hair of a bearded lady sitting in a retro pneumatic salon chair. "Wrong way," she says, without turning around. "Ticket booth is out front."

"We were wondering if you could help us," Henry begins. The skinny girl with the rough complexion swivels the chair around to face us. A wide grin spreads across the bearded lady's face, and she begins to twirl her mustache suggestively with her finger. "Oh, I can help you, I'm sure of it," she says.

I feel the earth tilt on its axis from the strangeness of it all, but Henry doesn't miss a beat. "Have you lovely ladies, by any chance, seen this little dog?" He steps forward, and proffers a flyer to the seated woman.

"Real cute, ain't he, Darla." Darla takes a moment to consider it, staring hard at the photo of Hudson. Finally, she nods.

"Real cute," she confirms.

"Have you seen him?" Henry asks sweetly. "It's only that he's been missing since yesterday and I'm quite worried for his safety. He isn't, as you might say, street smart."

"That's a pickle," Darla says, returning to her project of curling the bearded lady's lush, glorious tresses into a multitude of sausages.

"Grandma," the bearded lady shouts to the man in the clown suit. "This gentleman here lost his doggie. You seen it?"

"Nope," Grandma replies, not bothering to look up from his paper.

"Old grouch," she hisses. "Grandma has a lot to learn in the way of manners," she apologizes sweetly to Henry. "But I'll tell you what. You go through that way, take a left, then take another left, and you'll wind up in the Big Top. Jenny's in there working with the porcupine and the goat. Her dogs might be in there, too. She's practically Doctor Doolittle, that girl is. If anyone can spot a stray, it's her."

Is it my imagination, or does Henry bow before stepping forward to, and I kid you not, kiss the bearded lady's hand. "Thank you for your kindness," he says, backing away without breaking eye contact. "Good day to you all," he says as he walks briskly in the direction of the Big Top. I hustle to catch up.

"Are you *kidding* me with that? Who do you think you are, a rogue-ish duke from a Regency romance?"

"You get more flies with honey than you do vinegar," he says, not slowing down. "Give the people what they want, as the old saying goes." I follow him through a narrow passageway that smells like damp hay and cotton candy. Every time I think he might be a decent human being, he rekindles my suspicion. I push my frustration aside. If he is the devil, I'll have to turn a blind eye to ethics for the time being. At least he's using his evil power to help Hudson.

Henry pushes open one more flap, and I gasp at the sheer expansiveness of the room. Standing in the circus Big Top, it's really hard to imagine we're in the middle of New York City, surrounded by fleets of taxicabs, and chrome and glass skyscrapers.

A muscular woman in a lycra suit waves a baton at a wooden box and a low, lumbering porcupine waddles out. She holds the baton high in the air, and the prickly creature ascends a ramp, and triumphantly comes to a halt on a hip-high platform. It sniffs the air, but I'm not sure that's part of the act.

A flurry of motion catches my attention, and I see that a rambunctious white goat comes flying out from backstage, lips flapping, and hooves thumping. It sets its sights on me, and panicked, I dive behind Henry. "Help!"

"Buddy!" Jenny the trainer calls.

Like a ninja, Henry crouches into a squat, waiting for the goat to charge him. He expertly takes hold of the goat's horns. The impact throws Henry backwards, into me. I land on my rear. From my sitting position, I see that Henry and the goat are in a battle of force. The goat is pushing Henry; Henry is pushing right back. They stay locked in this wrestling hold until Jenny arrives. She takes the horns out of Henry's hands, turns the goat toward the door, and makes a clicking noise with her mouth.

"Beeeeeh!" Buddy calls as he hightails it to the door. Still running, he takes one last look over his shoulder and calls out "Beh!" for good measure.

"Sorry about Buddy," Jenny said. "But you're not supposed to be back here. I don't have insurance to cover that."

"Understood. We won't stay long. We were told you might know something about a dog."

"I know a lot about lots of dogs." She pulls a whistle out of her cleavage, and toots three sharp blasts. A parade of various-sized canines file out from the goat-door. The fifth dog in the line of six is largely beige with calico splotches and scruffy fur. My heart gets caught in my throat. In a split second, tears blur my vision.

He's digging into the sawdust for all he's worth. "Huddie!" I cry running toward him. I bend down and scoop him up in my arms. All of the other dogs start jumping up and banking off my knees, delighted at this unexpected interruption of the routine.

But the second I bury my face in the dog's fur, I know. This is not Hudson. I squeeze my eyes shut tightly to flush out two fat tears. Whimpering, the little dog licks my face. He knows I'm sad, I think. I give him a squeeze and a nuzzle.

I hear *clicka-clicka* and the five dogs on the ground obediently sit.

"We were looking for information regarding her dog, you see," Henry explains to Jenny. "Not dogs in general."

"You lost your dog?" Jenny asks me, expression sympathetic. Still holding the patchwork mutt, I nod. "I'm real sorry to hear that. It'd break my heart if I lost one of mine."

Henry hands her a flyer. "We'd be very grateful if you'd keep an eye out for Hudson, here. He was last seen in the general vicinity."

Jenny takes a long look at the flyer, and her eyes soften. "Your boy looks a lot like Teddy, there. I've got lots of dogs, but that one's special. Found him at a supermarket, upstate, huddled in a towel in a rusted shopping cart. Someone must have dumped him." As she's saying this, I cling tighter to the sweet, warm bundle of dog in my arms. "At least they left him where someone would find him. Best thing that ever happened to me, and that includes both of my marriages."

She approaches us, gently rubbing the wild hairs back from Teddy's eyes. "Who's a good boy?" Teddy's tail thumps against my coat.

"That dog's my bread and butter. Smart as a whip, and born to the stage, but it's more than that. I'd love him even if he didn't work a day in his life. That dog's my baby, know what I mean?"

"I do know what you mean." When I hear myself, my voice sounds small. Jenny nods to me. "Yep, you get it."

"Tell you what," Jenny says to Henry. "I'll pass a stack of them pictures around to the folks here. We're onsite till after New Year's. I'll get people to keep an eye peeled."

"Thank you, Jenny. That would be very helpful." I notice that

Henry doesn't pull his curtseying ways with Jenny. It's pretty clear she wouldn't fall for it. Like they say, "know your audience."

"We're based upstate, even though we're on the road a lot. All my animals are shelter kids and rescues. I'll put the word out, and post on the pet adoption websites I work with on Facebook."

Reluctantly, I give Teddy one last kiss on his bony little head, and set him on the ground. Instead of wandering off to join the other dogs, he sits on my foot.

"There's Buddy," Jenny says, waving toward the goat at the backstage curtain. "He knows what time it is. If I don't feed him soon, he's likely to start more trouble to get attention.

"Beh!" Buddy declares staring right at us. Instead of charging us again, this time the goat pointedly reaches over and begins chewing on the plush red velvet drape covering the backstage flap.

"Buuuuuuuuhdy!" Jenny warns, stomping off in the goat's direction. "I'll call you if I hear anything!" she shouts.

I gently slide my boot from under Teddy's rump, and give him a final neck scratch.

Empty-handed, I follow Henry out into the expanse of New York City.

****

"Shall we walk?" Henry asks me, as we're waiting for a cab. Holiday shoppers and tourists ensure that yellow taxis are scarce around now. Our next move is to go back to where Hudson was lost. I don't have a much faith in the plan, but I'm on a downswing and I can't think what else to do.

"I don't know." I'm losing momentum.

He takes a long look at me. "All right?"

"Not really," I tell him. Whereas the air felt crisp and promising this morning, all I feel now is cold. "Seeing Teddy in there, holding him in my arms, it really drove home that Hudson isn't going to be waiting for me at home when I get there."

"He might not be, but wherever he is, we're going to find him. See that statue of Dante Alighieri there?" He motions to the centerpiece in Dante Park, the little triangular oasis nestled across from Lincoln Center and above the historical Empire Hotel. "I see that as a sign of hope. You know *The Divine Comedy*?" I nod. "Then you know the story of a man who went through hell and came out the other side refreshed. It ends with him peaceful and in Paradise."

I try to match his optimism with a smile. I can tell by the alarm on his face that I'm not quite pulling it off.

"Even the park itself is a beacon of hope. This idyllic little green space, from which you can cool down by watching one of the city's most spectacular fountains in the summer, or warm up by drinking in the lush greens, golds, and reds of the Christmas tree in the winter, was once a condemned property. Did you know that?"

"No, I didn't." I wonder how he does. I survey the scene. Several stalls are set up to vend handmade gifts. There's a farm-stand selling burlap-wrapped loaf cakes, and jars of jam tied with tartan ribbons. Another sells raffia ornaments. Still another offers CDs of the dulcimer-rich Christmas carols the proprietor is piping out from a speaker.

"It's true." He suddenly shouts, "Taxi! Darn, lost another. Anyway, did you also know that the final scene of the film *Annie Hall* was shot here?"

I perk up. "Really? Seeing that when I was really young made me want to come to New York!"

"Same here," he tells me, with a tilt of his head. "Huh," his eyes twinkle, and I can see him filing that bit of information away. "How old were you?"

"Twelve."

"Weren't you a bit young for something that sophisticated?"

I'm embarrassed, like I always was in front of normal, traditional moms who'd raise an eyebrow at what my mother allowed me to do. "My mother didn't believe in censorship. People called

89

her Bohemian. She didn't care, though. After she got pregnant with me, a lot of the family's old friends snubbed her in their boxes at Wimbledon, and at weddings and deb balls. She didn't care. And the fact that she didn't really rankled some of those who ran in her circles, and who'd been at school with her, and especially annoyed my grandparents. They died when I was small. From what I hear, she infuriated them along with everyone else. I still don't know if she was freethinking or crazy, but I will tell you that it was downright horrible watching *Eyes Wide Shut* with her. Stanley Kubrick may well be a genius, but come on. After that, believe me, I wanted all the boundaries."

"Hold on a minute, was your mother Lily Bell?"

"Yes, I thought you knew that."

"Why would I know that?"

"From Miranda."

"No, I didn't. You mean Lady Lily Bell?"

"Yes."

"I see," he says. "Taxi!" He tries to hail another cab.

"You see what?" I ask. He doesn't answer. There are no taxis with their lights on anywhere up or down the avenue. "You know, let's just walk," I tell him, steeling myself for the exertion of it.

Brrrring Brrrring!

"Hello! Great, it's our lucky day," Henry says as a pedicab brakes to a halt in front of us. "Climb in."

"I've never ridden in a pedicab," I saw warily as he boosts me aboard. "It feels a little colonial if you know what I mean. How lazy are we to sit back and relax while this poor guy pedals?"

"Nonsense! What do you charge, sir?"

"Five dollars each minute," the wiry Russian driver answers.

"Do you like your job?"

"I love my jobs. I have two. This in the day, gymnastic coach in the night. This keeps me fit and strong. An office job would make me perish."

"Can you take us across to the entrance of Central Park?"

90

"Of course!" He bears down hard on the pedal to get us going, and we're off to the races. I'm quite surprised at how fast we're going.

"Don't you get cold?" I holler up to him over the sounds of the wind and the traffic. I wind my fuzzy scarf one more time around my neck, and pull the hood of my jacket up.

"I love cold!" the driver shouts, turning around. He's standing and pumping his legs, and we're darting in and out of traffic. It's kind of exhilarating. "If you're cold, there is blanket. Have your man wrap you up."

"No thanks, I'm good!" I say quickly as Henry reaches for the folded quilt. "Really, it's only a short trip."

"I've been meaning to ask you something, Charlotte?" Henry says to me. I have to lean in to hear him. "Why didn't Mrs. Rabinowitz know your name? She knew Hudson's. I'm surprised she had to ask yours."

I'm uncomfortable with this line of questioning. "I just never told her, that's all. Why?"

"She certainly cares about you. I found it curious."

I stare forward, watching our driver's shoulders rise and fall rhythmically as his legs power the bike. Just because I don't get all pally with everyone I meet, it doesn't mean I'm "curious." It's just who I am. People don't have to go around calling me "quirky" and "offbeat". If you ask me, the way I operate is perfectly normal.

"So when was the last time you saw *The Nutcracker* again?" I ask irritably. "If you want to get all personal." I'm aware that I'm pouting, but I don't care. I'm cold and I need coffee, and besides, he started it.

"Here we are, edge of Central Park," says our driver, braking abruptly near the 67h Street entrance. "Here is OK?"

"Perfect," Henry says, avoiding my question and paying the driver. "Say, if you happen to see this dog, would you call me?"

"There is reward?"

"Hmm, I hadn't thought of it, but yes."

"Is big reward?"

"Bring me the dog, and I'll let you know." Henry tells him.

"You are more Soviet agent than English gentleman," the pedicab guy declares, eyes narrowed. "I like it!" He bursts into a raucous belly laugh. "I try to find this dog."

"Come on," Henry says brusquely, leading me through the mossy stone wall that borders this part of the park, "let's walk in as far as Sheep Meadow and see if we can find that dog of yours." He's walking very fast, with his hands jammed into his coat pockets. I think I've struck a nerve.

I stop.

"You know, I think I've got it from here. Thanks for your help so far. Why don't you go back to your office?" I pull out my phone. "I'll text Aunt Miranda that you tried."

"Don't be silly," he says, ignoring me and marching forward. "I implore you not to text Miranda. Trying isn't good enough. Besides which, I am not accustomed to failing. Hudson!" he calls out. "Here Hudson! Come!" With every shout, Henry's steps become more aggressive and determined. "I am quite happy to be on this assignment."

"You're just saying that because of Aunt Miranda." Actually, I really wish he would go. I'm not used to spending so much concentrated time with any one person. I like having my own space. "She's making you do this."

"While that was certainly true in the beginning, I am now invested in this challenge," he says, picking up speed.

I trot to catch up. "You are not hearing me," I say, trying to catch a deep breath. "I am releasing you."

"You can't release me," he says, looking around. "Hudson! Here, boy!"

"Maybe I can't give you permission to go back to the office, but I can give you permission to leave me. Take the rest of the day off. Finish your Christmas shopping."

"Thank you, no. I don't have any Christmas shopping."

"That sounds like you. You probably had everything bought by October and wrapped by November."

"That's not accurate at all."

"Oh, you probably hired someone to do it for you, Don Draperstyle. Like those men who have their secretaries buy scarves for their wives."

"For your information, Miss Know-It-All, I don't do Christmas shopping." He stops to closely examine a pack of six dogs, all being led by a professional dog walker. The guy gives him a dirty look. "Sorry," Henry says.

"Creep," the guy replies.

We go through the fence into the big, open, grassy area called Sheep Meadow. In the summer, the place is packed shoulder-to-shoulder with people picnicking, throwing Frisbees, kicking balls around, and sunbathing. For now, it's simply a rare and sprawling open space. I look up to see Belvedere Castle towering over the Delacorte Theatre where free outdoor Shakespeare is played yearly to the citizens of New York. If I concentrate hard on only that view, it's easy to believe I'm in a medieval kingdom.

Swinging my eyes over a little, however, I can see the tops of the skyscrapers that signal the beginning of Midtown to our south. The juxtaposition of the former farmland and the concrete jungle never fails to make my head swim. Henry just keeps plowing forward, and shouting for Hudson.

"I'm confused. What do mean you don't do Christmas shopping? You just said you don't use a service or make some intern do it for you. Where do you get the presents?"

"I don't. I simply don't participate in Christmas."

"How can you not participate in Christmas?" Have I missed something, I wonder? I'm feeling dizzier as this conversation goes in what I feel are circles. "Are you Jewish?"

"No. My father is Church of England. That's where I went to chapel when I was at school, but my mother is Irish Catholic. She took me to mass with her when I was a small child." He smiles fondly. "That part I liked. Leaning on her arm as we sat in the pew, smelling the scented talcum powder on her soft, jiggly arms. Listening to her sing the hymns. She has a lovely voice. She could have been in the choir."

"Then what's the problem with Christmas?"

"I just choose not to participate," he says sharply. "Can we leave it at that and find your dog?"

"You can leave me," I respond hotly. "Because I don't want to have to hear you say 'participate' one more time. I told you I don't need you, so why are you still here?"

He stops in his tracks, growling a throaty noise of exasperation. "I've explained myself. Are you thick, or are you just trying to wind me up?"

"Neither! I'm just telling you that I don't need some huffy brownnoser following me around the park and slowing me down when I have important work to do. Now why don't you go?" I plant my hands on my hips. "Go!"

He swings around to face me. "I am not going to leave you alone, not matter how many times you tell me to. Is that clear?"

"Is there a problem here?" A familiar voice calls from above my head, about a yard behind me. "Because I think the lady is telling you you're not wanted." It's a helmeted Scrivello, sauntering up on a shining, muscular bay quarter horse. The animal sniffs at Henry, nostrils flaring.

"Not at all, Officer," Henry says, placing his hand on the horse's cheek, pushing his long face to the side. I see Henry swallowing his annoyance, and attempting to look relaxed and casual.

"Hey, I know you," he says, lighting up. "What are the chances? Craig, it's Charlotte. He was just gonna call you." He says nodding to his partner riding astride a rippled ebony-colored steed of his own.

"Do you have news about Hudson?" I feel a flutter in my chest.

"Sorry, Charlotte. We followed up on a few reports, but they were false leads. I was just gonna call to see how you're getting by.

Looks like it's a good thing I found you in person." He pulls back on his horse's reins, and the animal raises its head, veins popping underneath the gloss of its short, black hair. "'Cause I don't like the tone of your boyfriend's 'friendly discussion.'"

"He's not my boyfriend," I declare.

"I'm not her boyfriend," Henry blurts at the same time.

"Well, call it what you want, there are laws against any kind of violence against women, domestic or not."

"Violence! I assure you, I wouldn't lift a finger against her or any woman. Charlotte, please tell the officers."

I hesitate for a second. I could make my wish come true with just the tiniest implication. As much as I'd like to be alone, I can't bring myself to do it. This is the second time I've passed up a chance to throw Henry under the bus. If I were colder, I could have had him fired *and* arrested. "There was no violence, in any way, shape, or form. He's a decent man," I say begrudgingly.

Henry nods vigorously, as Scrivello's horse nibbles on his scarf.

"He's helping me find Hudson. It was a silly argument."

"Exactly!" Henry concurs, lightly patting the huge animal's neck. "Nice horsie."

"Don't eat his clothes, Flannel," Scrivello says, "that's not nice." He makes no attempt to stop his horse's munching, however, and I stifle a giggle as I watch Henry try to stealthily pull away, only to tighten the scarf into a makeshift noose.

"Charlotte, would you come over here with me, please," Craig says. The police officer steers his horse to the side, and beckons me with a crooked finger. Once we're out of earshot, he asks, "You're not protecting him, are you? Just say the word. You know I got your back."

"Honestly, it's nothing like that. And thank you." I'm moved by the formidable officer's warmth. I feel a little swimmy, as the emotion of having a friend like that washes over me. I reach out and lean on his horse's shoulder to steady myself.

"Hey, you all right there?" Scrivello calls. "You look a little pale."

"I'm OK. Just a little lightheaded."

"I'll bet you need something to eat," Craig lectures. "You've been working yourself to the bone without stopping to eat a decent meal." He turns to Henry. "What are you doin' marching her all over the park in the cold with no food in her belly?"

"I didn't…Charlotte, are you hungry?" Henry stammers.

"I could eat," I say, realizing that I really was running on fumes.

"Did you hear that?" Craig demand. "She's hungry."

"Yes, I heard." Henry is ducking and weaving in an attempt to thwart the attentions of Flannel. "I'd be happy to take you for a meal, Charlotte." Flannel's flapping lips engulf Henry's ear, and he emits a strangled, high-pitched noise. "In fact, I'm quite ready to go now."

"Well, then. Get the girl somethin' to eat!"

"Craig. It's fine. I will get *myself* something to eat."

"Girl's hungry, upset about her dog, traipsin' her all over the damn park," Craig mutters.

"I will put her in a cab, and take her someplace to get lunch," Henry says, hands up, trying to calm the police officer down.

"Oh, you'll get her lunch alright," Craig tells him. "You'll get her lunch, then you'll find her dog. That's what I'm talkin' about. Isn't that right, Scrivello? Isn't Hugh Grant over here gonna feed that girl, and then go find her dog?"

"You heard the man," Scrivello agrees good-naturedly. "If I were you, I'd get on the job. All right, Flannel. Enough playing. Time to get back to work. Speaking of lunch, we better head back to the station, Curtis." Henry breathes a sigh of relief as Scrivello guides his horse to the side, to walk with his partner.

"You take it easy, Charlotte, and don't think we forgot about you. A friend of mine on the force in Edgewater's got a soft heart when it comes to lost animals. He's spreading the word around Jersey."

"Thanks, guys. You'll be the first to know when we find Hudson."

"You have any trouble, you call me. You've got my cell." He gives Henry a warning look. "Any kind of trouble. At all."

Henry looks affronted, but is smart enough to stay quiet.

"Thanks, Craig," I call as the two policemen head uptown.

I start out across Sheep Meadow, but Henry sprints up and catches me by the elbow. "Where are you going?"

"To look for my dog in the park."

"Oh, no you don't. Now you've called your thugs on me, I have my orders. Come with me, young lady. I know neither how to carve a shiv from a bar of soap, nor how to make toilet wine. I'd venture to guess I wouldn't last a day in prison.

He frog marches me over to the 65th Street traverse and hollers, "Taxi!"

Chapter 5

"This is really over the top."

Perched high above the die-hard joggers and cyclists on the path along the road, in a horse-and-carriage, I'm embarrassed. "I'm not an invalid. I can walk, you know."

"There were no taxis to be had," Henry replies, talking loudly over the steady pounding of hoof beats. "I'm in direct compliance with the New York City police department. I've been told to take care of you, and I'm obeying the law." He unfurls the lap blanket and drapes it over my knees.

"I'm not a ninety-year-old grandma."

He looks at me enigmatically. "Yes, I can see that." A faint smile plays on his lips. "Never-the-less, it's cold. It must be near the freezing mark. Can you take us to the edge of the park, driver?"

"And why not? We're licensed to go as far as 5th Avenue and Central Park South," the driver says in a Dublin brogue. "Aren't we, Whiskey-girl?" Whiskey the pony trots on, head high, and tail flicking.

I had never, not even once, been in a horse-drawn carriage. I look around to see if anyone is staring. People might think I consider myself a princess. Or that Henry was a doting suitor who'd bundled me up here to pop the question.

"If you're cold, you should take the blanket," I say, shifting it over to Henry's lap. A few fat snowflakes are starting to fall. One sticks in my eyelash, and I blink it away.

"No, I insist." He shifts it back.

We wrestle like that for a moment, till our driver calls out, "Don't be daft. Share the shawl. No sense in catching your death. Sure, don't I wear thermals under me own kit? I'll wager you're wearing no such thing."

"The man has a point." Henry says. "May I?"

I have to admit, the warmth of the wool blanket does warm me up. A sandwich and a hot, caffeinated drink would probably do me a world of good too.

I stop fussing and Henry smoothes the cheery red, black, and gold plaid blanket across the tops of our thighs. I jump when he tucks it around my waist.

"Sorry," he says.

"'S'ok," I mumble. I can't remember when a man had touched me with more than a handshake.

Riding in a horse-and-carriage is preferable to walking, given how out of steam I am at the moment, but no one could accuse this mode of transportation as being high-speed. At this rate, it's going to be awhile before we reach any Midtown diner. I lean back against the quilted leather banquette, and relax. Another carriage approaches going in the opposite direction, that one with a sleek, black horse and a purple interior. The family of four inside wear matching expressions of wonder. As they pass, the young girl, ruddy cheeked and wide-eyed looks like she might burst with joy. She waves at us with ferocity. "Hello, hello! Hey look, it's snowing!"

Her excitement is contagious. I can't help waving back.

"Good day, young lady," Henry says, doffing an imaginary hat. "I hope you have a very, merry Christmas."

"Mom, he's English!" The mother nods, impressed. They must be from some small town in the middle of America. I put myself in their shoes. Riding in a Central Park buggy, seeing the pretty tinseled decorations on the lampposts, and being greeted by a man who seems Dickensian to them must be very exciting. I'm happy for them. That little girl will never forget this day. "Merry Christmas," I shout, getting in the spirit.

"Merry Christmas! Merry Christmas!" She calls as the carriage disappears behind our backs. Once again, Henry has nailed it with the ladies. He really knows how to read a crowd.

"Have you ever taken a carriage through Central Park?" I ask. He takes a minute to answer. "Yes, once."

"Tell me the story." He dons an expression of protest, but I insist. "You owe me."

"How do I owe you?"

"I want to be on foot right now, looking for my dog, but somehow I've ended up on a holiday excursion. But I agree," I tell him, waving a hand to keep him quiet, "we need to eat. I'll agree to take a time out before we get back on the hunt. So for now, it's your job to distract me."

"And how shall I do that?"

"Tell me a story. Take my mind off my troubles. Give my brain a rest. Help me think about something else for now. If I can't calm down, you're going to have to detour this buggy to the nearest psychiatrist to get me a big, fat bottle of Valium. So, go." I close my eyes, and rest my head. I can feel the increase in the number of snowflakes drifting down; they tickle my face.

"All right, then." He clears his throat. "Once upon a time there lived a mighty king…"

"Stop. I mean tell me a story about you. Tell me about the first time you took a buggy ride."

"I never have. This one with you is my first."

"Hey, come to think of it," I say, stopping to take a big breath of the crisp, snowy air, "you never told me about *The Nutcracker*."

He doesn't speak right away. I wait, listening to Whiskey's hooves, lulled by the motion of the carriage.

"I was first in New York seven years ago," he begins slowly. "For work."

"Go on?" I encourage.

"This part is difficult to put into words, but even then I knew I had to come back. I felt at home, like I had wound up where I was supposed to be."

I open one eye to look at him. He's not looking at me. He stares ahead into the middle distance. "I was here on my own for nearly two weeks. You see, I'd just been through a bad break-up, so I jumped at the chance for a change of scenery. New York City represented the polar opposite of where I'd come from. Where I'd been trying to get away from, I suppose. In the end, Patricia made it clear that my pedigree wasn't quite up to her or her family's standard." He laughs a mirthless laugh. "She wasn't the first to point it out, however, and I'd venture to guess that she won't be the last."

I concentrate on keeping my face placid, but I'm listening intently. I'd have laid money on the fact that he'd been born with a silver spoon in his mouth. I brush aside the little drift of snow that has piled up on my cheeks.

"During that first project, my employer provided me with a furnished apartment. I was earning more than I ever had up to that point, and feeling very confident and strong. That being said, I was working long hours that first week, and barely saw daylight.

"Out of the blue, Patricia got in touch via Facebook, and asked if we could be friends again. I had my doubts, but I said yes, and before you know it we were Skyping constantly. I surprised her with very, very expensive last-minute plane tickets, and she joined me here for a wintry week of Manhattan magic. In retrospect, I'd have done better to spend my time sightseeing instead of bedded down behind closed doors. I gave up seats at the ballet, a chance to see a Broadway show. I never even made it to the Empire State Building. I still resent not having seen the city when I had that chance."

I peek at him from beneath half-closed lids. His mouth is twisted into a wry knot. "She told me she was in paradise, and never wanted it to end. By the time I returned to England in mid-December, we were back together."

101

"That sounds nice," I respond cautiously.

"It was, for a time."

Henry stopped talking, and I don't push it this time. I lie back, savoring the rocking motion of the carriage and pull my half of the blanket up to my chin. It's nice to just close my eyes and rest.

"Was it the edge of the park you were wanting?" the driver calls to Henry.

"That's right, but there's nowhere for us to get a bite to eat here. Can you drive on to 5th Avenue?"

"Of course. On Whiskey-girl!"

I wait for Henry to continue the story, but he doesn't. Hoofbeats rhythmically clip-clop, and the air smells like snow. I don't feel the need to speak. I'm surprised how companionable being around Henry is starting to feel. Or maybe I'm just very tired.

"This all right?" The driver asks Henry. "I can't take you farther, but it's only steps to 57th Street. You'll find diners and cafes along there."

"This is fine. Wake up, Sleeping Beauty." Henry gently pulls back the blanket and the shock of the cold rouses me. I take the hand he offers, and step down from the carriage. We're in front of the Plaza Hotel.

While Henry pays the driver, I move in close to the side of the building, and flip up the fingers of my gloves so I can text Aunt Miranda.

Still no sign of Huddie. I'm feeling really down. :(

I look up to see Henry gesturing with animation while conversing with the driver. He takes a flyer from Henry, and nods solemnly.

Sorry to hear, Charlotte. Couldn't be busier! Tell Henry to hurry up and find that dog of yours. Need him back at the office ASAP. Big love to you xo

That's about what I expected. Not much of anything in the way of sympathy. I slide my phone into my pocket, and start walking toward Henry. He's right; we probably should get something to eat very soon. I'm definitely feeing kind of dizzy, now. There's a little newsstand on the corner. I wave to Henry to hurry, but he doesn't see me. He's shaking the driver's hand, and both of them have smiles on their faces. In the meantime, I pull a flyer out, and head for the guy in the little corner booth. It couldn't hurt to ask if he's seen Hudson. We're not far at all from where the Elfie booth was set up. The proprietor is making change for a customer who seems to have one of each of the papers the guy has on sale. As I wait my turn, I squeeze my eyes together to shake off this dizziness.

"Yes, miss? What would you like?"

"Hi," I say, handing him a flyer. My vision is starting to darken. I concentrate hard, and manage to ask, "I was wondering, have you seen this dog?"

"Charlotte!" Henry calls, catching up to me. There's a look of concern on his face, and he bursts into a sprint.

The newspaper man looks at the flyer, and then picks up the *New York Post*. He knits his eyebrows together, and holds up a copy of the late edition.

The headline shouts,

Times Square Fashion Shoot Goes to the Dogs!

Underneath is a photo of a jubilant Hudson, his one black eyebrow raised. He's wearing a heavy gold chain encrusted with emeralds and rubies, and cuddling in the arms of one of the world's most recognizable supermodels.

"You mean this dog?" he asks.

Reeling, I stumble backward off the curb.

"Lady!" The newspaper man's eyebrows shoot up and he shoots out from the door of his newsstand. A cacophony of voices with accents from all over the world begin shouting, "Watch out," and "Get out of the way," and "Move!" People on the sidewalk wave their arms and point west.

I look to my right just in time to see the panicked expression of a man piloting an out-of-control pretzel cart zooming down the hilly section of 57th Street.

And suddenly, everything goes black.

*****

I try to open my eyes, but there's too much glare. Finally, I force open my leaden lids and am blinded by a million tiny lights. I have to close them again.

"There she is," a strange voice says from far away. "Welcome back."

I feel a cool hand brush the hair back from my face. "Charlotte." This voice I know. "Henry," I manage to say. My mouth is so dry. "I saw Hudson."

"I know," he says. "I think we've found him."

"Do I smell mustard?" I ask.

"Shh, try to rest," Henry urges.

I try to sit up, but a pair of firm hands lays me back on the, on the what? I feel the surface with my hands. I'm on a divan, or chaise, and the silk under my skin is cool and fine. I'm not wearing my coat. I look up to see the top of a lush Douglas fir tree, bedecked all in white lights of varying shapes and sizes. Gossamer fabric drapes the branches like a ballgown, and delicate crystal snowflakes dot the surface.

A good-looking young man of about twenty-five picks up my wrist and squeezes it firmly. He keeps his eyes on his watch, as his partner, a baby-faced older guy writes something on a clipboard. "Pulse steady?" he asks.

The good-looking one stands up, and gently tucks my arm back into my side. He smiles a dazzlingly white smile inches from my face. He's still holding my hand when he pronounces, "She's perfect."

I like him, I think. I try to sit up, but my head throbs. He seems nice. I'm aware that I'm smiling back, and I'm also aware that it's likely I look dopey. He doesn't seem to be the judgey type, though. I keep staring. We stay that way until Henry interrupts.

"Very good, then." He takes my hand from the medic, lays it down, and pats it, maiden aunt-style. I take stock of the room. The tree is the centerpiece, surrounded by a multitude of shiny golden boxes festooned with splendid gilded lace ribbon. The tree is cordoned off with velvet rope, and all around us in the spacious hall are perfectly round live wreaths, taller than men, accented by antique blown-glass ornaments.

"It's really something, isn't it?" The gorgeous guy asks me, face alight with wonder like a little kid's. "The Plaza Hotel ain't messin' around when it comes to Christmas." I nod in agreement with him. It's magnificent.

"Back to the welfare of the patient," Henry says, redirecting us. "You're sure she won't need to visit the hospital?"

"No, her vitals are stable, and there's no sign of heavy trauma from the crash," the less dashing of the pair says straightforwardly. "Let's sit her up. If she feels well, we can sign off on leaving her in your care."

The handsome EMT slides his arm around my back to pull me to a sitting position. Henry swiftly jumps in on the other side, scowling. "Allow me," he says.

"I got this, brah," he tells Henry, expertly righting me. "It's my job." I have to admit, that was pretty smooth.

Henry ignores him, and speaks directly to the other technician. "Once again, you think the fainting could have been caused by an anxiety attack or possibly dehydration? Or do you think it was a blow to the head with a stale, oversized pretzel?"

"Please, Mr. Wentworth," a pulled-together man in a very crisp suit says, taking a glass of water from a tray held by a waiter in a tux. "Here's a glass of water for the young lady. If she needs medical care, the Plaza will happily accept the bill. On behalf of this establishment, I'd be pleased to offer the two of you a room so she can rest. Let us know how we can make both of you more comfortable."

"Should we book a room, Charlotte?" Henry asks me. My mouth falls open. I'm still one step behind. "So you can lie down, of course," Henry says. "By yourself. I'd be delighted to come with you if you want me. To attend to you. In a medical way." He clears his throat. "Should I call Miranda?"

"I'm fine," I say.

Mr. Hermes Tie With Matching Pocket Square sighs dramatically. "Well, thank goodness for that."

The efficient EMT tears off a sheet of paper, and hands it to Henry. "Get her hydrated, and make sure she eats. If there are any signs of blurred vision, dizziness, or nausea, get her to a hospital or call 911 immediately. Let's go, Leo."

Medic McSteamy gives me one last burning, tango-worthy look. I can only imagine he must do this to every living, breathing female. I cannot imagine that I, with my flattened hair and questionably laundered tracksuit could merit such ardor. "Feel better. And call if you need something."

"Grab the gurney, let's go," the baby-faced guy waves his finger in a circle above his head, and a doorman has already opened one of the heavy doors before the smoldering medic moves. With a flourish, he embraces the wheeled stretcher and conducts it through the hall. Pocket Square nearly collapses with relief. Medical equipment and emergency technicians conflict directly with the understated luxury the Plaza Hotel no doubt wishes to project.

"When you're ready to walk, miss, we'd be pleased to escort you to the Palm Court for Afternoon Tea. Unless you need a wheelchair," he adds, looking alarmed.

"I'm fine now," I say, standing up. Henry rushes to take my elbow. "Really, I'm fine," I tell him. He keeps my arm linked with his.

"Be that as it may, this isn't the time to take chances. Shall we?" Henry asks.

"I can't go to tea at the Plaza in my Gap sweat suit." I look down at myself. "Especially with this glob of mustard on my thigh."

"Of course you can," Pocket Square says wearing a pinched smile. He pulls out his handkerchief, dips it in my water glass and kneels down to scrub at the stain. "You've been given medical advice to take refreshment. We at the Plaza won't rest until we're sure you're feeling one hundred percent healthy. May I give you my card?" He asks, brandishing a tasteful gold square. "If there's anything I can ever do to be of service, I hope that you won't hesitate to call. Now, we'd be delighted for you to be our guests for tea. Please, follow me."

"Henry, I can't. We need to go find Hudson."

He holds up the front page of the Post. "Does this look like a dog in distress?"

My limbs tingle as relief floods my body. Hudson has been snapped in mid-wriggle, and the usually arch super model has her head thrown back in laughter. I feel like my face might break as my lips pull into a huge smile. "No. Exactly the opposite."

"Precisely. We'll fortify ourselves with strong tea and all manner of sandwiches and cake, then we'll head to Times Square and collect your pooch. Doctor's orders!"

*****

The steaming hot, milky tea warms my mouth. It acts like a miracle drug; I swear I can feel it coursing through my veins, restoring and revitalizing me. Hudson is not only fine, he's happy. I take another sip of my excellent hot drink, sink back into the high-backed banquette, and practically float away on the dulcet tones of the harp music.

"Feeling better, are we?" Henry smiles knowingly. "A strong cup of real English brewed tea is what was called for. I put sugar in yours, for the shock."

"Do you really think that helps?" I look at the tiered plate stands featuring tiny crustless sandwiches, bite-sized scones with double

Devonshire cream and fruit-rich jams, and an array of pastries ranging from parti-colored macaroons, to eclairs, to individual New York-style cheesecakes. "There's no shortage of sugar in this delicious food," I say, helping myself to an egg salad on white toast, and a roasted turkey and cranberry on whole grain with what appears to be French mustard. I make a mental plan to come back for the new red potatoes topped with crème fFraîche and ossetra caviar.

Henry's phone rings. "Please excuse me," he says, quickly pulling it out and switching off the ringer. He checks the number, scowls, and pockets it. "Sugar in tea helps shock, it's a proven fact." His face relaxes into a smile. At least that's what I was taught by my gran and mum down on our farm on the outskirts of what can loosely be called our village, Harrogate. Drive past it quickly, and you won't have known it was there."

"You grew up on a farm?" I'm gobsmacked. I can't stop picturing a little Henry toddling around a manor in baby Prince George outfits.

"Have you never been warned about judgment, books, covers, and so forth?" He looks at me levelly. "You shouldn't make assumptions."

I'm intrigued. "So that's where you learned to goat-wrestle?"

He nods as he pours his own tea through the strainer. With perfect manners, he serves himself several sandwiches. "It is." He doesn't elaborate.

"Am I right in remembering that Aunt Miranda said you went to Cambridge?" I'm trying to untangle the story in my head. I had him pegged for being the most tedious kind of entitled twit.

"Yes, and Eton before that."

"You must miss your family. Do you talk to them often?"

"Hmm." Henry replies, avoiding the question.

"Champagne, sir," declares the sommelier, indicating a busser setting up a silver bucket on a stand next to our table. "Compliments of the Plaza Hotel." He opens it and pours some for Henry to taste. He nods.

"Champagne, miss?" he asks, holding the bottle at half-mast above my flute.

"I don't think I should. Henry?"

"Have a glass. It will be good for your nerves." He nods, and my flute is filled. "Once we've retrieved Hudson, you can go home and have a nice long sleep."

I cannot wait. Being back home, quiet and alone with my best little friend sounds like heaven. Although, I have to admit to myself, there's something to be said about being treated like a princess in one of New York's finest hotels. It's funny that I've lived here so long, and it's taken a foreigner to show me a whole different side of my own home city. Starting with Henry's sitting me down in the fairy-tale holding area behind the skating rink at Rockefeller Center, it seems like I've been on an insider's, behind-the-scenes adventure in my own beloved Manhattan. I feel warm thinking that Hudson would be pleased. He'd want me to feel excited.

"To finding Hudson," he says, and raises his glass.

I raise mine in return, and sample the Moet & Chandon, Brut Impérial Rosé. Drinking with Henry was starting to become a habit. First the glass of wine he gave me in VIP waiting at Rockefeller Center, and now this. The wine smells fruity and dry, and the bubbles tickle my nose.

"In a few hours," he says, "this sleuthing will be a distant memory. Our job will be done, and it'll be business as usual." He smiles as he chews his sandwich.

A waiter approaches the table, and says, "Pardon me, sir? Are you Henry Wentworth?"

"I am," Henry says, brow wrinkled.

"You have a telephone call at the desk."

Henry frowns. Thank you," he tells the man, laying his napkin aside. "Would you excuse me, Charlotte? It must be Miranda." He rises and follows the waiter.

My sandwich plate is cleared, and I move on to the scones.

Back to business as usual, Henry had said. He didn't have to look so happy about it. I survey the gorgeous table in front of me, planning what I'll eat after the scones. What's his hurry? Sure, we all want to get back to our lives. I have work to do, too, Henry Wentworth, I pout to myself. I certainly wouldn't have signed up to spend the day like this, either. But, was spending time with me in one of New York's top restaurants really that bad?

Henry returns to his seat, and puts his napkin back on his lap. "Apologies," he says. He chooses a scone and sets it on his plate. He seems content to be here, so I relax.

"You know," I tell him between sips of champagne, "when I get my hands on that rascal, I don't know what I'm going to do. At the very least, he's getting a stern lecture." The waiter steps forward and refills my glass the second the base of it hits the table, then fades backward as quickly as he appeared. "I mean, he told me he's been dying to get out more, but he could have just asked again."

"He told you that?"

"Well, not in English. But you know."

"I'm not sure I do."

"I'm just saying that Hudson has always wanted to leave the apartment more, see the city. Really, this is so like him."

"Are you seriously implying that your dog had a plan when he slipped out on the Japanese elves?" Henry scans the pastry platter, and selects a salted caramel tartlet and a slice of opera cake.

"Obviously," I say, staking my claim on a lemon meringue bar and an individual dark chocolate ganache. "He's always trying to drag me places. He's always like, 'You should get out more.'"

Henry is slowly shaking his head at me, mouth wide open.

"What? Didn't you see the look on his face in the photo in the paper? He went looking for adventure and he found it. That little so-and-so! At least I can relax for a little while knowing he's happy. And not being experimented on in Canada. He found a way to get what he was craving."

"I feel I might need to stage an intervention. Did you hit your head in that fall? Charlotte, it's a *dog*."

"Yes, so?" I take another long quaff of my delicious bubbly. "By the way, Hudson is a 'he,' not an 'it.' You grew up on a farm, right? You must have had dogs."

"Yes, but they weren't magical."

"I didn't say Hudson was magical. I just said he planned to go on an adventure."

"You really believe that, don't you?"

"Wait till you meet him," I say.

"I honestly cannot wait," Henry says. I'm suspicious. Does he mean that he wants to meet Huddie, or that he wants to get this whole thing over and done with? And why do I care? I turn my attention back to the lovely morsels in front of me, and let the harp music dance over my mind. It could be the champagne, or it could be the fact that I'll be reunited with Hudson momentarily, but I feel happier than I have in years. Of course, it could be the company. Nah, it's probably just the high ceilings and skylights, and this bellyful of sublime food making me feel so uplifted.

Henry smiles at me over the rim of his glass. His eyes really are the most unusual color blue. I look away, and concentrate on the visual splendor of the myriad tabletop trees peppering the Palm Court.

No, it's definitely the atmosphere.

Chapter 6

By the time we step out of the cab, there's a light dusting of snow covering the streets. Flurries still fall, and Times Square's multi-colored lights sparkle and bounce off the flakes. Crystal droplets magnify the glare of the headlights and taillights of whizzing cars, trucks, and cabs. Henry takes my arm to hurry me out of traffic, whisking me across to Duffy Square. It feels like we're inside a life-sized snow globe.

The red bleachers backing up to the half-price Broadway theater ticket booth on the north side of Times Square, TKTS, have been wrapped up like an enormous holiday package, and roped off from the public.

Huge crowds of tourists surround the scene. Many take selfies with the iconic setting in the background. Others jockey for space in line to get an inexpensive seat for a hot-ticket show. Off to one side are the Naked Cowboy, and his myriad imitators, playing electric guitar in their Y-fronts and ten-gallon hats despite the freezing temperatures.

Astride the mammoth present is Ruby, the single-named, androgynous beauty usually seen gracing the covers of *Vogue* and *Harper's Bazaar*. She balances a giant bow on her toned shoulders and outstretched arms. The fashion designer has crafted a gold shawl with the simultaneous effect of both wings and an elaborate holiday ribbon. Beneath it, the model wears a slim green bodice that looks like nothing more than a skein of velvet ribbon wound around her flattened chest, and a pair of billowing, triangular palazzo pants. A lanky photographer whom I've seen profiled in *Vanity Fair* slithers around the bleachers like a lizard, stretching and retreating, and snapping shots with a vintage flashbulb that blinds with every pop.

"Wait here," Henry says, and strides purposefully up to the rope guard. All around me are workers associated with the shoot. There are trailers that serve as dressing rooms, and craft services trucks producing full, hot meals that are handed out to everyone on the crew, from the model down. I see that Henry is still talking to the bouncer in the headset, so I wander up to a heavyset man holding a Marie Antoinette wig on a wooden head. My hands fly to my own head. I realize I've left my hat at the Plaza. No time to stop and think about it, I think to myself, now's the time to track down Hudson.

"Excuse me," I say, "Have you by any chance seen this dog?" I hold up the front page of the *Post*.

"Ha!" he cackles, "Ruby's going to plotz! She loves that dog. She said if we don't find the owner, she'll start working on the papers to bring it back to Australia when she goes home." He uses the rapier-sharp point of a rat comb to coax on errant wig hair back into its respective curl. "How'd they get that picture in the paper so fast? The sheer wonder of modern technology, don't you know? Never fails to astonish."

"I'm the owner," I say, excitedly. "I'm here to pick him up. I'll have to thank her for looking after him. Do you know where he is?"

"Well, Ruby's back on set, as you can see. Last I heard, someone took him to craft services to get him something to eat." He touches his index and pointer fingers to the radio in his ear. "What's that? You need me? I'm on my way."

He takes off in the direction of the bleachers, and says over his shoulder, "Craft services is over by Toys R Us. Ask Zahava where your dog went."

I rub my hands together to stave off the chill, and I look around for Henry. I can't see him anywhere. He's disappeared into the bustling crowd. I realized I don't even have his phone number. What if I can't find him after I pick up Hudson? Part of the fun was going to be introducing them and I can't deny feeling a little disappointed at the thought that might not happen.

As I approach the craft services table, a cornucopia of mouth-watering smells wafts my way. Standing at the service line is a tall, striking woman with corkscrewed, reddish-blonde hair twisted in a high knot and secured with two chopsticks. I hope she's the person I'm looking for.

I get in line, and wait for the various crew people to get their plates, coffees, and hot chocolates.

"Next!" she shouts, even though she's only six inches from my face.

"Hi, are you Zahava?"

She gives a curt nod in affirmation. "Great! I was wondering if you have my dog." I hold up the photo.

"He was here a few hours ago," she tells me. "I made him a grilled steak, no salt, cut into small pieces. Salt is not good for dogs. I know. I have two at home. I cook all their food. Meat and vegetables only. Fresh, every day. That dog," she points at the picture, and her harshness melts, "he wolfed his meal like he had never eaten before. I made him a second fillet. I only hope Francesco, the photographer, is in the mood for chicken today."

"Do you know where he went?"

"The last I saw, Ruby's little brothers took him to the toy store to try buy him a coat. Wait, I have a text." She scrolls through her phone. "Ah, here it is."

She shows me a photo from her iPhone screen. It's of two very cute teenaged boys flanking Hudson in the My Little Pony-themed car of the Times Square Toys R Us 60-foot indoor Ferris wheel. The boys are giving the thumbs up sign, and Hudson's tongue is

114

out and flapping like he's in the co-pilot seat of a big rig truck.

"Where are they now?" I'm starting to feel the slightest edge of the old panic creeping in. I thought we'd be home on the couch by now.

"Hang on, I'll text."

Just then, Henry comes rushing up. "Did you find him?" he asks me. "Apparently Ruby hasn't seen him since this morning. Her assistant was supposed to babysit Hudson until after the shoot, but she fell off the bleachers and twisted her ankle, so she handed the job to someone else."

Zahava interrupts, "The boys say that they haven't seen the dog in maybe forty-five minutes. Teenagers! You can't rely on them for anything. Hang on, another text. They say they might have seen him heading downtown."

"He's gone again?" I moan.

"Don't worry," Henry says, obviously trying to maintain an air of calm. "He can't have gone far on foot."

"Hang on," Zahava cuts in. "Look up there." She points to the giant Times Square Jumbotron, the massive TV screen that dominates the landmark every New Year's Eve when it's used to televise the ball drop. "Look."

We do as we're told, and we're treated to an image of Hudson wearing a tiny red cap with a white pom-pom on the top, sitting on Santa's lap beneath a sign that says, "Winter Village, Bryant Park."

"That's it," I say, slitting my eyes. "I'm going to kill the little devil."

*****

It's late afternoon by the time we step out of the cab, and into the brisk air at the corner of 42nd and 6th Avenue. It's nearly dusk, as East coast cities' days are short at Solstice time. I practically gasp at how this relatively small plot of city land has been transformed for the winter holidays. Bryant Park is a gem at any time of the year, but this season it dazzles me.

"Gosh, that's gorgeous," Henry says, eyes alight.

"I thought you didn't like Christmas," I accuse.

He's quiet for a second, almost reflective. "In the face of this, it's somewhat harder to hold my position."

All around the periphery of the park are rows and rows of small, seasonal shops. The clever way the designers have conceived the roofs, and lit the plastic drapery from inside makes the rows of uniform structures appear as glowing ice palaces. Lit from within by white lights, the fountain looks more striking than usual dressed up in the purple beams illuminating it from above. Decorated this way, the fountain serves as a perfect complement to the Christmas tree across the park, standing in front of the elegant Bryant Park Grill building that backs up to the world-famous New York Public Library. The tree is bedecked in deep amethyst and rich sapphire lights and ornaments, so thick one can hardly see the branches. At its pinnacle sits a modern, multi-faceted crystal star.

Even with all of those spectacles for the eyes to drink in, the real showstopper is the combination of the Ice Rink and the Celsius Bar. Blindingly white, the two-story temporary restaurant towers above the rink, clean and sleek. Fashionable tourists and the New York after-work crowds gather to be seen while listening to the smooth holiday music, and watch skaters both glide and fall on the ice.

"We'd better find Santa's Corner and collect Hudson," Henry tells me. He leads the way past a stand selling Nutella-stuffed Chimney Cakes, a luxury soap and body scrub stall called *Sabon*, three outdoor ping pong tables, all of which are in play with lines of expectant challengers, garlanded and ribbon-wrapped gas lamps, and countless numbers of bundled revelers seated at the very French-looking little metal tables and folding chairs.

As we approach the grotto space, Henry gets ahead of me. A sea of bodies comes toward me, like an ocean wave, pushing me backward.

"Henry!" I call out.

A leather-gloved hand slices through the crowd, and takes my own. With a firm hold, Henry leads me.

Here we come a-wassailing among the leaves so green, here we come a-wassailing so fa-ir to be seeeeeeen, love and joy, come to you...

Without preamble, we are surrounded by Santa's caroling entourage. He is being led, parade-style, to a waiting sleigh parked on 42nd Street. Maybe not so much a sleigh, as a convertible Jeep with fake reindeers on wheels attached to the front, but I'm alarmed that he's leaving.

"Henry!" I call over the din of carol singers, "Grab Santa, he's leaving."

Henry lets go of my hand, and begins jogging along the outside of the group. "Santa!" he hollers. "Mr. Claus!" I see his head popping up as he strategizes about how to reach the jolly old fellow.

"Pardon me, pardon me," he says, elbowing elves and snowmen aside, "I need to speak urgently with Father Christmas."

...may God send you a happy new yeeeeeear!

The second the singing dies down, Henry swoops in to commandeer the attention of the big fat man in the bright red suit. I see him grab Saint Nick's arm, talking very fast as he continues to jog alongside the procession, but I can't make out what he's saying. Santa answers with an impressive belly laugh, palms cradling the legendary bowl of jelly, before looking both ways furtively before leaning in, and giving Henry an earful. He pulls a flask from the pocket of his velvet suit, and offers it to Henry. I see Henry hold up a hand to decline, and the flask is put away. Ranting away, Santa gesticulates wildly, pointing at an imaginary watch on his wrist. Henry nods solemnly, and crosses his heart.

We wish you a merry Christmas, we wish you a merry Christmas...

Santa's crew strikes up the chorus, and the elderly elf joins in with gusto. He dances along in the procession with his arms around the shoulders of a young, blonde elf in a short, fur-trimmed skirt. He's belting out the carol and punching the air with gusto. As the parade moves on, his hand slides farther and farther down the elf's back until he's cupping her rump with his black-gloved hand. She shoves him hard with her shoulder, and he's knocked sideways. Not missing a beat, a couple of the burlier elves catch him and set him upright, while he adjusts his wig and hat. It looks to me like they've been down that road before.

We pull over in front of a candle vendor to get out of the pressing crowd. We have no choice but to stand still and watch in silence since conversation is impossible when they're singing so loudly. We're shoulder to shoulder as we squeeze together to allow the revelers to stream by. Our fingertips brush, and Henry pulls his hand away, making a show of needing to cough into his fist. I remember the feel of his hand as he held mine, pulling me through the throngs of people. It felt big as it engulfed my smaller be-mittened hand, and warm and substantial. James and I never walked holding hands. I wouldn't let him. We just…weren't that way.

When the din decreases, Henry fills me in. Turns out, Hudson was there earlier. One of the snowmen saw him tap-dancing around the sleigh. She (it happened to be a she, so, maybe one of the snowwomen?) saw that people were giving him treats like pieces of steamed pork bun, and shish-kebab in exchange for little tricks like "paw" and "sit." She thought it would be a great idea to take a hat from one of the animatronic Santa puppets in the Christmas Tree Shop, and put it on Hudson's head. He was game, and patiently sat on Father Christmas's lap during the reading of *Twas the Night Before Christmas,* much to the delight of the crowd. After that, he'd slipped back into the crowd. Someone said they saw him riding on the little French carousel with a boy in crutches, but nothing after that.

"So what was with all the secrecy?"

"Oh that. He explained that he'd double booked and was due at Grand Central Station's Holiday Market and Train Display ten minutes ago. He didn't want to spoil the illusion of being the real

Santa so he had to leave quickly."

"Of course he's not the real Santa."

"Obviously, as there is no real Santa, but he didn't want to spoil it for the children."

"No, I mean the real Santa is at Macy's."

He raises an eyebrow. "First a magical dog, and now this? You're going to ruin your image as a Puritan pilgrim from the Mayflower and Carson from Downton Abbey."

"You make me sound all spinsterish and uptight! That's not me. I'm plenty of fun. In my own way."

"Be that as it may, it's clear to even the most innocent tot that this gentleman is no way Father Christmas. Did he think people wouldn't cop on when they saw the ear hangers on the back of his whiskers? It's his busy season, he said. In his own inimitable words, he told me 'Everyone wants a piece of Santa, if you know what I mean.' I assured him that I did not."

I cannot help laughing. Once I start, I just can't stop. Maybe it's a release from carrying all the worry about Hudson. Or maybe creepy Santa imposters are simply hilarious. At first, Henry looks worried. As I keep laughing, his worried look turns stern, and I think he might scold me for improper behavior. Finally, a smile spreads across his face, crinkling the corners of his cerulean blue eyes. It widens, and suddenly he's laughing, too. We laugh like that, then catch our breaths. Just as I'm wiping my eyes, and stretching out the aching muscles of my face, Henry squeaks, "Everyone wants a piece of me!" and we're both doubled over, clutching one another for support. We cross over to the point where we're not even making noise, just pantomiming what people dying of laughter might look like. Out of the corner of my eye, I notice that Bad Santa has ascended his makeshift sleigh, and is waving goodbye to his fans. Just before the door closes, I see a multicolored streak duck into the vehicle.

"Hudson," I gasp, trying to swim up to the crest of the laughter. "Henry, it's Hudson."

I point to the departing parade float. Henry immediately gets it, and regains his composure on a dime. "Let's go!"

He takes my hand, and we're off.

*****

We arrive panting and flushed at the Vanderbilt Avenue entrance to Grand Central Station. 42nd Street looked like a parking lot, so we travel the several long avenue blocks on foot. We stand at the top of the twin marble staircases for a moment, and survey the scene. The departure boards are to our right, a level down. We're looking down on the well-known opal-faced clock above the information desk, which has been adorned for the holidays.

We could not have chosen a more hectic time to be here. "Like I said, Henry. When I find him, I'm going to kill him."

Henry's eyes are sweeping the station. "Do you hear how ridiculous you sound? Charlotte, he couldn't have pre-planned this. It's not like he's been googling New York Christmas holiday events with his paws."

The sheer number of commuters and shoppers is staggering. College students and young city interns wait in line with their backpacks and duffels, eager to train home to their parents' houses where their laundry will be done and plates of food will be set before them. Travelers from all parts of the world are arriving from their US tours to experience a real New York Christmas in the heart of the city. Local families hustle to the Christmas Village to do last-minute shopping and bask in the atmospheric holiday train exhibition. And finally, we've managed to arrive at the end of the workday. Tired-looking men and women in suits wield coffee cups and newspapers for their journeys home to Croton-on-Hudson or Connecticut, pushing through the last few days before the blessed vacation week.

I look left and right, trying to pick out clues from among the swirling dots at the bottom of the staircase.

"I didn't say he planned it, exactly. But this is the kind of thing Hudson wants me to do. You know, get out there. Be in the mix. I'm always telling him crowds aren't my thing, and he just shakes his head and snorts."

"Has it ever occurred to you that he's just doing that because he's allergic to dust?"

"Stop being such an old Scrooge. You just don't know Hudson, that's all. Once you meet him, you'll get it."

"Look. There," Henry points to a woman walking in the opposite direction, with a dog tucked under her arm. He takes off running down the sweeping staircase, and I follow hot on his heels. "Madam!" he calls. About 20 women turn around, then keep walking. "Hello? Lady in the red coat! Excuse me."

Finally she turns around. "Yes?" I get a clear look at her dog's face. Not Hudson. I shake my head.

"Never mind," Henry says, "Merry Christmas."

We cover every square inch of the terminal, and even venture out onto the train platforms, where we hand out flyers to the porters known as redcaps and to passengers alike. We go down to the lower level to the elaborate food court. It's difficult to traverse, it's so packed with diners-on-the-go. The enticing aromas of the various cuisines from around the world begin to call to me. After my sumptuous tea at the Plaza, I thought I would never eat again, but that had been hours ago.

We look around Golden Krust, the Jamaican beef patty vendor. We go to the very end and inquire at Two Boots, the pizza place fusing recipes from both boot-shaped Italy and her sister boot-shaped locale, the state of Louisiana. I hand a flyer to the Middle Eastern proprietors of Eata Pita. The salt-of-the-earth New Yorker at the counter of Frankie's Dogs to Go tapes a flyer to the front of his counter, and offers us free red hots with kraut, but I don't feel we can afford to stop.

Finally, as we're crossing a long hallway in the vault below the main level, Henry stops me. "Charlotte, you're running yourself ragged again." I put my hand against the cool, tile wall and gaze around at the series of domes and arches. The air is cool and damp. It's almost like being in a Roman catacomb. I feel tired.

I know Henry's right about spinning my wheels, but we were so close. "We almost had him. We let Hudson slip right through our fingers."

"But that's a positive, right? You saw that he's not only alive and well, he also appears to be thriving. According to you, he's having the time of his life. You said yourself that he's looking for adventure."

"You don't believe that," I tell him, narrowing my eyes.

"Well, no. I don't. But, it's clear that he's not in danger. Forget what the stereotype is of New Yorkers being rude and cold, Hudson has been embraced at every juncture. Everyone who has met him has offered him food, companionship, and even a home if he needed one. People are good, Charlotte."

I gaze down at the square, brown tiles on the floor and think about that.

"I understand that hasn't always been your experience," he says gently. But given the chance, most people want to help. Trust them," he says, tilting my chin upward with his index finger. "Trust me."

I take him by the shoulders and situate him in one corner of the vault, at the base of one of the arches. I hold up a finger, warning him to stay put. He nods. I cross over to the opposite corner of the vault and turn my back on him. Relying on the magic and the physics of the Grand Central Terminal Whispering Gallery, I say very softly, "I trust you, Henry."

I turn around and see his face across the vault. His eyes are soft, and it looks like he's holding his breath. He heard me.

*****

With its vintage marquee lights lining the arches of the low vaulted ceilings, and its jaunty red and white Italian checked table cloths,

122

Grand Central's world-famous Oyster Bar is reliably festive at any time of the year. At Christmas, with the addition of dressed-up potted pines and swags of greenery and red satin bows, the cheer outdoes itself. Just stepping through the glass doors would even lift the spirits of the most hardened Scrooge.

Rather than join the diners in the main room, I motion to Henry that we should sit at the counter. Once again, he has convinced me to slow down and eat. He's never been here, so I'll enjoy the fun of watching him eat their unparalleled oyster stew or chopped clam pan roast for the very first time. The thing about sitting at the counter is that you are treated to both dinner and a show.

We slide ourselves onto the padded, swiveling, low-backed stools, and slide off our coats. There's a chalkboard on the wall announcing today's selection of oysters and clams, and the market price. The entertainment factor begins with the greeting from the ancient career waiter that could be described more as a grunt. Probably installed here since the forties, this man is here to supply us with beer and shellfish, not to make friends.

We each order the oyster pan roast, and before long, I'm taking a deep pull from a frosty mug of beer.

"I'm as thirsty and tired as I was this afternoon," I tell Henry.

He's checking his phone, brows knitted. "Could the lady have a pint of water, please? Thanks very much." The crusty white-shirted waiter plonks down a glass in front of me. "For heaven's sake, let's avoid calling the ambulance again."

"I don't know. It might be fun to see Leo again."

"He was highly unprofessional," Henry mutters into his beer.

"Oh, come on. I'm cured, aren't I?"

"You're cured, that's all I'll agree to. And a good thing, that. I was roundly chewed out by your aunt for allowing you to be mowed down by a runaway pretzel cart. I'm not sure those mustard stains will ever come out of your track suit. Won't happen again on my watch."

I don't respond, and instead nurse my beer. Behind the counter, a chef expertly chops the jumbo fresh oysters into pieces using a cleaver. I watch as he turns the valves on two of the tureens and I hear the hiss of steam. The kettles are similar to double-boilers, and hang from stands pivoting to decant finished soups directly into bowls. He tosses in generous, unmeasured lumps of butter, pours in clam juice, and slides in the chopped clams.

"Something the matter?" Henry asks.

I screw up my courage and ask, "Was Aunt Miranda the only reason you cared if I lived or died?"

"Of course not. How could you ask that? I was only saying that she was worried as well." He glances at his phone again, and says, "Excuse me," before typing into it.

Our chef pulls two expansive soup plates from a stack, and lines them both with triangles of white toast. He pours a generous amount of cream into the tureens, gives a stir, then adds a spoonsful of chili sauce, dashes of celery salt, and shakes of Worcestershire sauce. Quickly, he fishes out the oyster pieces, and layers them onto the toast. Then, he tips the tureens, submerging it all in a thick, creamy broth. The bowls are filled to the brim, and I'm impressed that the waiter so quickly ferries them to the counter without spilling a drop. Behind the scenes, the chef fills the kettles with water, cranks up the steam, tips out the liquid, gives a wipe with a fresh kitchen towel, and he's ready for the next order.

Henry puts his phone away, and leans over his bowl, inhaling the fragrant stew. He takes a sip of his beer and proclaims, "Now this is about as perfect a moment as I've experienced for a long time." He swivels his stool to face me. "Are you happy Charlotte?"

"I am, but I feel torn. How can I enjoy this cozy atmosphere, the warmth, the indulgent food and drink, when I know Hudson isn't curled up at home in the window seat waiting for me? Before I go out, Henry, I always fluff his nest and arrange them just how he likes them. I didn't bring much with me from England, but I did bring each and every knitted afghan blanket Bridget ever crocheted for me."

"Who's Bridget?" he asks.

"She was our cook." I stir my soup, and float a few round, puffy oyster crackers on top. "My nanny, really."

"Are you in touch?" he asks.

"It didn't really work that way. Anyway," I shake my head hard to clear the memories, about Bridget and Hudson. "Once his nest is ready, I always call to him. 'C'mon, boy, time to dig in!' He burrows way down deep, thinking he's camouflaging, so he won't be spied and disturbed. You should see it Henry," I'm laughing now, and I dab at the corner of my eye with my heavy white napkin. "With his combination glossy and wiry coat, with its wild patchwork of colors, he looks like he was knit together from the scraps from Bridget's yarn basket, just like the blankets were. Before I leave, I always kiss him on the muzzle and promise to come back. I wish that he'd be there tonight when I go home."

"Me too," Henry says, facing me, his elbow on the counter and his cheek resting on his knuckles.

"So I do feel happy, Henry. But I also feel guilty. How can I enjoy all this when Hudson is out there alone?" Steam rises from my bowl and warms my face. I take a deep breath.

"Another round?" the waiter asks. I say no, as Henry is saying yes.

"Have another drink, Charlotte." I hesitate. "Please." He nods and the waiter retreats. "Surely you've heard stories on the news about owners moving and dogs showing up six months later having tracked their owners down all the way across America? Don't you think Hudson is as smart as those dogs?"

"I know he is."

"Then believe. Believe that people are looking out for him. Trust that he'll either make his way back to you, or make himself known. Allow yourself an hour to have a nice meal and relax with a drink, and take care of yourself. Can you do that?"

"I do really like this soup," I tell him, spraying bits of oyster cracker.

Henry breaks into a wide grin. "Then, for God's sakes, woman.

125

Grab it while it's hot."

While we're eating our dinner, evening falls. They dim the overheads in the restaurant, making the strings of vintage lights along the arches seem even more like stars. The volume is turned up on the music, and jazzy versions of slow, wistful holiday favorites such as *Have Yourself a Merry Little Christmas* and *I've Got My Love to Keep Me Warm* waft at the edges of the din of conversation and clinking of glasses.

The beer loosens Henry's tongue, and he tells me that he and his dad don't really talk. "When I phone home, he'll say hello, and then immediately it's, 'Hold the phone, I'll get your Mum.'" His features look soft in the subtle light. "Mr. Cooper, the headmaster of my school, was my champion. He saw something in me, and refused to stand by and watch me leave school at sixteen to work on the family farm."

"What would you have done on the farm?"

"Same as I had done, even as a child, but with more responsibility. Make cheese from the goats' milk, help out at the sewing-machine repair and fabric shop Mum runs on the edge of the property, that sort of thing."

"Working with your parents doesn't sound like a bad life to me."

He sips his beer. The buzz of conversation all around us soothes me, like the hum of a fan on a hot summer's day. "It wouldn't have been. But I wanted more. Mr. Cooper saw that. He made sure I was admitted to the best schools, in the best places, and that there would be funding to pay for it. My father saw it as well, but he didn't like it. He felt like my wanting more was a judgment on him and my mum."

"Everyone judged my mother," I laugh, pushing back my bowl. "But it didn't bother her. She had a thick skin."

He leans over and plucks a piece of fuzz from the collar of my sweater. "Not like you."

"I do fine," I say, tracing the condensation on my glass with a fingertip. "I'm just not 'out there' in the way she was. That's just not me. I'm happier at home with Hudson." I smile thinking about the way Hudson sighs when he curls up in his nest in the crook of my legs on the sofa, happy to be there whether I'm crabby, happy, dressed-up, sick, peaceful, or worried. He just wants to be with me, because I'm me. "With people, I do much better one-on-one than with groups and crowds."

"How is this?" He rolls his sleeves to his elbows as he talks. The restaurant is full; the extra bodies have warmed the place up. "Being here with me?"

I think about it, looking him over to do a self-check. He looks expectant, his aquamarine eyes filled with light. I look away. "OK."

He bursts out in a guffaw. "Just OK? I generally get higher marks than that."

"Of course you do, you're a gadfly. You play crowds like some play a violin."

I watch as his eyes darken, and his laughter dies down. "I'm very good with crowds. I have spent the majority of my life learning manners and proper behavior. My mate Will from school, he took me on as a special project. He was born to everything an Englishman could dream of. A title, land, money, reputation. We were true friends, though, still are. Over the years, he and his sister Cas really put me through the paces. They gave me the full Eliza Doolittle treatment. Their parents were quite happy to have me around; I was polite, kept my nose in my books, never got into trouble or caused a scene. They took me skiing in the Alps, taught me how to dress for the hunt and bought me the clothes to do it, showed me how to order wine, and on and on. I learned a lot from the experience, part of which was how to sing for my supper. As a consequence, I'm the perfect dinner guest and I'm rising up the ladder in my career by leaps and bounds, but inside…Inside, I never quite feel I fit in. Not at home, and not out in the world."

I raise my almost-empty glass. "Here's to not fitting in."

He clinks my glass, tilting his head. "Are we celebrating that?"

"No," I say, "just acknowledging."

Relaxed, I go on to tell him how I ran wild in our grand house when I was little, born of privilege just like his friends Will and Cas, and about how I never felt there was ground beneath my feet, apart from when I was in the kitchen with Bridget. She had a little television on the counter, and together we'd watch that British TV soap *EastEnders* and bake. Twice a week, she let me choose what we were having for dinner. She'd make whatever I suggested, I told Henry, be it sausage rolls or chateaubriand with béarnaise sauce. Searching for new dishes taught me to use cookbooks for reference. "One time, we even made lobster Thermidor, and neither of us liked it. We went out into the cold that night, and threw it over the fence for the neighbor's cat."

"Bridget sounds like a wonderful lady," he tells me. "But losing your mum must have been very, very hard." He picks my hand up off of my knee, and squeezes it before laying it gently back down, and giving it one final long stroke.

As we talk on, I surprise myself by answering all of his questions about the car crash.

He surprises me by simply listening. "Thanks for not trying to make it better," I tell him. "Most people want to 'fix' it, somehow. Some things just are what they are." He gives my hand another squeeze.

I'm just about to suggest ordering another beer, when his phone pings. He checks the screen and says, "It's nearly the witching hour. I'd better see you home."

Before I can argue, he's laid down his credit card, and is holding up my coat. He's quiet as we make our way up the stairs, and into the main concourse. "What's wrong?" I ask him.

"Nothing. Nothing for you to worry about. Your aunt's not pleased that I haven't found your dog, that's all."

"Well, it's not your responsibility," I say, defending him to my absent relative. He starts to speak, then decides better of it.

We reach the revolving door at the southwest corner, and Henry motions me forward with an "After you."

The nip of the air opens my eyes, and I'm suddenly aware of the hugeness of the city. Cars whizz by, and there's a Salvation Army bell ringer clanging her bell and calling, "Merry Christmas, please help," over and over again. I'm nearly knocked over by a group of twenty-or-so drunk college kids, all dressed, in some form, like Santa Claus. Stragglers from Santa Con, a Christmas-themed bar crawl around Midtown, they must be heading to catch last trains out to bridge-and-tunnel suburban towns.

Henry takes me by the arm, and steps forward to the curb to hail a cab.

"Henry, wait." I step back from him. The insidious tentacles of panic that I'd managed to stave off for the last few hours were beginning to wend their way around my heart once again. "I don't think I can go home without Hudson. It's too hard. I'm going to keep on looking."

He turns to face me. "I don't understand. I thought you were feeling better."

I try to organize my racing thoughts so I can explain. I pull on my mittens, and tell him, "Going home alone to my apartment last night was really hard. Luckily, I passed out cold I was so tired with worry. But tonight…I was sure I'd have found him by now. The sight of his dishes on the mat in the kitchen, and the empty tangle of blankets…No, I'd rather just stay on the move."

He nods. "I understand. But you cannot keep circling the city in the cold and the dark until you collapse. Let me think." He stares into the middle distance as he considers something. "I'm calling Miranda. You need someone. I don't care how busy she is. Don't stand in the cold, come with me." He leads me back to the door, and gently pushes me inside. Through the glass, I see him punch in a number, then come alive. He paces as he talks, and at one point it looks like he's getting very terse. Is he yelling at Aunt Miranda? Finally, he nods, looking resigned if not entirely satisfied. He catches my eye, and waves for me to join him on the sidewalk.

"Come with me, please. I have a new plan."

Chapter 7

The French-accented steward throws open the door to the suite and says, "Welcome sir and madam, to the Waldorf-Astoria Towers Penthouse Suite. I'll bring up your luggage the very minute it arrives."

"We don't have any luggage," Henry informs him, as I take off my coat and drape it over one of the three silk damask divans.

He runs his eyes up and down my body, and throws a sly look Henry's way. "But of course, sir."

"Oh stop it," I tell the bellhop, "he's being paid to be here."

"Très cosmopolite," he says, raising his eyebrows suggestively and nodding his head. "Chapeau," he says sideways to Henry, tipping an imaginary hat and giving a surreptitious thumbs-up.

"OK, thanks," I say, standing up. Dear lord, the Oriental rug must be three inches thick. I practically sink into it as I cross the room to open the door. "You can go now."

"I'm sure you're anxious for your privacy, so I will leave you love birds." He proceeds to then stand in one spot, not moving a muscle.

Henry fishes his wallet out of his coat, and hands him a bill. "That will be all."

The second the door closes, I say, "Now will you finally tell me what we're doing here? And why we came in through the private

50th Street entrance that I didn't even know existed. "

He presses his lips together, deep in thought. He begins slowly. "Your aunt wanted to be supportive." He's choosing his words carefully. "It was mentioned that she might invite you to stay at hers, so you wouldn't have to be alone in your time of need. It just so happens, however, that she is very busy. Hardly home at all, she explained to me." He has a look of deep concentration on his face as he surveys the room. He fiddles with a small, antique globe sitting on one of the fine, wooden desks.

"And…"

"Naturally, someone should be with you for support." He opens what appears to be a Chinese cabinet. "Oh, look! Minibar." He holds up two small bottles. "Red or white?"

"White. Go on."

"Seems to be a Fume Blanc. Will that do?"

"Yes! So…"

"So I asked your aunt if there was a friend I could call, or maybe another relative. Well, to make a long story short, it was decided that, naturally, I should spend the night with you. In a two-bedroom suite, of course!" He pops the corks, and pours. "It's a very good thing your aunt has both deep pockets and connections in high places," he mumbles. "You must know the rich rarely pay for their luxuries."

"Again, Henry, we are here because?"

"First thing tomorrow morning, this room will be Hudson Central. This will be the headquarters for Operation Find Hudson. I'm having my laptop sent over from the office, and we're going to step up this game."

He hands me a glass of wine. I take a sip. I like the sound of this. Just as I'm beginning to unclench, there's a knock at the door. "Room service."

A waiter wheels in a cart with an ice bucket and a bottle of champagne, and lifts a silver dome to reveal a plate of chocolate-dipped strawberries. There's an ornate silver bowl filled with

131

grapes, mandarin oranges, plums, and bananas, and a chilled bottle of Evian, beaded with water droplets.

Right behind him comes a porter with several oversized Macy's red-star shopping bags and hanging garment bags in each hand. "Excuse me please, delivery for Henry and Charlotte." He pronounces the "Ch" in Charlotte as if it were "chair."

"I'm Henry Wentworth." The man then hands Henry an array of bags. In all the flap of Henry tipping, and the bottle being put on ice, I spy a card next to the tray.

Dearest Charlotte,

So sorry I couldn't invite you to stay tonight. Am barely managing with the two events I'm running. You know, of course, about the Radio City Music Hall engagement on Christmas Eve. What you don't know is that there's a pop-up restaurant launching in Macy's Cellar where the Bar & Grill used to be. On Christmas Day, when the store is closed, the mayor's daughter is getting married! Guess which genius suggested the venue and pulled it all together at the 11th hour. That's right, moi.

Not a word about the pop-up! It won't be open to the public until after the wedding.

So sorry, pet, but Christmas dinner is off this year, too.

To make up for it, I'm having the hotel deliver some yummies. Also, we're here at Macy's staging. They're so grateful for the publicity with the mayor and all, they're eating out of the palm of my hand. They're all over the surprise launch of the pop-up to follow the wedding. The publicity team is working round the clock.

I figured you could use some pajamas and whatnot since you aren't going home tonight. I sent some for Henry as well! And some clothes for tomorrow. And probably the next day. And perhaps the evening. The store manager was apparently feeling very generous. Forgive if sizes are all wrong!

Mwah mwah, back to work!

Oh, P.S! I didn't tell you who's in charge of the pop-up… drumroll please... James Keyes! He's hoping to wow the bigwigs at Macy's and reopen the restaurant under his brand. Drop by, darling! Once you're both in the same room, maybe bygones will be bygones.

Mwah again,
Auntie Miranda

The last thing I needed was to hear about James right now. Was the woman born without a sensitivity gene? I'm gripped with the sudden urge to scrub away the very mention of his name. Steam is coming out of my ears. "Would you excuse me? I need to call my aunt."

"No," he says loudly. "Don't do that. I mean, why bother doing that right now? It would be better if you simply relaxed and tried to put the day behind you."

"Good point," I acknowledge. If I call right now, I'm likely to say something I'll regret. "I'll be back in a few minutes. I'm going to jump in the shower. To clear my head."

"But what about all this?" he asks, waving a hand over the room-service cart. "It'd be a shame to let it go to waste."

It does look tempting. And I need a drink after getting blind-sided by The Miranda Treatment.

"Tell you what. Give me fifteen minutes, and I'll meet you back here to tackle that champagne." I tip back the dregs of my Fume Blanc.

"That sounds like an excellent idea. I'll do the same." He picks up his shopping bags, loops the hangers of the garment bags between his fingers, and disappears through one of the doors, closing it behind him.

I gather my spoils and head through the other door. The luxury of this room must be in direct proportion to Miranda's guilt. It's stunning. Done up in rich ruby and gold, it looks like it belongs in a palace. The heavy brocade drapes drip with cords and tassels, there's an overstuffed double chair with a cunning antique reading lamp, and the bed might have been designed for the eponymous

133

star of *The Princess and the Pea*.

In the cavernous bathroom, I strip off my funky sweatsuit, and slip under the powerful spray. Between that first glass of wine and the hot water, I'm starting to relax. Tomorrow will be a fresh start, I think, breathing in the divine scent of the Salvatore Ferragamo shampoo I'm massaging into my hair. A good night's sleep will set me right, and if Henry doesn't convince me that his way is the best way, I'll cut bait and set out on my own. After a nice scrub, and a conditioning treatment for my hair, I towel off and slip on the designer robe and slippers that are waiting at the ready. I'm not normally fussy with my beauty regimen, but there's a full range of Ferragamo toiletries that are far too good to waste. I slick on some lip balm, moisturize my face, dab on eye cream, spritz my face with facial mist, and cap it all off by dabbing some eau de toilette behind my ears and on my wrists.

Hoping for a clean pair of underwear, I dump out the bags Miranda had sent onto the bed. I'm speechless. There's not a pair of Jockey-for-Her high-rise cotton briefs to be found. The selection of undergarments seem to all be made by Agent Provocateur and are of the decidedly non-granny panty variety. I check the labels. They do all seem to be my size, in theory, but I'm finding it hard to believe the little wisps of fabric will do the job of covering my average-girl booty.

I somehow knew I wouldn't be unearthing fleece pajamas from the pile. Instead, I find a satin chemise and a white silk nightgown/ lace negligee set that looks like it came from a 1930s film star's wedding trousseau. What on earth had Aunt Miranda said about me when the Macy's manager offered to pluck overnight essentials from the shelves and racks for me? Certainly not that I just need to catch a few hours of shut-eye before pounding the pavement in search of my lost dog.

I consider my choices. 1) Put my grubby sweatsuit back on, 2) Stay in my room and forego eating the yummy dessert and tasting that top-shelf bubbly, or 3) as Tim Gunn would say, "Make it work!"

Determined to get my hands on those strawberries, I select a pair of cream-colored stretch lace and organza silk undies, and am shocked to find that they not only make it past my knees, but cling nicely to my hips in a flattering way. I'm surprised that they're comfortable. I gasp when I pull off the dangling price tag. I guess you really do get what you pay for.

My only foray into the world of naughty panties thus far had been a present from James marked "Fredrick's of Hollywood," given to me on our first Valentine's Day together. I'd been hoping for a red, heart-shaped Le Creuset casserole dish. One whose picture I had cut out of a high-end kitchenware catalogue and left on his computer keyboard. But, it was so like James to make my Valentine's present *his* Valentine's present. What he'd picked out was a cheap, lurid lavender bustier and thong set, as scratchy as it was trashy. I wore it once, reluctantly. It felt like a costume made for someone else. But James never really saw me for who I was.

I pull the chemise over my head, and top it with my bathrobe, for modesty's sake. It's not like I can sashay out in company wearing Betty Davis's honeymoon set. Stepping into my cloud-soft hotel slippers, I open the door to the main sitting room of the suite. Henry stands with his back to me. He's wearing what can only be described as a dressing gown, even though that sounds old-fashioned and stuffy even in my head. It's a heavy silk, with a burgundy and gold paisley patter. It's paired with navy blue pajama bottoms, and deep brown leather slippers. The personal shopper clearly has a penchant for high drama. Maybe she should transition from Macy's to Broadway.

I stand quietly, and take him in. I find myself assessing him, as if he's a specimen, an example of a man. Without his winter coat, I see the outline of his body. He has effortlessly good posture, broad shoulders thrown back without any stiffness. The belt of his robe is cinched closely. His waist is slim, giving his upper body that perfect V-shape seen on models in *GQ* or *Men's Fitness*. His legs are long, but a lot of his considerable height comes from his long torso. I imagine that line from his hipbone to his chest, and how long it would take to trace with my fingertip.

When Henry turns around, he's holding an open book that he has selected from the shelf. I see he's not wearing his glasses. Unveiled, his eyes are even bluer, if that's possible. They're as captivating as a wolf's, or an Alaskan sled dog's. His wavy, brown hair is damp, and combed back from his forehead, instead of laddishly gracing his forehead, as usual.

"Oh!" I breathe, involuntarily. "I mean, hi. Hello."

"Hello," he says, with a quizzical look on his face. "I hope you don't mind," he says, waving a hand to indicate his outfit. "After a day of running round the city, a fresh change of clothing was welcome. This, it seems, is what your aunt had sent from Macy's."

"Of course not. You look really good. No! Well, you do, but what I'm trying to say is you're usually so uptight, it's like you have a stick up..."

His eyebrows fly heavenward.

"You're just usually more serious. You know what I mean."

He closes the book and shelves it. "Do I?" A smile twitches at the corner of his lips.

My mouth is dry. I head for the champagne bottle, and start untwisting wire on the cage around the cork. "It's like you're always on the job."

He frowns. "I'm working for your aunt, as you know. I don't think it's fair to criticize me for taking my career seriously."

"I didn't mean that," I say, turning my head from the bottle. It's hard to uncork champagne with your eyes squinched shut. I've never liked popping balloons, or decanting sparkling wine. "It's just between your ambition and your Englishness, you're not exactly a barrel of laughs."

He takes the bottle from my hands. "That's a bit of the pot calling the kettle black." He expertly drapes a linen napkin over the cork, twists gently a few times, and I hear a faint 'pop.' He pours the champagne down the sides of the two flutes very slowly. There's not a hint of foamy head on either glass. I watch as an explosion of bubbles rises from the bottoms, sparkling to tiny *pop pop pops* on the surface.

"You don't have the authority to comment, one way or the other. Shall we?" He carries the silver tray of strawberries to the low, intricately carved oak coffee table. I take a seat on the adjacent sofa, and Henry follows with the champagne, and napkins, and sits down next to me.

"I think I have a pretty good handle on the situation. I've spent nearly every minute of today in your company." He holds his glass up to clink, and lets me take the first drink. While I savor the taste of the luscious wine, I think about today and how much of it was spent with Henry. There's no one I've spent this much time with, nonstop, in years. Except, of course, Hudson.

Not Aunt Miranda, not Beverly, and not James. When we were together, he spent most of his time schmoozing, courting investors, wangling invites to parties. It paid off, sure. He got the backing for his first restaurant in record time after we graduated from The Culinary Institute. That suited me. After a dose of his concentrated company, I found myself itching for alone time. He asked me to move in with him several times, but I just avoided the subject until one day, it no longer mattered.

"And you think you know me after one day?"

"I think that there's more to know," I say, measuring my words.

He bites into a strawberry. After a beat, he asks, "And do you want to know it? I got the sense from you that being in my company was a form of torture."

I pluck a strawberry from the plate, and nibble it to buy time. It's true that I felt that way at first. But I can't deny he's grown on me. How can I explain that being with anyone for too long makes me uncomfortable? I usually find a comfortable place in the periphery. I'm less a spotlight girl, than a shadows girl. I observe; I'm not observed. But today, the longer I've been with Henry, the more he's really seen me. I can't hide in the shadows any longer.

"Hello? You're miles away, Charlotte." He arranges a few of the overstuffed pillows, and lies back. "Did I put you on the spot?"

"You asked me a question…" I begin, when there's a knocking on the door.

"Excuse me," Henry says, getting up.

It's the French porter from earlier. "Turndown service," he says, blowing past Henry and heading for my room. He disappears, and Henry turns to me, confused. "Don't the maids usually take care of that?"

After a moment, he emerges and heads for Henry's room. We look at one another, bemused. When he comes out, he says, "If I can be of service, in *any way,* it would be my pleasure."

"That will be all," Henry tells him. He heads to the closet and takes out his wallet.

"Sincerely, if I can make the stay more pleasurable for either one of you, it would make me happy to do so."

"Charlotte, I don't seem to have any more small bills. Could you possibly?"

I run into my room, and grab my wallet. I pull out a five and press it on Henry.

"Or, possibly for both of you? At once?" the French guy says, leering, as Henry shoves the bill in his hand, and pushes him out the door.

"Euw!" I say, jumping up and down with a shiver, as Henry opens the door, checks to make sure the guy is gone, and hangs the "Do Not Disturb" sign on the outer handle. "Was that what I think it was?"

"Only in New York," Henry says. "Now sit down. There are a lot of strawberries to eat, and you, miss, are falling behind on the job." I flick my eyes across the champagne to check the level. Half a bottle left. I'm surprised that I'm looking forward to having another indulgent glass or two. I'm more surprised that I'm looking forward to having it with Henry.

"Let me just put my wallet back in my bag." I cross into my room where the lights have been dimmed, my shopping has been neatly moved and arranged on the chair, by covers have been folded back into a neat triangle, and my pillows have been graced with a selection of dark chocolates flavored with passion fruit, ginger, and Tahitian vanilla. I pop one into my mouth, and rush out, saying, "Hey Henry, did you get chocolates, too?"

He doesn't hear me. He's leaning against the frame of his bedroom door, half-in and half-out, with his phone to his ear.

"...told you before, Mum, working for a lady like Miranda Nichols has me run ragged. I'm knackered and then some. Of course spending Christmas at home would be nice, but I've told you before that it's our busiest season."

I retreat back into the dimness of my own doorway, and perk up my ears. Henry sounds terse. Weirder still, his voice sounds less like Prince William's and more like Daphne from the sitcom Frasier.

"Yes, they know what Christmas is in America, but the clock doesn't stop for Christmas for Miranda Nichols...That's what the job means, I'm on call day and night...Yes, but if I was home and working on the farm, I'd be there instead of here, now, wouldn't I? I'm not trying to insult you, but this is my life...Then I suppose it's better that I'm not coming home for Christmas. I wouldn't want to spoil your holiday with my fancy ways! Sorry you took it that way, but I'm stressed to the hilt. I've been on a wild goose chase all day, trying to find a lost dog...I don't have the time or energy to explain to you how that is a career, you'll just have to trust me...Yes, I think we'd better end it too, before I say something I'll regret. Tell Dad I'll talk to him next time. Goodbye, Mum."

I watch as he storms out, and slugs down the rest of his champagne, and pours himself another. He's breathing like he just ran sprints, and his face is as closed as a liquor store on Sunday.

"Don't stay up drinking champagne on my account," I tell him. "You must be exhausted after your 'wild goose chase.'"

His face springs to life with irritation. "Were you listening to

139

my private phone call?"

"Last time I checked, private phone calls were made behind closed doors." I park my hands on my hips.

"Anyone with manners would have stepped away."

"Anyone with manners wouldn't yell at his elderly mother on Christmas."

"She's not elderly!" he sputters. "The woman gets up at 6 a.m. to milk goats. She hauls sacks of feed larger than you around the farm before breakfast, which she cooks, then she opens the shop for a full day's trade."

"She sounds like a hardworking, respectful woman who doesn't whine and complain. Maybe you should take a page out of her book."

"You have no idea how hard I've worked to get where I am. No idea." He grows deathly quiet. "And you have no idea what it'll cost me if I'm not up to your aunt's standards."

"If I were you, I'd forget about Aunt Miranda, and worry about being up to your parents' standards."

"Then it is a good thing you are *not* me because you'd find that impossible."

My mouth falls open. "All your mum wants is to have her son come home for Christmas. It must be the middle of the night there."

"All the more reason she shouldn't be tracking me down."

"How is calling her own son to check in and invite him for the holiday 'tracking him down'? How hard would it be to make your parents happy? Just inform Aunt Miranda that you need a vacation."

He snorts derisively. "One doesn't inform Miranda Nichols. One stands at attention, preparing to take orders. And as far as my family are concerned, if I give them an inch, they want a mile. Every time I set foot on our land, it's like they've ensnared me. I'm considered a traitor when I leave again. My mum cries, and my dad lectures me once again how he should never have let me

140

go away to school."

"They're your family. You should grit your teeth and bear it if that's what it takes to make them happy." I think what I'd give to have a mother who would do anything just for a few days of my company. A hot feeling rises up from the pit of my stomach, and lodges in my throat. "You're just a selfish snob," I erupt.

He's on his feet in a split second. "And you're a spoiled brat!" He rounds the coffee table until we're standing inches apart. "You live your little life in your perfectly arranged brownstone, resting on your family laurels. Your aunt told me that you keep to yourself, avoiding people and never dating."

My mouth falls open. I ball up my fists in anger.

"She said you stay in by yourself, writing your cookbooks and blogging so you never have to talk to anyone. It's easy to think you're perfect when you live in a vacuum. Your manners are never tested because you never have to deal with anyone. You just avoid people altogether and pretend to have a relationship with your dog!"

It's like he fired a cannonball into the middle of my rib cage. I can hardly breathe for the dull pain. For a second, I think I might cry but blessedly anger takes over, radiating out to the tips of my fingers and the soles of my feet. Then, I'm numb. I feel nothing but coldness.

"You jerk. You don't know what it is to not to have people around who care about you. Do you know what I'd give to spend Christmas with a pair of doting parents who want nothing more than to lavish love and attention on me? All I have is an aunt who does a drive-by every month or so, and whose idea of support is throwing expensive things at me and hiring people to pretend to care about me." I walk to my bedroom door. I'm about to close it but instead turn around at the last minute. "For half a second today, I thought you were nice. I thought you got it. That little dog is my family."

I take a long last look at him. He looks back at me, barely

blinking. He's quiet and still.

"If having relationships with people means being grateful for little scraps of attention tossed to me by people like you, then I'll take the dog every time." I say, and I close the heavy door between us.

*****

I toy with the idea of ordering room service from my bed, with strict orders that my tray be brought into my room, but reconsider when I imagine that French guy showing up and offering to butter my muffins. The alluring aroma of coffee tickles my brain, and before I know it, I'm on my silk-slippered feet. My driving need for caffeine overtakes my angry desire to avoid Henry, and my body answers the compulsion to seek Java.

I plan to ignore Henry at all costs. I'll make a beeline for the liquid heaven I crave, and bring it back to my room. Then I'll make a plan for the day, one that doesn't include a pompous, callous, workaholic. Chin stabbing upward, and bathrobe cinched tight, I open my door planning to snub an unfeeling Henry who's likely on the phone brown nosing my aunt or charming some politician or TV personality in his race to the top.

When I walk in Henry is surrounded by piles of photos, flyers, and printouts featuring Hudson's image. "Good morning," he says dispassionately not bothering to look up. "No more amateur hour. Today, I intend to find your dog."

He's showered and dressed. On the table in front of him are three laptops, two phones, a scanner, a tangle of computer cords, a half-drunk cup of coffee, and the remnants of a continental breakfast.

His eyes are determined, and I can feel the energy coming off of him in waves.

Against my will, my heart softens. A surge of hope swells my chest. My head feels like a shaken snow globe. I cross to a sideboard where a breakfast spread has been laid out, and pour myself a cup of coffee, hoping to balance myself.

"I have a screenshot of Hudson with Santa on the Jumbotron. There's no one on earth who won't find that adorable. I've scanned the photos you brought from home, and we've been posting them to Twitter, Instagram, Snapchat, Tumblr and all the others. We're doing a full-on social media blitz. We're taking no prisoners. I have a good feeling about today."

Who's we? I wonder, pouring milk into my coffee and giving it a stir. The first swallow thrills my tongue and warms my throat. However, my moment of calm proves to be fleeting.

"Charlotte?" calls a distinctively feminine voice from behind me. "Do you have any photos of yourself and the dog in which you look more, hmm, I don't know, youthful? I'm working on something for Vine and I want people to, you know, respond favorably. What I have was fine for Pinterest, so that's already up and running."

"Who are you?" I blurt. I censor myself before I add, "And why are you coming out of Henry's bedroom at seven o'clock in the morning?"

"Oh hiiiiii," she coos sympathetically, making a cartoon frowny face. "I didn't introduce myself. First off, let me say I'm sorry for your loss."

I stiffen. "Hudson's not dead."

"Yeah. I meant I'm sorry for your lost dog." She tilts her head to the side, wrinkling her nose. She's wearing some sort of jumpsuit. It reads as a combination of Japanese haute couture runway piece/hostess pajama/vintage costume. My gut tells me it's the height of fashion, even though I know nothing about these things.

"I'm Landry," she extends her hand. Her nails are shortish and perfectly manicured, polished in a deep royal blue hue with a touch of iridescence. Reluctantly, I take her hand. As predicted, she wiggles her cold hand weakly. Fish grip.

"Henry, I just took care of Tagged, and ask.fm. Oh, and Charlotte, I brought you a laptop in case you want to check your, you know," she seems to be fishing for the right thing to say, "email...or maybe Facebook?" She scrunches her nose as if she's smelled something bad.

"Henry," she drawls, bending down to pick up one of the phones and exposing the landscape of her cleavage, "did you hear about everything I took care of? I did all that you asked, plus I took that scrap of video of the dog on the Ferris wheel, and made a GIF. I also put it up on YouTube." She's beaming at him. I get the feeling she's waiting to be petted, like a good cat.

His face is buried in his own phone, and he answers distractedly, "Great, sifting through responses now. Don't forget to call the *Daily News* and *The Observer*."

She stands back up, looking disappointed, and makes a note in her phone.

I select a cheese Danish the size of a pizza from the offerings, and take a huge bite. "Oh my holy yum," I keen, "cheese Danish is my favorite."

Henry looks up, over his glasses. "I know."

"How do you know?"

He buries his face back in his laptop, typing away. "I called Miranda." As I sip my coffee, I imagine Aunt Miranda's intense irritation at being interrupted in the middle of staging a pop-up restaurant complete with celebrity wedding to answer questions about what baked goods I prefer. She must have bitten Henry's head off.

"*News* and *Observer*, done and done!" Landry brags enthusiastically to Henry.

"Thanks," he answers, still typing.

"No need to thank me," she says, "We all just want to help Charlotte, right?" She turns to me, face scrunched into a sympathetic countenance. "Try not to worry. Our team is going to find your little dog. Before you know it, you can go back to that apartment of yours, where you're more comfortable, put this all behind you. And good for you! You should totally eat that huge pastry.

Breaking a gluten fast is perfectly fine in a crisis. Whatever you need to get you through."

"I'm not gluten-free," I tell her through a mouthful of buttery flakes.

"Oh, well, at a time like this butter and carbs are fine. Really. You shouldn't worry about your body."

Before I can tell her that I wasn't worrying and that I was simply having breakfast, she tosses a curtain of shiny black hair over one shoulder and puts on a grown-up, serious face. "Henry, I'm prepared to stay all day and into the night if you need me. Tell me what I can do for you, and I'm on it. Name it."

He tears his eyes from his laptop, and looks around. "I think that will be all."

She looks panicked. "But I told them not to expect me back at the office until late, if at all. I'm really dedicated to the project. Isn't there anything you need? Coffee? Anything?"

Henry stands up, takes off his glasses and rubs a fist into his eye. "I think we've done about all we can do for the moment. Now, we sit back and wait." He stretches, and the front of his shirt comes untucked, exposing a scant inch of firm ab adorned with a faint line of sparkling gold hair. I look away, while Landry gawps like a trout. "If you'll excuse me, ladies," he says, walking toward his bedroom.

Landry follows, clicking on the bare wood part of the floor with her impossibly slim, metal, cigarette heels. "Let me help!"

Henry turns around, and casually holds onto the doorframe, extending one long arm. "I'm planning a trip to the loo. Thanks for the offer, but it's more of a one-person job."

"Of course. Take your time," Landry concedes, lowering her head and holding her hands out in front of her. "When you're through, er, when you come back out, we can keep working."

"Thanks, again, but it's a wrap. I'll call Shanna back at the office and tell her you're on your way." She looks stricken. "And I'll let her know what a bang-up job you've done this morning. See you back there soon," he says, and closes the door.

I pour myself a second cup of coffee, and take a bite from a triangular brownie dusted in gold powder. As she shrugs on her long, camel-colored overcoat, she observes me like I'm a lab animal. "Wow," she breathes. "Good for you."

"Want one?" I ask, motioning toward the heaving platter of goodies.

She laughs and shakes her head. "Ahh! You're hilarious." She throws a glance over toward Henry's bedroom and whispers, "What is it about Englishmen that make them so hot?"

"Henry?" I ask. "Hot?"

"Oh, no," she backs off. "Are you two an item?"

"Ho, ho, no way. He's all about the work."

"I bet I could take his mind off it for a day," she smirks. "Or a night."

"Good luck with that," I say, draining my cup.

"Aww. Thaaaanks." She clearly doesn't understand sarcasm.

"Charlotte," Henry says, striding purposefully back into the room. "Oh, Landry. You're still here. I just spoke to Shanna. She said go directly to Macy's to support Miranda, and don't bother going back to the office first. She said to take a cab. Apparently it's all hands on deck there."

"In that case," she says, as if an idea were just occurring to her, "hadn't you better come with me? You said yourself that there's nothing to do here but wait."

"I'm where I'm supposed to be," he says, turning his back on her, and filling a glass with sparkling water.

"All right, then. I'm going to go now," she says, backing slowly toward the door leading to lobby. "If you're absolutely sure you're OK."

"Fine, thanks." He doesn't turn around. One thing's for sure, he has the status part of the job down-pat. Henry Wentworth puts the authority in Authority Figure.

"Bye," I say to her. I don't like her, but I feel like someone should make an effort at manners.

She mouths, *He's soooooo hot,* before composing herself and saying, "Nice to meet you. Good luck with Houston!"

"It's Hudson," I point out.

"Same thing!" And with that, she's gone.

Henry spreads butter on a croissant, and sits back down at his station. He doesn't say a word to me, just keeps typing. Slowly, I walk around gathering used cups and plates, and stack them on the sideboard. Henry appears to be engrossed in whatever it is he's scrolling through.

I clink a few glasses together. Still nothing. I steal a glimpse of myself in the giant mirror hanging over the umbrella stand near the foyer. Not good. Not good at all. My hair is wild, shooting out in all directions from the banana clip I dug out of the bottom of my purse so I could wash my face this morning. There are dark circles under my eyes, possibly from worry, possibly because I'd consumed what's normally my month's ration of alcohol last night. I cringe thinking about Landry and her fashion-forward fingernails, and limited edition leather carry-all.

Oh who cares, I think. I'm here to find my dog, not win *America's Next Top Model.* I may be in dire need of a good haircut and a layer of bronzer, but that doesn't mean I don't deserve an apology.

When I can no longer stand the silence, I probe gently with a "Sooo, Landry seems nice."

"Uh huh," Henry replies, still engrossed.

"And pretty too," I say, arranging the unused water glasses in a neat row.

"I guess."

"What, don't you think she's attractive?" I press. I hate myself for asking, but I can't shut my mouth. It's like picking at a scab. I don't really want to know the answer, which logically has to be, 'She's the most perfect girl I've ever seen in the flesh.'

"She's pretty, but she's what? Maybe twelve?" He looks up at me. "She's an intern. I felt like a babysitter." He closes the laptop, and once again takes off his glasses, and rubs his eyes. "I've been at this since 5 a.m. The groundwork, as they say, has been laid. Now, the waiting begins. I need to clear my head."

"Fine," I say. "Do what you need to do. I'm going to take a shower, then hit the streets again." I think about heading out without Henry. Searching alone after yesterday will feel so different.

"I didn't say I was leaving." He examines his shirt cuff, and toys with a loose thread. "Just that I need to clear my head."

"OK, then. You don't need my permission. Go to the gym, go for a walk, whatever." I'm still furious. I should really just go get in the shower. I rearrange the glasses into a diamond pattern. No one says anything. It's wondrous how silent luxury hotels can be.

Henry stands up, and crosses toward me. I don't turn around. The glasses might look nice in a circle, I think, shifting them around. I catch my breath as I feel Henry's hand on my shoulder.

"Please," he says to me.

I want to answer, but I can't. On principle. Please what? I want to know.

"I want to apologize. I confess that up to this point I hadn't thought of the situation from your viewpoint."

I turn and give him a long look, considering him. When my head hit the pillow last night, I'd written him off, and not for the first time. I had decided today was going to be different. It was turning out to be different, but not in the way I'd planned.

"Charlotte, I don't like seeing you unhappy. I'm going to make sure you get Hudson back."

I know my face is closed off. He's Miranda's puppet. He's just doing his job. I blink, not saying anything.

"I'm going to make sure you get your family back."

I cross my arms, waiting for more.

"You deserve to be taken care of. From this point forward, there will be no more crumbs of attention. You've had enough of that treatment." I realize he's talking about Aunt Miranda, but is too polite to call her out. "From here on out, I'm giving you my full attention."

I breathe out. "You mean you'll give *Hudson* you're full attention?" I tease.

"Of course," he says, face the picture of innocence. "I believe that's what I said." His eyes twinkle. "Will you let me?"

I'm all in.

"I'm going to get dressed," I say. "Don't leave without me."

*****

"Wow," Henry says, standing up as I stride into the sitting room. I really cannot help striding. It's the boots. "You look," he stops and shakes his head. "You look very well indeed."

"Thanks," I say. Normally, I'd brush off the compliment and take a shot at myself. Today, I can't help but agree with him. Maybe it was standing next to Landry in my bathrobe that prompted me to dip into the array of Lancôme, Bobbi Brown, and Laura Mercier cosmetics that Macy's sent over, or maybe it's the feeling that for once, I'm wearing exactly the right outfit for the occasion. Nah, it's probably the boots.

Tall and cherry red, with an asymmetrical military-style rise over my knee, my fiery new boots feature a modern silver buckle accent on the side. At once structured and slouchy, they are the pinnacle of architectural design. With enough of a heel to push me up and out at all the right angles, but enough of a base to keep me grounded, these boots make me feel relaxed and in command. I have to hand it to Calvin Klein. Anyone who can make footwear beautiful enough to display in a museum and manage to engineer the foot bed so the wearer feels like she's walking on air deserves the Congressional Medal of Honor.

After unwrapping today's selection of garments, I feel awful for characterizing my personal shopper as frivolous and flighty. She sent me the most perfect sleek black Michael Kors trousers; they're not clingingly tight nor do they bag in unfortunate places. They

149

stretch without appearing to be stretchy and feature elongating pleats up the fronts and backs of my legs. I'm not sure what miracle fabric comprises the backside and waistband, but suffice it to say I am duly lifted and tucked.

To top it all off, I've been given a camel-colored Ralph Lauren ribbed turtleneck and a black swing cardigan with a hood, and thumbholes in the extended sleeves. I love being cozy in the wintertime, and I'm amazed I can feel this wrapped-up and comfy in close-cut, flattering sweaters. This is a different universe from my zip-up North Face fleece and Uggs, let me tell you.

Henry's gaze still rests on me, and despite the confidence my new look has infused me with, I'm not comfortable standing in a spotlight.

"What?" I ask to break the tension.

"You just look…wonderful." His eyes are soft as he stares. "That's all. Wonderful. Anyhow," he says, snapping back to efficiency mode, "how are we going to kill time, as they say, while we wait? I've been posting and reposting on all the social media platforms, but so far nothing concrete has come up as to Hudson's whereabouts."

"Oh no!" I wrap my cardigan tightly around myself.

"Don't despair. I sincerely think this is going to yield results. That being said, you know the old adage about watched pots, don't you?"

I nod.

"At this point, I think the only sensible thing to do is to make space and allow the seeds we've sown to take root." He runs his fingers through his wavy brown hair. "To be honest, I feel like I'm trapped in a box."

I hesitate. I know it's irrational, but I feel like I'm keeping Hudson safe through sheer force of will. If I'm not vigilant, what will happen? "You know, Henry, I think I should stay here and wait. You take your walk. I'll man the battle station."

"At the risk of sounding like an old country doctor, I think some fresh air would do you a world of good. It's not healthy to

150

stay holed up all the time."

I wince internally. Staying holed up is kind of my thing. Was he getting in a dig about the way I live my life? "Actually, I think most people on the planet would hole up if given suites in the Towers at the Waldorf-Astoria."

He smiles, and crosses to the closet to get his coat. "You've got a point. Conrad Hilton did call this 'The Greatest of Them All.'"

"By the way, don't you think it's a little crazy how Aunt Miranda splashed out on this? I really could have gone home," I say, knowing in my heart that I really couldn't have.

"Don't forget that women like your aunt have a lifetime of connections. One hand scratches the other's back. You'd be astonished what she doesn't pay for. It's like the swag bags at all the big Hollywood award shows. Every person who's given one could afford to buy the contents. But, they never have to. It's how the rich get richer. I encourage you to shrug off any guilt you may have been harboring. I, myself, am enjoying my brand-spanking new Kenneth Cole boots, and my new jeans and shirt, compliments of Emporio Armani. Don't look at me like that, part of my job is knowing about fashion design."

"You could teach me, then, because I'm clueless," I tell him, pulling my brown puffy coat off the hanger.

"For starters, you'll want to burn that," he says with a wicked grin.

"Hey!"

"You said you wanted the benefit of my vast wisdom. Go check your bags. See if they sent a replacement. If they did, put it on. I'm taking you out on the town. Doctor's orders!"

Sure enough, when I dig deeper, I find an Anne Klein slim belted trench and a leather Dooney and Bourke cross body bucket bag. I change purses, throwing out months' worth of used tissues, starlight mints, wrinkled receipts, and empty packs of gum.

When I emerge, Henry closes the laptop, and declares, "All systems are go. If my pleas of 'Can you reunite this girl with her dog' along with the irresistible photos of your impish pup don't mobilize the holiday-besotted citizens of New York City, I don't know what will." He gathers his keys and wallet from a silver salver on the mirrored umbrella stand.

"You know, Hudson loves Christmas almost as much as I do," I tell Henry, as I button and tie my coat.

His lips twitch in amusement. "Is that right?"

"Look, I know you don't believe a dog can have feelings, but you haven't met Hudson." I go stand next to him as he waits by the door. He smells really good. A little like the Ferragamo toiletries, but also like freshly cut grass and rain.

"I'm sure that when I do, he'll forever change my mind about dogs."

"He'll change your mind about Christmas, too." I pull my bag over my shoulder.

"I'm doubt even the magical Hudson has that power." He drapes his winter scarf around his neck, letting the ends hang.

"Don't be such a scrooge. Are you seriously telling me that no part of Christmas in Manhattan was enjoyable to you yesterday?" I cock my head and wait for an answer.

"We were very busy. I hardly had time to notice," he says. "Shall we go?"

"Really? The carriage ride? The gorgeous tree at The Plaza Hotel? The shoppers in Times Square? The skating rink in Bryant Park? Nothing? Is your heart a block of ice?"

He considers this. "For the last several years, I've seen Christmas from an office window, or over the top of a spreadsheet." He pauses. "That was my choice. But, I admit that there was something, yesterday, that made me think I could someday change my mind on the matter."

"Then there's hope," I say. I tie the ends of his scarf together. "Let's kill some time and go take a big bite out of Christmas in the city."

"Was that, or was that not, fun?" I ask as we climb the stairs from the subway into the bright December sunshine. An older, dark-skinned man wearing very dark shades, wails on an electric guitar and belts out James Brown's *Soulful Christmas.*

"Do you mean the subway ride? It was different, I'll give it that. I'm embarrassed to admit that I've only traversed Manhattan by van, town car, and cab."

"And you called me spoiled?"

He holds up his hands in innocence. "These are the hazards of my line of work."

"I think most people would call them perks, not hazards. Anyway, I wasn't talking about riding the subway, I was talking about the trip to the Statue of Liberty and Ellis Island. What are you doing? Are you cold?"

Henry is standing by one of New York's ubiquitous Nuts 4 Nuts Carts, holding his hands up to the metal wall for warmth. The guy inside, bundled in a knit cap and scarf gives him the stink eye.

"I'm afraid to say yes. You might call me names again," he replies, grinning. "What was it you called me on the ferry to the statue? A big baby?"

"Well, who gets seasick on a five-minute ride on the river?"

"I believe the ice chunks in the Hudson made for choppy waters. I have science on my side, so there." Henry inhales deeply. "Do you smell that? That must be what it smells like when angels bake."

"Haven't you ever had nuts from a nut cart?" I ask.

"As I've told you, I've largely seen your city from the darkened windows of Sedans."

"Give me a bag of each, please." I watch as the guy scoops out the sugar-encrusted peanuts, almonds, cashews, and chunks of coconut from their pans beneath the multiple heat lamps keeping them warm. "How much?"

"Normally two for five. But you are very pretty. Give me five

153

dollars and blow me a kiss." I'm flummoxed. I'm torn between indignation at being asked to prostitute myself for candied nuts, and the thrill of being treated like an alpha girl. Normally, I pass through the streets unnoticed.

Henry quickly pulls out his wallet, and gives the guy a five. "Go on, then." He teases. "Don't be a big baby."

"Would a handshake and a wave do?"

The guy hands over my packages, thinking about it. "Yes, I would accept that." Because he proves himself to be nice and not creepy, I shake his hand, then blow him a kiss as we walk away.

"Very pretty, indeed. Your husband is very lucky!" he calls.

"Believe me, I know it!" Henry calls back over his shoulder. I punch him in the arm. We're both laughing, giddy with the cold and the pre-Christmas excitement in the air.

"As if! I cannot imagine, in my wildest dreams, you putting a woman before your career." He stops laughing, and looks at me seriously.

"There's a Starbucks," he says. "Let's have a coffee and talk."

*****

"What did you do after she said no?"

He looks down at his latte. "It was awful," he says in a low voice. "More awful than you can imagine. My mother had champagne on ice in the kitchen, and my father had put on a tie. Of course, they make an effort to spiffy up for holiday meals, but they had really pushed out the boat. I feel such the fool for not seeing it coming, but it was beyond my imagination. I mean, when someone says to you, point blank, 'I wish this would never end. Wouldn't it be bliss to spend the rest of our lives together,' it paints a certain picture."

I choose a coconut chunk from among the torn-open bags on the table between us. Henry hasn't picked up so much as a peanut. It makes me sad. I was so looking forward to his reaction.

"Did she just say the word no? Just like that?" I tried to visualize

154

what it would be like to be on the receiving end of a proposal.

"If only. The horror went deeper than that. She burst into tears. My aunt and uncle, and my parents, and the neighbors from down the road…"

I groan.

"Oh, yes. And the teacher who set me on the road to boarding school, and even the vicar, all took that as a sign of joy, and began clapping me on the back, and trying to clasp her hands. She looked panicked, like a caged animal. And then, things turned. She got angry."

"You're kidding me."

"No, it gets worse. Fasten your safety belt. She roared at me, wet-faced and snot-nosed, 'Henry, you have *embarrassed* me. Did you think my parents would just stand by and watch me marry you? I thought we both knew we were just having a bit of fun.'"

My stomach felt sick just hearing about it. "I'm sorry."

"You cannot fathom how bad it was. The vicar turned purple. It appeared that my teacher Mr. Cooper, was going to, as we English say, have very strong words with her. My dad practically had to push him into the next room. My mother still talks about how she wishes she'd never popped that cork." He shakes his head, looking pained and confused as if this were happening now, and not years ago. "The hour after that was excruciating. My mother had set Patricia up in the guest bedroom, and she'd unpacked, planning to stay through the end of the week. It was Christmas morning. There were no buses running. Everyone in England was hunkered down in his family home celebrating the joy of the season. Nearly everyone had started the morning with an Irish coffee or two, and the mulled wine had been passed around, so the only one sober enough to drive, apart from myself, was Mr. Cooper, who's teetotal. In order to get her out of our house, the poor man had to give up his Christmas and drive her the all the way across the country to the North coast to deposit her back into her parents' waiting arms. No one was sure he wouldn't stop his truck and

155

leave her on the side of the road."

"What happened after she left?" I feel awful for Henry. To take a risk and put your heart out there, only to have it stomped on. No, thank you. I think back to James. Did I really ever put my heart out there with him?

"As I recall," Henry continues, interrupting my thought, "my mother asked to be excused every fifteen minutes, and would reappear with a tense smile and red, watery eyes. My father polished off the champagne because no one else would go near it. He spent the better part of the day muttering about water not rising above its own level. As for me, I went on automatic pilot. One might say that I executed Christmas. I felt I owed it to the poor people around me to put on a brave face and go about the business of eating the joint and roast potatoes, and playing the piano so we could all sing carols."

"You play the piano?" I sat up straight, impressed. I love it when people play instruments. He really is full of surprises.

"Yes, I play the piano. That's your takeaway from this story?"

"Sorry! I'm paying attention. I really am."

"I cut my holiday short, and made my way to London on St Stephen's Day. I flew straight to California to work in the trenches for Miranda, who was in charge of the Tournament of Roses parade for the New Year's Day Rose Bowl football game."

"How did you manage to focus on your work after that?" I push the opened wax-paper bags of sugar-wrapped treats in his direction.

"You see," he says, shaking his candy at me. "That's just it." His eyes are bright, and he looks like at me, alive with fervor, as if he's giving me the secrets of the Masonic order. "I *only* focused on work. I forgot all about Patricia and threw myself into my career. That was really the turning point. During that job, Miranda took notice of me. After that, I was no longer a PA or a lackey. I became an assistant." He pops the nugget of candy into his mouth. "It won't be long," he says, filled with fervor and enunciating through his chewing, "till I'll be in charge. This may be my first and last Christmas in New York. I plan to become the Miranda Nichols of London."

In the passion of his speech, he has taken off his glasses, and tucked them into the breast pocket of his French blue shirt. I stare at him, trying to figure out if he looks more like a sexy professor, or a sexy car mechanic in a 1950s uniform. I can't tear my eyes away as I ask myself, why is he a "sexy" anything?

"Henry," I say. It comes out far huskier than I imagined it would. I clear my throat and try again, "Henry."

As if hit with a blow dart, he leans back in the chair, and closes his eyes. "Oooh," he moans. "God, woman." He sits up, and looks at me with intensity. "What have you done to me?"

What have I done? I wonder.

He lunges for a piece of the coconut, and holds it aloft. "Why would you set something so delicious and utterly addictive right in front of me?"

"You mean…?"

"The coconut is even better than the almonds. You're like a drug dealer. I don't dare try the cashews," he rants, "oh, who am I kidding? Of course I'm trying them. I'll probably finish them as well," he says choosing a handful of the nuts and piling them on the napkin next to his hot drink. Nearby, his phone vibrates, dancing sideways on the table.

"Right, I forgot to turn the ringer back on after the security guard gave me that filthy look back in the Ellis Island museum." Stuffing more almonds into his mouth, he picks up his phone, and checks it.

"What is it?"

His eyebrows spike as he turns it around for me to view. "And so it begins," he says, with the smug look of a winner on his face.

On the screen is a photo of Hudson, held up and surrounded by a group of high school cheerleaders on the top of the Empire State Building.

"Look up," I tell Henry, as we stand in line to talk to the guard at the desk.

"Incredible," he says, staring upward, mouth agape. The lobby's ceiling features a twenty-four-karat gold rendering of the planets and stars arranged in an assembly line of gears in a 1930's homage to the mechanical age. "Art Deco is easily my favorite movement. I doubt I'd have noticed that had you not pointed it out."

"Different than seeing New York from your office, isn't it? Stick with me, kid," I say in a black-and-white film voice, "I'll show you things you've never seen."

He turns his clear blue eyes to mine, holding my gaze. "I believe you."

I clear my throat. "Almost as soon as I landed in New York City, Aunt Miranda taught me to look up. There are so many wonders that aren't right in front of your face, you know?"

"Good advice. But there's something to be said for appreciating what is."

I take him in. In the crowded lobby, we're pushed close enough that I can smell his now-familiar scent, freshly mown lawn and rain, with a touch of earthiness, and I feel the warmth coming off of his skin. Pretending to look ahead for the end of the line, I'm still aware of Henry. His height, the rhythm of his breathing, the confident stillness with which he stands. Could he have been talking about me?

"Look, we're next. Perhaps the guard knows where Hudson is."

"Yes, Hudson." I reply. Eye on the prize, Charlotte, I tell myself. This is no time for fantasies and what-ifs? I ask myself, WWAMD? What *would* Aunt Miranda do? She'd take charge and demand access. I gird my loins, and approach the desk.

"Excuse me," I say to the bald, square-necked, uniformed guard. "My dog was up on the top deck earlier. I wonder if you know where he is now?"

He eyes me suspiciously. "Is your dog a service animal?"

"No, just a mutt."

"Only service animals are allowed into the building. Next!"

"But he was in the building."

"No he wasn't," the guard says, craning what on anyone else would have been his neck to look behind me. "Can I help you, sir?"

"Henry, show him the photo!" The guard glances.

"Doesn't prove anything. There is no way a dog could get past our security."

"But he did," I say loudly. Henry puts a hand on my shoulder. "My dog is in this building and I want you to find him."

His answer is drowned out by a chorus of shrill, happy voices. Coming down the escalator to the lobby is a gaggle of teenaged girls, all wearing maroon and white short pleated skirts and leather-sleeved jackets with huge letter "B"s on the front. The guard throws them an irritated look when they start chanting, "New York, New York, what a town, the Bronx is up, but the Battery's down!"

I abandon the guard, and head for the group of cheerleaders. "Girls! That dog you tweeted about. That's my dog! Where is he?"

"Oh, you mean Patches?" drawls one of the chaperones, wearing the same jacket as the girls, but with "Coach" embroidered on the chest. "We asked everyone up there if he was their dog, and everyone said no. We were fixin' to take him back to Texas with us, if no one spoke up for him. We have our own tour bus," she said proudly. "The Beaumont Bears Cheerleading Squad and Drill Team marched in Newark, New Jersey's Santa Day Parade yesterday, didn't we girls?" She beams with pride. "We were thinking Patches could be the squad's mascot. Kiley Anne!" She calls authoritatively. The girls' hush at the sound of her voice. "Where's Patches? You had him last."

"Oh my word," says a girl wearing blue eyeliner and bubblegum-colored lipstick. She's holding a shopping bag printed with an Empire State Building logo in each hand, and a caught-out look on her face. "I set him down when we were in the gift shop. I told him to stay." Tears well behind her spidery eyelashes. "I was picking out a sweatshirt for Billy. You know how wide his shoulders are. I couldn't decide between the large and the extra-large. I meant to get Patches. I'm so sorry." She bursts into tears and ten girls surround her in a mobile huddle, moving its way toward the front doors. Like ducks, the other girls and chaperones join the maroon-and-white wave.

The coach rolls her eyes heavenward. "Billy's the quarterback for the football team. He broke up with her before Thanksgiving, but that dizzy girl won't take no for an answer." She shakes her head and tuts. "Can't keep her mind on the routines to save her life. Nearly lost a leg under Santa's float after she got whacked in the head with Connie's baton."

Henry cuts through the fluff. "To confirm, the last time you saw the dog was in the gift shop?"

"Near as I can tell," she says. "Sorry, they're moving out, and I'm gonna lose track of them." Henry hands her a flyer, asking her to call if she has any other information. "I hope you find your dog, miss. He's somethin' else. I'd have taken him home in a heartbeat."

We run up the moving escalator to catch an elevator to the 80th-floor gift shop. "You know," Henry says, slightly out of breath from the chase, "at first I thought you were crazy. But now I wish I had Hudson's power. He gets into more restricted places than even your aunt." We catch the elevator and bolt to be the last two in before the cut-off. Packed in like proverbial sardines with breathless tourists from around the globe, Henry and I are pressed chest-to-chest. With my new boots on, my chin nearly reaches his shoulder. I have no place to put my arms. I'm forced to draw my elbows in tightly to my sides, and hold onto Henry's upper arms. He hooks his hands under my elbows, to brace himself against the jostling.

I look away, politely, pretending to watch the floor numbers rise, but I can't help noticing the feel of Henry's flexed biceps under my fingers. My mind wanders, puzzling out how he stays fit when he seems to do nothing but work.

We are siphoned out the elevator doors and down the short hall to where the gift shop is. Henry talks to the cashiers while I look around. I check behind displays holding key chains and tiny telescopes printed with the trademark ESB logo. I push aside shirts and hoodies hanging on a round rack, and call Hudson's name. I see a door that's cracked, and look around furtively before opening it. It's a broom closet, and on the floor is the tiny hat Hudson wore when posing with Bryant Park's bad Santa. I pick it up, and put it in my pocket.

Dogless, and on my way to join Henry, I pass a display of pet accessories. There are water dishes with the building painted on, leashes with a repeating pattern of yellow cab, Empire State Building, yellow cab, Empire State Building. A tiny sweater catches my eye. It's knit with a map of the island across the top, where a dog's back would be. There are blue areas on either side of the slim island signifying the rivers. In large, plain letters, one side says "East" and the other says "Hudson." I think about how sweet my baby would look wearing this, and my heart constricts.

"This lady, and the other cashiers tell me it's been a madhouse in here today. No one even had the time to glance up, so unfortunately the trail is cold. What's that?"

He reaches for the sweater, and examines it. He hands it to the cashier, "We'll have this, please." He pays for it and hands it to me. "Put this in your bag. It's my Christmas present to Hudson."

I tilt my head, and narrow my eyes. "I thought you didn't buy Christmas presents."

His eyes twinkle with mischief, but he doesn't answer. "Come on, let's go to the top floor and see if we can catch your furry rapscallion."

I laugh. "OK, but only if you say 'rapscallion' again."

"Rapscallion."

"You really do think you're a gentleman from a Harlequin Historical novel, don't you?"

161

"I've never heard of Harlequin," he says, pushing me gently forward in the line to the elevator. "Rapscallion, rapscallion."

"You lie! Everyone's heard of them. I'll bet that's what you do for fun. You probably ride the London tube with a copy of the Financial Times in front of a paperback called 'The Duke's Dark Desire,' is that it?" I poke him in the side and he grabs my finger like a ninja, holding it very still and looking me in the eyes. "That," he says, "I will neither confirm nor deny." He smirks, and gives my finger a final squeeze before letting it go.

We ride the elevator to the top, smashed in with the crowds, and the whole trip, Henry sings very softly, in my ear, the word "rapscallion" to the tune of *We Wish You a Merry Christmas*. I can't stop laughing. My heart is filled with helium. We're so close to finding Hudson, I can feel it.

After half an hour of inspecting corners and crevices, and a brief pause so Henry can gaze out over Manhattan from our bird's-eye vantage point, Henry checks his phone. We pull over to one side to avoid getting trampled.

"Ho, ho, Charlotte. It's all happening."

"What?" I ask breathless. "What's happening?"

"Hudson's breaking the internet, that's what. Messages are pouring in on every platform."

He flips and scrolls, occasionally holding out the phone for me to read something. Some of the Twitter messages are pure support. "I hope you find your dog!" and "Sending prayers to you and Hudson."

Some of the Facebook messages are suggestions, with maps and links to places a dog might wind up in the city. "Have you checked the 'Bark the Herald Angel's Sing' Santa-and-Pet photography event in Prospect Park, Brooklyn? It's at the Picnic House, sponsored by Love Thy Pet. They donate all proceeds to animal shelters."

Some of the Instagram messages seem to include genuine photos of Hudson with various people from around town. There's one of RuPaul, the drag queen and some of her cohorts in full, dramatic make-up, holding a dog that may or may not be Hudson in front of the makeover counter at the Mac Cosmetics store near the flatiron building. "This could be Hudson," I tell Henry. "It's not far from here. It's just hard to tell with that feather boa and the tiara obscuring his face."

Still another on Tumblr shows a man in dark clothing carrying a patchwork-colored dog under his arm as he boards a plane. "Oh, Henry, you don't think…"

"Breathe deep, Charlotte. This dog is the right size and colors, I'll give you that, but he has a full tail, see? Not a stubby one." I heave a sigh of relief.

"From here on out, we're going to have to treat this forensically. Information is pouring in, and we'll have to sort the wheat from the chaff."

I feel a twinge of regret as I say, "We should probably head back to the hotel and sift through some of this." This morning has been really fun, I think to myself. Fun. When is the last time I had fun, I wonder. Of course I enjoy being with Huddie, and he makes me laugh. I'm content, and peaceful. But fun with another person?

"New plan," Henry says, interrupting my thoughts. "Miranda wants me onsite ASAP."

I feel a letdown in my gut. Next on my agenda was a trip up 5th Avenue to see the window displays in the department stores like Saks and Lord & Taylor, and maybe even Barney's. He's typing furiously into his phone as he speaks, thumbs flying. "I'm texting Shanna at the office to send Landry and one or two of the other interns to the Waldorf to manage the social media accounts to figure out what's useful intel and what's noise."

In a split second, Henry's demeanor has changed from jolly partner-in-crime to ace coordinator. This must be what he's like at work. I can't help noticing that he hasn't assigned me a role. I'm indignant. Hudson is, after all, my dog. I don't have to sit around and wait to be told what I'm allowed to do.

"And where do you see me fitting in to all of this?" I ask.

He stops typing and looks up from his phone. "You're with me," he says, eyes searching my face. "Don't you know that? We're a team."

Chapter 8

"Do you think today will be the day we find Hudson, Henry?"

We're crossing west to 34th Street and 6th Avenue, and our eyes are pulled like magnets to the exterior of the world's most famous department store.

Henry points to the word "Believe" written in expansive, dreamy script and lit up like white fire. It arches above a decorated Christmas tree that proudly stands atop the iconic awning above the entrance that features the original Macy's sign, and the graceful old-fashioned clock. "Looks like someone is trying to tell you something."

Henry heads for the entrance, but I take him by the arm. "Before you have to go to work, just one more touristy thing." He glances at his phone. "Please?"

A relaxed smile blooms across his face, and he squints to keep the glare of the waning December sun out of his eyes. "All right. Lead on."

I walk him around the whole building and back to see the store windows. Every year, Macy's decorates four windows on the 34th Street side of the store with scenes from the classic film *Miracle on 34th Street* to pay homage to the store's role in the timeless story. But it also elects a theme and the top designers in the business deck out the windows with fanciful scenes weaving the conceit into a

165

Christmas fantasy. Over the years, the themes have been inspired, running the gamut from traditional *to au courant*. 1963 gave the world "Santa's Enchanted Forest." 1971 got with the times, offering "Santa's TV Studio." Sometimes popular characters from books and movies are showcased, as with Dr. Seuss's *How the Grinch Stole Christmas* in 1977 and *Harry Potter* in the year 2000. This year's confections revolve around the theme "Planets in Space."

The first window we view shows an animatronic puppet boy with wavy hair and glasses perched on his bed wearing moons and stars pajamas, lifting a telescope to his eye.

"Oh, look," Henry says, jumping and pointing, "I had that exact telescope." He beams, waiting for me to nod. I do.

"And I had glow in the dark stars on my ceiling, too." For a moment, it's easy to see what Henry must have been like as a child. A bright, engaged boy who knew, even at a young age, that worlds existed far beyond his little village. Cool as a cucumber in most situations, he must have unlearned that natural enthusiasm in order to succeed in business. Imagining it, I felt a little burn in my heart, as though I missed that boy whom I'd never met.

We circle the outside of Macy's, looking at each window from every angle. There's a scene of Santa and the boy's dog floating happily in space, wearing fishbowls on their heads. Another scene depicts sweet-faced aliens opening wrapped packages, ostensibly left by the retreating Santa and his reindeer. We peruse all of the windows, bopping to the upbeat jingle-bell music, until we come to the last one, depicting the dark and vast universe, with a tiny replica of Santa's sleigh circling the earth.

Gazing in at the scene where the little girl pulls Santa's beard in the movie, I ask Henry, "Do you watch that film over and over too?"

"I'll be honest. I've never seen it."

"Oh, you have to watch it. It's my favorite of all the Christmas movies. It's about a man who says he's Santa Claus, but no one believes him. They just think he's crazy."

"Like you with your magic dog?" Henry smiles devilishly.

I punch him in the arm. "Turns out, the guy actually *is* Santa Claus, so there."

"And maybe that dog of yours will give us the secret to world peace."

I stick out my tongue at him, and he laughs. When we finally exit the bracing cold, and enter the store, I feel all of my senses light up. On top of its usual visual delights, the store has been heightened with touches of Christmas everywhere. Red and green lights are projected into pools on the floor, swags of silver tinsel drape down from the atelier level, and along the bannisters to the Visitor's Center, and even the employees are spiffed up in seasonal neckties and silk scarves. I inhale the new-car smell of the luxury leather handbags before it gets trumped by the rich tapestry of aromas emanating from the fragrance counters.

As we move from section to section, the music changes along with the mood of what's on offer. From jazzy, to classical, to pop, to hip hop, but every refrain is holiday-themed.

Before leading Henry to the original wooden tongue-and-groove escalators that were built at the turn of the twentieth century, I pull him on a detour to the 34th Street Memorial Entrance where I show him a century-old bronze plaque affixed to a marble wall. The tribute had been purchased by grieving employees in honor of the deaths of store owners Ida and Isidor Straus caused by the sinking of RMS Titanic.

"They say Isidor encouraged Ida to get aboard one of the lifeboats, but she wouldn't do it. She wouldn't let him die without her."

He takes in the plaque with a faraway look in his eyes. Abruptly, he turns away. "I'm not sure I can imagine such a thing."

"Me either," I tell him, feeling a little hollow inside. "Why would she stick by him when she could save herself? It's not logical." I set out toward the down escalator, and he follows fast on my heels.

"Hey," he calls, shouting to be heard above the clinking and whooshing of the store, and the excited chatter of the shoppers. "You're moving at quite a clip. Everything all right?"

Before I have to answer, Aunt Miranda spies Henry from the bottom of the moving staircase. She points to him, and then crooks her finger, beckoning him over. When we're delivered down into the Cellar, she gives me a quizzical look. "Charlotte? What are you doing here?"

Henry steps in. "She could hardly be left on her own, wouldn't you agree, Miranda?"

Aunt Miranda doesn't look like she agrees, but she puts on her public smile. "Certainly, though, you could have asked Landry or one of the others from the office, to sit with her. I spared you yesterday, but things are heating up here, as you can see," she says between clenched teeth. Aunt Miranda pulls Henry to the side. "Are you here to tell me that the dog is still missing? You've had a whole day! What have you been *doing*?" I can see the muscles in Henry's jaw set. Knowing him the way I do by now, I know he's barely keeping himself under control.

Miranda steps back and points to a tented-off area into and out of which armies of workers are carrying everything from chairs, to trash bins, to pots and pans, to gallons of olive oil. "I need Henry here, Charlotte. Restaurants don't build themselves. Take a look! Things are happening! It's all hands on deck."

Henry and I both look as James, wiping his hands on a kitchen towel, steps out from behind one of the canvas walls. I'm not sure I can say he smiles, but his eyes light up and he throws back his shoulders as he crosses the room to greet me. "Charlotte," he says, holding his arms open for me to walk into. "You look gorgeous. Better than I think I've ever seen you look." He makes a throaty sound that I think is supposed to indicate desire. I recoil. "Whatever you're doing these days, you should do it more often." I certainly didn't expect this. I'm mute.

Henry steps in, bellowing "Henry Wentworth" by way of intro- duction. It's very "American Guy", in a way I've never seen Henry behave. "And I know you from the media." Henry throws an inscrutable look my way, before turning away from me to shake one of James's outstretched hands. "I wasn't aware you knew Charlotte, though. She's full of surprises, isn't she? Good to meet you Mr. Keyes."

"James needs rush approvals from fire safety, so get on that, Henry, plus you'd better work your magic with the food safety and the alcoholic beverage people if that's going to be an issue. James's assistant, Mila, has been on the phone all morning to no avail, but I told her to leave it to you, Henry. You can do this sort of thing in your sleep." Standing behind James is an almond-eyed beauty in chef's whites with her heavy black hair wound into a bun that covers the entire top of her head. She stares at me through narrowed eyes.

James runs his eyes over Henry, and I watch as my ex sizes him up, then dismisses him as nothing, and moves on. I've seen him do it a hundred times at parties. Instead, he focuses every ion of his charisma on me. "Charlotte, since you'll be flying solo, why don't you come back with me and see how the kitchen is shaping up?"

"Ah, I'm afraid we can't spare her just now, Mr. Keyes. Jane!" Henry calls to one of the nervous underlings circling Aunt Miranda waiting to pick up a dropped pen or fetch a cup of coffee. Jane has very big hair, and a very short skirt, hinting that she might be a native of Staten Island. Her makeup is just a tad too bright, and her earrings just a bit too dangly. I silently will her to stay as far away from Aunt Miranda as possible. That bright plastic jewelry-slash-extra-hold hairspray look has been known to draw Miranda's derision like fresh blood draws a lion to the kill.

"Jane, I'll need you to take Miss Bell with you, I'm afraid," Henry continues, "I'm going to need a photo of her for social media. A publicity shot, of course. You understand, don't you Mr. Keyes? I'm sure you can spare her."

James looks confused. I can see the wheels turning as he tries to work out why I'd need PR. Henry turns to Jane and says, "It'll need to be on Santa's lap."

"What?" I demand. "Why?"

Henry ignores me and speaks to Jane instead. "Darling, would you please find one of our Macy's partners and see that Miss Bell gets escorted to the front of the line up on the eighth floor? Is there someone who can help with that?" Henry has turned the full power of his sea glass eyes on the poor, aspirational Jane, and she is done for. "Can I count on you?" he asks meaningfully.

"Yeah, Henry, sure," she stammers. Staten Island accent confirmed. "That girl Penelope, the one who did all that personal shopping when Miss Nichols asked the other day. We're, like, buds now. She'll do me a solid."

"I can't tell you how much I appreciate that, Jane. Thank you." She basks in the light of his praise. No doubt she's never heard words like that from my aunt.

"Henry," Miranda cuts in, "Charlotte should stay with James. It'll give them a chance to catch up." She gives me a not-subtle-at-all eyebrow waggle. "They're old friends, you know."

Henry looks like he's just tasted lemon. "I didn't know."

I shrug, and turn away, pretending to be engrossed in an array of hand-painted ceramic and hammered tin Christmas ornaments with New York City and Macy's themes. There is very little on earth I loathe more than posing for pictures, but the alternative here seems to be a personal tour of my ex's hot new restaurant endeavor, given by said ex. I steal a glance at him. I can only see his back. He has his hands on Mila's shoulders in a placating gesture, and she's shooting him the look of death. Yes, sitting on the knee of Father Christmas and saying "cheese" for the camera sounds like a breath of fresh air compared with standing the heat that's likely to be in the pop-up kitchen.

"Miranda, may I have a word," Henry asks in an upbeat, polite tone, pulling her to the side. He says, sotto voce, "You're missing the big picture."

I strain to hear. I can, but just barely. "The sooner we find your niece's dog, the sooner you can tick it off of your to-do list. Then, I'll be back here giving the job my full attention. I'd turn the job

170

over to someone else, but it would take me longer to hand off the intel than to wrap this thing myself. I'm nearly there." She seems about to veto his plan, but he presses, "I'd be surprised if there wasn't a resolution by end of day, today."

She huffs and nods, waving him off with a flicking gesture. "Fine. Might as well. When else will I ever get a decent picture of the girl? The last time she agreed to sit for a portrait was when she graduated from high school, and that was only because I told her if she did, I'd stop badgering her about Barnard and let her enroll in the Culinary Institute."

Turning to the crowd awaiting her orders, she shouts, "Back to work people! Why are you standing about gawking? Do you think the mayor of the capitol of the world wants her daughter to get married in a stripped-down, low-rent beach cabana? I don't think so! Start hauling Steuben ornaments and Swarovski crystal before you all get pink slips in your Christmas stockings!" Back in work mode she must have forgotten I was there because she clicks off and boards an elevator without bothering to say goodbye.

Henry glances at me over his shoulder and smiles, as he smoothly slides a congenial arm around James, guiding him through the tent flap leading to the as-yet-in-progress restaurant. The exotic Mira follows the men, pouting. She also throws a glance back at me before crossing the canvas divide, but there's no trace of a smile this time, only daggers.

I jump when Jane entwines her arm through mine. My whole body had been coiled like a spring, completely on the defensive. "Sorry," I say to the brash, gum-popping girl as she leads me to the ascending escalator.

"Don't be afraid, hon," she says conspiratorially, giving my arm a friendly squeeze. "You're in good hands. No one here at Macy's is going to stand by and watch you go into that photo session when you're not looking your best." She pulls out a radio, and says into the mouthpiece, "Penelope, come in Penelope. Meet me at the Benefit counter. One word: unibrow. We have a situation."

Situation? Five minutes ago, I would have told anyone who'd listen that I was looking pretty darn good. Now, shoppers on both the up and down escalators were scrutinizing my face like they were an army of eagle-eyed Eileen Fords from the Ford Modeling Agency.

"Copy."

"FYI, I'm escorting Miranda Nichols's niece."

There's silence on the other end of the walkie-talkie as we get off the escalator and walk onto the first level of the World's Largest Department Store along with tourists and other holiday shoppers.

"Jane, come in Jane," says the voice through the radio.

We walk through brightly lit areas featuring cosmetics and perfumes, each brand's crew of salespeople glamorous and beautiful in their own way.

"Go for Jane."

"I'm at the Brow Bar. Claude-Marie is standing by. Out."

We turn toward the southern wall of windows, and I see a petite young girl with clear, creamy skin wearing a cashmere twinset and a neat, matching headband. It's Penelope, the girl with the exquisite taste who chose all the clothes that got delivered to me. Next to her, in a lab coat, stands a Diana Ross lookalike with skin so rich and dark it's nearly a shade of midnight blue.

Jane points to the striking beauty with the glossy red lips and doe eyes. "That's Claude-Marie. She's the best, you're lucky." She leans in and whispers, "Emma Watson's look? Claude-Marie. Rihanna's first shaping? Claude-Marie."

"I've really only ever trimmed my eyebrows with nail scissors," I explain. Jane laughs, and I see Penelope the personal shopper and fashion plate furrow her brows, and mark something down in the Moleskine notebook she's carrying.

Before I can argue, I'm seated on a high stool and the girl with the wild, glossy hair is dabbing warm wax above my eyes. She lays on strips of linen and *riiiiip.*

"What the HELL!" I scream, sitting bolt upright. Several women, and one man, seated in stools around me glance over.

"One more to go, so sit back and breathe," Marie-Claude advises, "unless you want to go around looking like you question everything anyone's saying."

I submit, clenching my fists around the seat of the stool. When she tears the second strip, I manage to contain myself with a subdued, "OWCHIE *Mama!*"

The three girls analyze my skin and discuss my coloring while Marie-Claude finishes the exquisite torture of my brow shaping by using a precise and pointy pair of tweezers to pluck and pull. From time to time, she dabs at the corner of my eye with a tissue to stave off fat tears.

She shows me how to use several different light and dark sticks, powders, and pencils to correct my brow, highlight it, and accent the brow bone. She lines my eyes with a bluish-white stick that she declares is "Like a nap in a tube."

When I look in the mirror, I'm astonished. I look confident, rested, and bright-eyed. "Now she needs color," Marie-Claude counsels. "I have a client due, so you'll have to walk her over to one of the other counters."

"Oh, I know!" exclaims Jane, "Let's do Urban Decay!"

Penelope closes her eyes, and shakes her head patiently. "Baby steps, Jane. We don't want to throw Charlotte here into the deep end of the pool. Clinique it is."

After seeing Jane's bold and bright makeup, and Marie-Claude's theatrical visage, I'm worried that my makeover will leave me looking like I'm going to the West Village Halloween Parade. Luckily, Penelope steers the ship and I leave Clinique with a flawless complexion, accented in creams, pale pinks, and sheer corals. I should have trusted her. After all, she's responsible for the classic outfit I'm wearing. I make a mental note to ask her about the meringue of a nightie, but she's on a mission and she's not wasting time with chit chat. Jane, on the other hand, talks nonstop.

"You look like a bride," Jane fawns, as I'm frog-marched over to

Blow, the Drybar for a touchup on my hair. "I see your finger's bare. Hold out for a big solitaire. Your man looks like he can afford it."

"What man?" I ask. Penelope plunks me down in a hydraulic chair, and a veritable pit crew of hairdressers rushes at me, throwing a cape around my shoulders, spritzing my hair with water, and combing it out with a wide-toothed comb.

"That sexy Henry! God, I'd give my right boob if a guy like that would look at me the way he looks at you."

That's plain silly, I think. Before I can protest, a loud dryer blasts on cancelling out all conversation. He's just one of Aunt Miranda's "people" who's helping me find my beloved baby. Or maybe these past couple have days have taken us a step further. He's a friend, a good friend, who's helping me out in my hour of need. That's as far as it goes, though.

I'm nudged forward until my head is between my knees. Should I tell the stylist that all the blood is rushing to my head, I wonder? How long could this really take, I ask myself, and decide to just go with the flow. I'm feeling very Zen at the moment. I keep replaying Henry's pledge that he'll find Hudson back on a continuous loop in my head. The repetitious and rhythmic pull of the round brush, the warmth of the air, and the need to close my eyes all conspire to lull me into a dreamy state.

An image of Henry appears in my head snuggling Hudson to his chest, my little dog's muzzle nestled in the crook of Henry's neck, and I drift off in a half-hallucination. My hand reaches out to pat Hudson, and Henry turns his face to gently kiss the back of my hand. I can't tell if I'm watching the movie, or I'm in the movie.

Henry's face is soft. He's mouthing something, but I can't hear the words. I'm reaching out to touch his face, but he takes my hand instead, and slides a ring on my finger. The cold of the metal is electrifying. He puts Hudson down at my feet, and my boy is jumping and twisting in the air, barking and barking. I'm so happy I cannot stop laughing. Cut to us running as fast as we can, Hudson chasing us with his tongue flapping. Henry and I are beaming at each other, me holding up my dress so I don't trip. Henry calls "C'mon, boy," to Hudson, and we fall. He lands on top of me. We're rolling, and rolling. Hudson licks both of our faces, walking over our bodies with his needle-sharp, little paws. Henry's on top of me, but I don't feel crushed, just warm. I love you, I try to say, I love you, but no sound comes out because Hudson is barking, and we're kissing and kissing...

I'm pulled up by the shoulders, and the dryer snaps off.

"...but it wasn't cancer in the end," Jane is saying in her high, nasal voice. "After all that, it was just a boil, so they lanced it," she continues. "And she went home with a Band-Aid and some sleeping pills."

I'm dizzy, and I struggle to come up for air.

"Girl, you look green," my stylist says. "Here, drink this," he says, uncapping a cold bottle of Smart Water and handing it to me. "If you wasn't feelin' well, you should've said somethin'. It's not everyone who can stay bent over in that position for that long."

"That's what she said," Jane chortles.

"Stop it," Penelope hisses, jabbing the snickering girl in the ribs. "Well I, for one, think she looks gorgeous."

Once the room stops rocking, I look at myself in the mirror. I have to agree. Between the hair and the makeup, I've never looked better. "Now let's get go get that photo snapped." In no time at all, I'm de-caped and spritzed, and the three of us are on our way.

"When Henry sees you, his eyes are gonna pop out of his head," Jane says.

This time, I don't even make an attempt to protest. I just silently wonder if she'll be right.

*****

We get off the elevator on the eighth floor of Macy's, and the holiday buzz hits me in the face like heat from an oven when I'm checking a cake. The song *Toyland* plays merrily and as we walk closer to the action, I see children all around me looking like they're about to explode with joy. A cheerful sign with a cartoon Santa and smiling kids shows us the way to go, and we pass under an arch labeled, *Santa's Workshop*.

All around are life-sized scenes featuring statues of elves hammering jack-in-the boxes, Mrs. Claus passing out trays of cookies, and lettered blocks large enough to sit on. Behind a snow-capped fence sits a shiny train emblazoned with the name, *34th Street Express*, in swirling gold letters, and a proud father holds up his little boy in front of it while the mother snaps photos. The little boy has glasses, and it makes me think of Henry as a child. Would he have enjoyed the thrill of Christmas in the City, or would the sheer magnitude of it overwhelm a child from a simple village. I decide he would have loved it, and I imagine a tiny Henry beaming with wonder like the little tyke in front of me.

As we round the bend to pass through yet another Christmas scene, this one with Santa's sleigh, I see adults who I know aren't all parents, lined up with freshly scrubbed kiddies, decked out in everything from their Sunday best, to elf costumes, to superhero outfits. I scan the crowd, wondering who among the grown-ups are grandparents, godparents, guardians, and social workers. There's a pang in my heart. Every kid, to a tee, looks caught up in the magic. You all deserve this uncomplicated joy, I think. I wish you all happiness, I say silently, beaming goodwill over the crowd.

We pause, to let a twenty-something girl dressed in a green-and-red felt costume lead a group of kids holding onto a clothesline with handles spaced evenly apart, and wearing t-shirts that say *Samaritan's Home*, to the front of the line.

I watch as a family of mechanical statues in a gingerbread house open presents in front of a decorated and fully lit tree. In a repeating scene, a mother embraces a pajama-clad girl in pigtails after she holds her dolly high above her head. Over and over, the girl rejoices, and the mother pulls her in for a hug.

Had my mother known she'd be leaving me early, would she

have made more of an effort to hit these well-known benchmarks of childhood? Would she have bought me My Little Pony toys, and Silly Bands? Would she have taken me to sit on Santa's lap? Would she have taken me to Disney?

Penelope signals for us to come with her, and we follow the winding path until I finally see the big man seated on his oversized chair, smiling benevolently at a sincere toddler who's exactingly explaining the size and shape of the toy he wants this year.

When I have a child, I think to myself, I will make sure he or she feels normal. My child will feel safe, and whatever my child's friends are into, I'll make sure my child knows about it. I want my child to have hoards of friends, and riotous birthday parties.

I burst out laughing, surprised at myself. When James had talked about having a boy who liked surfing like he did, or a girl with my green eyes, I'd told him I didn't want kids. At the time, I didn't think I had enough to give. Or maybe I just didn't want kids with James.

"Come on, Charlotte, you're up," Penelope says, tugging at my elbow.

She signals the photographer, and leads me to a little gate in the fence that's barely knee-high. She pushes it open, and sends me through before it springs back shut. I walk the faux cobblestone path leading to Santa's big chair. There's snow on the ground that's scattered with giant pieces of foil-wrapped candy and all-day lollipops. Short fir trees dot the lawn, dripping with icicles and stuffed woodland creatures peek out from holes in the ground.

Santa smiles, his wire-rimmed glasses lifted by his rounded, red cheeks. True to form, he's wearing a thick red suit trimmed in thick white fur. His boots are the real thing not some costume overlay; they reach to his knees, and they have rubber soles. They're polished leather. Nice, but not as nice as mine, I think proudly. He beckons me over, and by the time I reach his knee, I'm stricken with shyness.

"Ho, ho, ho," he says theatrically. "Come tell Santa what you'd like this Christmas."

My heart is pounding, and I can't move my legs.

His demeanor changes, and he looks at me, really looks at me, with his kind, faded blue eyes. "Don't be shy."

"It's just, I've never done this before," I tell him. "Silly, really," I say, trying to laugh it off.

"I wouldn't say so." He stays very relaxed, breathing in and out like he has all the time in the world.

I make myself approach confidently and take my place on his knee. I notice that his white beard grows soft curls from behind his ears, unlike the beard of the skeevy Santa from Bryant Park. The photographer holds up his hand, and I raise my chin, and smile for the camera. I'm surprised at the big flash. It's been ages since I've had a photo taken with anything other than a cell phone.

"Again," the photographer says, "again." We do that several times until he signals that I should rest. He looks down, adjusting his camera.

"Well, then," I say to the man dressed as Santa Claus. "Thank you very much."

"But you haven't told me what you want for Christmas."

I feel myself blushing. "There are kids waiting."

He says, very calmly, "You've waited your turn. I'd say you've waited a very long time."

When I think about what I want, my throat constricts. I make a move to rise up from his knee, but he very gently pulls me back in. "What would you like for Christmas?"

"My dog is lost," I whisper. I clear my throat, and say a little louder, "I want him home."

He doesn't smile, but he fixes me in his gaze, nodding. His watery blue eyes sparkle. "Don't worry. You'll get Hudson back."

"Charlotte," Henry calls, waving above the heads of the crowd. "Over here!"

"Henry!" I'm so happy to see him. I look up and smile, and see one final flash, and the photographer says, "Now that's my shot!"

Penelope opens the fence, giving Henry access to the area, and I blink, taking in all of the activity around me. It's like I just woke up. Eager to get out of the spotlight, I hurry to the exit where there's an elf to lead me through. Looking back, I see Henry shake the old man's hand. The man says something, and Henry bends down to whisper in his ear. Penelope and Jane have crossed behind Santa's set-up to meet me, and Penelope signals to Henry to come through the elf exit.

"Do you want to wait for the photos?" she asks. "I can put a rush on them."

"Could you have them messengered to the Waldorf?" Henry asks. "If so, please put it on Miranda Nichols's account."

"Of course, sir." She smiles professionally. "Macy's would be happy to do that."

"I have to say, Penelope, Macy's has treated me unbelievably well. First these amazing clothes...the sizes are perfect and I never dreamed I would wear styles like these, but I love them. Thanks for everything you did."

"All part of my job."

"And the makeup, and the hair..."

"She's gorge," Jane says. "A real Macy's girl."

Henry sizes me up. "I thought you looked different."

"Men!" Jane laughs, a little too loudly.

"And prepping Santa Claus for my arrival. Do you do that for every kid?"

"What do you mean?" Penelope asks.

"You know, telling him who I am. Was that because of Aunt Miranda?"

"If I'd have thought of it I would have, but I didn't tell him who you are."

I look over at Santa Claus, jostling a giggling kid wearing a cowboy hat on his knee. He looks up from the boy and straight into my eyes. "Believe," he mouths.

"Come with me please, Charlotte," Henry says briskly, nearly breaking into a run. "I've a very important matter that requires urgent discussion." He grabs me by the hand, and we blow through the sitting room of the suite at the Waldorf, leaving Landry and the rest of the interns staring as we head directly into Henry's bedroom. He slams the door closed behind us and falls down backward onto the big, white down-filled duvet like he's making a snow angel.

"Are you well?" I ask.

He cracks up laughing. "Never better," he affirms.

"What has gotten into you? You practically skipped across town, and when we finally hopped that cab, I think the driver was fairly surprised that you not only caroled from the back seat, but demanded figgy pudding."

"Who's being an old Scrooge now? It's almost as if you wish I'd stayed onsite at Macy's to work through the night."

"No, I'm glad you didn't. Frankly, I thought Miranda might insist."

"Oh, she tried," Henry said, standing up on the bed. I stood gaping at him. "But you should have seen me. First she lunged, with a 'Getting on James Keyes' good side could be a career builder'," he mimed a fencing gesture, hand on hip, posture perfect. "But I parried," he says, dancing backward, "saying, 'your niece is distraught.' She nearly had me with, 'The mayor might drop by later for a spot check,' but I triumphed," he says, flicking his imaginary rapier, "by pointing out that she was leaving you alone at Christmas time."

"What has gotten into you?" I ask, shaking my head and laughing.

"Freedom? The holiday spirit? All I know is that I feel drunk, even though I haven't touched a drop. I haven't skived off classes or work since…you know what? I don't think I ever have!"

He reaches down, and grabs me by both hands. He pulls me up on to the bed, and starts jumping up and down like we're on a trampoline.

"Henry!" I scream.

"What? Do you think they're going to kick us out of the Waldorf for jumping on the bed? I've handled royals and rock starts in my line of work. Trust me, this is nothing."

Swept away by his sudden onset of festive joy, I start to jump in earnest, still holding his hands. At first, we're jumping at odds like a seesaw going up and down, but eventually we're in sync, bouncing together. We're staring at each other in collusion, gasping from the laughter.

"Excuse me, Henry," Landry is standing at the door, eyes averted. "I wondered if you wanted to do a debrief before we have to head back to the office." I freeze, and wind up wobbling. I fall toward the sunken middle of the bed where Henry is standing. I scrabble for ballast, and wrap my arms around his knees. He crashes down on top of me, and we wind up a tangle of arms and legs, flailing like upturned beetles, trying to find a foothold on the squishy bed.

"I'll leave you two alone," Landry says frostily, backing out of the door.

"Wait!" I call. I'm huffing to catch my breath. "Don't go!" I'm up on my feet and following her. "Do you have any information about Huddie?"

"Yes," Landry answers, speaking not to me, but to Henry. "As I was saying, Shanna needs us back at the office, so I'd like to download what we know, Henry, if you have the time."

Henry steps down off the bed, adjusting the tails of his shirt and running a hand through his tousled hair. "Of course. Go ahead. I'll be right with you." Landry stands in the doorway, not moving.

Eager to hear the news, I pass her by. "He's all about the work," she mimics in a high-pitched voice. "Yeah, right," she snorts.

I join the three other junior staff at the card table they've dragged over to annex the coffee table at Hudson Central. Folder, printouts, and photographs line every surface and the two young men and the young women all have their noses pressed to the screens of phones, tablets, or laptops.

Henry eases up, hands in his jean pockets, surveying the stacks. "Fill me in."

"This stack contains what we've deemed to be credible leads. There are photos of Hudson here from places we know he's been such as the Empire State Building, Times Square, etcetera, etcetera." I pick up a picture from the top of the stack. It's of a smiling, curly-tongued Hudson in front of the first-floor security desk at the Empire State Building just out of the sight of the guard who told us no dog could possibly have darkened the building's doorstep.

"This stack is a maybe pile. We printed out tweets and posts describing sightings of a mixed-breed dog, and made copies of photos showing various dogs that might be Hudson." I read one of the tweets:

Mutt dancing to Mariachi band on a train platform. QT! Only in NYC #vacay

Underneath is a picture of the backside of a dog wearing a scarf being led through Bloomingdale's revolving doors, but the dog is solid beige, and is as big as a Great Dane. "This definitely isn't Hudson," I say.

Landry snatches the picture from my hand, and lays it on a different stack. "Then we'll put that in the False Leads category."

"Talk to me about next steps," Henry says, back in business mode.

"We think that the most compelling leads should be handed over to the police," Landry begins.

"I can take care of that," I say. "I'll call my friend Craig. He's a police officer," I explain to the group. "If he needs the physical papers, I'll messenger them over."

"We've been contacting anyone with a likely story by phone,

text, and social media. Obviously, we haven't been able to get contact info for everyone, but we've left messages when possible, and we're fielding responses."

"The whole thing's starting to pick up steam," the red-headed guy in the hipster cardigan with the roll neck says to Henry. "Check it out," he says, holding his phone up to show a video. "*Animal Planet* caught wind of the story, and they're running an interstitial showing lost pets while they play sad Christmas music. Hudson's photo is the lead and the closer."

"Oh my gosh!" I exclaim.

"Gray's Papaya has posters up at every store in Manhattan, right next to the ones that say, '*We are polite New Yorkers*'. They say, '*Be Kind and Find*'."

The other girl hands me a sheath of papers. "The whole city seems to be having fun with this story. Look, Magnolia Bakery has a cake in the window with his face on it. This group from New York Road Runners doing a 5K along the river, are all wearing t-shirts that say, *Looking for Hudson on the Hudson*." She pulls out a picture of a group of firefighters. "I printed this one out in color." It says, "Engine 3/Ladder 12 of Chelsea asks HAVE YOU SEEN THIS DOG?" Four super-built fireman, wearing sleeveless, ribbed white t-shirts with braces and their fireproof trousers surround the front page of *The Post* on which Hudson poses with Ruby. "It's up on their website. After I saw that, I started calling fire stations up and down the island, asking them to do the same." She stops to smirk. "After work, I'm going out with one of New York's Bravest who I met on the phone. His name's Diego. Jealous much?"

Landry types into her iPad, and pulls up another video clip. "New York One News has picked up the story. Someone from the office saw it on TV in a cab about an hour ago and called to let us know." We all watch for a few seconds as Pat Kiernan, the news anchor famous for simply flipping through the papers at his desk and reading out what he finds interesting, holds up a *Daily News* with Hudson's picture in it.

"So cute and dorky," breathes the young woman, who's sorting paperwork. "LOVE Pat Kiernan."

"Everyone does," Landry coos back.

"Hey, that's the *Daily News*," I point out. That means the story is in two major local papers!" The other young man hands me a copy, and I flip to the story on Hudson. It's a picture of Hudson, wearing a thick sweater with the I Heart New York logo knit into it, sitting on the lap of a twenty-something in an electric wheelchair. *Service Pig Shares Slop*, declares the headline. Beneath the larger photo, is a smaller one of a potbelly pig and Hudson, front feet on the table at Serendipity, lapping up one of their signature jumbo Frozen Hot Chocolates while the young man and his family look on, beaming.

I start reading out loud.

"We have documentation for Daisy, because she's Bobby's service animal, of course. Bobby had a brain injury during birth, and his muscles get stiff. He communicates with a computer board. Like I said, Daisy has papers, but we had to sneak this little fella in," Lisa Shore, 48, tells The Daily News. "Ryan saw him on the sidewalk and let us know he wanted to keep him. I told my son that if the dog's a stray, we'd bring him back to Omaha when we go back after New Year's Eve. My boy's got such a big heart. We bought that sweater at the little souvenir shop around the corner because Bobby thought the little fella looked cold." Bob Shore, Senior, chimed in with a plea to find the now missing mutt. "We finished lunch, and in all the commotion of getting our coats on and making sure Daisy got a walk, the little guy disappeared. We hate to think of him alone in a big city like that." The Shores ask readers to call The Daily News with any information.

"I've saved the best for last, Henry," Landry says, ignoring me. "I talked to one of my friends who works for Rita O'Dowd. You know, the publicist."

"Of course. Her firm handles New York City's tourism campaign, The MOMA, and other high-fliers. She's huge."

"I know. Right? Well, my friend said they're pulling out all the stops to push Michael Bublé at the Rainbow Room tonight. The blizzards earlier this month had a real impact on tourism, as you know, and they aren't even close to being sold out like they thought they'd be. You aren't going to believe this! They're offering dinner for two, and cocktails with Michael to anyone who shows up with Hudson."

"Excellent job, Landry. And the rest of you, as well," Henry enthuses. "See Charlotte? I said we'd have Hudson back by the end of the day. All right, guys," Henry continues, glancing at his phone. "Shanna is getting quite cross with me for not jettisoning you back to the office. Don't worry about sorting this. I'll deal with it. Leave me the tablet, but you can take your laptops. We already have one each."

"All right, people, that's a wrap," Landry says, clapping her hands. "Henry, these guys can take off, then you and I can finish up here and cab it back together later, maybe after we grab some dinner." She sticks out her lower lip, and finally deigns to turn her focus to me. "You look exhausted, Charlotte. You've got huge dark circles under your eyes." My thumbs fly up to wipe away any errant mascara that might have smeared when I was crying with laughter earlier. "Why don't you go lie down while Henry and I nail this down?"

"Oh, OK. Maybe I'll call Craig at the station house." As pleased as I am with all of the news of Hudson, I feel like the air has been let out of me. After Henry's change in mood earlier, I had envisioned that he would continue playing hooky while we waited for things to develop. But finding Hudson trumped everything. If I needed to get out of the way, I would.

Henry types into his phone, answering a text. "Shanna's asking for you, Landry," he tells her, not bothering to look up. "Says she has a hot project, and you're the only woman for the job. My

185

loss. People," Henry says to the interns, "hang back for a moment. You'll be traveling back with Landry." He slides his phone into his pocket. "Right, let me get you your coat," he says, not wasting a minute before crossing to the closet.

There's a knock, and Landry answers it as if she owns the place, pushing all of her co-workers aside. "Delivery for Miss Charlotte Bell," the bellhop says. Landry takes the package, and closes the door without so much as a thank you.

"The photos from Macy's," Henry says. Without asking, Landry opens the envelope with my name written clearly on it, and slides out the contents. Inside are various sized images of me. It looks like a packet of school pictures, with the one large, farmable photo, then sheets of two, four, and eight smaller ones.

Henry takes them from Landry's hands. "These are great, Charlotte, come look."

I wince. I hate looking at photos of myself. He holds up the 8x10. "This is gorgeous. Look at your eyes." I force myself to look over his shoulder. My pupils are enormous, giving me the look of a Japanese anime cutie. "You look so, I don't know, alive?" he says. "Like you've got a secret."

He hands the largest photo to Landry, and she quickly slides it into her leather folder. "See that this gets posted everywhere, Landry. Once New York gets a look at this girl, its citizens will start working overtime to see that she's reunited with her little dog."

Landry turns her back on me, and glosses her lips in the hall mirror. The others are still rushing around, straightening piles of paper, stacking lunch dishes on the room service cart, and pulling on their coats and hats. Henry lays the rest of the photographs on a side table. I watch him glance at Landry before folding the smaller page into quarters, tearing along the edges before putting one of the 4x5s into his pocket.

"Look," says the redhead, hand-knit fingerless gloves in hand. I swivel to see what he's talking about. He's pointing to the corner windows. "It's snowing."

"Then you'd better hurry if you're going to find a cab," Henry says, pushing them out the door.

Just as Henry is about to push the door closed, Landry sticks her foot in to block it. Immaculate in her well-cut coat, and carefully selected winter hat, designed not to crush coifs, she makes one last-ditch effort. "What if I called my friend at Rita O'Dowd and had her reserve a table for us? We should probably have someone on the ground at the Rainbow Room, just in case the stunt pays off."

"You've just said it yourself, it's a stunt. Better to focus our energies where they're effective. Thanks all," he calls, as the door closes. "Bye, Landry," he says. I catch one last glimpse of her flawless face, her full lips rounded in an "O" of surprise, then she's gone.

Henry marches over to the divan and flops backward as if he's just gone twelve rounds in the boxing ring. He drapes his forearm over his eyes, and breathes. His shirt is pulled to the side, and I can see the slightest hint of the carved ab muscle rising up from his hipbone. I quickly focus on the window, as he sits up and sighs.

"I got pretty excited about the whole Rainbow Room thing. You think it's a stunt, huh?" I pull back the drapes, and take in the sight of this part of the city filtered by a screen of fluffy snowflakes. "I was hoping that might be the tipping point to getting people to bring Hudson back."

"On the contrary." He hugs one of the couch cushions, eyes glinting. "I fully expect to find Hudson there tonight."

"But you just told Landry it was a waste of time."

"Having dinner at the Rainbow Room with Landry would be a waste of time. Can you imagine me having to spend my first, and possibly only, night at the Rainbow Room forcing conversation with someone so fresh out of college that her stories are still regularly peppered with what she and her friends did in high school? I had to take a van with her to scout a location for one of Hilary Clinton's stump speeches, and I nearly opened the door and shoulder-rolled out after less than an hour. As you pointed out, up to now I haven't really experienced New York despite the

187

amount of time I've spent here. Soon, it'll be back to London, and with any luck, I'll be a big fish in a little pond there."

A wave of wistfulness passes over me as I imagine him no longer being in the country. At this point, I can hardly imagine being separated from him. These last two days have been about as intense as I've ever experienced.

"So," I say, feeling uplifted with hope, "you think there's a chance Hudson could turn up tonight."

He pulls out his phone. "More than a chance. I'm calling Rita now."

"You know her?"

"My world is a small world. Everyone knows everyone in this business. Miranda taught me early, don't make enemies because people hop around from firm to firm, and never, pardon my French, make *merde* where you eat. It also doesn't hurt that Rita owes me a favor," he says, dialing the number. "Fancy being my date for the Rainbow Room tonight? Oh, one sec," he presses the phone to his ear, "Henry Wentworth for Rita, please."

His date? My stomach does a forward flip. Apart from Kenny in the park, I haven't even contemplated going on a date since James.

"I'd hate to wait for Hudson all by myself," he says, covering the mouthpiece with his hand. "Hello, Rita! What impossibly good luck that you picked up, busy woman like yourself." He holds up the one-finger sign, telling me to wait, and heads into his bedroom and shuts the door behind him.

I gaze out the window at the snow falling on the Midtown street below. It's coming down at a steady pace. Even with the holiday traffic on the streets, and the melee of shoppers on the sidewalk, a light coating is starting to form, making the city feel sparkly and fresh. Surely he didn't mean a real date? Like he said, his world is small, and one shouldn't make *merde*. I'm Miranda Nichols's niece. It's his job to get my dog back. And once Hudson's back, we'll go our separate ways.

I fix my gaze on a couple running across the street in the middle of the block, holding hands and dashing around the slow-moving cars and cabs. You can just tell they're giddy from the snow, and that being in love is making them reckless. "Be careful," I want to shout but I'm too far away. "You'll get yourself crushed!" Before I'm too deep in my worry, they're safe on the sidewalk, stopping for a kiss.

"Charlotte," Henry says, "are you all right?"

"Yes. Of course."

"This all must be very hard for you," he says, approaching. "And I've been running you ragged all over town."

I try a smile, but I find myself searching his face. His expression changes from interested to concern. "How insensitive of me. I got caught up in my own fun. I should have been thinking about your welfare. I apologize."

"Really, I'm fine."

"Maybe it's better if we skip the Rainbow Room," he says. I shrug noncommittally. If that's what he wants, that's fine with me. The last thing on earth I want to be is a girl like Landry. I've always been fine on my own.

His phone dings in his pocket. He pulls it out, checks it, then holds it out for me to see.

U R Confirmed. Bublé @ Rainbow 8 pm, second seating. Enjoy! Rita

"Just give me the word, and I'll cancel the reservation. All the irons are in the fire. I can spend the evening catching up on work, and fielding any responses we get regarding Hudson. You can rest if you'd like."

I feel like a sea anemone, reaching out my thousands of branches toward him, trying to get a feel for what he's thinking. He seems tense. Did he sense that I might have sort of wanted it to be a date? Is he horrified, the way he looked when Landry was coming onto him with both barrels?

189

"What do you want to do?" I ask him.

"I asked you first."

I wait. I learned a long time ago that if you sit still and stay quiet, people will usually tip their hands. He doesn't fall for it. He stares at me, refusing to look away. The thought of sleeping in this big suite all by myself feels unbearable, and the thought of going home to my empty apartment feels even worse.

"OK, on three let's both say what we want to do. It's an old trick I learned at boarding school when the girls in my dorm went in together to order food. On three, we'd shout 'pizza,' 'Chinese,' or 'falafel.'"

He narrows his eyes at me. "How do I know I can trust you? I recall more than one instance when my mates and I counted to three on the side of a freezing cold swimming pool, and I'd wind up the only idiot in the water. And that's not the only time I've been left with egg on my face." His eyes darken, and I wonder if he's thinking about Patricia.

"How do I know I can trust you?" I ask, putting on a false bravado, pretending I'm only talking about the game. How do I know I can trust you, I think, when I don't trust anyone?

"I guess we'll just have to decide to trust each other," he says. "There's no way to find out but to do it."

I feel my breathing speed up. "OK then," I say, feeling like someone's stolen the oxygen from the room. "On three."

We count together, pumping our hands rock/paper/scissors-style, holding up the numbers. "One, two, three!"

"I want to go to the Rainbow Room!" I shout, unexpectedly loudly. All I could hear from him was "Blahbidy blah Rainbow Room!"

We both break into great, big grins. I feel like I've just gotten a pardon from death row. Henry looks like he's about to giggle.

"Right, then. Good," he says, blue eyes smiling.

"Good." I say.

"Meet you back here in an hour, scrubbed and polished."

Chapter 9

"Most girls I know wouldn't agree to walk in the snow, let alone suggest it."

The sun had set an hour ago, but there was no trace of winter gloom in the heart of Manhattan. The doorman of the Waldorf, in his lavish red-and-gold caped overcoat and velveteen hat whisks open the heavy glass door, and we pass under the awning's heat lamp, and trot past the taxi stand onto the white-blanketed sidewalk.

"Taking a cab seems silly. The Waldorf is only a few blocks from the Rainbow Room, and this way we can swing by and look at the window at Saks on 5th Avenue."

"It's very sensible of you to wear boots. I find it tiresome to wait patiently while women teeter along in shoes more suited for display in china cabinets than walking."

"I have to admit, I do have a pair of those in my bag." Penelope, the personal shopper, had thought of everything. Why she thought I'd need a gown, I'll never know, but I have to applaud her foresight in sending the slim-cut, charcoal Hugo Boss tux for Henry. Worn with a simple but shimmering necktie, it doesn't look stuffy at all. In fact, I'm shocked at how at-home he looks in it, given his what he told me about his upbringing. It's as though he's wearing jeans and a t-shirt. I suppose that's what they call panache. He's wearing that suit like a boss, in the manner of Daniel Craig or Colin Firth, or maybe David Beckham or Will Smith. When James used to dress up for events with a capital "E," he always looked like a wrapped package. Henry inhabits the tuxedo like a second skin.

I pat my oversized leather tote, brought to carry said shoes even though a teeny-tiny cocktail bag made to carry little more than a lipstick and a credit card would have been more appropriate. "Like all sane women in New York, I'll shuck my comfortable shoes right before walking in the door, and put them back on when I turn into Cinderella."

"I think you look cute as you are," he tells me, brushing snow off of his glasses. "It's very Annie Hall meets Cyndi Lauper, especially with that wooly cap."

The crossing light changes from a big red hand, to the outline of a person walking, and he takes me by the arm as we cross from Park to Madison. "I'm grateful that your hair isn't arranged in a great candy floss beehive, and affixed with can after can of gummy hairspray. I wouldn't want to breathe in all those chemicals when we're dancing later."

Dancing? I'd pictured eating dinner, listening to music, and a big reunion with Hudson, but dancing hadn't factored into my plan for the evening. I blushed just thinking about being in the middle of a dance floor under the scrutiny of strangers. "Sorry, I'm not a dancer," I tell him. Maybe he should have brought Landry after all.

"Nonsense, if you're breathing, you're a dancer." He grabs me around the waist, and pulls me in tightly as a food delivery man whizzes by on a motorized scooter. "Hey buddy, it's a sidewalk, not a side *ride!*" he chastises.

"Geez," I say, catching my breath. "Listen to you! Who says you're not a New Yorker?" I laugh as we walk along, hips bumping. "That was pretty brash for a buttoned-up Englishman."

"He almost took off your arm," he says. "There ought to be a law. Wait, there is a law," he says, chuckling. "And who says I'm buttoned-up?" As we walk, our bodies find a rhythm and we begin gliding in a fluid, cohesive motion, like ice-skaters. "I wrestled a goat, remember?" I crack up laughing at the memory.

"The positive ions in the air with the snow are making you goofy, you know that?" I ask. "I believe your kind are supposed to keep their voices at a reasonable decibel-level and stick to conversations about the weather and the roads, Sir England."

"My kind? That's rich, coming from you Miss Poshy-Posh Dainty-Lady. I'm making an effort at letting my hair down. You're the prissy one who refuses to dance."

"I just don't dance, that's all."

"Everyone can dance. What are you afraid of?" he asks, playfully, looking me in the eye. "That someone might see you loosen up? That you might show some *passion?*" He says this with a cartoonish Argentine accent. Letting go of my waist, he puts one hand on his belly, and holds the other out in a dramatic tango pose. "That, when you move to the rhythm, you might reveal your dark desires?" He does a very competent box step, wiggling his hips as he goes, and bobs his eyebrows at me.

I feel myself contract. That's exactly what I'm scared of. It's like a red laser has just been aimed at me, and I close down in fear. It had been a long time since I learned the value of a poker face. After the crash, Bridget had been helping me pack what I would bring with me to the States. Over and over, she told me how nice my Aunt Miranda was going to be to live with, and how exciting it I would find it to live in America. Her voice had sounded funny, like she was talking to an interviewer on a radio program, and not to me.

I shook my head no. "It's never going to be OK."

"Everything always comes right in the end," she said, gripping me by the shoulders, her eyes boring into mine. You have to believe that." I wondered who she was trying to convince, herself or me. "Believe."

"I'll try."

"You can't just try, Charlotte. You have to do it, with your whole heart. Will you do that, my angel?"

I nodded my head. "Believe," I told her.

I remember waiting with her in the foyer by the front door, for the car that would bring me to the airport. Surrounded by suitcases, and we sat scrunched together on a narrow steamer, holding hands. Her worn, crocheted sweater felt soft on my wet cheek, and it smelled like nutmeg and wood smoke. Up to that point, I'd held it together, going through the motions of the funeral, the goodbyes from my teachers and headmistress, the awkward visits from my mother's adult friends whom I'd wound up reassuring, without crying.

When I heard the machine-gun fire of the cattle grid as the car shot up our long drive, the tears had finally come. Bridget rubbed the back of my hand fervently, the strokes growing deeper and firmer as the sound of the tires came closer. I don't think she realized she was hurting me. I welcomed the burn as a distraction from the real pain I was feeling; the pain of knowing I'd be separated from her. When the car stopped, so did my heart. The uniformed driver stepped out to stretch his legs, and a social worker I didn't recognize climbed the stairs. I could see her ringing the doorbell through the glass pane, and without thinking I ran up the stairs and hid behind my bed.

What happened next is still a blur in my mind, but I know I begged Bridget to keep me. I swore I wouldn't be any trouble. She told me that I'd never been a bit of trouble, and that she wished she could take me home. She broke down crying until we were both hugging, rocking, and crying, her in a low-pitched moan and me in a high-pitched wail.

"Be a big girl, Charlotte. Time to go," the social worker had said, looking annoyed. "You don't want to upset Nanny." She gave Bridget a sharp look, as she pried my arm away, and led me back down the stairs. She opened the car door, and handed me a tissue without so much as a pat on the back. The driver wouldn't meet my eyes, he just busied himself with the luggage, coughing nervously between trips up and down the stairs.

Of course I didn't want to upset Bridget. The thought of it twisted my stomach in knots. I felt ashamed. I sensed I'd gotten her in trouble. And in the end, showing how I really felt hadn't gotten me what I wanted. Bridget still stood on the porch, crying and waving, and the new lady just stared out the window until I wiped my face and put on a smile.

I bow my head against the falling snow, and walk faster. I cross Madison at 50th Street, without stopping to look both ways, and Henry races up to stand between me and oncoming traffic. Between the snow, and the volume of cars, people are rolling along slowly, so he manages to hustle me to the other curb without incident.

"Hey," he says as we walk on toward 5th Avenue. "I got carried away. Of course you don't have to dance." The snow continues falling at a pace faster than flurrying without ramping up into a storm. We traverse the long avenue block in silence, until Henry finally says, "I wonder if we'll have a white Christmas this year."

"Maybe."

We keep walking past delis, and dollar stores, and hotel entrances. A door to a barbeque restaurant is open, and the sound of booming laughter and honky-tonk music spills out, along with a rush of warm air carrying the aroma of roasting meat. I feel Henry looking at the side of my face. I don't meet his stare. "Do you think Hudson will turn up tonight?" he finally asks.

"Hope so."

We keep walking, moving to the side to walk single file for a length of sidewalk to allow a group of business people to pass. I spot a lucky penny struggling to shine through the snow, and quickly bend to pick it up. When the crowd is gone, Henry and I fall back into pace, shoulder-to-shoulder. We walk like that till we near the end of the block.

"I haven't been with a girl since Patricia."

My heavy heart swells like a helium balloon and rises into my throat. "Why would you tell me that?" I ask, making an effort to keep my voice dispassionate. It's incomprehensible to me how happy that piece of news makes me feel.

We keep moving forward, crunching through the half-inch of snow. "To make us even."

I get it. If I'm exposed, he's exposed. I feel supported, the way people who lose their hair from illness must feel when loved ones shave their own heads in solidarity. A liquid warmth flows through my veins, as we round the corner to where St. Patrick's Cathedral, the Roman Catholic neo-Gothic church stands formidable and solemn, across from the Art Deco-influenced buildings around the Rockefeller Center.

"That," Henry says, eyes drawn heavenward by the arches toward the lofty spires, "is impressive."

"You've never been inside?" I ask. I'd been on field trips to the city from school in which we'd sketched various statues for art class, and studied the history and architecture of the landmark. In addition to being a New York City attraction and a standout example of its architectural movement, it's a fully functioning parish, with neighborhood members whose life-cycle events are celebrated there.

"I haven't, but if you don't mind, I'd like to go in now."

We file through the majestic bronze doors along with tourists, worshippers, and congregants, into the back of the grand house with its Tuckahoe marble carvings, and enormous stained-glass windows, some of which were designed and executed by Tiffany & Company. The floor is slippery from the tracked-in snow, and I take Henry's arm to make sure I don't fall down in the shuffle.

In the front of the church, at the tallest and most ornate of the altars, a richly dressed Cardinal officiates a wedding mass. I look up and around to see where the sweet and haunting music emanates from. One of two huge pipe organs, the one in the choir gallery is being played by a skilled musician, and accompanying her are the voices of the choir and the celebrants. I don't know the hymn.

Mother never set foot in a church again after having been dressed down by an ancient, horrible vicar who all but excommunicated her when she announced she had no plans to marry my father.

Unused to being in churches, during services, I stay to the back in an effort not to be disruptive. A plaque stating, *All Are Welcome*, sets me at ease. I take a seat on a red leather cushion in an antique carved wooden pew, and take in a breath, noting how calming it is to be in a space with such sprawling overhead spaces. The smell of the incense transports me. I feel a sense of otherworldliness.

There is a spray of bridesmaids wearing tea-length, cranberry colored satin dresses, and in lieu of flowers are carrying puffy white furry muffs. To balance them out, there stands an opposite row of men in black tuxedos, accented with gold and green tartan cummerbunds and bow ties.

I'm transfixed by the backs of the heads of the bride and groom. It's clear from their posture that they understand that this is a solemn and formal occasion. They kneel, side-by-side as the priest says prayers over them, and makes declarations about the sacred state of marriage. But they can't help themselves. They keep turning to one another, smiling. It looks to me as if they are about to die laughing, though the words of the sermon speak about sickness, burdens, and loyalty till death. They can't help acting goofy. They're obviously in love, and they're making it look like a lot of fun.

I turn to point this out to Henry, but he's gone. I search the crowd frantically. Finally I spy him, kneeling at one of the small side altars. He leans over and stuffs a bill through the slot of a simple and very old metal box. He takes a long stick in hand, lights it with the flame of a flickering votive candle, and transfers the fire to an unlit one.

I know I shouldn't spy on his private moment, but I can't help watching him. He crosses himself, and bows his head. Forehead to fists, he stays bent serenely in that position for a very long time. Around me, the music swells. The Cardinal descends, and leads a processional of what I assume to be other priests, some swinging smoking incense burners, and still others showering acolytes with holy water from a golden bucket. When the clergy are gone, the bride and groom stand, turn and follow, marching down the center aisle toward the double doors. I stand up and watch them leave, along with everyone else, and I feel a hand on my shoulder. Henry puts his arm around me, and gently guides me to the side exit, where he flings open the door.

The snow is falling faster and thicker now, and the shine of it is blinding after the subtle, dim lighting of the cathedral. The streets are loud and vibrant in contrast to the serene atmosphere from which we emerge, and I'm filled with an air of promise, like something is about to happen. Even after this many years of living here, Manhattan still does that to me.

I check my watch. "We have time before our reservation. Are you up for walking down to see the windows at Saks?"

"Your servant, M'lady," Henry says, helping me down the snowy steps.

I give him the fish-eye. "See, I knew you spent your nights at school under the covers with a flashlight and a Harlequin romance novel!"

He looks affronted. "And why, pray tell, do you not think I speak in the tone of the immortal Bard, Shakespeare himself?"

"Because you're goofball, that's why," I say scooping up a little snow and tossing it at him.

"Why, Miss Bell, I believe that's the nicest thing you've ever said to me. It certainly is a far cry from 'snobby asshat.'"

I feel color rise in my face like the mercury in a vintage thermometer, remembering back to when I first him. "Sorry about that." We cross the street, still arm in arm, dodging the urgent holiday traffic.

"Yes, well, you owe me one for that. And don't think I won't cash in when you least expect it."

"Oh look," I say, shouldering in among the crowds standing in front of the renowned Fifth Avenue Department Store.

"Cinderella!" According to the signs, the theme this year is *Fairy Tales in the City: An Enchanted Experience*. I hold onto Henry's arm as I drink in the opulence of the window. In it, a Manhattan skyscraper festooned with jewel-toned decorations and garlands dominates the background, expertly lit with a fantasy of sparkling, flashing, and dotted points of gel-covered lights. Down in front, a Mardi Gras-worthy Cinderella with hair half her own height, decorated with feathers and baubles, extends a pretty foot from where she's seated in a carriage crowded with life-sized wrapped packages and metallic, reflective Christmas-tree balls. Kneeling on a slanted, velvet-covered bench is her bearded prince, eyes filled with hope, presenting a glass slipper.

"Poor chap," Henry says. "Careful Charming," he warns, "things don't always go according to plan."

"This one's a happy ending, Henry. I've read the book."

"It's not over till it's over, isn't that what they say?"

Henry stands slightly behind me, so I don't have to meet his eyes. "I noticed you lit a candle," I say.

"I lit two, actually," he says. "One was for my parents."

I don't ask about the second one. "If I were Catholic," I say, continuing to gaze forward at the captivating scene in the window, "I'd light a candle for your poor broken heart."

"You sound just like my mother."

I wiggle out from the crowd, and head uptown, and Henry follows.

"Good. She sounds like a smart woman."

"Don't waste your prayers. Gruesome as it was, my heart and I dodged a bullet. We've survived on our own for a good long while. We're fine as we are, thanks."

The bells from St. Patrick's start to peal, and Henry looks down at his watch. "We're going to be late."

"Don't worry. It's right around the corner. We'll make it before the clock stops." I pick up my pace, dodging tourists, and walking like a real New Yorker. Henry is lagging behind, so I reach backward through the crowd and he takes my hand. We jaywalk across the white blanket of 5th Avenue, weaving through cabs, limos, and trucks. We are in the front door of the building, and make it through the elevator doors standing open at the ready. Before we know it, we're hurtling up to the sixty-fifth floor before the bells stop chiming. Quickly, I shuck off my red boots, and replace them with delicate silver high-heeled sandals with crystals along the straps.

Standing up, I take off my coat and fold it over my arm, and fluff my hair in the mirrored surface of the car.

"Well hello, Cinderella," Henry says, eyeing me appreciatively.

"I don't want to be her. You said her story wouldn't have a happy ending."

"No, I didn't say that. I said it's not over till it's over." The elevator door opens, and we're thrust into the middle of the most beautifully decorated room I have ever seen, enveloped in the sounds of a big-band orchestra. "That second candle I lit? It was for you. My wish was for your ending to be happy."

*****

"You said Rita owed you a favor. It must have been a big one," I say as I clink my Manhattan Perfect with Henry's 1915 G&T. He insisted we do old-school cocktails, the kind Bogey and Bacall would drink to complement the retro traditional American menu made with local ingredients. I didn't think I could be happier with our drinks, until the charismatic maître d' sets down a poppy seed-flecked amuse bouche in front of each of us. When I pop it into my mouth, it immediately releases a detonation of smoked salmon and tangy, soft cheese. I watch Henry savor, and I'm not lying when I say his eyes roll back in his head.

"Mmm…" he moans. "Dear God in heaven."

"Our table couldn't be any better. If Rita aimed to impress, she truly hit the mark," I say. We're seated at the edge of the dance floor, with the perfect view of the orchestra, and have a southern view of the city. It looks like I could leap out the window and grab onto the frilly top of the Chrysler Building.

My Manhattan must be going straight to my head, because the next thing I blurt is, "I'm glad you told me you hadn't been with anyone, or I'd suspect you and Rita had been an item."

"And what if we had?" He raises his eyebrows suggestively. "Would that have been too big a price to pay for this ringside table to Mr. Michael Bublé?" Circles of light rain down onto our crisp tablecloth from the jumble of crystal chandeliers adorning the ceiling. The affect adds to the otherworldliness of the experience.

I sip my cocktail, and look him straight in the eye. "If that were the cost, I would have just as soon cooked at home, thrown on a CD, and taken in the view on 77th Street."

I can see that the G&T isn't doing him a bit of harm, as he smiles recklessly and says, "Jealousy becomes you."

"I'm not jealous. Just concerned about your honor, that's all."

"What if pimping me out to Rita meant getting Hudson back?" he teased, signaling the waiter.

"Then I'd tell you when she says jump, you'd better ask how high, mister!"

"You're funnier than I imagined you would be," he says, giving me an appreciative look. "By the way, that shade of deep purple becomes you. I didn't say it before, but you look beautiful tonight."

"Thank you." I find myself twisting my napkin in my lap. Compliments embarrass me. Aunt Miranda tells me to throw my shoulders back and own it, but I'm not like that. Still, I feel warmth spreading over me. I can't tease apart whether it's from Henry's words or the cocktail.

"Do you know what you'd like to have this evening?" he asks, gazing at me with those impossibly clear cornflower blue eyes. I bite my drunken tongue before I answer with something flirty that goes one step too far.

The waiter shows up at our table. "I beg your pardon," he says to me, "but didn't I see a picture of you on the news? Sitting in Santa's lap? You're looking for your dog, right?"

"That's me."

"My name is Manuel. I want you to know you have my best wishes and prayers. I don't know what I'd do if Popcorn ran away. Especially at this time of year. Yes, you certainly have my best wishes," he says, shaking his head with a faraway look in his eyes. "Are you ready to order this evening?"

"We haven't had a chance to decide," Henry tells him. "Could we please have another round, and let you know in a few minutes?"

"Absolutely, sir. I'll be back momentarily with your cocktails."

Henry's eyes flick over the menu. "Have you decided?"

"I'd like you to order for me."

He cocks his head. "That," he declares, "is the last thing I expected to hear."

"Really?"

"Yes, really. You, Charlotte Bell, are not one to willingly relinquish control."

"I haven't been in control of anything since Hudson took off. Believe me, I'm used to knowing exactly what's going to happen next. I knew what I was going to eat, and when. I knew what time I'd be going to bed at night. When the cable guy would show up, within a four-hour window. I knew what coat I'd be putting on before I left my door. Nothing, and I mean nothing, in the last few days has gone as I expected."

"How has that been?"

"Uncomfortable. Nerve-wracking." I take in his crystal-blue eyes from across the table. "Thrilling."

"I'll toast to that," Henry says, raising his glass. "It's funny how life conspires to throw you off track, for better or for worse."

"Oh, I don't know if it was life that conspired," I tell him, helping myself to a lighter-than-air yeast roll from the breadbasket.

"Surely you don't mean that Hudson could be turning the gears that brought you here, to this moment."

I butter my roll, taking the time to make up my mind about whether I should bother trying to explain. "You don't know Hudson," I say, proceeding with caution. "Anything I say is going to sound really out there. I don't have any concrete, scientific evidence that Hudson, my dog, had a master plan. Of course I don't. But maybe the way Hudson has affected my life could be part of something immense and mysterious, part of a grand universal scheme." I check in with Henry to see if I've lost him. He's listening. Encouraged, I forge on. "In my heart, I know it that finding him that day..." I have to pause, and swallow. I don't want to cry in the Rainbow Room. "I know that finding him that day, when I really needed someone, was no accident. It was like he was waiting in at the back of that shopping bag, waiting for me. Are you with me at all on this?"

"Yes, I agree that it can feel like souls are brought together for a reason. If I hadn't met Will back at school, my whole life would be different." The expression on his face is hard to read. Our table's candle flickers and shadows play across Henry's face. "And of course, there's you."

That hangs in the air. Before I have a chance to react, the waiter comes to take our orders. "Are you ready, sir?"

"Let me ask the lady," Henry replies. "Are you quite sure you can tolerate my ordering for you? I know you requested it, but you're a chef. Do you trust me?"

"I'm finding that there's something to be said for surprises," I raise my glass to Henry in a toast, and he nods his head in acknowledgement.

"To pleasant surprises," he counters, raising his own glass.

"To start," Henry begins with an air of complete ease, "The lady will have the Maine diver scallop baked in its shell, and I'll have the Jersey farm beets with goats' cheese and cress." He has to speak loudly to be heard over the orchestra's swingy rendition of I Saw Mommy Kissing Santa Claus. To a member, everyone in the band could be a concert soloist. It's hard to believe the lily is

203

about to be gilded with the addition of Michael Bublé. For me, he's right up there with Frank Sinatra and Bing Crosby in the Christmas album department.

"For dinner, she'll have the crisp Long Island roast duck with orange-braised endive and huckleberries, and I'd like the Maine lobster pot pie with black truffle." He hands the waiter our menus. "And may we have a bottle of the Billecart-Salmon, Brut Reserve?"

"Of course, sir. Very good," the waiter says, backing away from the table.

"Thank you," Henry says, smiling graciously. I sit back in my chair, admiring how polite he is with the wait staff. When I'd first encountered him at the tree lighting, I'd chalked him up to being another James — one who sniffed out the importance of the people around, and saved good manners only for those in a position to help advance him.

"Pardon the interruption," Henry leans in to say. "We were talking about Hudson and his magic, weren't we?"

"Don't put words in my mouth. I never said he was magic. You're trying to paint me as a nutjob. I don't believe in astrology, and I don't think there's a guardian angel on my shoulder interfering in mundane daily occurrences like my grocery orders and my electric bills."

"I have never thought you were crazy." He smiles flirtatiously, raising that one eyebrow. "Eccentric, maybe, but not crazy."

"I'm not eccentric," I insist. "I'm as normal as rain."

"And in this day and age, in New York City, that makes you a standout, my dear."

"Back to Hudson," I say, staying the course. I really want him to understand me. "I don't think he's magic, like he's a witch or anything." I try hard to find the words. "But to me, it's not out of the realm of possibility that he wanted to throw me off kilter. For my own good." I shake my head. "He showed up in my life to make me comfortable when that's what I needed. And when I got too comfortable, he rocked the boat. I doubt I can make you

204

see what I see. Never mind."

"No, go on. Please." As we talk, the sommelier at Henry's elbow goes through the elaborate ceremony of uncorking and presenting the wine.

"It's like you lighting the candles. You have no proof that doing that makes a difference, but on some level you just believe. Anyway, let's forget it for now." I take the glass of bubbly I'm offered and sample it. It's delicious. "Like we said, I'm in the middle of something I can't control. I'll just jump off the cliff and see where the wind blows me. Take tonight for example. Will Hudson show up or won't he? I don't know." I take a long drink of my wine. "And that's going to have to be OK for now."

"That's the spirit," Henry tells me. His head bobs to the music, and his leg won't stay still. "I've informed the maître d' that we're here and waiting should the person show up with Hudson as promised." Our starters are served, and as we're enjoying them, the bandleader introduces Michael Bublé. Always inviting, he looks especially friendly tonight, and he treats the intimate crowd to a huge grin, and promises us a night we won't forget. He looks especially sharp in a slim-cut navy tuxedo and thin silver-cobalt tie reminiscent of Rat Pack style. When he launches into the first number, crooning like a champ, fingers snapping and heels tapping, I clap till my hands are sore.

I get lost in the music as my appetizer is cleared and replaced with my entrée. Henry can't keep still, drumming the table with his fingertips, and jiving along to the bass. I watch the animation in his body. For someone I had classified as a stick-up-the-rear type, he looked surprisingly free and fluid.

A couple glides by our table, doing a slickly executed version of the dance I recognize as the foxtrot, only because I saw it on *Dancing with the Stars.* They must be eighty if they're a day, but they dance like their bodies have never known aches or pains. When the music slows down, giving center stage to the smoky sax, my eye lands on a young couple, dressed in homage to 1940s style. I imagine that they saved for this big night out, and that it is likely a once-in-a-lifetime splurge, or maybe the only Christmas present they're giving one another this year.

Henry signals to the maître d' who bends close to Henry's ear. Henry asks the man something. He looks at me, then looks away quickly, shaking his head. I see Henry slip him a bill, and the man bows slightly, and heads off to attend to another table.

"Would you like dessert?" Henry asks, still bobbing to the rhythm.

"I would," I tell him, "But I don't think I have room for it. Listen, don't let me stop you from dancing. There are plenty of ladies around here who'd probably love to take a spin around the floor with you."

"Thank you, but I'm happy where I am."

"Really, I wouldn't mind. I'd actually like it if you did. As it is, I feel guilty of depriving you of a chance to dance to Michael Bublé at The Rainbow Room. I mean, honestly, how many people in this world have a chance to do something like this?"

"How many people, indeed?" he asks, devilishly, raising his rakish eyebrow. "Won't you regret having passed up the chance yourself?"

I blush. "It's just that I don't dance. You promised you wouldn't make me."

"And I won't," he says gently. "So please return the favor. I'd rather stay at the table with you than dance with someone else."

The rest of our wine is poured, and the bottle whisked away. As I soak in the smooth music and glittering atmosphere, it's as though time has stopped. It would be hard to imagine that down on the streets of New York City people are rushing home from work, picking up their dry cleaning, and popping out to the deli for milk. I breathe in the magic and allow myself to simply be. This moment, I think to myself, this is a very, very good moment.

The music dies down, to only the bass player keeping a steady beat, accompanied by the drummer whispering on the snare with

206

brushes, while Michael Bublé addresses the crowd. "This next song I'm about to do is a song near and dear to my heart, written by some amazing composers and lyricists. Tonight, I send this song out to everyone in the world who is hurting with a wish that they get what they need to heal. And I also send it out to the dreamers who dare to grab happiness where they can find it without worrying who might think it's right or wrong. You look like you know what I'm talking about, am I right, young lady?" He's holding out an arm, and pointing straight at me. The whole room turns to look, smiling with expectation. Eyes moistening, I give a small nod.

"That's right, I know you do," he says, giving me a megawatt smile that lets me know it's true. "There's goodness and right in this world, all we gotta do is believe…"

Smooth as cream, he segues into the lyrics of the lovely song as the orchestra swells to meet his voice. Couples drift onto the dance floor, in a slow sea of movement.

"Come on, Henry," I say, rising to my feet. I hold out my hand.

"Are you sure?" he asks.

"I want to."

He takes my hand, and leads me onto the parquet floor, expertly slipping one hand around my waist and letting it come to rest on the small of my back. His hand is hot through the silk of my dress's fitted bodice. He shows me how to hold his other hand, elegantly raised to ear level. And suddenly, I'm dancing.

Almost imperceptibly, he leads me with the palm of his upturned hand, and steers me with the flat of the hand on my body. I close my eyes, worried that if I think too hard, I'll fall over my feet. Michael Bublé's voice envelopes the dance floor like warm caramel around a marshmallow, and the smell of dessert wine and chocolate floats on the air. More couples join us on the floor, and Henry pulls me a little closer so that there's barely any space between us.

"Is this all right?" Henry asks, his breath warm on my neck.

"It's great," I say. "Wonderful." As the music swells to a crescendo, I lay my head on Henry's shoulder. His neatly trimmed beard brushes my forehead.

"What's your grown-up wish this Christmas?" he asks me. He hums along to the song, and I can feel his chest vibrating against mine.

"To be with you," is the first thought that scrolls across my mind. Content and safe in Henry's solid arms, this is how I want to feel. I squeeze my eyes shut tightly, and swallow. I feel confused. Admitting I want Henry, even to myself, is terrifying. I hardly know him, and besides, he's sworn off love. Add that he's going back to London, and I'm already mourning the end of an affair that never happened. Then there's the guilt.

"I want to find Hudson, of course," I murmur.

"That goes without saying," he responds, his rich voice making his chest rumble against mine. "But is there anything you want just for you?"

I hesitate. "Other than that, no."

Up on the stage, Michael and the band are bringing it on home, wrapping the song up with technical prowess and huge amounts of emotion. I open my eyes, and sneak a peek at Henry. I'm startled to find him looking right at me.

"I have a wish for this Christmas." He tells me, with no trace of teasing or flirting. "Would you like to hear what it is?"

"Yes," I whisper. And his lips are on mine. I slide both my hands high, encircling his neck, and he gathers me to him. The band eases out of the song, drawing out a high, sweet, poignant chord, and the cymbals ring to a fade. Gently, he pulls back from the kiss and rests his chin on my shoulder, embracing me. For a moment, we just breathe, together. Until I break the silence.

"Me too."

*****

208

"Please don't be sad," Henry says to me as he unlocks the door to our Waldorf suite. "I'm disappointed Hudson didn't turn up and the lead was false as well, but on the bright side going out to dinner took your mind off of the waiting for a few hours." He takes my coat, and hangs it in the hall closet.

I shake out my damp hair. The snow had really picked up, and we walked back from The Rainbow Room, holding hands the whole way. My mind had certainly been taken off of Hudson. I watch Henry as he takes off his overcoat, then his jacket. I take in the broadness of his back as he rolls up his sleeves, and the memory of my hands on his shoulders while we danced sends a jolt to my belly.

My conscience niggles me, so I urge my undisciplined mind to focus "Rather than distract myself, Henry, as much as I'd like to…"

He crosses the room and slides his arms around my waist. "Would you?" he murmurs.

Smiling, I lay both of my palms against his chest and push him gently away. The feel of his firm muscles under the crisp cotton shirt ignites memories in me that have lain dormant for years.

"We have to concentrate on Hudson," I tell him, forcing myself to disengage from his embrace.

He takes a bottle of Evian from the fridge, and pours us each a tumbler. "Absolutely," he assures, handing me a glass. "But it's very late. Our irons are in the fire and the only thing to do at this stage is to wait for developments. But first things first. I'll do a quick check of all our social media accounts, while you go dry your hair and take off those wet boots before you catch your death of cold. You won't do your dog a bit of good lying in the consumption ward of the hospital."

"Consumption! I'm not Camille, this is the twenty-first century. Further proof that you stay up late reading romantic novels."

"Maybe I do, maybe I don't. You can speak to my lawyers on the matter," he says with a mock-arch air. Now, get yourself into a hot shower while I take a peek at our accounts. I doubt much, if anything, has happened in the few hours we've been gone."

I hesitate.

"Go on, then," he says, taking off his shoes and sitting on the divan. He looks so deliciously casual in his shirtsleeves and socks. "I know you're worried about Hudson. But I'm not. So far, he's been treated like a king everywhere he's gone. It's just a matter of time before he's delivered back to your arms. Tomorrow is a new day, and we can tackle getting him back together after a good night's rest." He leans back on the couch, his long arm outstretched over the carved back. "Or after a good night, anyway," he says in a sultry voice.

I feel myself blushing, so I squeak out, "Sounds good," before turning on my heel and exiting into my room.

The combination of the hot shower with its soothing high water pressure and the effects of the cocktails and sparkling wine I enjoyed with dinner conspire to make me feel very languid indeed. Resting comfortably in the knowledge that capable Henry is on top of fielding all questions and communications regarding Hudson's search effort, I take the time to give myself the full spa treatment. I scrub, condition, buff, smooth, and anoint. By the time I slide into the plush robe, and blow-dry my hair, I'm feeling a confidence that I'm not used to.

I dip into the cosmetics that Penelope had sent over from Macy's, this time applying them with a surer hand after watching the in-store makeover artists. I go lightly on everything. I don't want Henry to think I have big ideas.

My bathrobe is damp, so I rifle through my clothes to find something to wear. There's my dirty sweat suit. Scratch that. After a day of wearing my fabulous new day wear and evening dress, it looks like an old skin I've shed, the way snakes do, because it doesn't fit anymore. I may have to burn it.

I could get dressed in what I wore today, or in another of the urban-chic day outfits that they sent over, but my hand brushes over the peignoir, and I get a wild tingling in my belly. I hold it up, examining the lace and ribbons. I've never worn anything this alluring in all my life. I check the white organdy panels and scrutinize how see-through they are. All opaque. Suggestive, but opaque.

Really, Charlotte, I tell myself, this covers more than your evening dress. And if I cinch the sash properly, I can cover all of my cleavage. I give it a try. Well, most of my cleavage. It's longer, that's for sure. It'll brush the tops of the slippers they sent. Oh, the slippers! I haven't even looked. I open the shoebox, and inside is a pair of ivory, kitten-heeled, satin brocade slippers with… wait for it… marabou feathers along the peep-toe strap. I've only seen these in black and white films or on the Victoria's Secret runway.

I slide my feet in, and am surprised at how comfortable they are given the wow factor. Maybe I'll just try on the peignoir, I tell myself, and if it's too much, I'll just put my turtleneck back on. Of course, if I'm going to do that, I have to put on the appropriate undergarments. Just for laughs, I slip on the ménage of silky, lacy, shiny, creamy lingerie, and take a look at myself in the full-length mirror.

I'm stunned. I don't recognize the woman I see as myself. She looks sophisticated, and self-assured. In an out-of-body way, I admit to myself that she's beautiful. I feel a pang of something I can't immediately identify. Is it sadness? Regret? It feels like a kind of a loss. I also see fear. What am I getting myself into? I look myself in my green eyes, and give myself a pep talk.

"Like Henry said, tomorrow is a new day. Change is good." In my own eyes, I see a slightly scared look, like I might bolt. I breathe in deeply, determined to take care of that girl in the mirror. I repeat my old mantra. "Everything will be fine. Believe."

Like magic, my spirit feels buoyed up, and a balloon of happiness and hope rises up to my throat and escapes through my mouth as a laugh. What am I worried about? Stepping out in a pretty outfit doesn't signify that I'm making a proposition. Henry is Henry. He won't take it the wrong way.

In the glass, I'm surprised to see my head tilt, and my eyebrows raise. But what if he makes a proposition? What will you do then? Quickly, I push the thought from my mind. "Time to go check in on Hudson's status," I tell my mirror self. She smirks. "Well, that's the first thing I plan to do, anyway," I insist, playfully sticking my tongue out at her and turning on my heel.

*****

When I finally work up the nerve to emerge into the sitting room of the suite, I see Henry sitting on the divan staring intently into his laptop as he types. He's taken a shower, too, by the looks of it. His hair is slicked back in dark waves, and he'd donned the signature Waldorf bathrobe. His glasses lay on the coffee table, and his electric blue eyes are like beacons in the dimmed light of the room. I consider saying something, but a cat has my tongue. He looks so handsome and inviting, that I'm afraid I'll repel him with my yearning.

I swallow, and force myself to stand still. I'm a grown woman, for heaven's sake, and he's a man who knows his own mind. After all, he kissed me on the dance floor. The thought of it turns my insides to liquid fire. I wait.

When he looks up, his expression changes from concerned to what looks very much to me like enchanted. Suddenly, I feel shy, and I want to retreat to the safety and anonymity of my bedroom. Before my hand reaches the doorknob, Henry has crossed the room and is standing nose-to-nose with me. He takes both of my hands in his, looking deeply into my eyes. His eyes close, and he leans in. My breath catches as I tilt my chin upward, and…his phone rings in his bathrobe pocket.

Immediately he turns away and pulls out the phone. "Yes, hello," he says urgently, holding up a finger to tell me to wait. He goes back to the coffee table, and starts typing very quickly. "No," he says. "No, that will not work. Are you listening? I said no. Hang on." Abruptly he stands up from the sofa, and crosses to his bedroom door. "Sorry, Charlotte, this is a real emergency, via Miranda. You'll have to hang tight."

Hang tight? I think. What am I, one of your buds? Some flunky from the office? Standing unmoored in the middle of the room wearing my come-hither negligee, I feel exposed and conspicuous. I cross my arms, and wait to see if he's coming back.

He does, but it's as a streak through the room. He hurtles out to the common area, picks up a stack of papers, and bullets right back to his bedroom, barking into the phone the entire time. He doesn't even glance at me. Now I really feel ridiculous. If a red-blooded Englishman would rather advance his career than pay attention to me, I clearly didn't have the enchanting effect I imagined I did. I try to catch his eye as he storms back through the room, holding up a hand to no avail.

"You must not have heard what I said," he hollers into the phone. "Do you enjoy being employed?"

That does it. Whatever scales had formed over my eyes had now dropped. Maybe it was the wine, but I must have invented the man who held me in his arms earlier. Henry was nothing more than Miranda's mini-me. Maybe he viewed me as a diversion while stuck on assignment here at "Hudson Central." Whatever the case, I wasn't going to stand around looking the fool. I stomp back into my room, and pull my frilly nightie over my head, replacing it with my terrycloth bathrobe.

I run the water hot as I can, soak a thick white washcloth, and press it to my face. I welcome the burn. It jolts me awake. I use the cloth to scrub off my makeup, and rake a brush through my hair. Just as I'm about to hurl myself into bed and shut off the lights, I hear a knock at the door.

"What do you want?" I yell through the door. I don't want Henry to see me.

"I want to talk to you."

"There's nothing to talk about. You're free to get back to work. Good night."

"Charlotte, open the door."

"No." I say. I can hear his feet shuffling on the carpet. I lean my face against the wood. "Go away."

"Charlotte, please."

"Just go and do your work." I close my eyes, feeling the coolness of the door on my hot cheek. "You wouldn't want Miranda to be disappointed."

The door jerks open, and I stumble forward, right into Henry's arms. He sets me upright, and pulls me by the hand to the coffee table. "We have a situation."

"I don't think 'we' have anything, Henry. In fact, don't stay here on my account. You should go to back to your office where you're obviously needed."

"Look!" he says sternly, pointing to the screen. Trending on Twitter is #HudsonStunt.

"I don't understand." I tell him, running my eyes over the various windows he has open on the two laptops sitting on the table. I can't make immediate sense of it, but judging from Henry's demeanor I can tell it's not good. Henry flips through various windows on the computer to show me how the public is saying the plea to find Hudson has all been a stunt. The PetCorps pet food Facebook page is filled with nasty jabs about the company playing on people's heartstrings during Christmas to make a buck.

Henry shows me a site called *Where on Earth is Hudson?* that has a moving circle, and a message board on which you can "share your adventures with Hudson." I scan the page. The stories range from being taken about a spaceship in an alien abduction with Hudson, to a tale about Hudson partying in Fiji with Jay-Z and Beyoncé, complete with photoshopped pictures, to something so obscene, I scream and flap my hands.

Another website parodies the Bill Murray sighting website, done up in the same fonts and formats as the one about the

214

famous comedic star. "It gets worse," Henry tells me. He googles Hudson + Lost Dog + Christmas and shows me that YouTube features parody songs to the tunes of *How Much Is that Doggy in the Window?* and *The Little Drummer Boy* talking about what a scam the Hudson story has been. On Gawker, there's a photo of a milk carton with Hudson's picture on it, with a caption that says, *Have you seen our scruples?*

I click on a few other windows he has up, and there's the photo of me sitting in Santa's lap prominently featured on Yahoo's landing page, under a headline that reads, *Grieving or Thieving: You Be The Judge.* I call up another story entitled, *Beauty and the Busted: Supermodel Ruby in Cahoots with Santa Scheme?*

"Ohmigosh! You have got to be kidding me."

Henry pulls the laptop from my hands. His expression is dark. "Don't read anymore. It will just upset you. Our hunt for Hudson has gone from a search and rescue mission, to a novelty reminiscent of *Where's Waldo* to a huge backlash. I am going to take control of this thing if I have to stay up all night." He turns his attention back to his phone, texting furiously.

I look at Henry with new eyes, feeling guilty. I should have been grateful, not judgmental. If there's anything I need right now, it's a Miranda clone. I feel sick at my stomach wondering if people will stop being charitable to Hudson now that these nasty rumors are spreading. My poor little dog. My hands start to shake.

"Henry, I'm scared." Up till now, Hudson really had depended on the kindness of strangers. I take a moment to send a plea out to the universe that people will continue being kind.

"Everything will be fine," he says, typing. He looks up, with an expression of pure conviction, "Believe me."

I do.

"Ok," I tell him. "What do I do next?"

He sighs, and puts his glasses back on. "To be honest, the very best thing you can do is leave me to it. I work better without distractions, and as diligent as I am, after seeing you in that nightie,

215

you are proving to be the mother of all distractions."

"You want me to go away?"

"Want isn't the word, no." For a moment, the driven expression he's been wearing fades, and flashes a wistful smile in my direction. "But it's for the best. The internet is a nasty neighborhood. You don't want to go there at night. When people are anonymous, they'll post all sorts of ugly lies and filthy language just to get a rise out of their victims. I don't want you feeling bullied. I'll have this sorted before morning. In the meantime, you should get some sleep and leave it to me."

"That doesn't seem fair."

"Sometimes what's right isn't fair. I want to get Hudson back for you." He rubs his eye under his glasses with his balled-up fist. "This really is the best solution."

As much as part of me wishes this night had played out differently, I had to agree. My only port in this storm is seeing Henry in action. He looks so capable and confident, and fully engaged in work mode. I will myself to pull away. My being emotional in front of Henry right now would blur his focus.

"Thanks for what you're doing. I'll leave you to it." Whatever I'd hoped might happen with Henry, however vague my plans might have been, at this moment Hudson's safety trumped everything. He nods in affirmation, lips a tight line, and ducks back into the laptop.

Just as my door is closing, I hear, "Charlotte."

I open the door a crack, and call, "Yes?"

"Tonight was a good night."

"One of the best," I reply.

*****

I wake up to the smell of coffee. The cracks of light around the curtains are dim. I check the clock on the bedside table. 6:49. I splash water on my face, drag a comb through my hair, and quickly brush my teeth. I pull on my hotel robe, and head out to check on Henry's progress.

"What happened? Do we have him back?" I ask, bursting through the door. Henry stands at the buffet, pouring coffee from a silver pot. His hair is wet, and he's wearing nothing but a white hotel towel around his waist. His face is serious. He doesn't seem to have heard me. "Henry?"

"Oh, good morning." He barely glances my way. He looks preoccupied, and I'm immediately worried. Given Henry's usual courtly manners, I'd have expected him to have dressed before coming into the common room, or barring that, to have pardoned himself for being half-naked. He doesn't even acknowledge it. He appears to have bigger issues on his mind.

"We don't have Hudson back, do we?"

"No, we don't." He says laconically. His phone buzzes on the table, and he darts to pick it up and check it. He takes a big slug of his coffee as he reads the screen.

"Were you up all night?" I ask.

"I'm fine," he says, avoiding the question. He sets his coffee down, and types something into his phone.

Then I see it. On the service cart that must have brought the coffee in lies Hudson's harness. "Henry? Where did this come from?"

He sighs and looks up. "Charlotte, why don't you try to catch a few more hours of sleep?"

"There's something you're not telling me." There's a torn envelope and a note on the coffee table. Henry sees me notice it, and he lunges to grab it. I get there first.

"Don't read that."

Ignoring him, I unfold it.

"Give that to me," he says, holding out his hand.

You Want Your Dog. I Want Your Money.
I'll Call Tonight at 3 a.m. To Give You Instructions.

"Oh my God!"

"It's more than likely a hoax," he tells me, hand on his forehead, massaging his temples. "I didn't want you to see that. I knew it would worry you. I had planned to be up and out before you woke up."

"But Hudson's been kidnapped! You weren't going to tell me." My blood is ice.

"I've been in touch with your policeman friend Craig since the middle of the night. The package showed up at the concierge desk not long after you went to sleep. He talked to his mates on the force who deal with this sort of thing. They all agree that it isn't credible. Nevertheless, they have detectives following up on it. It pays to have friends in high places."

I concentrate with all my might, trying to figure out what I should do next. Nothing comes to me. The panicky feeling comes back, the one from the beginning of all this, that makes my limbs go numb and my brain hum like a radio that can't be tuned in.

"I feel so guilty, Henry. Like I haven't taken this seriously enough. Like I've been playing a game."

"Nonsense. You've done exactly the right thing every step of the way. It's just different now." He clenches his jaw, and shakes his head. "Something has shifted. I have to change tacks. I've got a new plan," he says, eyes darting, "but I have to act quickly."

"What is it?"

"It would take longer to explain than to act on it," he says, taking the last drink of coffee from his cup, setting it down, and heading for his room. "I'm going to get dressed, then I have to go out. I think I know a way to get out in front of this thing."

"Henry!"

"Just let me dress. Won't be a minute," he says, closing the door.

I race into my room, and rip open the Macy's packages, looking for something to wear. I grab the first things I see that are suitable: A pair of dark-wash jeans, a long slim winter-white cashmere scoopneck, and a silver asymmetrical tunic sweater with a loose, lacy weave. I pull my hair up into a messy bun, and pull on some socks, and my red boots. I rip back the curtains. The sun is up, and snow is still coming down. There's about two inches on the ground, and it's still accumulating. Cars are moving, but cautiously. I wonder if Hudson is safe indoors. Oh, please let Hudson be safe.

By the time I hit the common room, Henry is already in suit trousers with a fresh shirt and demure tie, and he's sitting on the sofa tying his brogues.

"Wherever you're going, I'm going with you."

"You can't. I'm sorry. I've got to go call in favors and work my charm."

"To do what?"

He finishes tying his shoe, stands up, and pushes his arms through his jacket sleeves. He deftly buttons up with one hand, and shrugs on his overcoat.

"How do I look? And please don't say like a desperate mad man with ghastly dark circles under his eyes?"

He looks good. Better than good. Whomever he's going to charm doesn't stand a chance, I think with a twinge of jealousy. "You look great. But you have to tell me what's going on. Are you going to meet with Aunt Miranda?"

"No, this is bigger even than her. Listen Charlotte, I'm actually quite nervous. Would you please just trust me? Just for a few hours? Give me some space to do this."

I huff in exasperation. "OK. Yes! Of course." I know he has Hudson's, and my, best interests at heart. "But what am I supposed to do with myself while I wait?"

He has one hand on the doorknob to leave the suite. My heart flutters in trepidation. We haven't been apart for some time now. I don't savor the thought of being alone. "Why don't you make a round of calls to your friends?"

What friends, I think to myself. I don't say it out loud because it sounds pathetic.

"Charlotte? Are you going to be all right?" Henry pauses in the doorway, looking concerned.

"Go," I tell him, putting on what I hope is a brave face. "Everything will be fine."

I wonder if that's true as I watch the door close behind him.

Chapter 10

The bell to the shop tingalings as I push my way in the door. I realize I've tracked in a good deal of snow, and I stare down at my boots wondering if I should try brushing it back out onto the sidewalk.

"Don't worry about it," Mrs. Rabinowitz bellows, rushing toward me with her coat on. "A little snow, a little dirt...it's a floor. Floors can be cleaned." She barrels at me, arms open, and before I know it, my face is pressed against the mothball-scented shoulder of what I'm guessing is one of her best dress coats. She's paired it with a feathered pillbox hat with a puff of net emanating from the top. She must be on her way somewhere.

"I've been worried sick. Sick, I tell you! That Henry of yours should have been in touch every hour on the hour." She holds me at arm's length, scanning my face. "How are you holding up, my darling?"

"To be honest, just barely." It feels good to tell the truth. She clucks over me, "Of course you're a wreck. I heard all about it. Sheldon, my delivery boy," she says, tilting her head toward a tall young man with a long, skinny neck and choppy haircut, "is a computer genius. When he's not helping manage the shop, he's on the Apples and the Macs and all the rest. He told me what they've been saying about you on the FacePage and the Tweetings.

Shame on them! Some people are born to spoil the world for others." She pats my cheek. "But let's not dwell. My people have persevered through the ages by keeping our eyes on our own papers, as the saying goes. What brings you here? Not that you're not always welcome."

"I'm not sure." Heart in my throat, I tell her, "I guess I just wanted to see you. Henry told me to check in with my friends. And, well, I got in a cab, and wound up here."

"Good girl," she says, filled with enthusiasm. "You did the right thing! I'm always here to help. But here's the thing: I'm running out the door as we speak. I don't like to boast, but I happen to be chairwoman of Upper West Side Together, an interfaith social justice organization. I started off working with the ladies' Hadassah group at our synagogue, and the next thing you know, this! Who knew? It's a great honor," she tells me, puffing up her chest. "I'm on my way to a luncheon at Gracie Mansion, if you can imagine such a thing. We're presenting the mayor with a plaque in recognition of her work to fight homelessness, and a check for the funds we've raised for the cause. It's a real to-do. The local television stations are covering it, and National Public Radio, and the papers. The whole works."

"Oh, don't let me hold you up, then." I feel shy about the fact that I've come looking for sympathy when she's already done more than her part.

"What? You? Hold me up? For you and Hudson, I'd let the president of these United States wait. If you need something, I'm all ears. Forget the mayor," Mrs. Rabinowitz says, "I have all the time in the world for you."

An idea flashes through my head. But could I even ask for such a big favor.

"What? What is it, my dear? I can see you have something on your mind."

I decide to go for it. What could happen? Would Mrs. Rabinowitz really shun me for asking for a favor? She'd already more than proven her devotion to me. I take a deep breath, and blurt it out. "Mrs. R, do you think you'd be able to tell the mayor about Hudson?"

She knits her brow, clearly giving it some thought. For a second, I'm worried she might scold me, but then a wide smile takes over her comforting face.

"Charlotte, you've got a wonderful *keppy* on your shoulders. That's a stroke of genius! If you're thinking what I'm thinking, this could be the thing that brings Hudson home to you. Are you thinking what I'm thinking?"

"I'm not sure," I tell her. "Go on."

"You've seen pictures of our mayor at home, am I right?"

"Yes."

"Well, she hasn't yet been blessed with children, but who always shows up in her photos, besides her husband, the First Gentleman, of course?"

"Fritz and Freckles."

"Boom! You didn't even have to stop and think. Our mayor loves her dogs! We talked about it at the tea I was fortunate enough to attend after her inauguration. Such a smart girl you are." Mrs. Rabinowitz runs back and unpins the photo of Hudson from her bulletin board. "Leave it to me. Those no-goodniks badmouthing you and Hudson all over the social media won't hold a candle to the mayor of New York City singing your praises and asking for help."

I'm overwhelmed. "Mrs. Rabinowitz, that's a huge thing to ask of you."

"Asked, schmasked. I'm offering!"

"But I don't want you to waste a favor from someone so important."

"Bubbeleh, there is no wasting. You know those people that say a glass is half-full or half-empty. They don't know the secret. The truth is, the glass is refillable. Where there's goodness, there's always more available."

Impulsively, I throw myself into her arms. She hugs me back

tightly. "Such a good girl." She rubs my back before letting me go. "Now, you go get something to eat. You need your strength. Leave this to me and the ladies of Congregation Beth Israel! The mayor will be singing your praises on the twelve o'clock news, or I'll eat my hat."

I walk out with her into the snow-blanketed Manhattan morning, hail her a cab, and shut the door behind her, and wave goodbye.

*****

The aroma of espresso and yeasty bread in French Roast makes my stomach rumble, as I walk into the steamy-warm dining room and choose a cozy wooden booth near the bar. I'm checking my phone every five minutes waiting for Henry to check in and let me know what his scheme is and how it's progressing.

I order a cappuccino and a basket of bread with butter and jam, and try to still my mind. The mental picture of Hudson's harness haunts me. As much as I want to believe what Henry said about the note not being a serious lead, I'm not resting easy. I'm hesitant to bother Craig. He already spent so much time searching for Hudson. I sip my coffee, and it warms me. So does the memory of Craig, a virtual stranger, devoting so much time and energy to Hudson, and to me. I laugh out loud, remembering how he was ready to defend me against Henry in the park. It's funny to think that they were now partnering to find Hudson, exchanging texts and emails at all hours of the day and night.

Belly full, and nerves somewhat slightly quelled, I pay my bill and step back out into the street. I'm not sure where I should go, so I start walking. I find myself walking down my block, stopping in front of my brownstone. It looks different to me; the way one's home does after spending a year abroad. There's no reason I couldn't simply move back in tonight, except that I don't want to. I consider climbing the stairs to my apartment, and packing a bag with a few of my own things. I look down at my boots, gleaming red in the accumulating snow, and zip the zipper of my new coat to my chin. I like what I have on. I wonder if my old clothes will suit me when I return to them. Rather than think too much about the answers to these questions, I walk on.

I find myself walking along the edge of Central Park, the last place I saw my Hudson. The impulse to call Craig with questions overshadows my feelings of shyness and I pull out my phone. As it rings, my breathing quickens. I know I'm delicate right now. If he brushes me off, or chastises me for wasting a police officer's time with my calls on top of Henry's I'm afraid I might cry.

Just as I'm about to hang up, he answers. "Go for Curtis," he says.

"Hi Craig," my voice comes out softer than I expected. I clear my throat. "Craig, it's Charlotte. Charlotte Bell? Hudson's mom?"

"I know who you are," he says. I can hear the smile in his voice. "I was getting ready to call you."

"You were?"

"Yeah, I been trying to reach Henry all morning, but he's not picking up."

I'm walking faster and faster along the edge of the park. "Did you find something out?"

"Yeah, I sure did. I found out the joker who tried to bribe you is dumber than we thought he was. My buddy from the force is a detective, and he stepped in and pretended to be you. Told the guy he'd make the money drop, and to make sure to show up with the dog. The whole show was over in a matter of minutes. My buddy nabbed the guy, and brought him down to the station, threatening him with jail time for conspiracy to blackmail and he sang like a canary. He found the harness in a trashcan near the subway entrance by Columbus Circle. He and his other knucklehead pal saw the story about Hudson on New York One and decided to try and be big dogs. They're both in a mess of trouble now. Should've stayed on the porch with the other little dogs."

"Thank you for letting me know, Craig. I'm so relieved," I tell him. And I am, but also a tiny bit let down. As horrible as it was to imagine Hudson in the hands of kidnappers, it was a lead. Now we were back to the trail being stone cold. "Anyway, I should let you go. I know you're at work."

"Hold up!" he tells me. "That's not all I was calling to tell you. A bunch of my buddies at the station, and the other guys Scrivello and I have been reaching out to about Hudson are all torn up about the nasty stuff that's been showing up on Snapchat, and Instagram, and whatnot. Long story short, one of the sketch artists was doodling around and she made a sketch of you and Hudson."

"Could we send it out with a press release?" I ask excitedly. "Maybe that would help people see that Hudson and I really are real."

"Hold up. Yeah, sure, we could do that, but that's not the best part. We passed the sketch around, showing everyone what a cute dog Hudson is, and that got a couple of the fellas who go through security camera tape thinking. They said, 'What if we did a public service announcement-type thing? Like a rebuttal to the load of bull that this story got made up by the dog food company?' So, Scrivello and I started out doin' a real serious video where we were like character witnesses, ya know? Like a commercial, right? Thinking that if cops set the record straight, then people would listen. And then, heh heh," he starts laughing.

"What?" His laughter is contagious and I find myself starting to smile. He keeps trying to tell his story, but breaking up. He's so tickled he can't get it out. I keep moving, waiting for the punch line. I realized I've walked all the way to the Plaza, and I'm not even cold. Despite the temperatures and the occasional flurries, my fast-pumping blood has me nearly in a sweat. Finally, I can't take it anymore. "Craig! Tell me!"

"It's plain crazy, is what it is. So we taped ourselves being all sincere, then one of the guys starts buggin' out, and he does, like a rap version of what we just said. Just cutting up and being all silly. So then, this detective who's a hip-hop aerobics instructor on the

226

side, starts bustin' some moves. Hoooooooey!" He's laughing again, and I can just picture him wiping his eyes, grinning ear to ear.

"Tell her the good stuff," I hear Officer Scrivello say in the background.

"Hold up, I'm getting there. So, here's the deal Charlotte," he says, turning his attention back to me. "We did this whole video, with like sampling and choreography, and everything. That one guy from the video surveillance lab's got mad editing skills, and it turned out looking way more professional than anyone thought when we were just goofing."

"Tell her," I hear Scrivello nudging.

"I am, Leonard! Will you stop talking in my ear? *Damn!* Sorry about that Charlotte. So anyway, he put it up on YouTube, and it's got way more hits than any of those stupid parody videos saying you're a liar. They're calling us the Hip Hop Dog Lover Cops. You gotta check it out."

"I will, I promise. Craig, I can't tell you how much I appreciate everything you've done. And Officer Scrivello, too."

"Call me Leonard!" I hear Scrivello yell.

"Will you quiet down? Sorry, Charlotte, I got you on speaker. Anyhow, you don't have to thank us, we had fun. Besides, that's what New York's Finest do. We serve and protect. And we take care of our own."

I like the feeling of being one of "their own." Of being anyone's own.

It feels so much better than being all alone.

*****

I check my phone again for the one hundredth time. Where is Henry? I consider bothering Aunt Miranda to see if she knows where he is, but I don't want to get him in trouble. I don't know where he is or what he's doing. She could very well want him onsite at the pop-up restaurant. Best not to draw attention to him.

227

I'm right in front of the Plaza. I think about how much fun I had stuffing my face with five-star delicacies, and bantering with Henry. I smile to myself, remembering what a great mood I was in, despite my near-death-by-pretzel-cart experience.

I turn down 5th Avenue, navigating my way through the salmon-stream of window shoppers, taking in the delights of the decorated storefronts of the designer shops. New York really is the best place to be for Christmas, I think. I take in the sheer number of window shoppers, and marvel at the variety of accents and languages I hear in the snippets of conversations I'm over-hearing as I walk.

I feel a buzzing in my pocket, and dive for my phone. It's Henry!

"Yes?" I answer breathlessly.

"Charlotte. Where are you?"

"53rd and 5th."

"Good. Head to the suite. I'll meet you there in 20 minutes."

"Where are you? What's the matter?"

"I'll tell you everything in person. Talk to you soon," he says, and the phone goes dead.

My stomach sinks to my knees. This has to be bad news, other-wise he would have just told me what's going on during the call. I pick up my pace, eyes forward, and don't slow down till the doorman of the Waldorf Astoria tips his hat, and ushers me into the lobby.

*****

I race through the lobby of the Towers, and open the door to the suite. Henry is pacing around the common room, tie off and sleeves rolled up to his elbow. He doesn't smile when he sees me. He just says, "Hello, Charlotte. Please, sit down."

I do as he says. I feel that if I try to take control, I'll just delay getting the news I crave.

"Shall I order lunch?" he asks.

"Eating is the last thing on my mind. Tell me what is going on, now."

He sits down in the wing chair across from me. Leaning forward, elbows on his knees, he looks me straight in the eye. "I'm going to be blunt with you, Charlotte. What happened is not good. I take full responsibility. I should have seen that backlash of the type that occurred was possible. I feel I led you into a trap."

"No Henry, you had a good plan." I wish I could blame him. It would feel so good to channel my anger and frustration somewhere, but Henry didn't deserve it. "For a while there, it looked like we were getting somewhere."

He shakes his head. "I've worked in publicity, and I have experience with the media. I never should have let this get out of our hands. I've allowed them to make you a villain, and the Hudson story a representation of all that's wrong with big corporations taking advantage of the little people of the world."

I scoff. "There are no big corporations in this story."

"Of course," he says, closing his eyes and rubbing them hard. "But as I said, the story has gotten away from us. We're so far from the truth now, I wonder if we can ever steer this ship back there."

"I think I've made a start." I tell him about Mrs. Rabinowitz and the mayor, and Craig's YouTube video, and the Gay Men's Chorus.

He takes a deep breath, and lets it out. "All of that is great. Well done. But as I said, things are bad. Bad in an epic way. I've been wracking my brain to solve this, and I think I have the answer."

"Great," I tell him. "Let's hear it."

"I already know you aren't going to like what I have to say. So let's start from the top."

I sit still and listen.

"I've been talking with every spin doctor I've ever met. To a person, their advice to me was the same."

"What did they say we should do?"

"I'm getting there. Once they spelled it out, I spent the morning on the phone with every person I know in the news and infotainment world, from intern to hotshot. In fact, that's why I was up and out so early this morning. I was aiming to put you in front of a camera this morning, but I was too late. The best I could do was to get you booked on air for a breakfast show tomorrow morning."

I feel the blood drain from my face. "No way. I'm not going on a morning show, if that's what you're saying."

"But the good news is," Henry says, bypassing my refusal, "I pulled in a million IOUs and managed to get a face-to-face with Matt Lauer. I've never pitched so hard in my life. It was touch-and-go, but I managed to convince him the story would be a real heartstring-tugger with a unique Christmas twist. In the end, he agreed that it could be a real ratings booster. He's interviewing you on *The Today Show* tomorrow morning at 8:30. We need to have you at the studio by 6 a.m."

My head thrums. Every cell in my body is frantically sending out warning signals to my brain, telling me to run. "No," I say, sitting on my hands to quell the energy that's gathering to propel my body into a run. "I'm not going to do it."

"Yes," he says shortly, "you are. You have to go on *The Today Show* and prove that you are a flesh-and-blood girl who loves her lost dog. You'll need to be charming, and personal, and make viewers see that you deserve their help. You have to tell them your story. You have to make them believe."

"I was barely able to tell you my story," I say, hands trembling. "I can't go on national television. I'm not Miranda. I'm not you. I don't go around drawing attention and making a big show of myself."

Henry fixes me with a hard look. "This is an opportunity. I advise you to take this chance to show New Yorkers Hudson's disappearance wasn't some kind of stunt to dupe them."

"I can't. I just can't. We have to find another way."

"There is no other way, Charlotte. We have tried all the other ways. This is the end of the road." He's angry.

"You know," I snap, "you sit there and tell me I should do this, all smug and bossy. What do you ever do that's risky? Maybe I'll go on a morning show when you invite your poor parents over to New York for a proper family Christmas dinner? How about that?"

He's furious. I watch him swallow what he clearly wants to say, and measure his words. "We are not talking about me. We are talking about a plan to get your dog back."

I want to say yes, but I literally feel terror. He may as well be asking me to jump out of an airplane or go over Niagara Falls in a barrel. I press my lips together and shake my head "no."

"How badly do you want your dog back?" His voice is sharp.

Feeling under a microscope, I search my soul. I want Hudson back more than anything, but exposing myself the way Henry is suggesting is out of the question. It feels like life and death.

"I don't have time for this," Henry says, standing up and stuffing papers into his briefcase. He doesn't seem angry anymore. He just seems gone. "An array of experts have spoken. You have my recommendation," he tells me, tone detached and businesslike. He walks briskly to the coat closet, and suits up to go out into the snow and cold. "I'm going to work. You have my mobile number. Call me when you've made up your mind." He turns his back, and goes. I'm left with only the echo of the slammed door to keep me company while I search my soul.

*****

"Hello?"

"Hi, is this Vijay?"

"Yes, this is Vijay. I already told the other guy, I mailed the check on Wednesday."

I keep walking. I'm fizzing with energy, but I have nowhere to go and no place to be. I just walk. "This is Charlotte Bell," I tell him. "You probably don't remember me. I was in your cab once. I'm not really sure why I'm calling you."

"Charlotte, is that correct? Doesn't ring a bell. Ha! That is a small joke." He laughs at himself. "It's funny because it's true. You are right. I don't remember you. Can you tell me more?"

Now I'm really embarrassed. What was I looking for when I fished out his card and dialed his number? "I'm in my mid-twenties, I have dark blonde hair, you took me to Rockefeller Center."

"Yes!" Vijay exclaims. "Wait. No. Sorry, I do not remember you."

I'm tempted to hang up. I feel my face heating up and I'm not sure if it's from shame or the exertion of plodding along in the ankle-deep snow. "You were very nice to me. You let me bring my dog in your cab. Hudson?"

"Oh, for heaven's sake, yes! Even if I had not remembered you from the cab, I have seen the dog's photo in the paper. Also, my Twitter feed exploded with that cop dance video." He chuckles. "Those guys are hilarious. They should go on *America's Got Talent*. People love it when cops are funny. It's like when football players do rapping and dancing. It's entertainment gold. Believe me when I tell you this," he says with an intense gravity. "I am an industry insider."

"I remember that. You played Caroline's, right?"

"I did. And I killed it. You would not believe the tape I got from that show. I sent it in to *Last Comic Standing*. Mark my words, this is the year of Vijay Singh. Then, with luck, my parents will stop going on and on about how I am wasting my medical degree by doing my 'little shows.'"

"You're a doctor?" I marvel.

"I am a licensed internist. I made my parents a deal. We agreed on a salary figure. I told them if I was not earning that amount within five years, I would not only join my father's practice, but also allow them to arrange a marriage for me. It goes without saying that they are rooting for my failure. Ha!" He laughs. "Actually, that is more sad than funny. I'll work on that."

Blocks melt behind me as I chug downtown, race walking in an effort to relieve my tension. "I'm sorry, Vijay. You must be very busy. I'll let you go."

"On the contrary. I am waiting for my shift to begin. The guy before me is due to drop off the taxi we share any minute. Though I dread getting in today. Windows stay up on cold and snowy days, and I believe this guy's diet consists solely of burritos and egg salad sandwiches."

"Bleurgh, good luck with that. Anyway, I should let you go."

"Wait, do not hang up. In medical school I was told that my bedside manner and intuition were my best assets. I hope you don't mind my getting personal, but you sound depressed."

"Oh, it's nothing."

"I don't believe that is the truth. You can talk to me. Seriously, I am a doctor."

"I don't know..."

"Then talk to me as a comic. We've heard it all." I laugh, and begin to tell him my whole tale from Hudson running off to Henry storming out. He listens patiently, punctuating the conversation with appropriate murmurs of understanding and exclamations of indignation. By the time I'm finished, I feel lighter.

"I have heard what you had to say. Do you want my opinion?"

"Your medical opinion?" I ask.

"No, my show biz opinion."

"Go on."

"Your English friend is right." My heart plummets, but I keep pushing forward, walking at a clip. "You must seize this opportunity."

"I can't. You don't understand," I confess. "I know it sounds stupid, but I feel like I literally might die if I have to say personal things about myself in front of the whole world."

"Ah, but I do understand. You are talking to a former geek, nerd, and outsider. I was the skinny Indian kid who was good at math in a school of jock WASPs whose families were part of the Ivy League 'Old Boy' network. My family started out more Slum Dog than Big Dog. You try keeping a smile on your face when no

233

girl will go with you to the prom because they whisper in the halls that you smell like curry. I started doing comedy to protect myself. Then it developed into a way for me to have a voice. Having the attention of a crowd is a powerful thing. You have been handed that chance on a silver platter."

"Did they teach you all about tough love in medical school too?" I ask him.

"I am not sorry if I seem harsh. I lived in that kind of fear for too long. That fear robs us of our chances to get what we truly want. You must have sensed that I would say this. I think that is why you phoned me."

I keep walking, head muddled. "I don't know," I mutter.

"Yes, you do. Confusion is having information you don't want. You know what you have to do. I will tell you what. My shift today is short. We will meet around the dinner hour and I will coach you. By the time we are through, you will be able to do this."

"Why? Why would you give up your night for a total stranger who doesn't really even want to be helped?"

"Because I am human. Because you need someone. Because a guy did it for me once. The first set I ever did at a tiny place called Bananas in New Jersey bombed so badly I thought it would be my last time doing standup. Someone in the audience presented me with a bill for his wasted time. A veteran comic pulled me to the side, and as they say, 'schooled me.' Let's just say I'm paying it forward. Are you in?"

"I'm not sure," I tell him. "I have to be honest. All I can say is that I'll try. If I bow out, you'll have wasted your time."

"I'll try if you will. Like we used to say in medical school, 'you win some and you lose some.'"

"You really said that?"

"No, what we said was much worse. Black humor got us through. But you are not on a need-to-know basis, so forget I said that. Insider privilege. So, will we give it a try?"

I feel like I'm walking blindfolded through a snake-filled tunnel, but I give him the info he needs to find me at the Waldorf.

"And Vijay," I tell him with a lump in my throat. "Thank you."

"You can thank me by killing on *The Today Show*."

"You never give up, do you?"

"No, I don't," he says very seriously. "And neither should you."

Chapter 11

Breathless and exhausted, I hang up my coat and pour myself a tall tumbler of water. It's strange being in the suite without Henry. It's stranger still not to know when, or if, to expect him back. I drink the entire glass, then refill it and drink that. My legs are rubbery and my hair is damp. I had walked from Midtown all the way down to Ground Zero. I had paused to catch my breath in front of a plaque memorializing the rescue workers who, without hesitation, put themselves in harm's way to help those who couldn't help themselves that day. Gazing up at the newly minted Freedom Tower at One World Trade Center lifted my frightened, shivering heart. The soaring, glimmering structure was a concrete reminder that there are more good people in this world than bad. Breathing in the hope, I made a choice to believe that Hudson is under the care of someone kind, someone who simply wants the best for him, the way that Mrs. Rabinowitz, and Craig, and Vijay simply want the best for me. And then there's Henry. I wonder what it is that he wants.

I wobble my way to a hot shower, hoping the spray will loosen my now-still muscles. Eyes closed, I think about the brave people who really risked their lives on 9/11 and how inspirational those actions are. I picture myself walking on to the set of the morning show, and shaking hands with the host. My shoulders relax under the pressure of the warm water, and some of my fear rolls off and disappears down the drain. Standing up in front of a crowd isn't truly dangerous. It just feels that way.

I towel off and slide into my robe and slippers. Boy, when I go home for good, the static trickle of my showerhead isn't going to cut it. Maybe I'll get a new one, I think to myself. I'm not sure I'll be able to go back to the farm now that I've seen Par-ee. The thought of going home carves a hollow space in my core. Without Henry, it'll be so lonely, I think. Wait, I mean Hudson. I laugh at myself. Without *Hudson* it will be so lonely.

I have time before my appointment with Vijay. I consider calling Henry, but then I remember the look on his face when he left. I can't face him pressing me about the show. I push it out of my mind for the time being. The large, puffy bed calls to me like a siren. I crawl on, fluff the pillows, and lay down my head. Maybe I'll just rest my eyes for a minute or two. I feel small in the huge bed, in the huge room. The heavy curtains obscure the light, and as I drift on a wave of half-sleep, it's hard to remember if it's day or night. The only sound is the constant, gentle whirr of the climate-control system. At home, I think, my bedroom could use an update. I float, enjoying the feeling of the soft duvet along the length of my body. I'm in and out of daydreams. The Waldorf feels like home, and home feels like a distant memory, or a story I heard someone else tell. Then I remember Hudson, and as if someone flicks on a projector, the day that I found him plays against the movie screen of my brain...

Struggling against the wind, I shoulder the solid glass-paned wooden door to my building open, and squeeze my body through. The wind whooshes across my brownstone stoop and my hair whips my face. It's way too cold out for April. I look left, then right, wishing someone would tell me where to go. I'm hungry. At least I think that's what that hollow feeling is.

I pulled myself from the warm cocoon of my duvet to go get

food. I ran out of pretty much everything yesterday, or was it the day before? I fiddle in my raincoat pocket for my keys. I'll just go back inside and order a pizza, I think, even though my heart knows a New York pie won't satisfy me. It's not just my stomach that's hungry. But really I'm too tired to go all the way downtown to the Village to Tea & Sympathy just for an order of sticky toffee pudding.

I turn to go back in just as the older man from 2R pushes out, two squat and panting Corgis stomping over his feet toward freedom.

"Oh, excuse us. Dylan! Connor! Be polite, fellas," he chides the roiling dogs, who are trying so hard to overtake each other that their leashes are weaving together like a macramé basket. The man tugs his hat down tightly.

"Blustery!" he booms, as an empty plastic shopping bags flies by. I try to smile politely. Instead, I feel my eyes start to dampen. I wipe them on my coat sleeve, and pretend it's because of the gust.

"Yes, certainly is windy," I mumble.

"We're just on our way to the park," he says brightly, as the dogs rub against my ankles. Their fur feels soft; it takes the chill off of my bare skin. I'm still in my pajama bottoms and house slippers. "You flirts!" he admonishes. "Stop begging. The young lady doesn't have anything for you." He reaches in his coat pocket and cups his hand under one dog's nose, then the other. "There's your cookies, now leave her be."

The man's always polite, though we've never said much more than hello. To be honest, I don't know many of my neighbors very well. Any, really.

"The boys are just dying to get to the dog run before the rain starts. Very fussy about getting their paws wet, these two."

The stoop isn't big enough for him, his two eager Corgis, and me, so I get pulled down to the sidewalk in a mini canine stampede. "Dylan and Connor!" the man scolds half-heartedly, indulgently allowing the dogs to pull him east toward Central Park. He turns back to call, "Have a nice day!" and catches his hat just in the nick of time as it blows off of his head. It's a comical scene, the man hanging onto his hat for dear life, and the Corgis galloping forward on their stubby little legs, but no laugh rises up in my belly. I just feel...nothing.

I look at the front door, and try to summon the energy to climb the four steps. It would be so nice just to be home. I glance up at the brightly colored curtains in my window, three floors above. My limbs feel too heavy to climb stairs.

Oh, well, in for a penny, in for a pound, I think. I'll walk to the market on Columbus, and buy the ingredients to make sticky toffee pudding. I'm a trained chef, I think to myself, I aced all my pastry courses at the Culinary Institute of America no less, how silly to traverse half of Manhattan to buy one dumb dessert.

A few fat raindrops hammer down on my head, and trickle down my scalp. It's stupid to trudge to the market when I could order in pizza.

It's not stupid, it's lovely, a familiar voice echoes in my head. Beautiful moments make a beautiful life. It's worth the effort. I can almost smell sticky toffee pudding, warm and inviting. I have a memory of spooning the rich, dense treat into my mouth, so sweet and so substantial, washed down with strong, milky tea.

I cross the street, and my legs continue to carry me west, even though my brain isn't yet onboard. I look at the ground as I walk, blinking raindrops out of my lashes. I should have worn a coat with a hood.

A delighted whoop and the roar of a crowd startle me, drawing me back to the real world. I stand stock still, looking around me for danger. The double red doors of the church on the uptown side of the street have been flung open, and a crowd of shouting, cheering wedding guests emerges, the people holding umbrellas, newspapers, and wedding programs over their heads against the rain. As if choreographed, they part to make an aisle for the bride and groom. No one seems to care about getting wet.

A stout woman in a frilled dress and a wide-brimmed hat beams with pride. She holds fast to the arm of a silver-haired man in a tuxedo, and the couple recedes to the side, waving.

Halfway down the stairs, the bride whispers to her groom, lifts the train of her dress, and races back up the stairs. She beelines for the woman in the hat, and throws herself into her arms. The older woman rocks the bride like a little girl, tears mixing with rain and trickling down her powdery cheeks past her wide smile.

Now I'm crying in earnest. Rain snakes down my collar, and my slippers squish with each step. I've only made it two blocks. Standing in front of the Hudson Deli, I seriously consider catching a cab home. I fish in my bag for my wallet, and realize I've left it at home. Now I have no choice to walk back.

I step out to cross back to my side of the street, and a horn blares. I hear a whoosh, and stagger backwards just in time to avoid being hit by a delivery truck, but not soon enough to avoid the sheet of water that slaps me across the legs. I'm off-balance, and my bag slips from my shoulder. I fall against a row of metal garbage cans. Amid the thunder of the crash, I think I hear a yelp. Or maybe it's a baby crying. I pull myself to my feet, and stand very still, listening hard. The only sounds are cars, and the drone of the downpour.

I turn toward home. I never should have left it in the first place. I just want to be behind closed doors, alone. As I stoop to retrieve my soggy purse, a truck rattles by. Its headlights slice through the gray curtain of rain, and for a split second they illuminate something blindingly bright, deep among the trash cans. Cautiously, I inch forward, crouching down and squinting. I find it hard to believe, but there it is, right in front of me.

The glint came from a pair of eyes, clear and focused, staring straight at me from deep inside a big Macy's shopping bag, one of the ones with the red star on it. I get down on my knees, and see that they belong to a trembling, skinny dog, with a slicked-down, soaking-wet coat. I extend my hand to the poor creature. I expect

240

him to cower, but he doesn't even look away.

"Are you hungry too?" I whisper.

I stretch my hand a little further, reaching out to him. He lays his cheek against the fleshy outside of my fist, pressing his sweet face against my chilled skin like a hug.

Still crying, but now for a wholly different reason, I scoop him up and take him home.

Chapter 12

I wake to a knocking, and imagine that it's the elderly couple from 1F finally coming to thank me in person for having left a meal in front of their door. Struggling to surface from a murky soup of memories, daydreams, and real dreams I raise my head off of the pillow and squint in the dark. The feel of the duvet grounds me. I realize I'm at the Waldorf, and I leap to my feet to run for the door. Henry must be back!

I swing open the door to the suite, only to find a smiling Vijay standing in the hall. My befuddled brain recalibrates. Of course it wouldn't be Henry. He has a key. And I have a meeting scheduled with Vijay. "I am glad to see you don't stand on ceremony," he tells me, indicating my bathrobe. "It must mean you are comfortable with me."

I apologize, and invite him in, surprised that I am, indeed, comfortable with him. "I'll just go and change," I say.

"Don't do it on my account. For one thing, you are more covered wearing that than most women are on the city streets. On top of that, I have the most wonderful girlfriend on the planet. You could be a model standing here naked and I wouldn't even look. I only have eyes for my Nina."

"Really?" I ask.

"Well, if you want to pin me to the wall, I suppose I might

take a cursory glance."

"No, I meant to ask if you really had a girlfriend."

"Is that so hard to believe?"

"Of course not. Any woman would be lucky to have you, but what about the arranged marriage?"

"Yes, that will be very awkward," he says with a wry smile. "That is why I cannot fail. And we are not going to let you fail either. Just wear that, and let's get started. I'm doing ten minutes at Stand-Up New York tonight, so I only have a little more than an hour."

"Understood, but before we get started you have to let me buy you dinner. Or, to be honest, to let my aunt buy you dinner." I call room service and place our order. "Do you want wine?" I ask.

"No, thank you. I never, ever go on stage under the influence. The whole idea is that you have to be in control. You have to steer the ship. That's what I am going to teach you about tomorrow. But you go ahead." I order a bottle of wine, and hang up.

"The wine is for after. Understood? This is serious work."

"Understood.'"

"First thing first. Go stand in front of that chair. I am going to look at you. Don't try to do anything. Just be. Just stand there."

I do as he says, but after about ten seconds, I say, "I feel funny."

"From the top. Try again."

I go back and do it again. It's more exhausting than it sounds to do nothing. "Do not fidget with your sleeve. Try again."

I stand up, and once again attempt to do nothing. "Drop your shoulders. Breathe. Don't make faces."

We do that again and again. When Vijay finally tells me to shake out my muscles and walk around the room, I'm surprised to see that half an hour has passed. "Hold that sensation in your brain. Remember the feeling of doing nothing. That's what you need to access when you are being interviewed on that couch tomorrow morning."

"IF I'm being interviewed."

"Moving on!" He makes me sit on the couch and simply tell

him that my name is Charlotte Bell, that I was born in England, and that I moved to America where I have lived ever since. It's harder than I would have thought. "Simpler!" he coaches. "It is not complicated. Just tell the truth, tell the facts."

We do that until he is satisfied. When room service arrives, Vijay asks the server to stay and watch me. I go through my three-minute routine. "What do you think of this girl?" Vijay asks the man.

"I think she was born in England, she moved here and her name is Charlotte. She seems nice."

"Excellent, thank you boss," Vijay says to the guy, and gives him a fist bump. When the waiter is gone, Vijay turns to me and says, "You did great. He didn't say you seem nervous or stuck-up."

"I'm not stuck-up!"

"No, but nervous people can be read as snobby. That is the last thing you want when you are trying to get America on your side."

Hurriedly, we scarf down our burgers and fries and get back to work. "Now, you are going to tell me about Hudson." Again, Vijay puts me through the paces. At first, I tell him bits and pieces. His eyes are so kind that I find myself telling him more and more about my personal life. "Good!" he encourages, as I confess that Hudson is really my family. "More!" he hollers as I tell him that my aunt loved me in her own way, but didn't quite know what to do with an adolescent girl. When I get to the part about my mother, he's quiet. I can see that he's really listening. It feels very intimate.

"Anything else?" he asks.

I'm scared. I want to say no and move on, but I find myself nodding slightly. "Will you tell me?" he asks, moving to sit next to me on the sofa.

"I'm sorry, Vijay." Two hot, fat tears push their way out from under my eyelids and roll down my cheeks. "It's too much."

"It's OK. You are tired. And besides," he says, looking right into my eyes. "We have company."

Startled, I look up. "How long have you been standing there, Henry?"

244

"A while." His eyes are soft. "Should I leave you two to it?"

"Actually, mate," Vijay says, shaking Henry's hand, "I was just on my way out. Charlotte," he says, grabbing his coat and gloves from where he'd lain them on the wing chair, "I'm glad we did that. Call me later."

"I wish I could be with you tonight," I tell him.

"There will be many other nights," he replies. "See you soon."

After Vijay leaves, Henry remains standing. "Take off your coat," I say.

"I thought you might prefer it if I left."

"Don't pin it on me," I tell him, folding my arms. "If you're still mad at me, and you want to go, then go."

His eyes blaze. "Don't you throw it back at me. If I've interrupted something let me know."

"You haven't."

"What's the bottle of wine for?" he asks, eyes narrowed. "To christen a ship?"

"Since when is it illegal for me to drink wine?" I demand. "Where do you think you're going?" I say, grabbing his arm and pulling him backward as he stomps toward the bedroom. He surges on.

"Aha! Your bed is messed up. I knew it!" He jabs a finger toward my chest. "I knew it!"

I swat his finger away. "You don't know anything, Henry Wentworth. Nothing about me at all! Besides, what do you care? You left me when I needed you."

"I did no such thing."

"I wanted to tell you why I was scared, and you abandoned me!"

"I didn't abandon you," he says, trying to rip off his overcoat. "I was trying to save you from yourself." He manages to get himself untangled, and he throws the garment on the floor.

"I thought maybe if I cleared out, you'd calm down and have a think. I still maintain that going on *The Today Show* is the surest route to getting Hudson back in your arms." He sits down on the edge of the bed, and puts his head in his hands. "Don't you see?

Everything I've been doing, I've been doing for you. My foolish mistake! Out of sight, out of mind, I suppose." He looks up at me. "I wish I'd been the one you confided in."

I sit down next to him on the edge of my bed. "Henry, there's so much I've wanted to tell you." I look into his eyes, but he looks away. His jaw is set. I wanted to tell you how much it has mean to have you with me since Hudson's been gone, I think. I wanted to tell you how the blue of your eyes sends shivers of pleasure to my core.

He shifts his eyes back to mine. "Then why didn't you?" He looks hurt. "I told you my biggest secret. Don't you trust me?"

"Up to now, I haven't really let myself trust anyone. It's never been safe, you know? I suppose you have to choose to trust. Are you telling me I should choose you?"

"I'm telling you that I wish you would." He scoots closer to me, so that our thighs are touching, hip to knee. "The choice is yours."

I take a deep breath, and take his hand. He squeezes it. "Here goes. For starters, Vijay is just a friend who came to coach me. Nothing happened." Henry breaks into a smile, and angles his body a little more closely toward me. I continue. "Let me tell you about the day I found Hudson."

I talk for a long time, filling in the details of what it was like to grow up never knowing my father, wishing I were normal. I tell him about the loneliness of boarding school, and how painful it was to behave on the outside like I was one of the girls, but to feel like a different species on the inside. I told him about going home for holidays with Aunt Miranda, and how she made an effort on the rare occasions when she was home but never quite hit the mark, and how that made me feel like it was my fault. If I had just been a better girl, I could have made her mother me.

At some point, Henry pulls me to the middle of the bed, and we sit knee-to-knee, holding hands, faces just inches apart. "Sometimes," I whisper. I can hear that my voice is raspy and weak. "Sometimes," I try again, "I worry that my mother didn't stick around because I wasn't good enough."

"It doesn't work like that," Henry says softly. "You were a very good girl then, and you are a wonderful person now. It was an accident. These things just happen. It may not be fair, but that's life. I'm just sorry it happened to you." He kisses me lightly on the forehead.

"Thank you, Henry." I feel so tired. "I think I need to sleep now." Gently, Henry cradles me in the crook of his arm, and lays me back on the pillow. My muscles are loose, and I'm floating.

"Shh," he tells me. "You're all right now. Everything is going to be fine."

I breathe in Henry's scent. The earthiness is comforting. So is the after-rain aroma. It's fresh, like the world's been washed clean.

He kisses away what's left of my tears and strokes my cheek. I close my eyes, and let myself rest. It feels good not to be alone.

Chapter 13

I wake to an unfamiliar chiming sound. I feel Henry shuffling around in the darkness. I see the light from his cell phone as he shuts off his alarm. I do a big yawn and marvel at the fact that I slept the whole night in his arms. I could count the number of times I'd spent the whole night in a bed with James, and on the rare occasion when I did, I had always awakened several times throughout the night.

"Good morning, Sleeping Beauty," he says to me, switching on the bedside lamp. "It's 4:30. Have you made a decision?"

I sit up. I check in with myself and am surprised to find I feel refreshed, and well rested. "What happens if I say no?"

"Then you say no," he says, sitting up opposite me.

"I'm surprised you didn't cancel."

"I wanted to leave our options open. I can clean up a mess and do damage control, but I could never have secured this slot twice."

"Will I ruin your career if I bow out?"

"Please don't factor that into your choice. I want you to do what's right for you."

I think about Mrs. Rabinowitz, and my new friends, Craig, and Vijay. All of them have been willing to stick their necks out for me. All three of them risked something for me and Hudson. Each one of them called in favors and risked. Not to mention Henry. I look at gorgeous Henry, rumpled and wrinkled from sleep, rubbing his eyes and yawning. He's done so much for me. I can't believe I ever doubted that he was on my side. He's not Miranda's minion, he's my boyfriend. That thought flips my stomach like going down a roller coaster hill. Well, maybe he's not technically my boyfriend, but we're something. I'm sure of it.

I take a deep breath. "When do we leave?"

Henry breaks out into a huge smile. "That's my girl!" he says, and he gives me a quick peck on the lips before springing out of bed and running to his shower to get ready for my big day.

*****

I've been up for ages, drinking only coffee. There are platters of fruit and pastries everywhere in the green room of the NBC studios, but I couldn't eat if I wanted to. I have over an hour before my scheduled appearance, and I don't know what to do with myself. They've made an attempt to gussy up the bare cube of a room by draping a malnourished pine garland across the room-length mirror, and installing a wan two-foot-tall tree dotted with candy canes on the counter in front of the three Naugahyde swivel chairs.

There's a woman in the holding room across the hall from me, who keeps pacing and laughing. She's an army sergeant, just back from the Middle East, and they're going to surprise her children by having brought her home in time for Christmas. She's being fussed over by her own mother, and sisters, and aunts. They've all been sweet to me, popping in to introduce themselves. They're bursting at the seams with joy about having their girl home. I can't help wishing my life were like that.

It's really my nature to deal with things on my own, but I have to admit it's nice to have Henry here with me. There are moments when his knowing all of my personal business and being physically near set off a trigger in me. It's like my clothes are too tight, and I feel like I need to burst into a run. I'm not used to people being so close, not like the sergeant across the hall from me. She looks like she revels in it. But I know Henry is on my side; everything he's doing, he's doing for me. I focus on that. From the time we walked in, he's been acting as my agent, personal assistant, and body guard. Because of him, my nerves are holding steady, but just barely. I wish Aunt Miranda had shown up, though. I texted her when I was leaving the Waldorf, telling her I was going on television, but she never responded. I know she's busy with the mayor's daughter's wedding, but it stings.

I run a brush through my hair. I have no idea how much makeup to put on, so I swipe on some lipstick and hope for the best. My clothes look good. I'm wearing my first-day outfit from my Macy's delivery. I stare in the mirror and, suddenly, I see Vijay's face. I whip around to make sure it's really him and not a daydream.

"Vijay! How did you know I was here?"

"I have to say you did clue me in when you said, 'I am going on *The Today Show* with Matt Lauer tomorrow', and then we practiced together for over an hour."

"No, goofy! I mean how did you know I was *here* here?"

"I have a lot of friends in comedy who do very well. I don't want to name drop but let me just say Jerry Seinfeld."

"Shut up," I say, slapping him on the shoulder. "You know Jerry Seinfeld."

"No," he laughs, "but I wanted you to let me say it. I know some of the writers from *The Daily Show*. They were on and they told me how to get to back here. Once I was back, I told the girl guarding the main door that I am your brother."

My jaw drops. "But…"

"But what? I am a rich, deep brown and you are like a ghost dipped in bleach?"

I crack up. "Thanks a lot. I'll have you know I get a good suntan every summer."

"At the spray-on salon?" He winks. "That is the beauty of the story. After I told her you were my sister, I stuck out my chin

250

and dared her to question me. Slum dogs like myself can leverage people's need to be politically correct. Ah, I love it when the ends justify the means. Best part of the story? I was joking around with her, you know, and getting along. Another woman joined her behind the desk, and was listening in like she was bored on duty, are you with me?"

"Yes."

"So the first girl asks what I do. We were shooting the breeze, right? I tell her I'm a doctor but I do stand-up comedy. People love that backstory. So she says, as people do, if you're a comic, tell me a joke. So I launch into some of my act. The other woman asks me do I have a card. I give it to her, thinking she would look for me at one of the clubs. Turns out, she books the warm-up comics for the audiences. She invited me to send her my tape."

"That's amazing!" Hearing Vijay's story lights a spark of hope in me. If I can just get through this interview, maybe I'd get Hudson back.

"Charlotte," Henry says, bursting into the room at a clip. "Oh, hello." Even though I explained about Vijay, Henry seems suspicious.

"Just here for some last-minute coaching," Vijay says. "I had to creep out before dawn's early light so I wouldn't wake my girlfriend. She is not a morning person. Lovely in the afternoon, but you don't want to cross her before that first cup of tea. It's like disturbing a hibernating bear." His eyes fill with affection. "So cute."

Henry warms immediately, lunging forward to shake Vijay's hand. "Good to have you here. Thanks for coming to support Charlotte."

"Happy to do it. What goes around comes around. I firmly believe that."

"I came in to take Charlotte with me to hair and makeup."

I'm embarrassed.

"But you don't need a thing. You're beautiful as you are." Henry smiles at me. My insides feel warm and gushy. "It's standard

251

treatment. Everyone gets it, all genders, regardless."

"Go," Vijay says. "I'll wait here. I am going to pace. My rear end is due in the seat of a cab in two hours. It feels good to stand."

Henry hands me over to a woman wearing an apron with a hundred different brushes in its multiple pockets. She introduces herself as Annie and gets to work. She sprays my hair with water, and while she dries it with a fat, round brush, I go over the lessons Vijay taught me in my head. My goal is to make the audience understand, he told me. Take the focus off of myself and my nerves will settle. Pretend I'm talking to one person, and one person alone. Make Matt Lauer understand how important it is that I get Hudson back, and the whole television audience will understand.

"Flip up, now," Annie instructs. When I toss my hair and sit back tall in the chair, I see Aunt Miranda standing there with Penelope from Macy's.

My heart swells. "Aunt Miranda! You made it."

"I couldn't very well let you go on national TV wearing rags, could I Cinderella? Penelope, would you be so kind as to offer Charlotte the outfits you chose for her?"

Excitement begins to replace dread as Annie expertly applies a face full of cosmetics that give the effect of a fresher, more wide-awake me without looking like a mask. Once I'm out of hair and makeup, I change into my television clothes. I put on a denim nipped-waist shirtdress with an asymmetrical hem and Penelope quickly accessorizes it with simple zip-up booties and a statement necklace.

"Perfect," declares Miranda, as I come back to the green room. "You look sophisticated without being too urban or runway. Well done, Penelope."

"Yes, very well done," Henry agrees, not taking his eyes off of me.

"You look very nice, Charlotte," Vijay says. "Last minute pro tip: Don't fiddle with your costume. Don't touch your collar, don't loosen your belt, don't zip or unzip zippers, and don't roll or unroll your sleeves."

"Got it."

"Your friend Vijay here is a riot, Charlotte," Miranda says. "I didn't stop laughing the whole time you were gone."

I give Vijay a skeptical look, and he shrugs. "I told you. I am very, very funny."

The PA wearing headphones pokes her head in the door. "Five minutes. We're taking you to set in five minutes. Vijay, want to come watch the warm-up comic?" He jumps up and follows her, eagerly.

"Thank you," I call as she strides out, obviously in a hurry. "So, everyone, I made a decision while I was in the chair. I'm going to offer a reward for Hudson on the air."

"Yes, but darling, didn't Henry already post that there's a cash reward on social media?"

"He did, but it didn't work. No one has come forward."

"If you need to raise the ante, I'll cover the cost," Aunt Miranda says. "I'll get you the funds, Henry," she says in a loud whisper over her shoulder. "We need to get this dog back and put this thing to bed."

"No, I want to offer something money can't buy. I'm going to offer to throw a party. A Christmas feast. At my home. I'll cook it." Just saying it out loud gives me goose bumps. I've never had more than two people at a time in my apartment. But I know in my gut that offering something personal is the key to getting through to people.

"Are you out of your mind?" Henry demands. "You most certainly are not having strangers into your flat, and that's final."

I bristle. "Did you just give me an ultimatum?"

"Charlotte, that is how people get murdered on Craig's List. I forbid it."

I didn't want to feel irritated with Henry after the lovely stretch of time we'd had, but I did. "Henry, I'm a grown woman. If I want to have people in my house, I will."

"Let's not discuss it now. There's no point in getting upset before you go on air." He clamps his mouth shut, and looks away.

"He does have a point, darling," Aunt Miranda says.

"Oh, so now you're on his side?"

"There are no sides. We're just more experienced with this kind of thing than you are."

Maybe it's my nerves about going on live TV, or maybe it's the early hour, but my head is throbbing, and I'm buzzing with fury. Across the hall, the sergeant's family are all gathered round singing *For She's a Jolly Good Fellow* and giving her hugs. I wish I were alone.

"Excuse me," I manage to say with in a civil tone. "I'm just going to pop down to the desk to see if they have any painkillers."

I avoid all eye contact as I exit the room and walk the halls looking for a couple of aspirin. A kind young man in one of the reception areas gives me some, and a bottle of water. The walk did me good. I re-jigger my mind, and start psyching myself up for the interview. By the time I'm back in the hall where my green room is, the noise from the sergeant's room has ended. She must have been taken to set. My heart lurches. I must be next.

"...texting me at all hours of the day and night." I hear Aunt Miranda say, and I freeze.

"Miranda, I kept her busy. I kept her busy for days and nights, you know that." I hold my breath. I know I shouldn't eavesdrop, but I can't help myself.

"What you should know is that this is the last time of year I can spare you."

"Then why did you assign me to watch your niece?" I hear Henry demand.

"Because you're the best. I figured that you would have this done and dusted in record time. I never counted on having to handle Macy's without you."

"If you wanted me at Macy's, then why on earth did you put me on as a babysitter?" Henry replies with a harsh edge in his voice. I feel like I've been punched in the gut.

"You're right, Henry. The fault is mine. It's a weak leader who doesn't take responsibility for her decisions. But I told you that I couldn't be dragged off task, and you let her text and phone. I didn't need to feel guilty whilst trying to pull off a mayoral wedding."

"That's not fair, Miranda. What did you want me to do? Tie her to a chair? Do you honestly think I relished missing the chance to rub shoulders with influential people in order to...to what?"

"Charlotte Bell," the PA says, tapping me on the shoulder. I hadn't even heard her walk up. "You're up. Right this way, please."

Without stopping to tell Aunt Miranda or Henry that I'm going to set, I fashion my face into a smile, focus my mind on my story, and prepare to take care of everything.

*****

"In five... four... three... two... and –" the stage manager points, and Matt Lauer's face springs to life.

"In this next half-hour of the show, we have what we hope will turn into the feel-good story of the holiday season. If you don't already know her from Twitter, Facebook, Instagram, or other social media hangouts, please meet Charlotte Bell. Charlotte's dog Hudson has become something of a sensation here in New York City this Christmas time, and we're here to give you the straight talk. Welcome, Charlotte."

"Thank you, Matt." I remember to sit up straight, not to touch my clothes, and to keep talking to Matt as though no one else were around. The stage lights above me feel like a tanning bed, and I have to squint to see the faces of the audience with the dimmed house lights. They flash the picture of Hudson and Ruby up on a giant screen behind us as Matt tells the story of my dog gate-crashing the photo shoot. When the picture appears, the audience dissolves into a chorus of "awws."

"Now, Charlotte, is it true that lots of folks think this whole 'lost dog thing' is a scam? A ploy to separate people from the money in their wallets?" I don't like where this is going. Vijay told me to

255

stay in control.

"I've heard that, Matt," I say, shocked at the confident tone of my own voice. "And I'm here to tell you that nothing could be further from the truth."

"We have a surprise guest on the line to illuminate this story. Ruby," he says to the ether. "Are you with us?"

"I'm here, Matt. G'day Charlotte. I just want to share that I believe one hundred percent that the little doggie who appeared in the photos with me was a stray. I'd have taken him home to Australia and kept him forever had my knucklehead of a little brother not turned his back and let the little fella wander off."

"Those were beautiful photos, Ruby. Just gorgeous, and reminiscent of the season."

"I just wish you all the luck in the world, Charlotte. And here's an offer I'd like to make in front of God and everyone: When that doggie gets turned back in, I'll do a shoot with him and donate all the proceeds to the animal rescue charity of your choice. Good luck, m'dear!"

"That was supermodel Ruby, weighing in on the side of Charlotte here. That number you see on your screen there at the bottom is for your local animal shelter, and we're going to put up some national numbers later in the program. Watch for those. Back to you, Charlotte. Before now, has Hudson ever escaped or run off? Have you ever lost him in a huge crowd?" A photo of Hudson when he was a puppy, and first came home to me flashes up on the huge screen. Again, the audience makes appreciative noises, louder and higher this time.

"I'm a food blogger and a recipe tester. To be honest, I don't leave my house all that much." The audience roars with laughter. I turn to them in surprise. "I'm not trying to be funny, I'm just happiest at home with my hands in a bowl of dough."

Matt smiles at me, charmed. "Great, Charlotte, just great."

"We have one more guest, and this time, he's here in person. Please welcome Officer Craig Curtis of the New York City Police Department."

Craig walks onto the stage, takes a seat next to me on the couch, and squeezes my hand.

"Welcome, Officer Curtis. Can you tell me how you fit into what has become a very public story about a very small dog?"

"Certainly Matt. I'll start at the beginning. When I first laid eyes on Charlotte, I was suspicious. We see all kinds of things as cops, and I don't think I've ever seen a person crying as hard as she was." I get to relax and let my mind wander as he tells about the search and rescue efforts. Somewhere in the middle, they flash up a photo of big, burly Craig and his pack of tiny Yorkies that almost renders the audience apoplectic. I see Henry standing behind the cameras, biting his nails. He's staring right at me, and I look away. When Craig reaches the end of the story, the video of him and the other police officers plays on the big screen, and the audience claps along. He gives me a big hug before he's called off the stage, and whispers, "I'm rootin' for you, babe," into my ear.

"Now, your parents must be very worried about you, given all the angry words and accusations, and gosh, even threats aimed at you on the internet." He gives me a concerned look, and puts his fist under his chin.

I swallow hard. "I never knew my dad, you see. And my mother, well, she died in a car crash when I was only twelve." The audience leans forward in their seats. I can hear murmurings of sympathy.

"Would you say you're pretty close with your dog, then?"

I do what Vijay said I should do. I tell my story. "He's my family, Matt."

I feel like I'm watching myself talk from above my own head, but I launch into the story of finding Hudson on the day that I found out Bridget died. I start to cry, but will myself to keep talking, flicking away the few errant tears that manage to escape.

One of the largest cameras zooms forward for a close-up, and I hear it whirr as the lens extends. Off to the corner, I catch a glimpse of a stagehand wiping his eyes with the back of his hand.

257

By the time I get to the end, I feel as though I've been talking forever. Matt is staring at me intently, brows furrowed. "So I'm asking, please. Bring Hudson back to me."

When I look up, I see Vijay punch the air and mouth "yes." Aunt Miranda stands next to Penelope, wearing a rare look of approval. Henry stands off to the side, gazing at me. If I didn't know better, I'd think the expression he's wearing is one of pure love. But now I know. He's a better actor than Vijay could have ever coached me to be.

"That was beautiful, Charlotte. I think any doubters out there have been set straight." Matt turns back to me. "So, can you tell the viewers what you want Santa to bring you this year?" The screen melts and suddenly the huge picture of me on Santa's lap at Macy's appears.

"I just want my dog back, Matt." I stare straight at Henry. "Nothing more." His face dissolves into a stung expression.

"I believe that might just happen, Charlotte! I'll bet a lot of our viewers would like to lend a hand. I understand there's a reward being offered for Hudson's safe return?"

"Yes, a cash reward."

"And I believe we have that amount and the number to call up on your screen right now."

"But Matt?"

"Yes?"

"There's more. If anyone brings Hudson back to me today, I'll cook them a real feast. Homemade. It'll be the best celebration dinner they ever had."

"Did you hear that, folks? Sounds very personal and special, from a girl who just wants her dog back home. Now, how will people find out the details?"

"I've nothing left to hide." I smile, and he smiles back. I feel buoyant when I take in a deep breath. "My life is now pretty much an open book. I'll post details on the internet." I laugh. "People sure know to find me there by now."

He laughs along with me. "Charlotte, this has been a delight. Once again, Charlotte Bell, the girl at the center of the controversy surrounding a lost dog at Christmastime. We're all waiting to see what happens. Next up, how to spruce up your holiday bathrooms and leave them smelling like Christmas came early."

"And…we're out," says the stage manager.

Aunt Miranda barrels forward and kisses me on both cheeks. "Brava, darling! And Penelope says you can keep the clothes. We're tweeting a gif of you in the outfit, sponsored by Macy's. It's a win-win. Must dash. Glad we could do this. I'm so proud." She's halfway across the studio with Penelope scooting along behind her carrying all the garment bags before she turns around, and makes a telephone shape out of her hand, and presses it to her ear. "Call you!" she mouths, and she's gone.

There's a tapping on my shoulder, and I turn around to let Henry have it.

"I didn't do it!" Vijay hollers, stunned, holding up both hands. "Sorry, automatic response. I have three brothers, and that's the look my mum would get on her face when something was broken."

"Sorry, Vijay. I thought…I thought you were someone else."

"Never mind. I just wanted to say congratulations before I have to go pick up my cab. You did everything to perfection. Those tears looked real."

"They were real," I tell him, taken aback.

"It was brilliant. You couldn't have paid for better publicity. The call from Ruby, the real New York cop. I'd wager you'll have your dog back before sundown."

"I don't know how to thank you, Vijay. I cannot believe you showed up at this hour to support me."

"I'm a comic and a taxi driver. Day is night, and night is day. Besides, you don't have to thank me. I should be thanking you! This is one of the best days of my life. I have invitations to send my tape to CBS and to Miranda Nichols of Nichols Bespoke. That's like, five years' worth of dues taken care of in one morning. You

259

are a star." He leans in and hugs me. I'm proud that I don't even flinch. I'm getting more and more used to this kind of thing.

A young man comes up and starts untaping the microphone from the back of my neck, and gently fishing the wire out from the back of my shirt. While I'm standing there, arms out, like a gingerbread woman, Henry approaches. "You were brilliant," he begins.

Once I'm released from the mic cords, I begin walking.

"Charlotte." Henry says, trying to catch up with me. I walk faster. "Charlotte!"

I turn on my heel. "You can go back to work now. Your job here is done."

I hold my head high as I stride to the green room to gather my coat and bag. I concentrate on performing one task at a time, like Vijay coached me. Walk to room, pick up coat, exit to street, hold arm up to hail cab, climb in and shut out the world.

The first tear doesn't come until we've pulled out into traffic.

*****

"Stand aside boys," the round man from 2R says to the milling and seething Corgi pair. "The park will still be there when we arrive. No need to knock our neighbors over. Can't you see the lady wants to get up the steps? By the way," he says to me, "I should introduce myself since I already know you're Charlotte."

I set down my bags, careful not to crush either of the low-to-the-ground dogs.

"I saw you on *The Today Show* this morning. I wondered where you had been. I haven't seen your lights on in days."

It had never occurred to me that my neighbors noticed my comings and goings. I'd always been fairly certain I was invisible. He continued, oblivious to my surprise. "I'm Skip. Skip Fleming. I'm really sorry to hear about Hudson. Is there anything I can do?"

Normally, I'd just say, "no, thank you" and move on as fast as

260

possible. But there was something he could do. "Actually, if you wouldn't mind, it would be great if you could post about Hudson being missing on Facebook or Twitter. That is, if you're on social media."

"Oh, I'm on all right. I belong to a whole slew of online Corgi-lover groups. I'll be happy to spread the word."

"Also, could I slide a flyer under your door? Maybe you and the boys could show it around the dog park?"

"I can do that. I'll also bring it to my Swingin' Seniors Group tonight." I must have a horrified look on my face, because he quickly says, "Not that kind of swinging. We dance. I love the music from the forties and it's great exercise."

"I'd really appreciate that." I get an idea that makes me nervous, but I say it out loud anyway. "If you want, I could bake you something in exchange. Or, if you don't eat sweets, I could cook you something. I'm a pretty good cook."

"That's what I hear from Irv and Frieda. They told me they've wanted to invite you out to dinner for ages, but they didn't want to put you on the spot. Dylan! Quit that. There's plenty of room for everyone if you two would just settle down." He shakes his head fondly. "Can't live with 'em, can't live without 'em." As soon as he says it, his eyes fly open wide. "I'm so very sorry. I wasn't thinking. Forgive me, Charlotte."

"Nothing to forgive," I assure him. With great effort, I pick up all of my shopping bags, looping them over shoulders and wrists. Skip scrambles to open the heavy door for me. "And thanks again for offering to help."

"Knock if you need anything," he says, trotting to keep up with his eager Corgi boys.

I slide my key in the door, and turn the knob. I'm damp and breathless from dragging up what served as my luggage. I didn't even have suitcases; the front desk had to supply me with an outrageous number of carrier bags to supplement the ones I got from Macy's. I only hope I packed everything. I wanted to be in and out before Henry could even consider coming by.

I laugh bitterly. I didn't have to worry about that eventuality, it seems. Apparently Henry was more than happy to get back to work and put this whole chapter behind him.

As I settle in, and unpack my bags, I'm struck to find that my apartment has a smell. I try to recall whether I've ever been away long enough to notice it. When you're in your own home every day, your nose just gets used to it. I sniff, closing my eyes. I smell cinnamon, and yeast, and a touch of wet dog. I remember how I used to fuss at Hudson for coming in from the rain, and shaking off next to the furniture. I'd give anything to have him rub his muddy paws all over the rug right about now.

Walking into the kitchen, I inhale again, trying to imprint the smell of my home onto my brain. Through some sort of trick of my mind, I recall Henry's scent instead. Mossy, grassy, with a touch of earth. Close up, he smells like the air after a storm. Oh well, I tell myself, grabbing the milk from the fridge, I won't be smelling that smell again. I might as well forget I ever did.

I unscrew the cap, and sniff the milk to see if it's still good. Surprisingly, it is, and the smell pops me back to the present. I make myself a cup of coffee, and take a few deep drinks as I walk around the apartment, heading nowhere in particular. I go to the window seat where Hudson naps in the early morning while I write. A few white dog hairs glint in a sunbeam. I sit down, and stare at my rug. I'm beginning to feel the fatigue from waking early, and all the emotion. What if I really don't get Hudson back? For the first time since all this started, I feel like I could go on. It's the way this all happened that's so terrible. To just have someone go missing means you can never rest. To lose Hudson this way would mean there would be no closure. Losing loved ones is a part of life, but having it happen this way is particularly cruel.

Before I realize it, I'm dialing Aunt Miranda's number. To my surprise, she picks up. "Hello, darling. Any word on Hudson?" I'm touched that that's the first thing she asks me.

"No, nothing yet. But I just got home. I haven't even switched on the computer."

"Anyone with information will call the phone line we had set up, so you don't need to be right on top of it. Give your nerves a rest. Henry will let me know if there's news. Hold on a minute. *No, you cannot substitute polyester napkins for cotton ones. Were you born in a barn?* Sorry about that, Charlotte."

"I should let you get back to work."

"It's fine. These monkeys need to learn to figure things out on their own sometime. Now, you called for a reason. What did you need?"

"I forget. We can talk later."

"We can, and we will. But we're on the phone now, so we may as well talk. Listen Charlotte," she says, clearing her throat. "I meant to phone you myself but the day got away from me. I wanted to tell you that I thought you did a very good job on the show this morning."

"Thank you, Aunt Miranda."

"That story you told." She clears her throat again. "I suppose I knew some of it, but I didn't know it that way. Your way, I mean." There's a long silence.

"I wasn't sure if I could tell it."

More silence.

"I wish you had told me. I'm sorry."

"Sorry for what?"

"Everything, really." I hear her breathing. "I wish I'd done a better job. I wish I'd thought to fly you back to visit Bridget. I didn't realize how important she was to you."

"I never told you."

"You were a child, Charlotte. I just didn't know enough about raising a child. Hold on, darling. *Do you not see that I am on the phone? Go ask Henry. I'm not to be disturbed. Go tell the others. Please.* Excuse me. As I was saying, I wish I had done better. Just... just that. I wish I had done better."

263

My heart swells. Poor Aunt Miranda. "You did the best you knew how. And that's good enough. Hey, look at me. I'm pretty great, wouldn't you say?" I grin.

"I would say. Listen, about that reward you offered. I'll find you a venue."

"What do you mean?"

"I mean that I worry about you. I won't forbid you to have a party in your own home. I see where that got Henry. But I will suggest you let me help you do this in a more public place." She pauses. "Let me help."

There was a time when I would have just said no straight away. As if it would have cost me something. "All right," I tell her, heart open. "That sounds nice. Aunt Miranda, you know I didn't reveal all those things to hurt your feelings, don't you?"

"Of course, darling. I doubt that what you did was easy. As I said, I'm proud of you."

"I'm proud of myself."

"I'll tell you what. Let me rethink Christmas dinner. Surely I can juggle this and that, and put a few people in charge. The mayor won't miss me if I duck out for a few hours, surely. I can't make a blood promise, my dear, but I don't want you to be alone over the holidays."

"I'd like that."

"Good. Now, was there anything else before I hang up?"

"Yes, one thing." I swallow hard. "I love you, Aunt Miranda."

"Oh," she says, "I love you too, my darling."

Chapter 14

The phone wakes me early the next morning. Everything about being in my bed felt strange last night, from the sensation of something being missing because Hudson wasn't curled up against my leg, to the feeling that the duvet cover wasn't the one from the Waldorf, to a sense that I didn't quite belong here. I was itchy and raw, like a hermit crab who'd outgrown her shell.

"Hello?" I croak.

"Good morning, Charlotte." My heart sinks at the sound of the voice. "It's Henry Wentworth."

"I know who you are. You don't have to tell me your last name."

"Force of habit. Anyway, I'm phoning with news."

I don't say anything.

"Per Miranda." Even though I didn't want to hear from him, underscoring that he had to call me stings.

"Have you checked social media this morning?" I open one eye, look at the clock. 6:25.

"No, not yet," I tell him. "Why are you up so early?"

"There's been a crisis. Paparazzi have released photos of the mayor's daughter in a wedding dress on the shores of Fiji. Miranda just arrived, and is assessing the situation."

"I'm sorry to hear that for her sake, but why are you calling to tell me that before sun rise?"

"Unbelievable as this may seem, when I arrived onsite around 5 a.m., we heard a cluster of reports from management suggesting that Hudson, or a dog very similar to him, was spotted in several locations inside of Macy's by security before closing last night."

I struggle to process what he's saying. Then an idea forms that makes sense of it all in my pre-caffeinated brain. "Could it be because Miranda had Penelope tweet that my *Today Show* outfit was from Macy's? It's probably a prank, like when those people photoshopped Hudson in with President Obama, showing them going into the Waldorf. You know as well as I do how these things take on a life of their own."

"That's what I thought when I first heard. Which is why I didn't contact you. I wanted to give the story time to play out. The thing is, several of the night guards, independent of this, reported seeing what they thought might be a large rat or a small, hairy toddler."

"Hudson doesn't look like a rat!"

"And he likely doesn't look like a hirsute child, either. But night watchmen in New York City don't expect to see dogs running wild in major department stores in the middle of the night."

I roll over, and rub my eyes. "But they expect to see feral children?" I pad to the kitchen to make myself a cup of coffee. I really need it.

Henry sighs in frustration. "This is neither here nor there. I had Landry and the others go over this, and it looks like a credible lead."

"Oh," I say in a snotty tone. I know I should shut my mouth, but without coffee, the path from my brain to my mouth seems to have no filter. "You had *Landry* go over it. Figures!" I have to scoot trays and trays of Bakewell tarts, peppermint creams, Everton toffee, scotch tablet, and Irish flapjacks out of the way to make room to brew my morning cup. I'd distracted myself last night by finally catching up on my blog, and by testing numerous recipes from the English Meals cookbook. The fallout took up every inch of counter space.

"Figures, you say?" He snorts angrily. "What's that supposed to mean?" I can tell Henry is struggling to remain professional, but I can hear the cracks in his demeanor.

"It means I already told you not to bother calling me, and here we are on the phone!"

"I am doing my job. And for your information, the next part of my job *per your aunt* is to find you a venue for your reward party, so expect more phone calls from where this one came from," he blathers. "I may call you every hour on the hour, so strap in miss!"

"You'd better not!"

"Oh, just watch me. I'm likely to have lots and lots of reports and updates. Sorry if you find that annoying!"

I put the phone down on him. It rings again, immediately.

"What?!!" I scream into the receiver.

"Charlotte, it's Craig. We may have found Hudson."

*****

I exit the cab with shopping bags full of my homemade treats. Stress baking can really leave a girl with more than she can eat. I figure I give some to Craig, and hand a few around to Jane and Penelope. Even though it's just past 8 a.m., the streets are filled with shoppers and tourists. Families are taking videos of the moving puppet scenes in Macy's windows, children bundled up and sipping hot cocoa. There is already a line of women at the 7th Avenue entrance, faces determined. Two more days till Christmas, and people are eager to complete their last-minute shopping.

I text Craig, as instructed, to let him know I've arrived. Flurries dance in the chill air, but it's not bitterly cold as some Decembers have been in past years. I set my bags down on a dry patch of sidewalk under an awning and take in the scene. 34th Street looks beautiful with long garlands of pine and red ribbon twining around the light posts and the temporary planters of squat fir trees in planters lining the length of it. I wonder what next year's holidays will be like for me. For a minute or two, I allow myself to imagine what Christmas will be like if Hudson isn't found. I try to picture myself dealing with bad news gracefully, but I can't. I'm startled out of my reverie by the sharp cry of a toddler in his stroller. He's dropped his little snowman toy in the snow, and his father dives for it, and shakes off the snow before handing it back. The little boy snuffles, and tries to catch his breath.

I look up to see Craig standing at the glass door, waving. He's with a Macy's employee in a suit, who is turning keys in the door. "Stand back, ladies and gentlemen," Craig says, "Official police business, please let the lady through." I squirm through the crowd, dragging my shopping bags of baked goods, and the door is locked behind me.

"Where's Leonard?" I ask.

"I'm not officially on duty," Craig explains. "I just wanted to follow up on this lead myself. After that mess with the kidnapping and the harness, I didn't like the idea that someone might be baiting you."

"What do you mean by baiting me?"

"It's just an awfully big coincidence. The public knows your aunt is working with the mayor's daughter's wedding at Macy's. It's been all over the papers." I follow him onto one of the antique wood escalators going down. He looks right and left. "People know your aunt has money, and they sure as hell know the mayor has money." He surveys the store. "I just want to make sure all the bases are covered and there's no funny business."

We get to the Cellar, where the pop-up restaurant is, but there's no bustle of activity the way there was the last time I was here. I spy Aunt Miranda standing, holding an iPad, and staring into space. "Hi Aunt Miranda," I say.

"Oh, Charlotte, I was a million miles away. Can you believe all of this is for nothing?" she asks, waving her arm toward the now very chic pop-up restaurant space.

There are a few people working and I look around, telling myself that I'm not searching for Henry. "Aunt Miranda, this is

Officer Craig Curtis. He's the one who has been helping me look for Hudson."

She snaps out of her funk, and comes to life. Extending her hand, she smiles and says, "Of course. Lovely to meet you, Officer. I recognize you from that clever video you and your colleagues produced. I appreciate all you've done for my niece."

"Happy to do it for a friend," he says. "You haven't seen anything unusual down here, have you Ms. Nichols?"

"Nothing I can think of. I'll certainly let you know if I do."

"Alright, then. If you ladies will excuse me, I'm going to head up to security and interview the guys from the night shift. They're waiting to go home."

"Thanks, Craig," I say.

"Not a problem," he tells me. "I might go through some of the security camera footage as well. I've got my phone. Call me if you need me," he says and heads back up the escalator.

"How are you holding up, dear?" Aunt Miranda asks me. I'm moved. Up till now, it had seemed like she barely noticed I'd been upset about Hudson.

"About the same. How about yourself?" I ask.

She sinks into a folding chair. "Not well, I must admit." She sighs. "Pulling this off would have been a real feather in my cap. The sad part is, I chose to give up my holiday to work on this project, and now I'll have nothing to show for it."

"Surely they're going to pay you?"

"Yes, that's not an issue. In fact, they pre-paid the fee, and have paid for everything we've ordered so far. There are refrigerators and freezers full of food, and a storeroom filled with linens, crockery, and flatware. The list goes on and on. I have no idea how I'm going to break the news to James. He turned down a chance at guest starring on Martha Stewart's holiday special to do this. He'll be devastated to have lost the publicity."

I felt bad to hear that, even if James wasn't my favorite person. I wondered if they'd have to lay off all of the servers, bartenders, and other staff they had booked. It would be a huge blow to lose work during the holiday season. "It'll all work out, Aunt Miranda," I told her, only half-believing my own words.

"You're right, darling. It will. I just have to think of something. No ideas are coming to me at the moment. My brain is in lockdown." She looks at her watch, and sighs. "The store is going to open soon," she says, and stands up. "I'd better get what little staff we have here to straighten up. I hate to say it, but we may have to start breaking down and moving out."

"You don't have many people here."

"I sent most of them back to the office. Henry's there fielding calls about the wedding, and doing damage control. That wedding was going to launch this pop-up. Macy's had planned that it would be packed for the period between Christmas and New Year's."

"Can I help you with anything?"

"Not at the moment, but thanks."

"If you're sure?" She nods. "Then I'm going to see if I can find Jane or Penelope and ask them if they know anything about Hudson."

"Yes, go." Aunt Miranda has a faraway look in her eyes, as if she's thinking hard. "I hope you get good news." She gives me her usual European air kisses, but this time she ends by pulling me in for a squeeze.

*****

"Do you want a refill before the doors open?" Penelope asks me, holding up the carafe of the coffee pot. I nod, and she takes my mug. She and Jane and I had been sitting around the 8th-floor employee lounge chatting and drinking coffee for nearly half an hour.

"So, tell me again about the night guard. I'm confused."

"When I got here a little before seven," Jane says, "I run into Murray on my way to clock in. He looks really scared, like he's seen a ghost or something. I say to him, 'Murray, what's the matter with you? You look like hell warmed over,' and he says to me, 'Jane, I think I saw one of them *chupacabras* in the fine china department.' He said it had big yellow eyes, and moved real fast and low to the ground. I told him that *chupacabras* only live in like fields or forests in like Mexico or the Amazon or something. I told him they eat stuff like groundhogs or squirrels or something, and how was it gonna survive at Macy's, by going behind the counter at Mixed Greens and tossing himself up a salad?"

"He broke over five hundred dollars' worth of Mikasa dinnerware, Jane," Penelope says. "This wouldn't be the first time he was drunk on the job. He needed an excuse so he wouldn't be blamed for the damage."

"He does carry that flask," Jane says thoughtfully. "It's probably his mind playing tricks on him."

"The only thing that keeps me from writing the whole thing off," Penelope says, putting our mugs in the half-sized dishwasher, "Is that Bernice from lingerie said in her closing report that she had to call janitorial to clean up a pile of something she found in the fitting room."

"Hudson is housebroken," I say automatically. In all the time he's lived with me, he's never had an accident in the apartment.

"So am I," Jane says, "but if you leave me someplace without a bathroom long enough, and all bets will be off. Nature calls, you know."

"I won't go into gory details," Penelope says, reapplying her lipstick in front of the mirror by the door, "but you'd be surprised at the kinds of things we've found in the bathrooms and fitting rooms."

"I know, like…" Jane begins.

"Tsst!" Penelope hisses. "Too gross."

"But tell her about the…"

"Shh!" Penelope warns. "Too shocking."

"But what about the security cam tape where…"

271

"Stop!" Penelope says, hand in the air. "The lawyers say we can never, never mention that. Male politician. Brassiere," she whispers. "You didn't hear it from me."

"Macy's will be opening in five minutes," a smooth voice purrs over the loudspeaker. "Employees please take your positions. Let's make today a great day for ourselves and our guests."

"Hey, Pen," Jane says, "What say we take Charlotte down for a makeover again? If we tell the big managers that Ms. Nichols doesn't have much for us to do, they might make us start doing inventory early."

Penelope considers it. "Come on," Jane says, "You don't always have to be a goody two shoes."

"Why not? It's almost Christmas. We deserve a little fun. Maybe I'll get my own brows done while we're at it."

*****

I'm seated in a big, padded salon chair, while T'Kwon is working his magic on my hair. He's pulling it out, section by section, with a big, fat round brush while I'm bent over at the waist. So far, the three of us have spent nearly two hours hopping from one cosmetic counter to the next, having lips done here, eyes done there, and being spritzed with intoxicating scents. I wonder what, if anything, Craig has found out. I wish he'd call my cell.

At one point during our makeovers, a senior manager came by to check on Penelope and Jane, and Jane told such a convincing story about how we all needed to look good for a Macy's-based Vine shoot pleading for Hudson's return while putting the store's best foot forward, I almost believed it myself.

Once the boss was satisfied and had moved on, Jane shouted from her chair, "Where is your hunky boyfriend today?"

The coffee in my stomach curdles. "He's not my boyfriend," I holler back, just as T'Kwon shuts off the dryer. Everyone within fifty feet turns to look.

272

"Me thinks the lady doth protest too much," T'Kwon says, fluffing my hair with his splayed fingers.

"No, it's the truth. Turns out he never was. He was just using me to get on my aunt's good side. I was nothing more than a step on the career ladder to Henry Wentworth."

"That's his name? Henry Wentworth?" T'Kwon asks. "Mmm mmm mmm. That is sexy. That is real sexy."

"You're not helping, T'Kwon." Jane chastises.

"Oh, I'm sorry," the stylist says, getting his bearings. "I meant to say you're too good for him, honey." He circles my head with a fast-flowing can of hairspray. "You can do better than that no good ol' Henry Wentworth."

"That's right!" Penelope chimes in.

"Mmm mmm mmm. Henry Wentworth," T'Kwon murmurs under his breath. "That is just too sexy."

"T'Kwon!" Jane bellows.

"Sorry," he answers meekly. "Well alright then, Cinderella," he says, taking off my cape. "Get on with your bad self." I look at the result in the mirror. It's the best version of me I've ever seen. I flash back to the look on Henry's face when he saw me after my first Macy's makeover, and I feel an ache in my chest.

"Come along, ladies. We still have carte blanche to dress Charlotte up on the Macy's tab. Let's take her up to ladies' wear and play with our human doll while we can."

"You look hot," Jane says. "You'll find a new man in no time, right Pen? Maybe we could introduce her to Girard in Fine Leather."

"Gay," Penelope declares.

"How about Frank from up in Customer Service."

"Lives with his mom."

"That's not so bad."

"In Newark."

"Oh no," Jane responds. "Next! Jamal from the loading dock?"

"Girlfriend."

"Nicky from Menswear?"

"Divorced."

"So?"

"Three times?"

"Thanks anyway, girls," I break in, "but not everyone was born to be coupled up. I've tried it. I'm much happier on my own." With Hudson, I think. The idea that I might never get him back creeps back in, and I feel tears threatening to rise.

"I refuse to believe that," Jane says, as we ride up the escalator. "I believe there's a cup for every saucer. I'm not giving up till I find my soul mate, and neither should you."

Penelope motions for us to join her at a large rack of wrap dresses, and starts sifting through the merchandise.

"I'll cross my fingers for you, Jane. I'll even dance at your wedding if you invite me. But I don't believe it for myself." I rifle through a round rack of silk blouses, while Penelope holds first one dress, and then another up in the air for our votes. As I'm flicking through the hangers, I feel Jane step on my foot. "Ow!" I say, involuntarily.

"You OK?" Jane asks me from across the aisle. I feel it again. Quickly, I duck under the blouses to check, but there's nothing there.

My cell buzzes, distracting me. I see that it's Aunt Miranda, and I pick up.

"Hello?"

"Charlotte, darling. I've been on the phone with Henry over at the office. He's had the most marvelous idea. He told me not to tell you he suggested it, for whatever reason. No ego at all, that boy."

I snort.

"What's that, darling?"

"Nothing. Go on."

"I told him to find a space for you to do your little reward dinner if someone brought your dog back. Instead, he came up with an altogether new idea that I think is brilliant. Instead of throwing a party to reward someone for bringing Hudson back, he said, why not reverse the idea? Throw a party to *invite* someone to bring Hudson back? Why not have it in the pop-up, he suggested, since it's sitting empty?"

It's a great idea, I'm only miffed that Henry was the one to think of it. More brown-nosing at my expense. "When?" I ask.

"This evening."

Wow, I think. That's soon. But what if I could get Hudson back by Christmas? "OK!" I agree. "Let's do it."

"Wonderful," she tells me. "Henry said he has Landry lying in wait, ready to pull the trigger on the social media announcements. He tells me that she's turning out to be quite an asset. It seems she nearly as big an asset as he is."

"Almost," I say, fuming. "But not quite."

*****

Jane and Penelope have been stars, helping me set out a handful of the baked goods I brought onto platters, and make a cozy corner to offer treats to anyone who might find Hudson. We set a table for eight, even though that might be overkill. Anything smaller just didn't look festive, in Penelope's opinion. Aunt Miranda asked the staff to lend a hand, and a few of them helped us pull out carrots, celery, and radishes to make a crudité plate. While they were doing that, I spotted some phyllo dough in the freezer, along with some frozen spinach. I rooted around in the giant fridges until I found some feta cheese and I whipped up a tray of spanakopita.

"We need flowers," Jane chimes in. Before I know it, Miranda has one of her assistants on the phone with the florist that had been engaged to do the wedding.

"Wait till you see this," one of the other assistants tells me. She rolls out a cart with some electrical equipment on it, flips a few switches and suddenly the entire restaurant is bathed in a soft, welcoming light. It's a breathtaking contrast to the regular daytime store light. "How on earth did that happen?" I ask.

"Your aunt knows what she's doing. She called in lighting designers to make sure the bride would glow."

I have to admit, it's perfection. Jane and Penelope look lovely bathed in the pinkish illumination. "Hey there, Miss Charlotte," Craig says, strolling up with Officer Scrivello. "I've got good news and bad news."

"Hi Leonard," I say, and he tips his hat. "Give me the bad news first."

"The bad news is that we don't have concrete proof of anything. Turns out, about ten people posted things on Twitter last night saying that they saw strange things in Macy's yesterday. There were a couple of pictures, but they were too dark or blurry to tell anything for sure. One guy swears he saw a dog who looks like Benjy from those seventies movies sitting on the train in Santa Land, and he thought it was a publicity push for a remake."

"What's the good news?"

"The good news is that there haven't been any more threats or demands for cash. We were worried about copycat activity."

My heart falls a few notches. I was hoping for something better.

"Thanks, Craig." I say.

"When we were looking for clues, we saw your announcements everywhere. Word is spreading. People are reposting the tweets and photos about how you're waiting here at Macy's. They put it up on their blog, along with that picture of you sitting on Santa's lap."

"Speaking of that, Charlotte," Penelope says, staring at her phone. "I just got a text. They want to know if you'll come up to the main office to take a few shots. The management here really wants to see you get your dog back. They're going to stop advertising on the big screens outside the store today, and just put up a picture of you and a plea to bring Hudson back."

I swallow. "The big screens on the sides of the store?"

"Yes," Penelope tells me, "and even better," she says waving her phone in the air. "They're also going to put it up on all the electronic billboards they've rented around the city, and believe it

276

or not, on the Jumbotron space they've bought in Times Square."

"That all sounds awesome," Craig says. "But listen. Scrivello and I have to go check in at the precinct uptown."

"Oh," I say. It sounds sadder than I meant it to.

"But don't worry, we're still on top of it. We have our buddies on the trail, and as always, if we hear anything, you'll be the first to know."

"Thanks, guys."

"Charlotte, come with me. Let's go get this picture taken. The faster we do, the faster your face will be all over New York City."

As I follow her up, I wonder if Henry will catch a glimpse of my face. I wonder if he'd even notice.

*****

The store is mobbed with holiday shoppers, and it takes forever to make it back to the Cellar from the administrative offices. The deed is done. The guy who handles publicity showed me how he edited my photo so there would be an image of Hudson in the corner, and added a slogan and contact info. He hit a button, and the poster hit the streets of New York almost immediately. While he was working on the computer, he hopped from platform to platform showing me how news of the "Bring Hudson Home" celebration was spreading like wildfire. Matt Lauer tweeted,

Make a sweet girl happy this Christmas. Macy's 2nite. B there or B square. #BringHudsonHome

As the escalator conveys Penelope and me down to the pop-up, I see James's curly brown hair. He's in his chef's whites, with his back to me. I turn and start walking up the down escalator, before Penelope grabs my wrist, asking "What are you doing?"

Too late. James turns and sees me, a big smile spreading across his face. The little I can see of the restaurant looks lovely, and there is jazzy Christmas music playing. "Hey Charlotte. I caught wind of all the hubbub and thought I'd swing by to see if I could lend a hand. Your aunt told me you were cooking," he smiles a television smile at me. "We always made a great team in the kitchen."

"I'll give you that, James. That was the one room where we made a great team."

"Hey, hey, now Feisty," he says, holding up his hands to defend himself. "I really am here to help. I saw the pictures. I feel bad about your little dog. I never knew you were a dog person."

There was so much about me you never knew, I think. "Where's Mira?"

"Out of the picture," he says, shrugging. "From the looks of it, your guy is, too. No reason we can't keep each other company, isn't that right?"

"Charlotte," Jane says, poking me in the ribs. "It's Christmas, for Pete's sake. The guy is here to help you." From between her teeth, she says, "Be nice."

"Yes," I tell James. "Why not? Thanks for offering to help."

"Anytime. Hey, I made hummus and I'm thinking about making a salmon-cream cheese spread. I could make toast points. Stop back by the kitchen." He smiles a genuine smile that actually makes me smile back. "What do you say?"

"Sounds like a plan."

He flashes me one last smile before going back to his post in the kitchen.

"I cannot believe James Keyes is flirting with you!" Jane squeals. "I love his stuff on the Food Channel. Can I offer to help in the kitchen? Maybe he'll sign my spatula."

"Go for it," I tell her. She runs off eagerly. Maybe he's not that bad after all. Maybe he never was. Henry pops into my head and I sigh. Maybe I was born without the good judge of character gene.

No wonder I prefer dogs to men.

*****

I'm nervously pacing the perimeter when I see the elevator doors open, and a family emerges, including a young man in a motorized wheelchair with a small pig seated in his lap. The family from the news story about Hudson in Serendipity light up when they see me. Penelope appears by my shoulder, smiling, and greets them.

"I hope you don't mind that we're here, Charlotte. When Bobby saw the news story on the TV in our hotel room, saying that Hudson would be back tonight, he asked if we could come say hello. He fell in love with that little dog the day we met him. As disappointed as he is that we'll never be taking him home with us, he was happy to see you on the Today Show. He just wanted to know the little fella wasn't on his own."

"Oh! Well, I'm not sure that Hudson will be here tonight, Bobby. Of course I hope someone brings my dog back to me, but there's no way to predict what will happen." I feel bad. I hope I haven't led these people down the wrong path. I don't want to see them disappointed.

"He will be," an atonal, electronic voice says.

"That's how Bobby communicates. Lots of people ask us if he's related to Stephen Hawking because they sound so much alike," the mother says, winking at her son. Bobby cracks up.

"That joke never gets old," says Bobby's proxy voice. I laugh. His dad scans the room. "You've done the place up real nice. Why don't we wait someplace else? Looks like we crashed your party."

"Don't be silly," I say. I'm happy to have them with me. It feels like good luck. "Please, join us." Penelope, ever polite and proper, invites them to follow her with the promise of drinks and snacks.

The elevator doors open again, and this time there are two men pushing carts with countless flower arrangements and loose, long stems. "Delivery for Nichols. Where do you want 'em?"

"Erm, I'm not sure."

Aunt Miranda comes sweeping up beside me. "Good. You've arrived. You were due an hour ago, but better late than never."

"What is all this, Aunt Miranda??

279

"When we called the florist, we found out that they'd already started assembling the wedding flowers. The bill has already been paid by the mayor, so I told them to go ahead and bring what they had. Over here, men," she says, leading them through the entrance to the pop-up.

Looking at my watch, I realize it's nearly the time we'd publicized that the party would begin. Nervously, I glance up the escalator. Who do I see but Landry, standing tall and proud on the descending conveyor, like the figurehead on the prow of a ship. Behind her is a man holding a large camera emblazoned with the New York One logo, and a reporter whom I recognize from the news channel. What I thought was going to be a little incentive party to entice a kind citizen to give back my extraordinary dog, rather than hold onto him, is beginning to take on a life of its own. Feeling overwhelmed, I walk back to the kitchen area to get a drink of water.

"Charlotte, James here was just saying how wonderful you looked on *The Today Show*," Miranda said. "Let me get out of your way," she says, pushing me toward the stove where James is sautéing garlic in olive oil. "I'll just let you experts work." As she breezes by me, she whispers in my ear, "Together."

He tips a dozen or so long, green asparagus into the pan from a cutting board. "I've missed you, Charlotte."

"James, don't." I'm filled to my eyeballs with a wide variety of emotions, ranging from anticipation, to fear, to shyness. A confessional speech from James might just do me in.

"I really think you should hear this. I've been with women since you. Lots of women," he says. He adds finely chopped red pepper to the pan. "Look at that, Christmassy, right?"

"It's gorgeous," I tell him. "Maybe it's a bit on the nose, but at Christmas time, I think that's a good thing."

"Anyway, lots of women. Lots. In lots of different ways."

I roll my eyes. "Go on."

"You were the best of the bunch." He pours the tasty morsels onto a while platter, and sprinkles dark green chopped parsley leaves on top.

"That's nice of you to say."

He hands me the platter. I take it, but he doesn't let go. We're standing eye-to-eye. "If I knew then what I know now, I would have cherished you more."

I'm dumbstruck. I don't recall ever hearing James say much of anything that was self-aware or humble. "I, um, need to get out there. Just in case."

"Let's have dinner."

I take the platter. "I'm kind of in the middle of something," I say, deflecting.

"Not now. You name the date." He gives me a long, serious look. "Think about it."

I whisk the platter through the flap that cuts off the kitchen in the restaurant tent, and head for the food table. Someone has pushed in four more tables and there are people seated all around. In the middle of the table is a platter of gefilte fish I don't recognize. Suddenly, I'm squeezed from behind.

"Bubbeleh!" Mrs. Rabinowitz cries. "Any word about Hudson?"

"Not yet," I tell her, scanning the table. There's an open bottle of Manishewitz wine, and several people are drinking it from small plastic glasses.

"Sheldon, my delivery boy, such a tech genius he is. He read out to me all of the goings on about the welcome party for Hudson."

"It's not really a welcome party," I tell her. "I don't know if anyone is going to bring him back tonight or not. I had just planned to offer dinner for one, maybe two people…"

"Doesn't matter," she says. "What matters is I'm here. I couldn't stand the thought of you waiting here, biting your nails, by yourself. My husband Abe came to keep us company. 'You can't show up without some schnapps', he says, and of course he's right. We brought a little of this, a little of that. I didn't know you'd have so many guests!"

"Neither did I," I say, as more people stream down the escalator and head for the restaurant. Penelope is functioning as hostess, welcoming people, and seating them. Uniformed waiters are starting to pass trays of hors d'oeuvres. I give her a quick hug. "Will you excuse me, Mrs. Rabinowitz?"

I find Jane, and ask her what's going on. "Who are all these people? Did the mayor not cancel the wedding party?"

"Mayor?" she says. "These people didn't come for the mayor, they're here to see Hudson. "See that couple over there with the fanny packs talking to Bobby's family?" I glance over at a middle-aged couple wearing matching shirts, fussing over Daisy the Service Pig. Seated regally next to them is a tall, chocolate brown Standard Poodle, wearing a bandana printed with snowflakes. "Last summer, they lost Cocoa when they were hiking in the Catskills, and a ranger returned him two weeks later. They saw your story on *The Today Show* and wanted to come show support. And that guy over there said he waited on you during the Michael Bublé concert."

I wave, and the waiter holds up his little Peek-a-Poo.

"That's Popcorn," Jane continues. "Manuel, you know, from the Rainbow Room, just said he was on his way over to pick up his holiday bonus check, saw Macy's and decided to drop in and meet Hudson."

"Where did all the waiters come from?"

"From the agency we were going to use for the wedding, I guess. That aunt of yours is a force of nature. Between you and me, I just heard her tell the captain to tell James Keyes to unlock the wine fridge." In a sing-songy voice, she trills, "There's gonna be champagne!"

I look over the crowd, and see Craig and Leonard, still in full NYPD uniform, holding their mounted police helmets, and posing for photos with various smiling people who look like tourists.

Five handsome men are standing in a small circle, harmonizing to find a pitch.

"Um, Jane? Who are they?"

"Some guys from the Gay Men's chorus. Apparently, they saw you on *The Today Show* and planned to come over after their Carnegie Hall gig. They told me they were all not only singers, but the tall one runs one of those Adoption Day vans you always see down by Union Square. A bunch of random animal lovers, I suppose. They asked me if I minded if they did a few Christmas tunes as long as they were here. Is that OK with you?"

"Why not?" I ask, my head spinning. "What's next, trapeze artists?" I can't believe the way this simple event was mushrooming. Aunt Miranda sweeps by, and leans over my shoulder, "This is getting big. Really big! Landry just told me that the local network news feeds are being picked up by nationals. The combination of the mayor's daughter eloping, James Keyes doing a surprise eclectic pop-up, plus the Hudson story. We weren't prepared. The pop-up launch wasn't supposed to be for days, not until after we cleared out the wedding supplies and brought in the pop-up restaurant supplies. I haven't had this much fun since Julia Roberts cancelled her wedding to Kiefer Sutherland! The creative juices are flowing, my dear. Absolutely flowing. Walk with me," she says, "Keep up the pace, already in motion."

"Excuse me," I say to Jane and the chorus singers, and follow Aunt Miranda to the kitchen. There are four sous chefs, all in chef's whites with bandanas or toques, chopping, marinating, and filleting. "I called in the troops," James tells me.

To my surprise, Mrs. Rabinowitz is standing above a giant bowl of grated potatoes, cracking in eggs, while James listens to her instructions, flipping dozens of pancakes on the griddle. "Charlotte, you'll have a *latke,* maybe two? Your James here let me into his kitchen. What's a holiday party without *latkes?*"

James turns and smiles. "Your James," he mouths. I can't deal. I walk out in search of Penelope. She has a level head. If there's been any word about Hudson, surely she'd know it. Instead, I run into Jane. She's twirling a long piece of her hair, leaning against a wall. A man leans in, whispering in her ear, and she giggles. He turns and says, "Oh, 'ello! I was told to messenger the stray items you left in your suite, but I saw on ze news zat you were here, so I decided I'd deliver them in person." He holds up a small carrier bag that says, *The Waldorf-Astoria* on it.

"Oh, no. Come with me, young lady." I grab Jane by the arm, and pull her along with me.

"Hey! That guy was friendly."

"You have no idea how friendly. I'll fill you in later. For now, help me find Penelope."

A swell of music fills the air, and I look up to see that someone has put together a small dais, and covered it with cloth. It must have been here for the Bride's table. Standing on it are the tuxedoed chorus singers, doing a soulful a cappella rendition of *Rockin' Around the Christmas Tree*. More tables have been set up, and dozens and dozens of people, including several elves from Santa Land, are seated with flutes of champagne, eating from china plates, drumming their fingers on tables along to the beat.

We're intercepted by a very Landry on the way to find Penelope. "Excuse, me. Charlotte? I just need a moment of your time." She reaches out and slaps a badge on my chest that says, "HELLO my name is Charlotte." My hand flies to my breast. I feel violated.

Jane crosses her arms and tilts her head. I can already tell she doesn't like Landry. "I just wanted to let you know that I'm your point of contact now, per Miranda." She smiles a knowing smile. "I suppose I should really say per Henry." She brightens up when she says his name. "He's the one who gave me the promotion, in reality, even though she had to approve it." She tosses her hair back over one shoulder. "You're in capable hands. I wanted to tell you that personally." She leans in, whispering. "Henry briefed me that you're a little unstable."

Jane puffs out her chest. "Henry, her old boyfriend, said that?"

"Old boyfriend?" A shadow crosses Landry's face. "Henry didn't tell me you were together." She composes herself. "It must have slipped his mind." A sly smirk appears at the corner of her mouth.

284

"We haven't been getting a lot of sleep lately."

"Yeah, well you look like you could use a little more." She circles her own eye with her finger, and whispers, "Dark circles."

Landry scowls.

"Anyway," Jane says, linking her arm through mine. "It's a lie. She's not unstable. She's just very emotional."

"Jane!" I protest.

"In a good way."

"I'm sure Henry didn't mean anything by it," Landry says in a light voice. "You know Henry, ever taking care of the little people around him. I so admire him for that."

"Yeah, well, I gotta go admire a glass of champagne," Jane says, pulling me away. "Maybe I'll admire two after that conversation," she tells me out of the side of her mouth.

"Jane," calls a young woman sitting at one of the tables. "Have you eaten? I've never had such great food in my life. Her plate was an eclectic mix of food from all over the world, with ultra-high-end cheffy morsels thrown in for good measure. I look around to see where it's all coming from. In addition to waiters passing trays, there's now a long buffet table set up with stacks of the *latkes*, trays of lasagna, the rest of my baked goods, pans of curried chick peas in sauce, and more. Standing at the end of the line, scooping beans and rice onto his plate, is Vijay.

"There she is! My girlfriend and I came to say hello to Hudson. When I told my mother about this idea for getting your dog back, she asked me to drive by our family house out in Queens. I told her how you got me the warm-up comic gig on *The Today Show*, and she wanted to show her gratitude. She sent four trays of food... palak paneer, channa masala, and lots more. It's a good thing you decided to have a party! Her food alone was enough for an army."

"You got a gig doing the pre-show warm-up? That's amazing, Vijay. You deserve it."

"Wait! You didn't read my email?" He sets his plate aside and throws his arms around me. "I didn't just get the gig doing warm-ups, the producer liked my story about being a cab-driving doctor so much, I'm going to be featured on a segment called 'Ordinary Folks Who Follow Their Dreams.' I can never thank you enough. Do you have any idea what kind of exposure something like that can get a person?"

I gesture to the room. "I think I have a pretty fair idea."

Vijay points, "Aw, look at those short, fat little dogs. So cute."

Jane says, "The Corgis? They're not fat," she coos protectively, "they're just big-boned."

I swing around to see Skip. He's hand-feeding Dylan and Connor from his plate. I approach the table, and give the dogs pats on the head. They're too busy scarfing down jumbo shrimp to pay me much attention. "Oh, hey Charlotte. I was looking for you," Skip says. The webmaster for the Corgi Club website called me to tell me there was a big public party for Hudson. Dylan and Connor and I wanted to be here for you, to help pass the time while you wait. We have his photo up on the site, you know. On the way out, we ran into Irv and Frieda, so I brought them, too. I don't think you've all formally met."

We shake hands all around, and they thank me for always leaving food at their door. In appreciation, they tell me, they had their son send over several cases of the craft beer he makes in Brooklyn. Half the people at their long table are slugging back longnecks, and singing along to the harmonious holiday tunes the chorus guys were belting out. "Thank you," I tell them. "I'm glad you're all here. Will you excuse me for a minute?"

I'm overwhelmed. I push my way through the crowd, not knowing exactly where I'm going. I check my watch. The store is officially closed. When I get to the first floor, I see two bouncers sitting on stools by the far west 34th Street entrance. A well dressed, pretty woman, and a camera guy walk up, and are waved in. I keep walking, wondering if I'm going to be allowed throughout the store. I know there's a lounge in the restroom in the back of the kids' section, near the McDonald's. I just need to sit down by myself for a minute or two, to be alone. I head to the elevator and hit the button for the 7th floor.

It's odd being in the huge department store with no shoppers around, lights dim, halls quiet. I can't ever recall being in a Macy's elevator without pressing shoulder-to-shoulder with at least ten strangers. I take a deep breath in, enjoying the peace. I watch the numbers on the floors light up, consecutively. 5, 6, 7.

On 7, the door doesn't open. I buzz right past it, and the door opens on 8. It looks like I pushed the button, but my head is practically spinning from all of the activity of the evening. I walk out, and head left. The corporate offices and employee lounge are on this floor. That would be as good a place as any to rest by myself for awhile. The regular showroom lights are soft, with most of the illumination coming from the display cases and mannequin spotlights. I see colored lights in the distance. Santa Land. Surely Macy's planned a bathroom in the section where thousands and thousands of kids wait in line each year to see Santa.

I head in that direction, taking in the beauty of the life-sized Christmas-themed circus scene. It's amazing to walk through and gaze at the various scenes with a wholly unobstructed view. I hear something fall, and I freeze. It must be the night watchmen. I listen hard. Maybe it's just something settling, like in an old house. I read on one of the plaques outside that the store's been here since 1902.

I walk past the scene of a family opening presents on Christmas morning. A man and a woman are smiling in their bathrobes. Seated on the floor, under the decorated tree is a toddler in her pajamas, and a spunky dog sniffing a wrapped gift with his nose down, and his tail up. The mom is smiling, holding a gift up to her ear. The man has glasses.

I think about Henry, and how he looked so handsome and cozy in his terrycloth robe from the Waldorf, and I'm sad. For a short while, I thought I might have what the family in the diorama before me has. I had even let myself think I could have it with Henry. That ship has sailed, Charlotte, I tell myself walking on past a scene in which elves and aliens compare toys, and another featuring a schoolroom filled with gingerbread children decorating the tree.

When I continue down the hall, there it is. Santa's big chair. The only light comes from the gleam of the Christmas tree lights all around the grotto. I open the gate, and let myself in. I climb the steps, and take a seat. I close my eyes, thinking about all of the people downstairs and how awful it'll be to send them all home if no one brings Hudson back to me. I breathe, listening to the silence. For a moment, I almost forget where I am.

"Hello, Charlotte," says a deep friendly. I open my eyes.

Standing all the way across the room is an old man with a white beard. He's wearing jeans and a checkered shirt, and work boots. I squint to see him better. Could it be the man whose lap I sat on in this very chair?

"How did you know my name?" I ask. I glance down to see my nametag. "Oh, silly me. Of course." Could he have read it from way back there?

I could have sworn he was wearing glasses before. "Your vision must be very good," I say.

"There isn't much I can't see," he tells me with a wink.

*****

"There's your ride," Chris says as the elevator doors open to carry me back down to the party. "The important thing to remember is that you are not alone." He smooths his beard thoughtfully. "There's a lot of power in love."

I still can't believe I sat with a complete stranger for half an hour, telling him the whole story about Hudson. It was a nice break from all the energy of the party, but like he said to me, it's time to get back to all of those friends, and strangers, who came to support me. "Whatever is supposed to happen, will."

I hold the door with my hand. "Are you sure you won't come downstairs for awhile? Or maybe we can sit and talk a little more."

The truth is, I'm scared. If I go down there, and Hudson hasn't been returned, I'm going to have to send everyone away. This was the last chance. Tomorrow, I'll have to start my new life resigned to the fact Hudson won't be coming home.

He shakes his head. "I have to catch a flight." He waves as the doors close.

I check my watch on the way down. It's later than I thought, nearly midnight. When the doors open, I'm surprised to find the gathering in full swing. Vijay is up on the dais, microphone in hand, "...and THAT'S where I found the stethoscope!" A huge wave of laughter sweeps the crowd. "Thank you very much, I am Vijay Singh. I host a show every Tuesday at 10 at the Broadway Comedy Club. Come out and see me!"

I look around, hoping that maybe Hudson was brought back while I was gone. I catch Jane's eye, and raise my eyebrows. She shakes her head no, and mouths, "Sorry."

As the applause is dying down, he spots me. "Ladies and gentlemen," he says to the crowd, "please give it up for Miss Charlotte Bell." The clapping picks up. I have no choice but to take the stage. To my surprise, I'm not scared. Vijay is smiling as he hands me the mic, and when I turn to look at the crowd, I see Jane and Penelope, Mrs. Rabinowitz, Skip, Aunt Miranda and even James, along with so many other people who have proven they're in my corner. I'll never have to face tough times again if I don't want to.

"Hi everyone," I say.

"Hi Charlotte," they all boom back, and there is a collective laugh. I see Manuel holding Popcorn upright in his lap, waving his little paw at me.

"I want to say thank you to each and every one of you for the love and support you've shown for Hudson and me. I've never felt this kind of friendship, and I know if Hudson were here now, he'd love every minute of this. I'm really happy that everyone has gotten to have fun, and celebrate. I know you all want what

I want: To see Hudson back. It's getting late. I want to stay positive, but eventually we're going to have to call it a night. Yesterday, the idea of moving on without Hudson was unthinkable. First and foremost, I couldn't bear the idea that he might not be safe and cared for. I'm honestly not worried about that anymore. As much as it would break my heart not to have Hudson in my life, I am comforted by the fact that I absolutely believe, one hundred percent, that someone out there who is as kind as all of you is taking excellent care of him. Thanks, friends, for proving to me that the world is good."

Everyone claps as I step off the dais. Vijay, who knows how to handle an audience, takes the mic from my hand, and says, "Ladies and gentlemen, please welcome back our wonderful singers from The Gay Men's Chorus of New York City." Without missing a beat, they step up onto the stage and launch into a harmonious *Last Christmas.*

Aunt Miranda walks up to me and hands me a glass of champagne. She gives me an awkward side-hug that's meant to be a spirit-lifter. She's trying, even if she's not quite there yet. "It's not over till it's over, darling," she says. "Hudson might show up yet. The night is still young."

"There's always a chance, and I'm really hoping that I get my boy back. But I have to be a grown-up." I squeeze her back. "Hudson came into my life when I needed him. He changed me. Maybe that was the gift, and I have to appreciate that I had him in my life at all. What's that expression? It's better to have loved and lost, than never to have loved at all?"

"Speaking of that, darling, what happened with you and Henry?"

"Like I said, it's better to have loved and lost." My heart constricts at the sound of my own words. I love Henry. Well, loved him, I guess. "Why are you asking me that? I thought you wanted me to get back together with James and rule a food empire as his queen."

"It's just that Henry hasn't been well, not since he left *The Today Show* Studios. His clothes are rumpled, he walks around in a fog, and he has great black circles beneath his eyes."

"So does Landry. I guess all the late-night hanky-panky is wearing them both out."

"Pfft!" Miranda dismisses the idea. "Not bloody likely! She's been working round the clock, picking up his slack, because he's been useless. She's barely left the office, and when she has, I've had her on call."

"Oh, well. It's none of my business."

"Isn't it? Why do you reckon he's in such a state, then?"

"I don't know. Flu?"

"Could it be that you changed Henry the way Hudson changed you?"

I stiffen. I heard it with my own ears. Henry was just doing his job. "I don't think so."

"Well, I'd say Henry might have changed you. The Charlotte I knew a week ago would never have run all over New York City, making friends with strangers and getting people on her team. And she certainly wouldn't have made an eloquent speech like that in front of a whole room. But have it your way, darling. I'll just leave you with one thought." She turns and looks me in the eyes. "I had a man once who looked at me the way Henry looked at you. Words were said, feelings were hurt, and there was a standoff. I had my pride, or so I thought. In the end, I won." She puts her hand on my shoulder. "But I didn't really, darling. I may know about *The Art of War*, but I wish I'd learned about the art of love. My bed is awfully cold at night." With that, she gives my shoulder a squeeze, and disappears into the kitchen.

Suddenly, I'm very tired. I look around the room, at my friends laughing and chatting with the strangers who came to sit vigil with us. This is the end, I think with resignation. My last, best hope is gone. There's no point in stopping the party. I want to go around and hug each and every one of them, and tell them a personal goodbye. I look around at their happy faces, and decide against it. They would feel the need to comfort me about Hudson not showing up. I don't want to put them on the spot. Might as well let them enjoy the fun for now. I sneak up the escalator, careful to avoid notice. I'll grab a cab, I think. I'm looking forward to falling into bed, and sinking into oblivion. I'll deal with the fallout of not getting Hudson back in the morning. I've got to start afresh sometime, but it doesn't have to be now.

When I get to the main floor, I see that the snow is coming down hard. It's sticking, and a thick, white rug covers 34th Street. There's little traffic, and what's there is moving slowly. I'm so exhausted, I nearly walk out past the one remaining bouncer without my coat and bag. It seems like days ago that I was up in the office drinking coffee with Penelope and Jane. At the elevator bank, I push in Floor 8. When I get out, I head toward the lounge, briskly walking through Santa Land, past the scenes and dioramas.

I hear a man's voice, and I stop. "Chris?" I call, even though I know it's not him; he left ages ago. "Hello?" I try again, hoping it's a night guard. I hurry through Santa Land, to the dark corridor where the corporate offices and lounge are. I'm nervous. I don't like being alone up here at what must be midnight by now.

"Hello?" calls out a rich voice with an English accent. "Who's there?"

It's Henry. Bubbles rise in my heart. Until I heard his voice, I hadn't realized how much I wanted to see him. I think about what Aunt Miranda said about winning. I think about what Chris said about how what is supposed to happen will. "Henry!" I find myself shouting. I run right into the darkness. "Henry, it's Charlotte. Wait for me. I'm coming!"

I round the corner to see Henry sitting in a chair, holding my coat against his face. His mouth is hanging open. He looks disoriented.

"Henry. Are you alright?"

"No, I'm not."

My elation shifts to embarrassment. He doesn't know what to say to me. He doesn't want to see me.

"Never mind," I say, trying to let him off the hook. "I was just leaving." I reach for my coat, but he holds it firmly, and stands up. The rapture he seemed to be in is broken.

"Charlotte," he says to me very seriously. "I wasn't planning to come. There was a message. A man said it was urgent. You just..."

"Henry?"

Just then, I hear skittering on the linoleum floor, and turn around. Hudson slides around the corner, jumps onto the chair, and starts dancing on his back legs.

"Hudson!" I scream. I bend down and gather my wiggling, joyful dog to my chest. He's whining and moaning, and I'm crying and kissing his furry snout.

"Henry!" I shout through my tears. "You brought Hudson!"

"No, I think Hudson brought me." He still looks dazed. "The man said I needed to meet him in the corporate office to sign an insurance waiver to cover the early pop-up launch. There's no one here. I saw your coat, and..."

I'm rocking Hudson in my arms. "And?"

"And I was smelling it," he says, smiling. "I sat in that chair, and I was inhaling your scent, eyes closed, because the coat belongs to you." His eyes shine. "Because I have missed you so much. And then I felt a scratching on my leg." He laughs an unbridled laugh. "I wanted that dog to be Hudson so badly. But you see, we've never actually met. Please tell me that's him."

"It's him. It most certainly is." I squeeze my little dog tight. "Hudson, meet Henry. He's the man I'm in love with."

*****

"Would anyone care for more kugel? Craig! You've hardly eaten a thing," Mrs. Rabinowitz chides, carrying a tray and pushing her ample girth between the various folding tables and card tables taking up nearly every square inch of my living room.

Craig pats his stomach, and says, "You have got to be joking,

Mrs. R. You must have scooped gefilte fish onto my plate three times when I wasn't looking, and I just ate my weight in those cookies you made. What do you call them?" He leans down and scoops up two tiny Yorkies in one large hand, and balances them on his lap. Vijay reaches over and offers the bigger one a scrap of meat. The little one beats him to it, and Vijay laughs, grabbing another scrap for the big guy.

"Rugeleh, my dear. Let me say, those scalloped onions you brought were perfection."

Craig smiles proudly. "My grandma taught me right down south. The boys learned to cook as good as the girls. Sturdy old southern cooking will stick to your ribs."

"You know that's right," Beverly, my agent says. He pats his stomach under his vest and watch chain. "Helped me to grow up to be quite a big boy." Everyone laughs.

"You'll have to come to our house some night and I'll make you a whole meal. Bring your husband."

"I'll take you up on that," Mrs. Rabinowitz says, heading toward the kitchen.

Vijay raises his glass. "To Charlotte! And the best Day-After-Christmas Dinner anyone has ever thrown."

"To Charlotte," everyone responds.

"And to the book she's going to write for me the very minute she tests the last recipe for *Traditional Meals*."

"Beverly," I say in a warning tone, "I never promised to write my own cookbook." I check my watch as I gather plates and cups. Henry's over an hour late, and I haven't had a text or a call. I'm starting to worry.

"But darling," Aunt Miranda chimes in, "Money cannot buy the kind of exposure you have right now. Strike while the iron is hot. Hudson is the new black." She's reclining on the sofa next to Jane in front of a fair number of shot glasses. I've never in my life seen her let her hair down like this.

"I thought tequila was the new black," Jane argues with a little bit of a slur.

"How about I get you both cups of strong, black coffee, and *that* can be the new black?" They both snort, and wave me off.

"Skip!" I holler to my neighbor over the din, making my way toward the kitchen. "I'm going to give Hudson some beef pot roast. Is it OK if I give some to Dylan and Connor?"

"Only if you want two new roommates. After being fed like this, those little Corgis won't want to come home to me. You're taking spoiled to a whole new level."

In the kitchen, Hudson and Popcorn are snoozing together in Hudson's oversized donut. Irv and Frieda, my old neighbors and new friends, are seated at the table with Manuel drinking after-dinner cappuccinos and talking about Guatemala, where Manuel was born and where the older couple own a mountain home. "Hold still," I tell them. "I want to get a photo of you for my blog." I cannot believe how full my kitchen is, and how many friends I've made in such a short time. My face hurts from smiling.

"Pay attention, everyone," I shout. "'Charlotte's Chefs' have been begging me to post more pictures of the friends I've been writing about. Say 'queso!'"

I begin piling morsels of meat into small bowls for all the dogs when I hear the buzzer go. "Penelope," I call. "Will you please make dinner for the dogs while I get the door?" I'm so glad she got the day off from her job so she could join us. People in retail always work on holidays. I'm especially glad she insisted on showing up early to do my make-up. I'm starting to like the girly-girl thing.

"Sure," she says, coming through to the kitchen and setting her fussy, pale Chihuahua called Macy Gray down on the floor. The spindly little dog, wearing a pink turtleneck sweater toddles over to sniff Hudson and Popcorn. Hudson lifts his head and raises an eyebrow. Macy turns away to inspect the perimeter of the room, unimpressed as I predicted she might be.

Ruby pops her head through the swinging door, and asks, "Can I help with anything?"

"No, but thank you. Just relax and enjoy your downtime." She smiles and retreats back to the living room. When she called to congratulate me about Hudson, I hesitated to invite her, knowing the grand lifestyle she was used to leading. I could almost hear her jumping up and down on the other end of the phone. She told me she couldn't wait to have a homemade meal. Turns out, she's very down-to-earth, and she showed up not looking like a model at all, but wearing a very simple sweater and long skirt without a trace of makeup.

I push my way through all of the tables and chairs to reach the door as the buzzer sounds a second time. "Can someone buzz them up?" I call. Mrs. R's husband does a sprightly half-jog to the intercom, and presses the button, while I'm still weaving in and out of tables and chairs.

"Sorry, Leonard," I tell Officer Scrivello. He's made fast friends with James. It turns out that they both have an interest in sleight-of-hand magic, a new development since I had been part of James's world. They're palming coins and doing card tricks for Ruby's brothers, and Beverly. I'm happy James is at my table, in my home. I figured a meal was the least I could offer him after he worked to feed all of my friends at the welcome party. I never thought I'd be friends with him; it's a wonder how things can change even if you never expect them to.

I open the door expecting Henry, but instead see a stout, graying couple in somewhat formal clothes holding packages. "Happy Boxing Day," the woman says.

I stand there, staring. I know I'm being rude, but my brain scrambles to figure out how I know them. Did I meet them at the pop-up party? "I'm Charlotte," I say, stalling. "Happy belated Christmas."

"Same to you," they say in unison, still waiting.

"Do you have the wrong apartment?" The buzzer goes again, and I press the button to buzz open the front door to the brownstone.

"I don't believe so. 3R isn't it?"

I hear someone thundering up the steps, two at a time. I crane my neck to see Henry flying around the corner, panting and red-faced. "I'm so I'm late. Mum and Dad, this is Charlotte Bell."

Mum and Dad? "Mr. and Mrs. Wentworth! Come in, please," I say, standing aside. "Here, let me take your coats." Mrs. Rabinowitz swoops in with welcomes and introductions, ushering the Wentworths in and getting them drinks. "Henry," I say, "would you help me with these coats?"

He follows me into my bedroom, where everyone's winter gear is piled on the bed and says, "Remember the fight we had at the Waldorf?"

I laugh. "Which one?"

"The one where you told me I should appreciate my parents. After you sent me away from the TV studio, I felt more lonely than I ever have in my life. I called my mother, and told her everything. We must have talked for an hour. I had her get dad on the phone, and we talked for nearly five minutes, which was an achievement. The point is, I was happy they were there."

"That's so nice. But what happened to Ebenezer Scrooge?"

"You look lovely, by the way," he tells me.

"Thank you, but back to the story," I say, blushing. I begin organizing the coats by color.

He moves closer. "You have been very bad indeed to put off seeing me until now. One kiss after the Hudson reunion, and then banishment? What a cruel mistress."

"I needed to bring Hudson home alone that night. You understand, don't you?"

"I do, but that didn't mean I didn't yearn for you. I not only yearned, I believe I pined. The torch I carried nearly set New York City aflame."

I start putting gloves and mittens in neat piles. "Do not ever tell me again, Henry Wentworth, that you don't have a stack of Harlequin Romances in the back of your closet. Anyway, you and Aunt Miranda were up to your eyes in work once the news hit the media about the pop-up restaurant launching. I still can't believe she's able to be here today."

"Let Landry and the rest handle it. There are more important things in life than work."

"Again, what happened to Scrooge?"

Henry smiles. "He sent the boy to buy the biggest goose in the window, didn't you hear?" He looks at me seriously. "I'm sorry if I ever rained on even one moment of your Christmas joy." I wave him off. "But I promise I'm a changed man. I arranged to send my parents plane tickets, and to take off from work. It's only a shame they couldn't make it on Christmas Day." He sidles up to me, and slides his arms around my waist. "Besides, I wanted them to meet you."

"That's sweet."

"No," he says turning to face me. He takes both of my hands. "No, *I wanted them to meet you.*"

"Oh." I look up at him. "Oh!" I feel a lightness in my chest. "Would you call us an item?"

"I would and do."

"Would you say we are a couple?"

"I would say it on the record at a news conference."

"Would you say we're getting serious?"

"Serious as a proverbial heart attack, but with no threat of demise or perishing."

A smile spreads across my face, and I raise an eyebrow in imitation of Henry. "Then let's go tell everyone, why don't we?"

"That," he says, kissing me lightly on the lips, lingering slightly before drawing back, "is my plan exactly."

*****

"I knew Charlotte was keeping secrets when I asked her if Henry was her boyfriend," Jane says loudly to Leonard. "I have an intuition, you know. People say I have the gift."

"So does my Nana," he says, sliding closer to her on the sofa. "Tell me more." Hudson jumps up into his lap, and Jane reaches over to scratch the dog's neck. He's wearing a little red stocking cap that Mrs. Rabinowitz brought him as a present from the pet store. "Would you ever want to have a dog someday?" I can tell Leonard likes her by the way he's sitting up straight. "Or kids? I mean, if you got married, of course?"

I smile, and look around the room. Henry's parents brought crowns for everyone to wear, the way the English do at Christmas dinner. They also brought crackers, the paper tubes shaped like wrapped candies, that make a noise and pop out small favors when you pull them apart. They're spread among the tables. I can't wait to see them in action. Everyone looks sated and happy. Dogs are running around between everyone's feet, and revelers are taking turns leashing and harnessing them for quick walks in the foot-deep snow. It takes a village, I think to myself.

"Charlotte, do you mind if I turn on some music?" Henry asks.

"No," I holler across the room. "That would be great." The sun is just waning outside the windows, and the street lamps have gone on for the night. Ruby is circulating the room, pouring the champagne she brought to the party into my guest's glasses.

"Charlotte, could you come help me with this?" Henry calls from the front of the room, where's he's fiddling with the speakers. Hudson leaps down from the sofa, and hops up onto the window seat next to Henry. Henry reaches over and gives him a treat. "Good boy, Huddie. Good boy."

"Here, let me try," I tell Henry. But he doesn't need my help. It was a ploy to bring me in close. He puts his arm around me as the room swells with Michael Bublé singing *I'm Dreaming of a White Christmas.* Henry picks up a champagne glass, and tings the side several times with a butter knife. Every head, including Hudson's, swivels to watch as Henry drops to one knee, and says in a loud, rich voice, "Charlotte Bell, will you marry me?"

He pulls a ring from his pocket and holds it up in the air,

waiting for an answer. His face looks confident, but I can see his hand shaking.

"Yes. Yes, Henry Wentworth, I will marry you," I say, and he slides the ring onto my finger. I watch as if it's slow motion. The ring is a rich, deep garnet, surrounded by small emeralds, and set in yellow gold. It's perfect. I never was and never will be a diamond solitaire girl, and the fact that Henry knows that melts my heart.

As we kiss, I hear yipping and thumping from Hudson in the window seat, and the *pop pop pop* of Christmas crackers. We pull apart for a moment to look at the friends and family surrounding us, to bask in the warmth. And then we find each other again, this time for good.

Epilogue

We applaud wildly when the huge cast of the Broadway show finishes their big old-fashioned song-and-dance number, and file off the stage by the entrance to Macy's. Henry is holding Hudson in his arms, and I'm taking deep breaths waiting to be introduced.

"Like I told you a year ago," Aunt Miranda says, "no one could have dreamed up this kind of publicity. That dog of yours is a genius."

"I'll say," Beverly chimes in. "That dog bought me my villa in Italy. I've never seen an auction for a book go that high, that fast."

Ruby has taken the stage.

"Oh my word," says Mrs. Wentworth. "She's a vision. It's hard to believe that's the same girl who sat with us at dinner last year. Isn't she the most beautiful woman you have ever laid eyes on?" she asks, poking her husband in the ribs.

"No, because I married the most beautiful woman I ever laid eyes on," he tells her. She brushes him off, but she looks pleased. "I hope my son treats you half as well as I'm treated, Charlotte."

"He's a good man, Mum." I say. I love calling her Mum. She insisted on it the night we got engaged. I'll never get tired of it.

Behind Ruby, they've projected the picture of her and Hudson in Times Square last Christmas. She's talking about how meeting Hudson inspired her to donate so much money from the photo's sales to animal charities.

"I'm just glad that such a huge portion of the proceeds from *Hudson's Adventure's in Santa Land* are going to help support animal shelters around the world," I tell them.

"Oh, come on now, tell old Beverly the truth, aren't you just the *teeniest* bit excited about your own book? *Charlotte Bell Cooks for Friends and Family* isn't going to suffer one bit from having a picture of you and that magical dog on the front cover."

I smile. "Yes, I'm pretty excited." After all of the post-Hudson return interviews and photo shoots last year, and the focus the media put on my and Henry's wedding, I've gotten quite used to being in the public eye.

"I can't wait to see what's behind those curtains," Mrs. Rabinowitz says, squeezing Abe's arm. She motions to the purple curtains with swirling gold script that say *Coming Soon: Hudson's Adventure's in Santa Land.* "How about you Abie?"

"If it means I can keep my limbs then yes, bring it on in good health!"

"Getting married in Macy's was a stroke of genius, Henry." Beverly drawls. "You are not Miranda Nichols' protégé for nothing."

"I wish I could take credit, Beverly, but it was all Charlotte's idea. You know the bride is always right."

"Beverly, they got married in Macy's because it was romantic, not for publicity," Jane protests. "You make it sound so cheap. They met there! That's why we're getting married in Macy's, right Leonard?"

"That's right, Sweetie. But I hope you're not disappointed if the paparazzi don't turn out for ours like they did for Henry and Charlotte's."

"As long as you're there, nothing could disappoint me," Jane says, giving him a peck on the cheek.

"We're almost up, Huddie," Henry says. Hudson looks especially festive tonight in a red sweater with white faux-fur at the collar, and a pair of reindeer antlers, all courtesy of Mrs. Rabinowitz.

Gently, he hands me my dog. "Media genius or not, I know what the public wants to see, and that's not me, but Hudson with his mommy."

The window designer is speaking, talking about this year's theme. They've partnered with the publishing company to create Christmas windows featuring the book cover. He also asked us for wedding photos with Hudson as Best Dog, wearing his tuxedo, and "going up the aisle," by riding the wooden escalator. Those have been blown up as backdrops for some of the windows along with pictures from photo shoots showing Hudson at Blow Bar wearing a hairdresser's cape, Hudson standing in two pairs of men's shoes, Hudson being gift-wrapped by a sales girl, and Hudson eating a plate of spaghetti Bolognese in James's new permanent restaurant in the Cellar called, fittingly, 34th and Hudson.

There are animatronic Hudsons, puppet Hudsons, marionette Hudsons, Lego Hudsons, and stuffed animal Hudsons.

"...I'd like to introduce to you the inspiration for all this magic, Hudson," booms the emcee.

Henry and I ascend the stairs to the platform, amid flashing cameras and roars of applause. "And now, allow me to present this year's Macy's Holiday Windows." The designer holds his arms up in the air. "Hudson in Santa Land!"

Fireworks shoot off from the roof of the building as the curtains drop, revealing the windows that are alive with lights and motion. Glitter cannons shoot gold sparkles out of the third floor windows, and the sides of the building light up in red and green. Hudson pants, smiling. We turn our backs to the clapping crowd, and survey the splendor of the building. Henry slides an arm around my waist whispers "Are you happy?"

"I have everything I have ever wanted." I choke up. "I got my grown-up Christmas wish."

Above the clock, in sparkling gold letters two stories high, a sign lights up.

Believe.

Acknowledgements

I send out deep thanks to my editor Charlotte Ledger. She's as nice as she is smart. She makes my stories better, and boosts me up. Thank you to Alexandra Allden, a real artist, for my perfect book jacket. Thanks also to the whole team at Harper UK.

I wouldn't have had the gumption or momentum to face writing the words "Chapter One" without the support and encouragement of my friends. Heartfelt thanks to Kate Bushmann, Molly Sackler, Meirav Duffey, Anne Hulsman, Laura Feldman, Kenny Feldman, Dan Diggles, Susie Felber, Jill Bennet, and Zahava Tzur. Special thanks to Cathy Yardley for all of her kindness and wisdom. Thanks to my Kentucky and Erie family, too. If I have forgotten anyone, please forgive me. My brain is a sieve. If I tell you I remember something clearly, don't believe it. Challenge me. I won't be offended. I haven't been right since I gave birth for the first time.

Thanks to all of my FB and Twitter friends. You guys keep me going, and give me laughs. The wonderful reviews and support I get mean more than you can know.

Thank you to the other HarperImpulse authors who have been in my corner. It's appreciated.

Thanks to my husband, Sam, and our kids for keeping the household going while I write. Once upon a time, I lived in a clean house. I swear it. And as God as my witness, I shall someday again. Try to work around that pile of dirty dishes for now.

And to my fellow New Yorkers: Thanks in advance for not pointing out that I fiddled with the dates of time-honored traditional holiday events. I'm not going to lie… I love how fiction is forgiving. It works for me. We all know I'm fairly lazy, and I prefer being loosey-goosey.

Finally, and mostly, thanks to all of my readers. Even after all of these books, I'm still humbled that strangers choose to spend their precious time reading the words I've put on pages. You made my dreams come true. X

Lynn Marie's Holiday Delights

Did you know that Lynn Marie Hulsman is also a chef? Well, she is! And she's agreed to share some of her wonderful festive recipes with us! We've got three recipes from her exclusively for you, starting with this yummy-sounding *Sweetly Spiced Holiday Popcorn* recipe! Enjoy...

This tasty treat is a wonderful light offering, packed with show stopping flavor. Salty and sweet, it's perfect as a cocktail snack for adults at a sophisticated Holiday Open House or as a pre-dinner nibble on the special day itself. I suggest making big batches of the spice mix, and having it on hand in your pantry – since it only takes minutes to pop corn, you'll have a nearly instant snack to serve chilly carolers or gift-delivering visitors. Packaged in a decorative tin, or a plastic bag festooned with ribbons in holiday colors, this gorgeous goody becomes an elegant hostess gift!

Makes 8 Servings

Non-stick spray, for coating
1 dried bay leaf
Zest of 6 large clementines or 3 medium oranges, finely grated

Zest of 1 large lemon, finely grated
1/2 teaspoon ground clove
1 teaspoon ground cinnamon
1/2 teaspoon ground nutmeg
1 vanilla pod, split and scraped *(Reserve the seeds)
1 teaspoon salt
5 cups / 1 kilogram raw sugar (or use granulated or caster sugar, if that's what you have)
2 tablespoons butter, for popping
3 to 6 tablespoons olive oil, for popping
1 cup / 200 grams popping corn (more or less, adjust spice mix to popcorn to your taste)

To Make the Sugar-and-Spice Blend

Preheat the oven to 200°F / 120°C. Lightly coat a 9-inch by 13-inch / 23-centimeter by 33-centimeter baking sheet with non-stick spray, and set it aside.

In the bowl of a food processor, combine the bay leaf, clementine zest, lemon zest, clove, cinnamon, nutmeg, vanilla pod, and salt. Process until finely ground and well combined, about 1 minute.

Add the sugar to the zest and spice mixture, and pulse until well combined, about 10 pulses. (The sugar will look damp.) Spread the mixture in an even layer on the prepared baking sheet. Bake in the oven set to very low heat, stirring occasionally, about an hour. Make sure to watch carefully, so that the mixture doesn't burn. The goal is to bring the oils out of the zest and vanilla pod, and to take the dampness from the mixture. Once the mixture is fragrant and dry, transfer the baking sheet to a cooling rack, and allow it to come to room temperature. One cooled, transfer the mixture to a colander or sieve and strain, then discard any large pieces of zest or pod. Use immediately, or store in an airtight container in a cool, dark place for up to 1 month.

*Don't waste the seeds from the pod! Combine with 1 cup granulated sugar, and seal in an airtight jar and make vanilla sugar to spoon into tea and coffee!

To Make the Popcorn

Before you pop the popcorn, prepare one or more bowls. You'll need a bowl large enough to hold the whole batch of popcorn with extra room for tossing and coating, or you'll need to work in batches using several smaller bowls.

Combine the butter and the oil in a very large, heavy-bottomed pot with a tight-fitting lid set over medium-high heat. Stay with the pot, stirring occasionally with a wooden spoon. You want the butter to melt, but not scorch.

Once the butter has melted, add the popcorn kernels, stir to coat, and cover the pot. Once you hear the first several pops, shake the pot to distribute the heat and prevent burning. Do not lift the lid! Continue to shake often until the popping dies down. When popping slows and becomes intermittent, remove the entire pot from the heat. (It's better to waste a few kernels than to burn the batch!)

To Assemble

Spoon the spice mix into one large bowl or divide it among two or more smaller bowls.

Add the warm popcorn and toss lightly, distributing the spice mix, until the kernels are evenly coated. Serve immediately or store in an airtight container for up to three days.

Of course holidays are for family, but I think every hardworking gal should make room on her schedule for a Girl's Night amid the hustle and bustle of the season. After all, it's the support of your girlfriends that gets you through the dreary mundane Tuesdays of the year. It's only right to allot a celebratory night to bask in that friendship, and relax surrounded by feelings of gratitude and appreciation.

Here's a drink I recommend serving after the last night of your office job, right before the holidays start! You can make the chocolate stir-in in advance, so when your girlfriends gather to kick off their heels, snuggle on your sofa wrapped in throws, and share wishes about holiday gifts to come, these decadent warmers will be ready in a flash.

These smooth and warming drinks go down like a dessert, but there's no denying that they pack a punch. But why not? Letting down your hair with friends and a bot drink during the holiday rush is the perfect way to spend a cold, wintry night.

Makes 6 mugs

1/2 cup / 90 grams dark chocolate chips
1/4 cup / 60 milliliters white corn syrup (or substitute golden syrup)
1/4 cup / 60 milliliters water
1/2 teaspoon pure vanilla extract
1 cup / 240 milliliters heavy cream (or substitute double cream)
1 quart / 1 liter whole (full-fat) milk
6 ounces / 170 milliliters good Irish whiskey
Dutch cocoa powder, for dusting

In a medium-sized, heavy-bottomed saucepan, set over low heat, combine the chocolate chips, syrup, water, and vanilla. Warm the mixture, stirring often, until the chocolate has melted. Chill in the refrigerator for at least 15 minutes.

Put the cream in a medium-sized mixing bowl (this will work best if you use a metal bowl that you've chilled in the freezer), and beat using an electric mixer set to medium-high, until soft peaks form.

Gradually add the cooled chocolate mixture, and beat on medium-low until it mounds. Chill in the refrigerator for at least 30 minutes.

To serve, heat the milk in a medium-sized saucepan set over medium-high heat, stirring occasionally with a wooden spoon. If bubbles form at the edges of the pan, reduce the heat. Aim for steaming hot milk, but not boiling.

Divide the warm milk evenly among 6 large mugs.

Add 4 tablespoons of the chocolate mixture to each mug, and stir briskly to combine.

Add 1 ounce of whiskey to each mug, and stir one turn. Serve immediately.

Store in the refrigerator, in a tightly lidded jar or bottle, for up to one week. Shake to combine, and heat before serving.

Dried Cherry & Dark Chocolate Loaf

I love this simple-to-make loaf as both a gift and a sweet treat for the table. If making it as a hostess gift or a present, I suggest including a tag listing the dry ingredients that are included in the jar, along with the list of fresh ingredients needed to complete the recipe, and the directions for baking. If you're crafty, the jar itself or the handwritten recipe can become keepsakes that rekindle memories for holidays to come. Holiday shopping already complete? Treat yourself! Served with a milky cup of tea, this moist, decadent loaf is the perfect pick-me-up for exhausted tree trimmers.

Makes one 9 x 5-inch / 23 x 13-centimeter loaf cake

1 1/2 cups / 180 grams all-purpose flour
1 teaspoon baking powder
3/4 teaspoon salt
1 cup / 200 grams granulated sugar
1/2 teaspoon ground cinnamon
1/4 teaspoon ground nutmeg
1/4 teaspoon ground ginger
1/2 cup / 75 grams dried cherries
1/2 cup / 80 grams dark chocolate chunks (I like Ghirardelli)
1/2 cup / 75 grams chopped walnuts

Sift together the flour, baking powder, and salt and then spoon into a canning jar. (You can use large resealable plastic bag, but you won't gorgeous layered appearance.) Tap the jar gently on the countertop to settle the flour. Combine the sugar, cinnamon, nutmeg, and ginger in a bowl and pour over the flour in the jar. Continue the layers with the dried cherries, then the chocolate chunks, and finally the walnuts. Put the lid on the jar and decorate as desired. Store in a cool, dark place until ready to use, up to 6 months.

To make the bread, you will need:

1/2 cup / 120 milliliters sour cream
4 tablespoons / 60 grams butter, melted

1/4 cup / 25 grams Confectioner's sugar
2 to 3 teaspoons whole milk

Preheat oven to 350°F / 175°C and grease and flour a 9 x 5-inch / 23 x 13-centimeter loaf pan.

Pour the jarful of dry ingredients into a large mixing bowl and stir well, using a wooden spoon. Using your hands, make a well in the center and crack in 2 eggs, beating lightly with a fork. Add 1/2 cup / 120 milliliters of sour cream and 4 tablespoons / 60 grams of melted butter. Stir just until incorporated; the batter will be lumpy. Transfer the batter into the prepared loaf pan and bake for 45 to 50 minutes, or until a toothpick inserted into the center comes out clean. Let cool slightly in the pan before turning out onto a cooling rack to cool completely. In a small bowl, whisk together 1/4 cup / 25 grams of confectioners' sugar and 2 to 3 teaspoons of milk (adding a little at a time to reach the proper drizzling thickness) and drizzle the glaze over the top.

Rich Winter Chutney

Even home cooks who swear they can do little more than toast bread and boil water can pull off this simple chutney recipe with aplomb. For beginners, though, I don't recommend learning the ins and outs of canning (though this condiment lends itself nicely to that method of preservation). My philosophy is that it's so easy to make, and gets eaten so quickly, why not just store it in the fridge and plan to eat it daily? And believe me when I tell you that delighted holiday-gift recipients won't mind stashing jars of your homemade treat in their own fridges. I suggest serving this as an accompaniment to sweet and salty roast pork, or on a platter alongside a wheel of brie and some hearty crackers. Or, give your overnight Christmas guests something to remember by spreading it onto sandwiches made with leftover slices of turkey or goose.

Makes about 2 cups / 480 milliliters chutney

1/2 cup / 75 grams chopped walnuts
1/2 cup / 80 grams chopped pitted dates
1/4 cup / 50 grams chopped dried apricots
1/4 cup / 50 grams chopped dried figs
1/3 cup / 50 grams raisins
2 large apples, peeled and chopped
3 teaspoons ground cinnamon
1/4 teaspoon ground cloves
3 tablespoons grape juice
2 teaspoons honey

Place the walnuts in a food processor fitted with the chopping blade attachment. Process the nuts until coarsely ground. Add in the dates, apricots, figs, raisins, apples, and cinnamon and pulse 4 to 6 times, until mixed. Scrape into a bowl and mix in just enough grape juice to make a pasty consistency so the mixture sticks together (you may wind up using more or less than a few tablespoons). Stir in the honey. Serve immediately, or ladle into clean jars with tight-fitting lids and store in the refrigerator for up to 1 week.

Festive Holiday Mulled Wine

Nothing fills a home with the holiday mood like the spicy-sweet fragrance of mulled wine. Guests adore being called inside from the dark and chill of winter by having a steaming mug of winter cheer pressed into their hands. Tread carefully, though! This delicious warming beverage goes down easy. I'd go so far as to call it a wolf in sheep's clothing. That said, when the jolly chatter of convening with friends rings in your ears, and the worries of workaday life melt away with the season, why not indulge a little? Christmas comes but once a year!

Makes about 12 mugs

2 large, thin-skinned oranges
1 small lemon
2 bottles Cabernet Sauvignon
1 bottle Pinot Grigio
3 thick, coin-sized pieces of fresh ginger
2 cinnamon sticks
5 whole cloves
5 tablespoons granulated sugar
4 tablespoons brandy

Wash the oranges and lemon thoroughly. Using a sharp knife or citrus zester, remove the zest from the oranges in strips about the size of your thumb, being careful to remove only the outer layer, leaving the white-colored pith behind (it has a bitter taste, and will ruin the pot). Then, using a citrus reamer, juice the oranges and lemon. Pour the juice into a very large, heavy-bottomed, non-reactive pot.

Pour the Cabernet Sauvignon and the Pinot Grigio wine into the pot with the orange juice. Add the strips of orange and lemon zest, the ginger, the cinnamon sticks, the cloves and the sugar to the wine mixture. Stir lightly to dissolve the sugar.

Cover and set the pot over medium-high heat, and simmer until just steaming, stirring occasionally, about 8 minutes. Do not boil.

Reduce the heat to medium-low and warm the mixture for about an hour to allow the flavors to combine and develop. Using a slotted spoon, or a skimmer, remove and discard the fruit peels, ginger, cinnamon sticks, and cloves, and serve hot in mugs with a splash of brandy.